MADELYN ROSE

# BENEATH

## A SECRET SOCIETY

# BENEATH
## A SECRET SOCIETY

TitleTown Publishing, LLC
P.O. Box 12093  Green Bay, WI  54307-12093
920.737.8051 | titletownpublishing.com

Cover Designer: Erika L. Block
Interior Designer: Erika L. Block
Editor: Erin Walton
Proofreader: Megan Richard

PUBLISHER'S CATALOGING-IN-PUBLICATION DATA:

Names: Glosny, Madelyn Rose, author.

Title: Beneath : a secret society / Madelyn Rose.

Description:  Green Bay, WI : TitleTown Publishing, [2022]

Identifiers:  ISBN: 978-1-955047-00-5 (Print)
                        978-1-955047-01-2 (eBook)

Subjects:  LCSH: Secret societies--Fiction. | Friendship--Fiction. | Autonomy--Fiction. | Future, The-- Fiction. | Utopias--Fiction. | Young adults--Fiction. | Teenagers--Fiction. | LCGFT: Bildungsromans. | Romance fiction. | Science fiction. | Subterranean fiction.

Classification:  LCC: PS3607.L6646 B46 2022 | DDC: 813.6--dc23

# DEDICATION

To my fellow dreamers,
may we create a brighter future together.

To my family, whom I am grateful for beyond words.

# Prologue

SUNLIGHT BEAT DOWN ON HER THROUGH THE WINDOW, warming her skin like a blanket. In that moment of silence, the realization of her situation hit her like those rays of sun, filling every fiber of her being, though not nearly as gentle.

She blinked and tried to slow her racing heart, leaning her head closer to the window to focus on the outside sounds. The nearby Hydro Tube station was all hustle and bustle as usual, signaling the end of a work day and the beginning of rush hour. Most people from the sector would be taking some strand of the tube, waiting their turn like usual. Not everyone had the luxury of having their own car. Those were mostly owned by government officials nowadays; the ones who had all the money and power. *Figures.*

Too bad passersby couldn't see past the external walls of the house. Although, even if they could, they may not want to see what went on behind them. They'd probably run in the opposite direction.

Never in a million years, would she have guessed she'd be here. Was it possible she'd missed one tiny detail? That one slip-up had gotten her into more trouble than she was worth? At least those she loved were safe. Clarise with her love for books, Lilianna who lived in a cloud of innocence, Andre who could be so annoying it hurt but who was really sweet on the inside. All of them. She'd much rather be here alone if it meant nobody else had to endure this. They deserved to live their lives until they were all old men and women, watching their children grow up. They needed to watch them start their own combat training and eventually their careers. For a parent to be there any moment of the day for their child, there was nothing quite like that. She didn't know what she had until it was gone.

A door slammed, sending a nervous shiver down her spine. She moved to a kneeling position to get more leverage, but her tied hands didn't help the situation.

Her heart started racing again. *No, not yet!* She wasn't ready. They'd just finished with her moments ago, didn't they? Or had it been hours?

Time was no longer a concept for her here. Especially when she was forced to be locked up like an animal in the basement. The floor was dirty and disgusting, the air quality a perfect match. It was strange for her to have any chance to see the sunlight through the window. It was unlike them to give her a favor, but that must've been a sign that today was a "special" day.

She could hear them shouting in the other room. She sighed in relief; that meant she had at least a minute to wrap her head around what was about to happen again.

The sunlight hit her face just right, so she closed her eyes to let her sallowed skin take in the vitamin D. The shouting melted into the background. Thoughts of her friends and family washed over her in that moment. Her emotions would come back to bite her later, but she let herself feel them during that rare instant of calm.

It was somewhat comical how, not too long ago, she'd thought she was safe and well cared for. It had given her hope for her future.

No longer was she confined to a desk nor the government's rules; the Fortress had offered her *more* than her freedom. It had offered her a life. The raw kind, where she was never certain what would happen next, but was happy having the people she loved go through it with her. An existence where she got to choose whom she loved and to what extent. She had the ability to have as many children as she wanted, not the government-sanctioned limit of two. Down there, she could pick her own career path, her own way of life. Perhaps the others were doing that now. She hoped they were moving on with their lives, emptying out the contents of her room, making it seem as though she hadn't even existed.

She was alright with being an invisible hero. They didn't know what she was going through, and she would keep it that way if she could help it. She loved them too much to allow them to endure this kind of pain.

Almost as scary as what was happening to her here were the effects of her broken heart. Not everything was meant to last, but that didn't mean it hurt any less. Looking back, she admitted that her decision had been an impulsive one. Thanks to her naivety, she'd set aside her common sense and let her heart take control. That had condemned her to this, which she would classify as something close to death. She'd honestly take death over being dragged into that dungeon again, and she'd been through a number of horrifying adventures: bullet and stab wounds, poisonous shots, countless bruises, and worst of all, love.

Eventually, a flower without sunlight and oxygen was bound to perish.

Her breathing slowed and her heart quieted. This was what she needed to give her hope. If she just held on a bit longer, she'd make it through this. She'd make it back to them. To *him*--though, everyone and their uncle seemed to think he wasn't right for her, including herself. Love was weird that way; even when you had the opportunity to choose who you loved, you never actually made the decision for yourself. The heart was in charge of that and it didn't care about your opinion. She'd learned that the hard way.

Another door slammed. This time it was right near her head. She kept her eyes closed, telling herself to go to a different place.

A hand clamped down on her shoulder.

"Are you ready?"

# TWO YEARS EARLIER

# Chapter 1

## (ROSABELLA)

THE MOMENT SHE SNUCK OUT OF THE WINDOW, Rosabella's stomach dropped into her feet. She had a bad sensation in her fingers about ditching her family. It was almost like that feeling when she got hit in the gut with her brother's toy truck after he decided it would be fun to throw it down the stairs at her.

Then she remembered why she'd done it. And so what? Her parents were too controlling. It was about time she went through a rebellious phase. Up until now, Rose had been a goody-two-shoes with nothing to show for it. She still wasn't popular in school and her parents had been working her harder than ever with college coming up. They were always on Rose's back about making sure she had stellar grades so she could get into the college of her choosing...which basically meant they wanted her to go to the college of *their* choosing. Blah, blah, blah.

It hadn't really ever bothered her until now. Call it restlessness or whatever, but Rose was determined to live her life the way she wanted to from now on. She was as stubborn as they came and would let her parents know that they couldn't control her anymore.

Although her heart knew it was ready to explore the unknown, she *had* felt a twinge of guilt when her mom had knocked on the door to check on her. Less than a minute after she drove her mom away, she'd crawled out the window. She felt awful about yelling at her mom to give her space when she hadn't done anything wrong.

It wasn't completely a lie; she really *did* want space from her family. She especially loved her brother, Nicolai, but it was time for her to get a much needed break.

That's how she wound up at this party, having the time of her life. Parties in high school were few and far between, as everyone lived with a strict curfew. For some reason, Rose thought it a good idea to mention the party to her parents. She assumed they'd let her go since she was being honest with them, and honesty was a quality their parents stressed the importance of. She'd been so wrong. Her dad's head nearly exploded right in front of her. So what if he worked for the government? She didn't care if he *was* the highly regulated government itself; he didn't have the right to treat her as if she were a child anymore.

Besides, it was her birthday. In less than three hours, she would turn eighteen years old. Rosabella Mae Porter, born to Harley and MaeLee Porter, at 1:02 am on a Monday. How could they deny her a fun time on a day as special as this? Wasn't bridging the gap between teenagedom and adulthood supposed to be fantastic? Wasn't she entitled to some kind of special treatment now? Sure, she could legally drink alcohol and sign up for her own payments and everything; but what fun was that really? She'd been preparing all her life for adulthood--courtesy of her dad's rules and lessons--so that wouldn't be much of a change for her. The part she was supposed to indulge in included the extended curfew time. Once you turned eighteen, your curfew changed from 10 pm to 3 am. How exciting!

Parties weren't technically allowed, but they were never shut down in this neighborhood either. Not when they were hosted by many of the government officials' children. If they wanted to, kids like Rose could murder someone and still get away with it. Her dad was decently high up on the ladder, which gave him some influence; that made Rose valuable, and in her dad's eyes, a target. He'd always been fearful that she would be kidnapped for ransom or something stupid. He freaked out over the tiniest things. Neighborhoods and schools were so safe these days, you literally had to scan your thumb to go to the bathroom or walk in the school's front door. It was ridiculous.

Oh, who was she kidding. Rosabella was not one to go against the rules. She'd hardly ever complained about such things out loud. Staying submissive and quiet had grown redundant and tiresome to her. She yearned for a change of pace.

Rose sighed and leaned back against the patio chair. This was the point at the party when people initiated the losing-their-minds-stage. It was probably from all the alcohol. Even those under eighteen were drinking. Didn't they know how much trouble they could get into? Despite the drinking, Rose enjoyed watching people do stupid things. The comedy stemmed from her knowledge of each of their families and what their parents would say if they could see their kids now.

Rose paid close attention to a girl who, heavily intoxicated, jumped into the inground pool. Once she confirmed the girl was safe, she turned her attention back to people watching.

The Stevenson's had a really nice set up out here. Their property stretched from their back patio door to the edge of the sector's only nature preserve. Without a doubt, the Stevenson's had the largest lot in the neighborhood. Real grass, a commodity hard to come by these days, spread across the entirety of their lawn. Mr. Stevenson held a position as one of the sector's representatives, the highest governmental position possible. He had probably snapped his fingers and the lot was delivered to him. Rose wouldn't put it past them.

She reached down and ran her hand along the cool stone patio, refreshing against her warm skin. She'd been suffering under the heat from the nearby fire pit for a while now, but was too comfortable in the chair to move. The two-story pool was now occupied by a large group of guys and girls, the majority drunk or on their way to intoxication. Rose made sure to keep an eye on anyone who went under the water and didn't resurface for a while. She didn't know why she worried about others so much. Rose kept telling herself that if she was the only thing keeping them alive, it would be worth it. Life would forever be the most precious gift; the air in one's lungs the greatest reward of all.

Had she made the right decision, sneaking out of the house and going to this party? In reality, it had caused her more grief than it was worth.

"Rosie, why are you just sitting there? C'mon! Live a little!" Her best friend, Aire Gil--who's name suited her so well, since it rhymed with "I play"--ran over, carrying a cup filled to the brim. Rose smelled the sharp, potent alcohol on her the moment she crossed the pool deck. Aire squeezed onto the chair beside her and handed over the cup.

Rose took one look at the murky drink and pushed it back into her friend's hands. "No thanks, Rei."

Aire's round face hardened and she took Rose's face in her hands, spilling the drink all over the two of them. "Rosabella Porter, if you don't start having some fun, I'm going to kidnap you and drag you over there!"

She followed her friend's gaze to the booze table, where a group of senior guys made sure to fill everyone's drinks as they passed. One drink contained about seven or eight shots of liquor and a single splash of soda. It appeared more dangerous than fun.

"I don't know Rei. I'm just not feeling it right now. My parents don't even know I'm here. What if something happens to me?"

Aire wrapped an arm around her and dropped her head onto Rose's shoulder. Her dark brown hair tickled Rose's nostrils. Between the alcohol and the sweat, Rose picked up the scent of coconuts, Aire's favorite body scrub flavor. "Oh don't worry about that! Once you go back home and they celebrate your birthday tomorrow, you'll be right back to normal. You're the golden child, remember?"

It was meant as a friendly, teasing comment, but instead it felt like Aire had just scooped a part of her heart out and stepped on it. Still, even Rose had to admit, it was a little pathetic of her to be sitting alone in the corner. Maybe she *should* try to enjoy herself. Those guys over there seemed nice enough, right?

"I know that look...and I think it means I'm winning!" Aire giggled into Rose's shoulder. "I know what you're thinking too. It's too bad there's that whole marriage law or else I think I'd have found my forever soulmate here tonight. He's over by the pool."

"Oh shut up." She brushed her friend's hair out of her face. "You don't know what love even is, Rei."

Aire's eyes began to droop. "But of course I do! I love *you*, don't I?"

"I guess, but to love another person completely is beyond either of our comprehensions at this point. I guess we'll just have to see what happens when it's time for the *Union Ceremony* in a few years..." She trailed off, realizing that her friend had fallen asleep.

Rose sighed. Well, if she really wanted to have fun, maybe she should've stayed home, because now she was also in charge of making sure her friend stayed out of harm's way. This would officially go in the books as Rose's first and last high school party. It definitely wasn't all that her classmates hyped it up to be. Who did she think she was anyway? She wasn't friends with these people.

She was ready for a change of pace; Rose wanted to meet new people and discover more things about herself. She was *so* done with high school and learning the government's way of doing things. Their ways could be callous sometimes. She'd heard enough of her mother's sobs to know that when Rose's aunt passed away, it hadn't been an accident. Her aunt had no longer complied with the rules and was therefore made an example of. Maybe that's where Rose had gotten her attitude from.

She scooted over so Aire's head could rest comfortably in her lap and leaned her own head on the back of the chair. It wasn't long before she felt herself growing tired. Since Aire drove her family's car here, Rose would have to find her keys eventually and get them both home. Maybe she'd spend the night at Aire's instead of walking home. They only lived three blocks from one another, but in the middle of the night, that could be a dangerous trek. Great, now she sounded exactly like her dad.

Rosabella wasn't sure when she'd dozed off, but all of a sudden, she heard screams coming from the end of the massive yard. Her eyes snapped open, and her body jerked forward, knocking Aire from the chair onto the stone patio. *What on earth was that?* Aire, bless her soul, remained asleep; she had the alcohol to thank for that.

"Run!" Someone screamed. Rose jumped to action, hopping to her feet and looking around for the source of the screams. That's when she saw them. They came from the trees at the back of the property. The nature preserve to be exact. Rose wasn't sure if she'd seen them correctly for a second. She squinted to get a closer look. Instead of figuring out what they were, she watched in horror as one of them picked up a younger guy with one arm and ripped his head from his body in one sweep. She bit back a scream and knelt down beside Aire. The cool of the stone matched the icy fear in her heart.

"Come on! We have to go, *now!*" She shook her friend. "Aire, wake up!"

The screams were so deafening, she couldn't even think.

"Mhm?" Aire blinked lazily up at her.

"We need to run! There's these things--just get up. Please!" Rose grew frantic and tried lifting her friend up. Aire was just over six feet tall, while she herself was only 5'5"; it wasn't easy, but Rose was determined to save them both. "I'm not leaving you behind, but you need to help me help you."

Thankfully, they hadn't moved too far from the pool. Rose checked to make sure they were still far enough away from those things before dunking Aire's head in. After a few seconds, Aire pulled herself up, sputtering water. Her eyes wide and searching.

"Rosie? What the hell was that for?"

"No time to explain. Something's happening. Something bad."

Aire turned sideways to look over Rose's shoulder. She saw fear fill Aire's eyes. Nearly all the high schoolers who'd been playing games near the trees were now either decapitated, missing limbs, or running for their lives. Those running were headed straight for them.

"Rose! We have to get out of here now!"

She nodded, pulling Aire toward the patio door. "Gee, I wonder why I didn't think of that idea myself."

They made a beeline for the house. Some of the others must've seen them and followed suit. Before they could get to the door, one of the guys that had been hanging out near the booze table grabbed Rose. He spun her around.

"Don't let me die!" He cried, leaning forward. Without warning, he collapsed on Rose, pinning her to the ground. She screamed when she saw half his face missing. Soon she was covered in blood and some kind of greenish blue substance, oozing from the open wound in the boy's face.

"Rosie!" Aire helped shove the guy off of her. They both made it to the door, but not before she turned back to see what was happening. It was mass chaos. People were being attacked left and right. Those who weren't decapitated were stabbed with some kind of needle that was connected to the things' hands. Rose wasn't sure what to call them, but the one nearest them, only twenty yards away now, looked to be a cross between a human and robot.

Its body had the same shape as that of a tall human, but without eyes, a nose, or a mouth. Its "skin" was a creamy, white translucent material. She could see all the mechanical pieces inside of it; metal gears and gadgets filled the spaces where human organs were supposed to be. The final disturbing feature was the heart: the exact same shape and in the same place as a human's. The major difference: it was black.

Absolutely fascinating, the way they moved so gracefully. It took her breath away. She wouldn't share that with anyone--they'd simply think her crazy for finding a weapon of mass destruction beautiful.

There were too many to count now.

"We have to get in the house!" Aire dug her nails into Rose's arm. They were both nearly frozen with fear. One of them had to take charge if they were going to survive this. Rosabella felt a prick in her side, as if willing her to move forward. It expanded into a dull throbbing, which she took as a sign they needed to move.

"Keep going! I'll get the door open." She took a shallow breath and pulled the door open. It stuck once, but with a little extra pull, flew open. "You just keep going. Don't stop. Find a place to hide. Call the government guards."

She let Aire in first, and then a group of some other high schoolers slipped in behind her. Rose was just shutting the door when something in her friend's voice made her stop.

"Rose?"

She quickly spun around to see a man standing in the doorway between the back room and the kitchen. He was about six feet tall, with a built figure, but not the kind that made him look sickly ripped like those actors in the movies always did. He had caramel colored skin that shone in the lights mounted in the ceiling. Rose wasn't close with the girl whose family owned this house, but she knew her enough to know there wasn't a young man who lived with them. She was an only child, so it definitely couldn't be her brother.

"I know you must be scared...my name is Logan Clarke and I'm here to help you." He looked right at Rose when he spoke. Did she really look that afraid? Damn. She'd been trying to hide the terror on her face for Aire's sake if not her own. Obviously, she hadn't done too great a job if he spotted it from across the room. Everyone trailed him without hesitation. Rose wasn't sold on this mysterious man.

She took one more look behind her, at the chaos outside, and it was enough to make her lock the door and press the button to put the glass into night mode. They wouldn't be able to see inside...if they could see without having eyes.

"Don't worry, they can't see. They use some kind of sensory receptors to locate their victims," the man, Logan, said quietly from behind her, hands behind his back.

She scoffed and faced him. "Thanks, that makes me feel so much better."

He reached out and touched her arm. "I'm sorry, I didn't mean to freak you out...I guess I'm just used to this by now. I should be more sensitive to others' fear. My apologies...we've been through this before and we have a plan. You and your friends are going to get through this."

Rose wanted to pull away from his touch, but it was incredibly calming. She looked into his face, and where she expected to see lies, she saw only truth. He had such kind green eyes, it was almost difficult for her to look away.

"Okay, Logan. I'm going to trust you." She folded her arms and looked him dead in the eye. "But if you manage to screw this up and we all die, I'm going to make sure you suffer."

# Chapter 2

## (ROSABELLA)

DESPITE THEIR SITUATION, WITH THE CREATURES IN THE background searching around the yard for more people to kill, Logan laughed. He held out his hand for her to take. She hesitated for a moment before considering the alternative was being mauled by a murdering humanoid thing. She took his hand and followed him into the kitchen.

He gave her hand a gentle squeeze and left her at the back of the group. Once he stood before them, he held his hands up to silence the frenzied conversations.

Aire found her immediately and ran over. "What were you doing?"

"I was just making sure that Logan guy wasn't leading us to our deaths."

Aire looked down at her, brows furrowed. "And?"

Rose lifted her shoulders. "I don't know for sure, but it's better than having our heads ripped off by those things."

Logan began talking. His voice took hold of the room and all eyes glued to him. He had strength in commanding a crowd. Rose found herself impressed with his confidence and certainty.

"Now, I know you're all confused and scared, but please listen to what I have to say. I'm here to bring you to safety. We have a safe haven of sorts. I need you to know that before you enter, you have a choice to make. We are a secret organization, and therefore we have some--rather unfortunate--rules we must follow." He took a deep, steady breath. "You either join or you die. That is the rule. I don't want to kick anyone out, but I also don't want to force any of you to join a place you won't find a home in. But you need to decide quickly."

Rose didn't appreciate the sound of that. What was he thinking, giving them an ultimatum like that? Some of the others must have thought the same things, because they began whispering amongst themselves.

"Please, I don't want anyone to be uncomfortable." His frown convinced Rose he felt truly sorry. "It really is a safe place. But in order to maintain that safety, we have to follow these rules. Those of you who do not wish to move forward with us can try to fend for yourselves in this house. Those of you who wish to continue...follow me."

Without even thinking, Rose moved to follow him out of the room. Aire grabbed her arm and forced her to look up at her. The fire in her eyes made Rose fearful of her friend for the first time in a while. Aire had a way of making sure she got her way.

"Rose you can't be serious. He's probably leading us to our deaths."

"Aire, I'm not going to stay here and get killed by those things. You do what you want, but I'm intrigued by this safe haven...especially if it means I get to live." Without another word, Rose stormed out of the room after Logan. She knew there was no other option for her. The idea of leaving this world excited her. Nobody would be able to make this decision, other than herself. Maybe there would be new rules and regulations, but she could already see herself in a new environment; and who knows, maybe she'd be able to alter the rules to her liking?

Rosabella met up with Logan at the front door.

He smiled when he saw her crossing the threshold, revealing a row of shiny white teeth. "I knew you'd follow me. Now that you're here, I'm sure others will join."

She smirked. "Well, as long as you don't kill all of us, I'll be right behind you."

So relieved to see Aire join them, Rose could have cried. About half of the others filtered into the room after a minute or two, which wasn't saying much; they'd made it to the house with fifteen. Oh well, it was their decision to stay here. She wasn't even sure if she was making the correct choice; she could die the moment they moved an inch. She looked up at Logan and noticed him peeking at her. Was there something wrong with her?

When they made eye contact, he smiled at her and leaned in. "You're very brave. I was just admiring that about you."

She laughed, disregarding the strangeness of that comment. "Umm. Thank you. I guess you're not so bad yourself...again, if you don't get us killed, remind me to thank you."

"When." There was that smile again. His green eyes lit up.

"Excuse me?"

He laughed again. "I said *when* I don't get you all killed."

"We'll see about that," she muttered under her breath. He'd already turned his attention to the group so he didn't hear her. If he had, she was certain he would have smiled. What a happy guy. Even though they were in danger of being slaughtered by those things, he still managed an optimistic view of the situation.

"Alright everyone," Logan grabbed their attention with his strong voice. "Please make sure to stay close. I'm going to take the lead on this, and I expect all of you to follow me closely. If anything goes wrong, alert me at once." With that, he opened the front door. Rose and the other highschoolers, tucked in the house safely behind Logan, peered out at the brightly lit porch and an equally bright road. Logan poked his head out, looking in every direction before stepping foot outside.

Rose stepped down onto the porch after him. Aire grabbed her hand, holding her back again. "Rosie, are you sure about this? Maybe we can ride this out in the house."

Logan heard the scepticism in Aire's voice and turned around. "It's entirely possible you could do that here."

Aire sighed, a smile crossing her face. "There. You see? We'll be fine."

"It's not a guarantee though. The droids are unpredictable. You never know when they'll be done with their hunt." Logan shook his head and looked Aire in the eye. "We've been studying them for months now, but we can't get a good read on why they do what they do. I wouldn't trust this house at all."

Rose pulled her friend along. If Logan was telling the truth, they didn't have much time to get the hell out of there. She decided to follow him into the unknown. It would be better than waiting for a surprise death, helpless. At least she'd have a chance at survival this way. A chance for freedom. This time Aire didn't argue, but she also didn't let go of her tight hold on Rose's hand. She tried giving Aire a squeeze to tell her they'd make it through this. Hope was always better than despair.

They made it across the street before she dared to say anything. The only other sound came from the others and their nervous panting.

"Logan?" whispered Rose.

He didn't turn around but he did slow his pace so she could walk beside him.

She let go of Aire's hand to catch up. "Why is this place of yours so secretive?"

He breathed out in a long stream. "It's just a rule we've always followed. If we stray from tradition, who knows what could happen? We're already the minority in this sector." He gave her a sideways glance. "I shouldn't be telling you this, but if the government found out where we were located, they could obliterate us in minutes."

That didn't sit well with Rose. It chilled her to the core. "What does the government have against you?"

Logan smiled down at her, without teeth, probably to verify he could trust her. He'd just rescued them from a really patriotic governmental neighborhood after all; he couldn't be completely positive they wouldn't turn on him. That's what made Rose trust him. He put his life on the line for them: for people he knew absolutely nothing about.

"We've created our own society. We make our own rules, and we don't follow any of those put in place by the government. Basically, when people join with us, they become invisible up here."

She clutched his arm. "I'm sorry, did you just say *up* here?"

"Shh." He took her hand in his. "I don't want the others to freak out. We have to keep them calm or else the droids will detect their fear."

Oh right. She'd almost forgotten about being hunted by inhumane creature things. What a great time to have a birthday. "Okay, I'm sorry."

"Don't be sorry. Until today, you had no idea the droids existed." He gave her a sympathetic look and surrendered her hand. They'd woven through numerous houses and lawns already. She wouldn't begin to guess where they were headed, but at least she knew it involved going *down*.

"One more question--I'm sorry if this is annoying. I'm just really curious."

He let out a light laugh. "It's really difficult to annoy me. I'm a very patient person. What's your question?"

"How did you find out about this place? Were you rescued too?"

"No. I was actually born there--oh, watch your step." He grabbed her hand and pulled her out of the way of something. She took a closer look and nearly screamed. It was someone's head. Just the head, the body nowhere in sight.

He pulled her in close, lips in her hair. "Don't draw attention to it. If they don't see it, they won't be scared."

"Did those things--"

"Droids."

"Sure." She took a shaky breath and continued, "Did they really make it all the way over here too? I thought they came from the opposite end of the neighborhood--Wait! What about our families?"

"We've had countless patrols go through the nearby neighborhoods tonight. It just so happens that party was the last place we checked. Most of the people were given the same choice. We'll see how many of them trusted our men and women once we get there. But now you understand why we have to be vague. If we give too many specifics, they could discover our location."

She shook her head in disbelief. "The government can be pretty harsh. I used to just think they were annoyingly strict."

"That all depends on where you grow up and who your parents are."

They made eye contact. Something passed between them; an understanding. In that moment, she was sure Logan had had many of the same thoughts as her growing up. Maybe, just maybe, she'd find her place wherever they were going.

"Well, Logan Clarke, do you have any advice for me?"

"I don't know--what's your name?"

She faced forward, afraid to see his expression. She'd been picked on for her name all her life. Some said it was untraditional in that it contained four syllables. Names were better when they were short, she was told. It was easier for people to call you by name when it was two syllables or less.

"Rosabella."

His pace faltered for a second. She'd screwed herself over for a better start already. What had she been thinking? She'd gotten used to introducing herself as Rose because of that fact. For a second, she'd betrayed herself and thought she could trust him.

Face red, she looked to the ground. "I know. It's really long. I hate it."

He stopped walking altogether and stepped right in front of her. It forced Rose to look at him.

"I think it's a beautiful name, Rosabella. You shouldn't be embarrassed by it. We promote individualization and uniqueness where I come from. Your name would be embraced."

She didn't take compliments well, even from people she knew. So this was really off the table for her. Rose's face warmed; she was the type of person who'd blush at the thought of turning red. It was a vicious, never ending cycle. Before another wave of embarrassment could take over her, she decided to remind him of their quest.

Rose nodded her chin. "We shouldn't slow down."

He gave her one more look before conceding, "Alright. Come on."

After a minute, she couldn't take their silence anymore. She fell back to walk beside Aire instead, taking hold of her hand again. The two of them remained silent, but it wasn't the same as it had been with Logan. Being silent next to Aire was comfortable; Logan's silence made her feel strange. It hadn't been awful, but she'd felt the need to fill that silence with chatter, yet she couldn't think of anything to talk about. She'd save her other questions for when they arrived. There would be plenty of chatter for her then.

Logan held a fist up. Rose and the rest of the group came to an abrupt halt. Everyone started looking around. The air was thick with anxiety, their nerves all bundled up into a tight ball of fear. She felt tense and sick at the same time.

"Logan?" Rose whispered.

He turned his head to her, eyes dark and focused and...was that *scared*? What had he seen? Or what had he *not* seen? Were they lost? She wanted to ask all of her questions, but the look in his eyes silenced her. Eventually, Logan shook his head at her.

Their group was small, so they packed themselves together to keep a united front. Whatever those droids did to the people at the party, Rose was determined to not let it happen to them. She squeezed Aire's hand again, but it was much harder this time. Her friend winced before returning the squeeze, equally as rough. As they huddled in someone's backyard, Rose recognized the house across the street. They were near her house. She acknowledged the same muted grey siding of her house up ahead. Their porch light had been turned on. She noted it as out of the ordinary, as it usually cycled on a timer that shut it off by no "Rosie?" Aire must have seen the same thing.

Her throat squeezed. "I know."

A low whirring sound exploded in Rose's ears then. She cried out and fell to her knees, clutching her head.

Logan was beside her in an instant. "Rosabella? What's wrong?" He pushed her hair back from her face to get a better look at her. He touched her forehead, cheeks, neck, stomach, legs, everything.

The sound developed into a piercing sound, too loud for her to endure. If she'd taken the most annoying sound in the whole world and amplified it by one hundred, it still wouldn't compare to this debilitating penetration of her sanity. She would give anything for it to stop! She screamed again, pain taking full control of her body.

Logan picked her up and cradled her, breaking into a run. "Come on, we need to get out of here!"

She tried squeezing her head between her hands to see if that would relieve the pressure. It didn't work. Then she pursed her lips to keep from screaming again after her attempts failed. The others were already scared out of their minds; she didn't need to make it worse for them. She was only vaguely aware of them running toward a house.

"Here? Are you sure?" Aire's voice, nearly impossible to hear over the whirring in her head, was hesitant. Her side throbbed again, but this time it felt like it was ripping her apart from the inside out. Rose couldn't hear Logan's response. She didn't know what was happening. All that mattered was making it stop. Tears welled in her eyes. Damn it! She didn't want them to see her like this.

Soon, she was laid on a cold, flat surface, with Logan's face hovering right in front of her own. She barely heard him over the sharp whirring, "Close your eyes. Think about something else."

She shook her head, focusing on his green eyes. "I--I can't! It hurts!"

He ignored her comment and kept talking, "What makes you happy? Is there someone you love more than life itself?"

"Yes," whimpered Rose. Her brother. That eight-year-old bundle of joy she'd left behind tonight.

Then, just as quickly as it had started, the whirring stopped. Her muscles collapsed, turning her into a puddle of noodles. Logan allowed his own tense arms to release her, breathing heavy. He didn't take his eyes off of her for a second, but she couldn't bear to look at him anymore and tore her eyes away from his.

This kitchen...why was it familiar? Granted, she was on the floor and didn't have the best view, but she'd recognize this place anywhere.

"Can you please tell me why we're in Rose's house?" Aire blurted from a few feet away. She stared daggers at Logan. Rose observed their dishes from dinner, stacked neatly next to the dish chute. Tomorrow was dish day, one of two times the whole week they were allowed to use extra water for their dish chute, so they made sure to leave them out on the counter. It was likely they'd forget about them if they put them in the sink. It always happened if they didn't put things right in front of their faces.

Logan massaged his hands, lips tight. "This is where one of our entrances is housed."

Rose spotted him looking at her from the corner of her eye. She didn't want to feel helpless anymore and attempted sitting up. It was a weak attempt, but it caught Aire's attention.

"Rose, don't move!" She ran over, taking Rose's head in her hands. She began stroking her forehead, massaging her temples. It was a much appreciated gesture. Rose's eyes closed involuntarily.

She thanked her friend, "You're the best."

"Don't you dare come near her again," said Aire, anger dripping from each word.

Rose's eyes snapped open. Logan stood there sheepishly, looking down at her. She wished he wouldn't keep staring at her like that.

"Rei, it's okay," she calmed her friend before turning to Logan. "Why are we in my house?"

He ignored her, "Come on, we need to keep moving. We aren't safe up here."

Rose slammed her fist down on the counter. Several people gasped, some jumped. "Not until you tell me why the hell we're in *my house*."

Logan lifted her up again, cradling her as he did before. "Rosabella, believe me, I will tell you everything. But I need to get you there immediately. You've been struck."

As if on cue, her side throbbed again. She twisted in his arms, reaching for her side. If she could just see it, she'd be able to determine what was going on. He nudged her forehead with his chin.

"Trust me, you don't want to see it."

Oddly enough, that made her even more curious to see what was happening. After carefully considering his words, she decided not to check. If it was as bad as he implied, she definitely wouldn't like it. Besides, the movement sent a sharp shooting pain up to her shoulder.

She watched in amazement while Logan showed them to the pantry. Aire huffed something about not trusting him, but she followed right behind. The rest of their group filed into the pantry, all seven pairs of eyes wide and searching. Logan leaned in toward something on one of the shelves. A scanner popped out of the side of a bag. It scanned his thumb before extending a tiny microphone. He whispered some sort of passphrase into it. It recoiled itself, and for a moment, she didn't think it'd worked. Then the back shelved panel of the pantry slid open to reveal a white wall. She turned her head into Logan's chest when he stepped forward right into the wall. She braced herself for impact, but it never came. Instead, they went right *through* the screen. Straight into an elevator. Her gasp brought a laugh out of Logan.

"What--? How--?" She couldn't even speak. A haze of debilitation settled in over her, turning her head to soupy mush.

"If you think *that's* cool, wait until you see what's ahead." His shoulders shook with a small laugh.

Aire charged in after them. "This isn't very big. How many can fit with you Logan?"

"About five...but I don't want any of you to bump into Rosabella, so we should keep it to four."

She refused to leave people behind because she was in pain. "No. Put me down. If you support my weight, we can squeeze one more in if I press against the wall."

He shook his head. "If you can stand, I'll help you. But that still won't leave enough room for all of us to fit. I'll come right back up for them. It'll only take half a minute."

She searched his eyes. If he was lying, he'd look away briefly and then back at her. She'd learned that trick from her mom. She didn't see any tell-tale signs he was lying. In fact, he'd looked right into her eyes the whole time.

"Fine. But put me down please. We can at least let five people go down instead of four." She wiggled around, trying to get him to set her down. It hurt to move, but she wanted to save as many people as possible. A lot could happen in half a minute.

He sighed, a sure sign he didn't believe she could handle standing. Rose was committed to proving him wrong. So what if her legs were numb? If she could see the ground, she could see where to stand and when to move her legs. Unless it was dark.

Unfortunately, they all rode down in pitch black, a chorus of their breaths the only thing keeping her centered. How did people do this without falling over? Thankfully she had Logan to lean on, but had she been alone, she'd be on the ground already.

"I think you'll really like it here." Logan's voice made her jump, but he was there, with an arm around her waist to keep her from falling.

"What makes you so sure?"

She didn't get to hear his response. The whirring in her head returned. Rose wailed, losing her balance completely. She tried squeezing her head again, but it did no good. Now that it was dark, it was even worse. Claustrophobia kicked in and soon she began hyperventilating. There wasn't enough air. The walls were closing in! Her chest constricted. A bubble of pain formed at the base of her throat.

Logan wrapped both arms around her waist, keeping her on her feet. "Hold on, we're almost there!"

"Logan, what's happening to her?" Aire yelled over Rose's shrieks. The pain was too much. Every time she moved an inch, the sharpshooting pain came back, but now it was making its way from her shoulders into her neck. If it reached her head and combined with the whirring, what would happen? She'd probably explode.

"Rosabella, hold on. Hold on," Logan repeated until they finally came to a stop. Light flooded the tiny space. What was meant to be a fifteen or so second elevator ride had turned into an eternity for her. Logan scooped her up again. The others filed out into a wide open space. She kept shaking her head, willing the pain to stop. She honestly didn't know if she was screaming anymore since the whirring bounced against what seemed like every single one of her brain cells. Everything went dark. Or she closed her eyes. Or both.

Another man's deep voice cut through the pain. "Clarke, what's going on?"

"Clayton, thank goodness! She's been hit. I don't know how she even made it this far, but we have to get her to the medical wing."

"You know that it won't help anything."

Logan must have pushed past him, because Rose was jolted around.

"Clarke, stop at once. Please don't disobey my orders."

"If you don't let me pass, Clayton, I'll see to it myself that you have a world of hurt ahead of you." His voice cracked, "Just let me help this girl. I can't let anyone else die."

Clayton fell silent. What more did he need to think about? Rose just needed to be taken to the freaking medical wing or whatever it was called. Was she still screaming? The pain was definitely still there, and she couldn't feel anything below her neck anymore. At least that meant she couldn't feel the sharp pain in her torso. That was good, right?

"Alright. But I'll take her. You get the rest of these kids safely inside. We don't know if anything was following you."

Logan handed her off. "Shit, I have to go back up for the rest of them!"

Aire caught on to the exchange and joined them. "Rosie? What's happening to her? Who are you people? Oh my god, can you help her?"

The one named Clayton huffed, annoyed. "Not if you keep asking me questions."

Rose would've corrected him for talking to someone like that had she been fully functioning. As it was, the whirring was taking over her brain. She couldn't even remember how words felt in her mouth. All she knew was the whirring pain.

"If you know what's good for you, you'll stay here with the others. We'll help you, but only if you cooperate." He stormed away, leaving her friend behind. What if Rose never saw Aire again? Why were they being separated? Why had he said taking her to the medical wing wouldn't help anything? Surely he'd have yelled at her if she'd asked those questions out loud.

The farther from the elevator they went, the more the pain subsided. It reduced to a dull ache by the time Clayton stopped walking. She kept her eyes closed, afraid of what she might see if she opened them. Or what if that only brought the pain back? Through her closed lids, she could tell they were in a room with bright lights. What if that's what had set her off the first time? She'd been looking at her porch light when it started after all.

"I need medical attention for this girl right now."

Rose could hear people scrambling around.

"I said right *now*. If you can't move faster, I'll carry her to a room myself."

Rose wished she could speak. She'd give him a piece of her mind for acting like such an asshole. Didn't he know those were human beings he was talking to? Or maybe they had robots for nurses too. That had become the new thing these past few years. Many of the teachers, nurses and a few other professions had been replaced by robots programmed to perform the same exact work.

"Right this way. Please follow me, Mr. Taylor."

He scoffed. "It's about time. I could have grown a full beard by now."

Rose wanted to shake her head, but she still didn't have control of her body. Instead, she sucked in a breath, anticipating the whirring to start again. If she so much as moved her head, would it start? Clayton laid her down on a bed, surprisingly gentle for someone who had such a hard demeanor.

Once she felt him release her, she dared to open her eyes. The first thing she saw were eyes the color of chocolate looking at her with a strange expression. He had a confused look on his face, just as Logan had when he'd hovered over her on the floor.

"Just so you know, most people would be dead by now if they'd been struck. I shouldn't even be giving you special treatment if you're going to die anyway."

It was her turn to scoff. "Gee thanks. I'll be sure to send you a postcard when I'm dead."

"Hmm."

She felt good, rendering him speechless like that. It meant he was still somewhat human. It also made her feel good to speak again instead of scream. Rosabella watched him head for the door, leaving her alone in the bed. She was completely immobile save for her face now; even her neck was numb.

"Can we get a doctor in here?"

"You don't have to stay here you know." She spat at his back. "I'd probably do a lot better if your negativity wasn't making me too angry to focus on anything else."

She'd never seen another person turn around so fast. She took a good look at him then. He was very handsome; but he seemed to know that. He had curly dark brown hair--almost black, a built figure and those beautiful brown eyes. She wasn't sure if she'd ever seen a more attractive man before in her life. In person anyway. The actors in the movies Rose's mom made her watch were usually decently attractive, but that was all edited to make them appear that way. This was all natural.

She'd also never wanted to smack one as hard as she wanted to Clayton.

"Are you enjoying the show?"

Damn. He must have caught her staring at him. She supposed she'd made it pretty obvious. She must have looked as baffled as she felt, because he smirked and moved to stand at the head of the bed, right by her face.

"Can you move anything?" He moved a strand of her hair from her face, so it wasn't sticking with sweat to her temples. At least he'd picked up on that.

"Only my face."

"Well, that's all a person needs. If this goes south, at least you'll still have that."

She rolled her eyes. "Spare me the death jokes. I'll be fine."

He crossed his arms and glared at her. How tall was he? Looking up at him, she was a tiny ant compared to him.

She was interrupted from her examination by hearing shouts from down the hall. Aire! She could really use a friend right now. She almost started crying when she spotted Aire and Logan run into the room.

Logan looked around. "What's going on? Where's the doctor?"

"I don't know. I've told them like fifty times to get their asses moving, but here we still are."

She'd about had enough of Clayton. Attractive or not, he was being rude. "Seriously, shut up! If you can't, then I want you to leave the room."

"People don't talk to me like that." It was more of a statement. Nevertheless, it made her feel powerful. He had a terrible attitude.

She glared at Logan, who was now sitting on the edge of the bed. "I hope the other people here aren't like him. Otherwise, I'm out of here."

He laughed and took her hand in his, giving it a friendly squeeze. She couldn't feel it, but she could see it.

"They're not all like our Clayton. He's a special one."

"I'm right here."

She ignored Clayton. "Rei, are you okay at least?"

"I will be once you're back to normal." Her friend ran around to the open side of the bed and leaned down to hug Rose. They stayed like that until the doctor came in.

Clayton headed for the door once the doctor started her inspection. He looked over his shoulder at her. "If this is what you're like when you're literally dying, I don't want to know what your 'normal' looks like."

"Don't worry, you'll get to see it." She made a mean face at him to solidify her point, but he was already gone.

The doctor asked Aire and Logan to leave the room too. They told Rose they'd be right outside if she needed them.

Once the room was empty except for herself and the doctor, Rose tried making light of the situation, "Doctor? Am I really going to die?"

The doctor patted her cheek. She had a kind smile and a hoop in her nose. "I hope not, dear. Try not to be afraid. You've already made it this far. There's hope for you."

"I pray you're right."

"Close your eyes, this may hurt."

Hurt it did. She didn't even know she could still feel until the doctor started going to work. Rose could only guess what she was doing. Perhaps cutting her side to get at whatever that stuff was? Whatever the case, she was not going to let a little pain take her out.

She'd have to start really fighting when she woke up, because the pain was indeed too strong for her to stay awake now. Everything went dark again, but not by choice. This time she didn't close her eyes; pain darkened her vision until she passed out.

# Chapter 3

## (ROSABELLA)

A BRIGHT LIGHT BROUGHT ROSE TO HER SENSES. SHE refused to open her eyes just yet. For the first time in a while, she was truly comfortable. As she lay there, she tried to wrap her mind around what had happened. Had everything been real? Or had it been a dream? She remembered a man named Logan who'd helped bring her and the others to safety. They'd gotten there by going through her own pantry--when had that elevator been put in there? She remembered Logan arguing with another man named Clayton once they left the elevator, but at that point, the pain was so surreal, she could hardly concentrate. She'd have to ask Rei for the details later. If she was allowed to leave. How long had she been in the medical wing?

Rose decided there was nothing to lose by opening her eyes. She blinked until the bright lights didn't seem so harsh. It didn't help that everything she saw was white; the light reflected off of everything in sight. She sat up and rubbed her eyes, happy the pain in her head was gone. The machine next to her head started beeping.

Almost instantly, the door to her room opened and a middle-aged man walked in. He went to the machine right away and pressed some buttons, turning the annoying beeping noise off. He took her hand and checked some of her vitals before taking her head in his hands. He shone a flashlight into her eyes, her ears and nose. She let him go about his check-up, sitting there obediently. She didn't dare to speak so that he could focus on what he needed to do. The sooner he finished, the sooner she could reunite with Aire and their other classmates.

Only when he began putting his tools away did he say anything, "You sure are impressive. We were starting to worry for a few days there. We thought we'd have to induce a coma to keep you alive."

"Glad I could save you a step," she teased. "Now, if you don't mind, I'd really love to go see my friends."

He gave her a friendly smile. "Based on what the others have told me about you, I'm not surprised."

She was encouraged by his smile. At least Logan had told her the truth; not everyone else here was like Clayton--thank goodness. Rose let her legs dangle over the edge of the bed, ready to run out of the room to find everyone. The nurse took hold of her arm and gently pushed her back onto the bed. It wasn't meant to be rude, but Rose was still annoyed that he wouldn't let her up.

"Please don't push yourself. You'll be out of here in no time, I promise. But I have strict orders to keep you here until you can be released by Bernard." He smiled at her with sympathy. At least he felt bad about making her stay in bed.

She wasn't used to this. She'd been pushing herself all her life; what made now any different? To satisfy this man, she grimaced and nodded.

"Good. I'll go buzz for him right now. Be right back."

Bless that man's heart. She convinced him she was going to comply, when really, she was going to make a run for it. She double checked to make sure nothing from the machine was still connected to her. When she cleared herself, she hopped out of bed and made her way to the door. It wasn't a painfully slow process, but it certainly wasn't as fast as she would have liked. She poked her head out the door, finding herself near a desk. A young teenage girl sat in a chair behind the desk, papers in front of her. She hoped the little girl didn't have any authority to tell her to stay in her room or else they were going to have a problem.

Everywhere she looked, there was white. White walls, white shelves, even those who passed the room wore white shoes and shirts. She didn't know why they were wearing so much of the same color, but now wasn't the time to bother asking. The main doors were just past the desk with the little girl. She observed for a moment in order to confirm that they were motion activated. No thumb scan was needed.

It was actually fairly easy for her to sneak past the doctors and nurses walking past her room. She made sure to time it right, when nobody was in the hall. She knew the little girl was staring at her as she walked across the hallway, past the desk, and straight out the doors. She'd probably call for the nurse who'd been sent in to take care of her today, but by the time they'd receive word Rose was gone, she'd already be reunited with Aire and the others. The only thing left was to figure out where the heck she was. Easy, right?

***

## (AIRE)

Aire kept her head down, afraid to look Bernard in the eye. Everyone else in the room treated him as if he were a king. That was how people treated the government where she came from. She wasn't used to seeing one person leading the masses, so this was certainly a change of pace.

While she waited for him to start speaking, she thought of Rose. What on earth had happened to her best friend? She'd never seen Rose do anything like that before. It was terrifying. Especially when she thought Rosie was going to die. Looking at her lying there on that hospital bed was awful. She was so pale and cold. It really made her blue eyes stand out, but in a sickly flattering way. Her orange-red hair had taken on a matted appearance from thrashing around on the floor in her house. That was a whole new issue she didn't have a chance to ask about yet. How had Rose not known there was a door to an entirely different, underground, secret society in her own *house*?

She'd been dragged away from Rose's hospital bed that night against her will by Logan. He had no right to do that! She needed to be there for her friend and he'd taken that from her. Then they had the audacity to bring her to get a change of clothes and a meal in her? Who were these people? For days, Aire feared Rosie could be dying and she wouldn't even be there to hold her hand. They'd done everything together for years, and surely that wouldn't change because one of them was incapacitated, right? They met when they were both really young, and ever since then, they'd been inseparable. Anyway, she wasn't sure what was happening with Rose now. She hadn't been allowed to visit her since they'd first arrived nearly two weeks ago.

This was the first time they'd seen the so-called Bernard in person. Everyone had mentioned him, but they'd never elaborated. Now she understood why. He was too difficult to put into words. Bernard was much shorter than herself, probably only five feet seven inches or so, but he took over the room just by walking through the door. He had these eyes that seemed able to cut someone in half should they step out of line, yet he had a brilliantly wide smile. She couldn't decide what to think of him.

She stood on the end of the group, aware that they were meant to listen to Bernard, who was standing on a foldable stage. The room was humongous! It reminded her of their high school cafeteria but much larger. They even had similar light grey tile floors and off-white walls. Their high school had been very selective, and hadn't allowed more than a set number of students in each age level, which made for classes smaller in size than the national average and lots of opportunities to get to know their classmates.

Bernard made eye contact with all seven of the new "saves," as people here called them. "I know you've been here for a little while and are still uncertain about who we are and what we do, so I wanted to give you some answers. But before we get into that, I am here to welcome you to our peaceful home. Welcome to the Fortress!"

Everyone in the room besides herself and the six other rescues began clapping. Bernard waited for the hoots and hollers to die down before continuing. He had a booming voice that pulled her along and kept her listening. If only Rose could be here with her. It would make everything better. If her friend survived whatever poison had been injected into her by the droids, Aire vowed to get both of them out of here somehow. She'd do whatever was necessary. Maybe the people of the Fortress really brought all of them here for ransom. Pretty much all of their parents had connections in the government. If they wanted to, the government could supply any dollar amount to save their beloved officials' children. Aire didn't mind the hierarchy, so long as it aided her.

"It seems you're all still wary of us...and rightly so. We can't just expect that you'll fall right into step with our ways here, but we do ask that you try. If you are committed to staying in our safe haven, you'll at least comply with our rules. You don't have to undergo all of the intensive combat training sessions required of our members right away, but we still like our citizens to at least be trained in self defense." He looked around the expansive room. "Would anyone like to give a testimonial of their time here?"

She noticed a group of two other men and three women at the back of the stage, surprised to see Logan among them. He stepped forward and whispered something to Bernard, who stepped back to let him have the microphone.

"I was born here. My parents escaped to the Fortress and had the opportunity to start their new lives here. They seized the moment and decided it was the safest place for them at the time."

"Basically, I've lived my entire life in the Fortress and have found no issue to question our rules. We are safe because we work together. For those of you who are new, I can only imagine how you must feel." He seemed to look right at Aire when he said that. "I can speak for all of us when I say we don't want you to feel lost or forced into anything you can't handle. If you have a question, please ask right away. Don't let it build up so that you come to hate us and what we stand for. That is my only advice for you. Welcome."

What kind of testimonial was that? He basically just told them to talk about their problems before they got out of hand. Was there something Aire should be worried about? She'd already gotten the tour of the Fortress, and to be honest, she wasn't too impressed. Their technology down here was old fashioned compared to what they had above.

She did feel some sympathy for Logan. He was so brainwashed he couldn't see how controlling they were. If only she could have told her best friend all these things. Aire had so much to share! Similar to their home above, they were required by the Fortress's rules to go into a career in the hopes they would use their skills accordingly to keep order and structure to their social system. Unlike the world above, they actually had some say in what their career would be down here. Usually, the Government would pick a career for you based on your social standing and your skillset. There were still powerful families who had the ability to influence which careers their children or other family members went into, but that was only in the top one percent of their society. Personally, Aire believed her sister, Luna, could help get her anywhere in life if she batted her eyelashes at the right people. Luna held a lower position in the Government, but was fortunate enough to be employed in the corporate building in this sector.

Suddenly, Clayton took the microphone. He swallowed before speaking. He was the only good thing she'd seen since arriving at the Fortress. Aire had the biggest crush on him--but, come on, who didn't? With his chocolate eyes, he must've had every girl pining for him. She couldn't wait for Rose to meet him. He was awfully brutal and tough, but most of the best men were. They just needed someone to break down their outer shell to get to their heart. If Aire wound up staying here, she'd make it worth her while. Clayton had been the first to show their group of seven around the Fortress the day after they'd been saved, but that wasn't the first moment Aire felt something stir inside her chest for him. That moment had been when the elevator doors opened and she'd seen his face. God, those eyes were so beautiful. Oh, and his muscles!

She wasn't even sure what he said in his speech because all she could think about was how gorgeous he looked in his tight grey t-shirt and faded jeans. How could someone make such an average outfit look like a style fit for royalty? She could already see them together. She'd heard someone in the kitchen say something about how they were allowed to pick who they married here. What a concept! If that were true, she'd definitely make sure Clayton knew how great of a partner she'd make. She could already see their children. They'd look so great with his brown eyes and her light brown skin.

She waited patiently for the rest of the speeches to be made. She was getting annoyed with all these people who'd put down their lives for the Fortress. Rose wouldn't like this place one bit; she'd never liked feeling confined or controlled, which was funny, seeing as though her parents were so strict. Or maybe that's why Rosie was determined to not be controlled by others, because she was so used to it at home; they hadn't really given her any choices. She was just expected to be the best at everything. And everyone knew she was.

Bernard took the stage again. "Thank you for all your kind words. We all appreciate you taking time to stand in front of us and share your stories. Now, I would like--"

All heads turned to a middle-aged man running across the room. He wore a white nurse's uniform: white pants and shirt. From the looks of it, he was upset. He clearly had his sights on Bernard and ran right for him, when Clayton intercepted him at the foot of the stage's steps. Aire felt her heart speed up. That was so brave of him, to put himself between that man and his leader.

Bernard waved his hand at Clayton, using his last name to address him, "Taylor, let him pass."

They all tried to listen to what the nurse whispered to Bernard, but they were perfectly secretive about it. She couldn't hear a thing. If it was about Rosabella, she needed to be involved. She made a last second--uncharacteristic--decision to be brave herself and made her way over to Clayton.

He didn't notice her standing next to him, so she took it upon herself to ask him what was going on. He crossed his arms and looked at her. Maybe he had a few more inches on her, but that was about it. Nevertheless, he was the only man she'd met who was taller than her father.

"I'm not sure. But Bernard will tell me if it has anything to do with your friend Riley."

She giggled, a flirtation trick she'd learned by watching her sister interact with men in the Government. They were usually easily swayed, but Clayton didn't seem to even care.

He looked down his nose at her. "Did I say something funny?"

She wouldn't be discouraged yet. He didn't know her well at all if he thought she could be intimidated out of flirting by a harsh tone. "Her name isn't Riley. You probably heard me call her *Rosie*."

"Oh. I see. Well, I'll be sure to call her the right name from now on." He turned away, glancing up at Bernard, who still had his head bent next to the nurse.

Aire nudged Clayton's arm. "So what's your role in all of this?"

He sighed and turned back to her. "Weren't you listening to my testimonial? And why are you asking me so many questions?"

Oh crap. How could she tell him that she'd been too busy fantasizing their future together instead of listening to his speech? It was obvious she'd taken too long to respond, because he began walking away. It was a slight consolation when she realized he was following Bernard, who'd left the stage without her noticing. One of the women who'd been on the stage behind him had taken over the microphone. Aire had no idea what she was saying, she was too busy following Clayton to the huddle he'd formed with himself, Bernard and Logan.

As she neared them, she heard Bernard say Rose's name.

In response, Clayton shoved Logan back against the wall. "Clarke, weren't *you* in charge of her?"

He squinted up at Clayton, just as angry. "Don't touch me! I'm a member of the Cabinet. And I didn't even know she was awake!"

Aire ran up to them and tugged on Clayton's arm. "Rosie's awake?"

Clayton groaned. "Watch out, if you let her talk, she'll ask a million questions before you can answer one."

Tears pooled in her eyes. How could he say something so rude? She was in a foreign place she didn't even want to be in and he wasn't making it any better.

Bernard stood on his tiptoes and did his best to get in Clayton's face, though it was impossible with their height difference. "Silence! Clayton Taylor, if you don't start keeping yourself in check, you'll be demoted."

She fought the urge to shiver at the harshness of his voice. It was quiet but deadly. How anyone could hold so much power in a whisper was beyond her.

It didn't matter nearly as much as her friend did. Aire released Clayton and turned to Bernard. If she couldn't get through his beautiful head, she could at least try to convince their leader to let her visit Rosie. "Please, she's my best friend. I need to see her."

Bernard looked at her with sad eyes. "We don't know where she is right now. She could be anywhere in the Fortress."

"What I don't understand," Clayton said, running his fingers through his curly hair, "Is how one little girl could sneak past all of the medical personnel."

Wow, had she really done that? Aire couldn't help but smile. "That's Rosie for you. She's always been crafty. And stubborn." She laughed. "She won't come back without a fight."

She didn't know why Clayton and Bernard quickly shared a look at that. All she knew was that she had to help them look for Rose, or they wouldn't be able to reign her in. She could only beg so long, though if she was being honest, it was pretty pathetic. She wasn't sure, if her role was reversed with Clayton's, that she would let *him* help look for Rosie. "Please?"

Bernard nodded and immediately, Clayton groaned again. Was she really that annoying? Their leader wrapped an arm around her shoulders. "Of course you can join us. If she's as stubborn as you say she is, we'll keep the search party to just the four of us. We don't want her running off again and causing a fuss." He steered her toward the door. "Can you think of places she could be hiding? Somewhere she might feel comfortable?"

She thought for a moment. Oh, of course!
She nodded excitedly. "I have a couple ideas."

# Chapter 4

**(ROSABELLA)**

S HE WASN'T SURE WHICH ROUTE SHE'D TAKEN OUT of the medical
wing, there had been too many to count. This place was like a maze.
Nothing made sense to her. That was the most exciting part about this,
albeit scary as hell. Still, she'd asked for change and a fresh start, and here
she was in a completely new place. If only she'd been a patient person,
she could have waited for that man, Baylee or Bernie or something, to
come talk to her, maybe she'd have a better shot at fitting in. As it was,
she didn't really have any other option but to move forward.

She'd checked in every room that seemed important as she passed
it. There wasn't any reason for her to open every door. There were too
many anyway. She'd be caught before she even got down one of the long
hallways.

Logan had made this place seem small and cramped. From what she
saw, they had an entire network of underground spaces to use to their
advantage down here. That was so strange to her. She was underground
right now. Perhaps even right below her own house, a matter for another
time.

Was her family down here too? That was enough to make her slow
her pace. What if her parents had known about this place all along and
hadn't wanted to risk their children revealing it? She was sure they'd do
something chivalrous like that. Where her parents were extremely strict,

they were also compassionate. Even if they hadn't installed the elevator themselves, certainly, they would have done whatever they could to keep these people safe. If her *dad* trusted them enough to keep quiet, that was saying something. That could only mean there was something worth saving down here.

All the walls were the same bright off-white as the ones in her room in the medical wing. The tile floors were all a light grey in every hallway she'd found herself in so far. Every door matched the color of the floor, which is why the one at the end of the hall caught her attention. A set of wide double doors stretched from floor to ceiling, each made of a deep rich wood. As intrigued as she was, she knew she didn't have time to stop and explore, but something told her she should check this room out.

The door creaked and she paused, listening for the sound of footsteps running after her. She hadn't run into a single person yet which was strange. There were so many rooms here. When her heart slowed down and the silence resumed, she slipped into the dark room. To her dismay, the lights weren't motion activated like they were back home. Oh, well. It would be easier for her to hide here for a few minutes while she collected her thoughts. She made the choice to hunt around for the lights while she came up with a plan of action. She'd stand by the light switch and quickly turn it off if she heard anyone in the hall. That way she could have the power to turn the light on and off, blinding whoever came in this room. She'd be sure to catch them off guard that way. She meant no harm; all she wanted was to find Aire and the others that escaped with them. Was that really too much to ask?

She continued running her hand along the wall, surprised when she actually came across the switch. The lights weren't nearly as bright as the ones in the hall or medical wing. These were more rustic, a dim older version of their high tech LED power descendants nowadays. They must not have a ton of resources to keep everything as modern down here as the world above.

How many times had she gone into the pantry in her home, oblivious to the elevator that led to an entirely different world?

She took in the rest of the room and nearly fell over. It was long and spacious, with comfortable looking chairs and couches scattered all around the room. That wasn't what made her breath catch in her throat; the walls were covered in rows of wooden shelves. On those shelves were innumerable amounts of books. She couldn't wait to get her hands on each of them.

She was a nerd. Everyone at school knew that too, which was why she really only ever made friends with Rei.

Rose absolutely adored books that had been based in the future during the time they were written. It was amusing that people thought they'd be in space by now. They hadn't heard anything about having to move into space because of natural causes. There was this movie she watched with her family once, *WALL-E*. How funny that the creators of the movie thought humanity would be confined to chairs, just drifting endlessly around a ship in space. They certainly weren't drinking their foods from cups with straws, nor were they growing fat and lazy.

This room was exactly like one from her dreams. All the books at the local library were locked up tight day in and day out. The only way you were able to check one out was if you signed pages of contracts each time. Everything was online now, with easy access to various genres. Nothing would supersede the original format of a paperback or hardcover book though. Rose loved the smell of them, even the musty ones. Not many people could appreciate the work and art that went into making those books. It'd be difficult for people up there to appreciate anything anymore, what with everything being operated by robots and other forms of technology. At the end of the day, with all these advancements, the government needed people to perform certain tasks, which was why they decided on peoples' careers for them.

Time stood still while Rose wandered around the room, reading as many titles as she could. The section on the back wall was divided into all nonfiction works, most of them personal accounts of living through historical events. Rose made a note for herself to come back to one of them in particular, the cure for cancer. She'd heard how cancer could take either days or years to kill people, but it almost always succeeded unless caught right away...sometimes, even then it was unstoppable. Another one about the Coronavirus stuck out to her too. They were given shots for that virus when they were little kids. Rose didn't personally remember getting the shot, and she was glad of it.

She'd made it halfway around the room when she pulled one particular book from the shelf she recognized; a story about an outspoken girl who was chosen, along with thirty-four other girls, to compete for a prince's hand. How funny that the author assumed they'd be a kingdom right now. The main character finds herself rethinking everything she thought she ever wanted. It was a beautiful story about sticking true to yourself and falling in love. Even though the most powerful of people were against her, she still did her best to speak out against injustice and push for change. A lot could be said of that young woman. Though it was only fiction, Rosabella hoped she could be half of the person the character, America, was.

She didn't remember when she'd moved to one of the couches. Whenever she held a book, she'd devour the pages like a vulture. There was no way she'd be able to leave this room any time soon. She'd just have to hope the others didn't think to look in here.

"Are you enjoying yourself?"

Rose had never jumped so high in her life. The book tumbled out of her hands and hit the floor with a thump. She jumped off the couch, feeling as if her heart had leapt into her throat.

"Stay back!" ordered Rose. She did her best to stand her ground, even though Clayton was a full foot taller than her and looked like he could break her in half with his pinky. It was better than succumbing to his anger.

He smirked at her, amused. "Don't worry, I have orders to not lay a hand on you."

Well that didn't sound even remotely good. "Are you saying that if you didn't have those orders, you'd *hurt* me?"

Clayton's face went completely blank, rendered speechless again. Wow, she was on a roll with him. Perhaps she'd be able to whip him into shape. He could use someone willing to fight back. Somewhere along the way, he'd gotten too conceited for his own good. It was obvious he thought he was *all that*. Rose was prepared to knock that right out of his head. Maybe there was a human underneath the bitter exterior...or maybe there wasn't. The door swung open then and every bad thing she wanted to say to Clayton disappeared from her thoughts.

An older man she didn't recognize stood at the head of their little group. Logan followed behind him, eyes searching the room. When he saw her, he visibly relaxed; his shoulders caved in with the release of a breath. Okay, so she did feel a *little* bad about worrying Logan. He'd been the only one to really help her get here safely since Aire had been in too much of a panic to think clearly at the time. Speaking of, where was she?

Her friend ran into the room then. Aire had looked better, but maybe it was because she was in unfamiliar territory. She hated not knowing where things were and what was happening. They ran to each other and met in the middle. Aire was already crying before they embraced, and her tears ran down onto the top of Rose's head. It was gross, but she didn't mind. Her friend had been hurting without her, and she was here to make it better.

She rubbed Aire's back. "I'm so sorry, Rei. I've been such a terrible friend."

Aire replied by sniffling and hugging her tighter. The three men, one of whom she still hadn't been introduced to, waited off to the side. She appreciated them granting her a chance to reunite with her friend before they took her away again.

Logan leaned closer to the older man and said, "See I told you."

"Okay," Rose said, pulling out of Aire's embrace, "I'm ready to go. Take me away."

To her surprise, the older man started laughing. He slapped Clayton on the back, who jolted forward from the contact. Logan smiled at Rose and winked. What on earth was happening? Were they all crazy? Aire grabbed her hand and gestured to the older man.

She made sure to keep her voice low. "That's Bernard. He's their leader. Obviously you know Logan, and if you remember, that one is Clayton."

If Rose wasn't so close with Aire, she wouldn't have noticed the little rise in her voice at the mention of Clayton's name. Oh please, no. She could *not* like a guy like that. He was plain awful! They'd have to get to that later; for now, she was going to get some answers. Were they planning on taking her away from Aire or not?

The man named Bernard must have seen the look on her face and stopped laughing. "I'm sorry, we haven't been properly introduced. I'm the head of the Fortress. Name's Bernard. You can trust me when I say I want nothing but your comfort and safety."

Hmm. That's what the classic manipulative leader always said at first in all the books and movies she'd seen. The people who fell for it always wound up dying. Still, there was something about his kind smile that made her question that stereotype.

"I can see you're still skeptical of us. I'm sorry if we've done anything to make you question your safety here." He glanced at Clayton and added a shake of his head. "Our Clayton here is always getting himself in trouble for his attitude. Don't let it get to you."

Clayton threw his hands up. "Why do you guys keep saying that? Logan introduced me in almost the same way."

Rose couldn't hold back anymore. "Maybe because you're a terrible person? Even when I was in pain last night, I could still hear you speaking to people as if they were less than human. To be honest, I'm not even sure why Logan, Bernard and anyone else are kind to you when you clearly don't deserve it."

Logan burst into a fit of laughter. "Ouch, man."

Bernard bit his lip, obviously fighting a similar reaction. He crossed his arms and looked up at Clayton, shaking his head yet again. Clearly, they knew how he was. Perhaps it was best to just let him be.

Aire touched Rose on the arm and leaned down to whisper, "Aww, come on Rosie. He's not that bad. Just give him a chance."

Rose stole a peek at Clayton; his eyes locked on his feet and hands buried deep in his jean pockets. She tried to keep from smiling, a feeling of triumph nearly overtaking her mind. "I will if he's the last person in this place with me...wait, what did he call this place?"

Bernard held his hand out for her to shake it. "You're in the Fortress, my dear. And it wasn't last night that you were brought here. You've been out for two weeks."

Her hand went limp in his. "I'm sorry, what?"

"Oh my, it seems Clayton skipped that part." He sent Clayton a disapproving look. "He was supposed to brief you on that tiny detail when he reached you."

Logan glared at Clayton, annoyance evident by the look on his face. "What good was it letting you go on ahead if you couldn't even do your one job?"

"Shut up, Clarke. I didn't think I was going to be verbally attacked by a high school girl."

Bernard spun around and glared at them. "Boys, knock it off. I mean it. This is no way to behave in front of our new saves."

Rose tried to ignore their bickering. "I have so many questions--"

"Not you too!" groaned Clayton.

She stormed over to him and thumped her fist against his chest. "Would you please shut up? Your voice isn't the most important here. Why don't you take a minute--no a *second*, because obviously you can't think about anyone else for very long--to think about how we feel." She motioned between herself and Aire. "We've just had our lives completely flipped upside down. I watched some of the people I've grown up with all my life get mauled by things that I can't even conceptualize right now, escaped to a secret society underground, whose entrance is apparently in my own *house*, and nearly died because of some debilitating pain in my head. And not that anyone cares, but it was my birthday that night."

The room was completely silent. Even Aire stood frozen. Great, now she sounded like Clayton. Was she going to start disrespecting everyone else she knew too? She wanted to cry and scream and laugh all at the same time. It was all so ridiculous.

Logan left Bernard's side and took her arm, hauling Rosabella away from Clayton. He pulled her into a hug which caused her to stiffen. "I'm so sorry you had to go through that," he whispered into her hair. He had such a gentle touch, it almost made her cry. Instead, she fought the lump in her throat and awkwardly patted him on the back. It was all she could do. Everything else she thought she knew was completely wiped clean. She'd have to start building her life from scratch here--if they let her after that outburst.

Once Logan's hug ended, Bernard patted her on the back. "I completely sympathize with you, dear. Why don't we get you cleaned up? I'm sure a shower and change of clothes will do you a world of good. Your friend can go with you. Do you know the way, Miss Gil?"

She shook her head, looking bashful. Was she embarrassed that she hadn't impressed Clayton or something? Rose wanted to take her friend by the shoulders and shake her until her stupid crush on Clayton was gone. Besides him, the others here were genuine and seemingly good-hearted. When Rose looked down and fully saw what she was wearing, it was her turn to be bashful. She was wearing a thin paper gown from the medical wing. It was two sizes too big for her and kept sliding down her shoulders. Attire hadn't been at the forefront of her mind when she'd run out of the hospital.

"I'll show them the way to Prince's," Clayton jumped in, astounding all of them.

"Alright, but please keep in mind that if you upset Miss Porter again, I'm afraid you won't like what you hear." Bernard winked at Rose and whispered, "I give you permission to lay it on him if he acts like an ass again."

She smiled, grateful he didn't decide to toss her out. "Thank you."

"Alright, let's go," mumbled Clayton from the doorway.

Aire followed right behind Clayton. Rose was a little hesitant to follow the man she just insulted, but it was unlikely he'd lead them to a dangerous part of the Fortress. Or so she hoped. The firm set of his shoulders and his purposeful stride made her think otherwise.

# Chapter 5

## (ROSABELLA)

THEY STOPPED IN FRONT OF A GRAY DOOR with a handmade sign that read "Prince's."

"Well, this is it." Clayton reached for the doorknob, but hesitated. "Fair warning, Prince is incredibly chatty. But he's got really good intentions. Unlike myself apparently."

Rose rolled her eyes. "I'm sorry, okay? I didn't mean to go off like that. You just really pissed me off."

He actually smiled at her. The tiniest lift at the corners of his lips. "I know. I can be a handful."

Before she could ask what he meant by that, the door flew open. A skinny man with pale skin and spiky blue hair squealed. He wore thick blue eyeshadow, a perfect match to his hair. The makeup framed his eyes, a stark contrast to their natural hazel. He was dressed in bell bottom black pants and a flowy pink shirt. He looked like an advertisement for cotton candy with all those pinks and blues. She caught a glimpse of the room behind him and nearly had a heart attack. There were so many different colors and fabrics scattered about. It was as if a rainbow had puked on the floor.

"Rosabella! It's so good to finally meet you!"

She was pulled in for a hug before she knew what was happening. Prince squeezed her so hard she couldn't breath. He pulled back to get a better look at her. Then he clicked his tongue at her hair, her face, her clothes--or lack thereof. That basically left her feet the only desirable thing...but then he wound up doing a double take when he saw her unshaved legs.

Prince toiled with an orange strand of her loose hair. "Oh honey, we need to give you a full re-do. You've been asleep too long. You've absolutely let yourself go!"

Rose wanted him to like her, but she couldn't really control her mouth. "I'm sorry, I didn't really have access to a razor where I was." At least when it came out it sounded more teasing than accusatory.

"Aha! Feisty. We *love* our women to be fighters! Come, I fix you." He pranced into the room, beckoning the three of them to follow. Clayton stepped back for Rose and Aire to go first.

Rose fell back to comment on his chivalry. "Wow, Clayton. I'm impressed. There may be hope for you after all."

He laughed, a deep low chuckle. An actual, real laugh. It was a nice sound. She wished he'd spend more time laughing instead of insulting. He shook his head, at a loss for words yet again.

"Duck!" Clayton cried. Something sailed through the air right for them. He dove to the floor, dragging her down with him. An explosion of colors materialized directly above them. Feathers and fabrics rained down on the two of them. The feathers tickled her face and she found herself laughing uncontrollably. Soon, Rose was completely buried in the mess of colors, accidentally sucking in the feathers near her mouth. The smell of stale fabric hit the back of her throat and she coughed.

A hand brushed away the feathers from her face. Clayton reached out his hand for her to take. When she accepted, he pulled her out of the pile with ease.

"Are you alright?" He seemed genuinely worried. How peculiar. Her little lecture had gotten to him. At least, that's what she'd tell herself.

Rose laughed when she saw a flash of something fuzzy and pink in his hair. She reached up to pluck the feather and showed him her prize. He smiled and blew it out of her hand. It hit her face, tickling her again. A new round of giggles emerged from her. She hadn't laughed like this in a while. She felt really safe being here. Even Clayton's terrible personality wasn't able to put a damper on her mood.

He removed his hand from hers and trudged through the remaining feathers and fabrics toward the source of the explosion. Prince and Aire were standing in front of a closet, in a heated discussion about how to dress Rose. They would both be sorely disappointed if they saw her closet at home; she had a very dull fashion sense.

Clayton looked over his shoulder at her. "I was about to say that this is as far as I go, but now I think I need to stick around so you don't drown in feathers."

Prince caught sight of Rose waiting for further instruction and sashayed over. He took Rose's hand. "Oh, honey. Sorry to keep you waiting, I hope we weren't boring you."

She took an opportunity to look at Clayton. When they made eye contact, he smiled; Rose had to bite her lip to keep the giggles at bay. She didn't want Prince to feel insulted.

"Why don't you go take a shower? It's just over there, first door on your left."

This place really liked to give the illusion one was playing a mind puzzle. All the doors looked exactly the same; she couldn't even distinguish which one was the door they'd come in nor could she tell which one was the first door to the left. Prince picked up on her hesitation, because he directed her toward the correct door with a smooth hand on her arm.

Before he shut the door on her, he blew a kiss and said, "You'll soon learn our set-up. Don't worry."

Rose thanked him, but it was lost in the metal door, already shut. Prince was probably already halfway across the room; he never stopped moving. What a strange and funny character. She loved how he was so into fashion. She'd never met a man who was in charge of clothing people before. Sure, men have owned some of the online clothing stores up above, but she'd never interacted with them. Whenever she called the fashion hotline and an associate would answer, it was always a woman. How fitting that down here everything was flip flopped. It was quite refreshing, actually.

The bathroom was just as white as the other walls and the floor the same grey. What was the point of having everything so similar? It was the only thing she'd noticed that had any correlation; they certainly didn't have a dress code down here. That would be a really nice change.

Rose caught a glimpse of herself in the mirror and wished she hadn't. The amount of hair sticking off her head in all directions was atrocious! Why hadn't Aire said something to her? Her eyes looked really bright against the pale egg color of her face and the dark circles under her eyes.

She didn't understand how a person wound up looking so exhausted when they'd been asleep for two weeks. That would forever pose a mystery to her. She leaned against the sink, letting the cool of the metal soothe her warm skin. She wasn't sweating, but she was warm. She'd obviously worked herself up running out of the hospital like that. She wasn't even sure what she'd been thinking at the time. There was no way she'd have found Aire and the others on her own.

*Okay, you can do this,* she thought, remembering how the doctor had cut into her side that night. She pulled her hair to one side to get at the tie at the back of her gown. She took a deep breath and untied it. She undid the rest of the ties on the back and slipped out of the paper thin gown. Rose prayed they hadn't been able to see through it, especially with these bright lights. She would literally die of embarrassment if they had. If the droids couldn't kill her, that absolutely would. A big gauze bandage had been taped over her entire side, reaching from the side of her chest down to her hip bone. She squeezed her eyes shut, not yet ready to see what she looked like. What if she found her body completely changed? Unrecognizable? Doctors had the authority to do whatever they could to save a person's life, legally of course. Would that rule carry into a society like this?

After a minute, she nearly kicked herself. The sooner she looked at it, the sooner she could hate herself and move on. Rose slowly peeled away the gauze and stared at herself in the mirror. As luck would have it, she genuinely didn't think it was that bad. There was what looked to be a small entry wound directly in her side, between two of her upper ribs, right below her chest. She was fortunate it hadn't gone directly into her heart or she would have been done for. It was bordered by a huge nasty bruise that reached the edges of the gauze bandage. It was a blend of blue, black and green; an artist may have called it a work of genius had it been anything other than a bruise. Rose reached for the wound, wincing at her own touch; it was still really tender. She turned so her side was more exposed in the mirror and sucked in a breath.

Nobody could say she had an easy time fighting whatever poison had been in her system. That wound was proof of it, if her piercing screams hadn't been enough of an indicator.

In order to keep herself from crying, because she really wanted to let it all out right now, she pressed the button for cool water and stepped into the shower. It instantly made her feel better, and even chased the tears away. This was just what she needed. Hopefully they couldn't hear her sighs out there. But at that point, she almost didn't care. She'd found her happy place, if that kind of place could be found amidst such horrible circumstances.

# Chapter 6

## (AIRE)

Aire was beginning to see great improvements in Clayton's behavior. He was already treating her better, for one; and he'd even shot her a small smile when she put on a hat for fun and looked at herself in the mirror a few minutes ago. That was the first time he'd looked at Aire since she'd arrived. She would make sure it wasn't the last.

She plopped onto the couch beside Clayton, completely fashioned-out for the day. Rose had been in the shower for nearly an hour, and in that time, Aire and Prince had been sorting through his messy "office" as he liked to call it. They'd agreed on an outfit for Rose within two minutes, and since then, they'd been splitting everything up into color groups. Who knew a man could be so particular about his clothing? Aire had to say she'd never met someone quite like Prince before.

Prince found an empty square of floor to sit on and plopped down in front of the couch. "There! It's all done for the night!"

Clayton shook his head at the two of them. "I can't believe I watched you both sort *clothing* that entire time. I have so many other things I could be doing."

"Why did you stay then?" Aire nudged his arm, willing him to look at her. He didn't, but she wouldn't let that discourage her, even if she'd only changed into this outfit because she counted on him ogling her. Aire had been blessed with long, lanky legs and had gotten more comfortable with flashing them around over the years, thanks to many confidence speeches from her sister. Today, she'd decided on a pair of forest green short shorts and a pale yellow tank top. Her sister had told her once that those two colors were really flattering against her skin. She took pretty much everything Luna said to heart; even if she didn't accept it at first, she almost always took her advice. Today, Aire's hair was pulled back into a cute low bun to show off her round face; she was feeling herself. If Clayton didn't find her attractive today, she wasn't sure what else she could do. This was as good as it got.

Clayton looked down at his shoes and shuffled his feet. "I don't know."

Prince laughed and patted his knee. "Oh Clayton. Don't think too hard or you might implode!"

Aire threw her head back and laughed. Clayton really did look like he was in pain. She wasn't sure why he seemed to think there was a complicated answer. It was a simple question. Or maybe he was embarrassed to give the real reason: that he was still here because of her. It was possible she was growing on him. She'd only known him for two weeks, but she already knew she had feelings for him. Aire wrapped her arms around herself and winked down at Prince.

"Let's talk about something less stressful," Prince said, fighting back another laugh. "How is Clarise doing?"

At that, Clayton relaxed. Aire's hands tightened around her arms. Clarise? Who the hell was *that*? Whoever she was, Aire was going to beat her in the competition for Clayton's heart. Without question.

Clayton smiled at Prince and leaned back on the couch. "I'm just so happy we're back together again. When we were apart was the worst few days of my life. She and I were both so young then. I know I'm not perfect, but hardly anyone is."

Prince smiled approvingly. "Well you just tell your girl that she's always welcome here. She'll have a special place here in my office."

"I'll tell her when I get home tonight."

Aire's blood was so hot, it could have boiled a pot of water. Was Clayton seriously living with this woman? And after all the signals he'd sent her these last two weeks? He'd spoken about this Clarise girl with a kind of love she wished he felt for her. She despised herself for picking up on that. Well, whoever this woman was, there was no doubt he loved her...which only meant it would be harder for Aire to take Clayton for herself. She was up to the challenge. She figured the best way to learn about the competition was to go directly to Clayton for information.

She tapped the side of his leg with her foot. "Who is Clarise? I haven't heard about her yet."

Clayton pulled his leg away and rolled his eyes. "Maybe that's because I didn't want to tell you about her." He pushed himself off the couch and walked over to the bathroom where he knocked on the door. Hard. She didn't know why his mood had suddenly changed.

Prince stood up too, caressing her cheek on the way up. "Don't worry honey. He's just very secretive. If he wants to tell you about her he will."

An annoyed sigh slipped out. "I just wish he wouldn't be so dismissive. I'm worth it, aren't I?" Whoops. That wasn't supposed to come out. Thankfully, Prince didn't think much of it.

"You are definitely worth it, honey, but Clayton's a damaged man. Been through a lot, ya know?"

She looked over at Clayton, who knocked on the door again, this time in a panic. "Rosabella? Are you alright?" Clayton turned and saw Aire looking at him. "Aire, can you go in and check on her? She's not responding."

Even though part of her wanted to tell him to shove his request up his ass, the other part of her won over. The part that would do anything he asked. She ran over and knocked on the door herself.

"I already tried that."

"I know, but maybe she can't hear because of the water. I'm sure she's fine." Was she really sure? Everything she'd thought was fine lately wound up turning into a huge disaster, especially when it involved Rosie. She herself was starting to panic. She tried one more slap on the door. "Rosie?"

Prince flitted over to them, dark blue fabric in hand. Oh right, the outfit they'd picked out for Rose. It was a pair of black short shorts accompanied by a dark blue t-shirt. If it had been up to her, Aire would have given her something like a crop top to show off her curves, but she knew Rose would kill her if she had.

"Here. Fashion makes everything better." Prince shoved them into her arms. "And if the clothes don't do it, she'll need a friend after what she's been through. Just go on in."

She obeyed and took the clothes from him. Clayton stepped back, diverting his eyes away from the door. How noble of him; she hoped this *Clarise* appreciated how perfect he was. What was that he'd said…"I know I'm not perfect, but hardly anyone is?" Oh how wrong he was. Clayton was perfect; the only perfect man she'd met in her entire life. The more she'd gotten to know him these last two weeks had proven that.

Aire turned the knob and pushed the door open. She glanced behind her. Seeing that Prince was staring into the bathroom, she hesitated. "Umm, I don't want to be rude, Prince, but Rose is really modest. If she knew you'd seen her, I think she would die of embarrassment."

He laughed and flitted back to his work station. "Oh honey, don't worry. I don't play for that team."

*What?*

"He means, he's living happily with his *boyfriend* of two years." Clayton bit his lip to hide a smile. "You don't have to worry about him. Now go see what's going on with Rose."

People were allowed to date and even marry the same gender here? Wow, she'd only heard about that in history books. That was fantastic!

She'd been expecting the mirror to be fogged up and the room to be heavy with steam. Instead, it was rather comfortable inside the bathroom. Rose must've decided to take a cold shower. That was probably for the best; she'd looked flushed when they'd found her in the library.

"Rosie?" She slipped into the bathroom and shut the door behind her, just in case Clayton got any ideas, which he probably wouldn't. But still. She leaned close to the shower door--thank goodness for one way glass. "I have a change of clothes for you."

The only sound she heard was the water hitting the tile floor. It shouldn't have been that difficult for Rose to hear her. And anyway, Rose should've seen Aire come in by now. Something was off. She didn't want to open the one sided-glass door, but she also didn't want to leave Rose alone in there if something was wrong.

She knocked on the glass. "Rosie, fair warning, I'm going to open the shower door." Still no response. Now she was completely, one hundred percent sure something was wrong. Her hand shook as she slid open the door.

Oh god! Rose was just standing there, with a stunned expression on her face. Aire didn't like the way her eyes seemed to stare at nothing and how she couldn't hear a regular pattern of breathing. But the most appalling thing was the massive bruise along her left side. It was disgusting! Aire didn't want to look at it anymore, but she couldn't look away.

The knock at the door was the only thing that brought her back to reality. "Aire? How's it going in there?"

Aire shook herself and tried to focus on her friend. She had no idea what was wrong with Rose, but she knew she had to get her out of the shower so Clayton could help figure out what to do. In order to do that, she needed to get Rose into those clothes.

He pounded again. "Aire?"

She pressed the button to turn the shower off, hands still shaking. When she was convinced Rose wouldn't be moving anywhere, she ran to the door and opened it a crack. Clayton had his ear pressed to the door.

"Umm, I have no idea what's wrong with her. She's just staring off into space." Her voice faltered on the last few words. The severity of what had happened to her friend finally hit her. Rose had lost everything, and on top of that, she'd almost died. "I don't know what to do."

He pushed against the door, suddenly alert. "Let me in. I need to see her so I can help."

"No! Just -- just let me get her into some clothes first." Aire sniffled, finding it harder to fight a wave of fresh tears.

Clayton sighed, undoubtedly hating the idea of not being able to be in charge of the situation. "Fine. But hurry up."

She shut the door with a firm click and turned back to her friend. Rose hadn't even moved an inch. Aire honestly had no clue if she could do this on her own. Being the youngest in a family of four, she'd never had to dress another person before, especially not when they were unresponsive. She pulled the pair of underwear from the pile, hesitating for a second. If Rose suddenly snapped out of it, she'd be mortified to find Aire sliding a pair of underwear up her legs. How awkward would that be? She decided it was better than letting Clayton deal with a naked Rose...she'd be sure to explain that to Rose later. If there *was* a later, what with Rose's situation being so unpredictable.

Once the underwear was situated, Aire went for the sports bra next. It was the best of the best. Wherever the Fortress managed to gather its clothing and fabric from must have offered them some really good online deals because most things she'd seen people wearing here were so expensive! Or maybe they didn't get their clothes online; maybe they were given these clothes by someone who knew about the Fortress and wanted to help them. That person had to be either brave or stupid to deliver things to a secret society that was against everything the Government had in place.

She'd found it a challenging task to get the bra over Rosabella's head. Once she managed it, Aire maneuvered Rose's right arm through the hole. Success! When she finished the other one, Rose blinked and looked right at her, startling the hell out of Aire. She screamed and slipped on the wet floor, falling into Rose, who wound up tumbling to the ground on top of her, wailing in pain. Aire must have accidentally bumped her bruise on the way down.

"What's going on in there?" Clayton banged on the door, but neither of them responded fast enough for him, because he threw open the door a second later. He took in the scene: Aire's legs twisted with Rose's, both of them lying in a heap on the floor. He glared down at them. "What the hell is going on? Which one of you screamed?"

Aire looked at Rose, unsure of how to answer that.

Rose met her gaze and started laughing. "I guess it was both of us."

Clayton's scoff sent the two of them over the edge into slap-happy land. They started laughing hysterically.

"You two really are just a couple of girls." He rolled his eyes and approached them, pulling Aire up first, then Rose. He held onto Rose for an extra moment, as if she'd fall to the floor again without someone to hold her up. "You freakin' scared me. Don't do that again."

"It's not like I chose for that to happen...I've been saying that a lot lately." She stopped and looked around. "Wait, what happened?" She was clearly trying to cover up that she was in pain, thanks to Aire, who felt so horrible for hurting her best friend. She held out an arm and helped Rose step out of the shower--without slipping this time.

"You were in the shower for a really long time so we tried to check on you, but you didn't reply."

Clayton nodded. "I banged on the door a few times, but you never responded. I figured, if you'd heard me pounding on the door, you'd probably yell at me...so it was strange when you didn't." His eyes travelled from Rose's face to her bare stomach, then her legs. He forced himself to face the door frame and rambled on, "Then, Aire went in to go check on you and said you were just staring off into the distance. My guess is that it was probably shock. Were you thinking about what happened to you?"

"Oh. Umm, I have no idea. I don't really remember much after I rinsed the soap out of my hair." Rose wrapped her arms around herself, shivering.

Clayton grabbed the shirt from the pile Aire left on the floor and tossed it, along with the shorts, to Rose. She accepted them, her face turning bright red.

"Oh, and Prince has sweatshirts if you'd rather wear one of those to warm up." He walked out of the bathroom to give her some privacy to get dressed.

"Thanks," she mumbled. "Rei, can you please shut the door?" She nodded, happy to do anything she could to help. She was halfway out the doorway when Rose stopped her. "Hold on. Please don't go! I don't want to be alone again."

Aire slipped back into the bathroom and pushed the door shut. "Of course. I'll always be here for you, Rosie."

# Chapter 7

## (ROSABELLA)

ROSE STUCK CLOSE TO CLAYTON SO SHE DIDN'T get lost. Aire had been here for two weeks, but unfortunately she was still unsure of which hallway led to what part of the Fortress. Rose preferred to be with someone who knew every inch of this place.

Clayton pointed to some of the rooms as they passed by and informed the girls on facts that didn't mean anything to Rose. She wouldn't remember any of what he told them after they reached their destination; in all honesty, she'd already forgotten most of it by now. Given that the Fortress was an underground secret society that housed hundreds of free people, Rose was certain the information Clayton presented them was interesting and important, but she just didn't have it in her to engage in a tour at the moment.

When Clayton faced forward, Aire bumped Rose's shoulder. "I wish he'd smile more. He'd look so good with a happy face."

She bumped her back, not as excited by Clayton's presence as Aire. "I don't know. He'd probably look mad either way."

Clayton turned his head to explain another one of the grey doors to them and fixed a curious gaze on Rosabella. They were caught. Rose implored him to continue on their merry little walk like he hadn't heard any of that. Clayton Taylor was the most indecent, rude man she'd had the pleasure of meeting. She'd made it very clear a few times already, but the more he heard it, the faster he'd do something about it--hopefully.

"I can see that you're both bored out of your minds right now." He said with a slight tilt of his mouth.

Rose threw all the sarcasm she could into her voice, "Who, us? Never! This is such an *invigorating* tour!"

"Hmm." He gave her another strange look and turned around again, expecting them to follow no doubt.

She held her ground. "Why do you do that?" Aire nudged her again, but this time it was more a warning than a playful action.

He turned around so fast she thought he might tip over. "Do what?"

Rose rolled her eyes at him. As if he didn't know! "Act so condescending? Whenever you say 'hmm' I just want to smack you across the face."

Clayton started to laugh, a full blown, belly laugh. Rose stepped back, entirely taken off guard, what with him being so angry all the time. Aire shared a look with her. He sounded as if he was going crazy.

Finally, he leaned against the wall to take a breath. "I must say, I've never heard anyone speak to me like that...until you."

She threw up her hands, rolling her eyes for dramatic effect. "Well, it's about freakin' time!"

"Maybe you should be giving me lessons on how to be a better person." He must have seen her actually consider that, because he shook his head at her. "Oh no. I was just kidding."

Rose strode right up to him and stood on her tiptoes. "Clayton, if there's anything I know about people, it's that they usually *don't* like being insulted."

"It's true," Aire chimed in. There was no need for her to say something, Rose had it handled. But she let it go. No use in shooting Aire a frustrated look for trying to be helpful.

Rose tapped him on the chest for emphasis. It was hard as a rock. "So I think you should really consider talking to someone--it doesn't have to be me."

He looked down at her. "Now you're suggesting I need to see a *therapist* or something? You seriously don't know me at all."

Crossing her arms, she glared up at him once more. "You're right, I don't. But you need to prove to me that you're worth being around, or else I'm never going to speak to you again. I can't have your negativity around me. Clayton, my whole world just flipped completely upside down...I don't have time to deal with your rude behavior."

Rose would not back down. Clayton seemed to understand that about her now, as he sighed deeply before running his hand along his jawline. His beautifully chiseled jawline. Just because he was really nice to look at, didn't mean he was really nice to speak to.

He threw his head back and stared at the ceiling for a minute. Rose wouldn't budge. It was his turn; she was going to force him to make the next move.

"I'll consider what you said." He looked back at her. "But for now, can we please continue? I want to show you the rest of the Fortress before dinner." Before she could say anything, he sped along in front of them, heading for the next hallway.

Rose eyed Aire, who seemed just as exhausted as she did. "Clayton?"

He looked back at her, halfway down the hall. "What is it now?"

She shook her head again. "Nope. How about you rephrase that question?"

Clayton's eyes radiated frustration, and he looked ready to strangle her, but seemed to change his mind. He swallowed and stuffed his hands in his pockets. "Okay. What can I help you with, Rosabella?"

She beamed at him. "Much better. I just wanted to tell you that we're both beat. Can you just show us where we're going to sleep? And honestly, I'm not going to remember any of this stuff. Can you just draw me a map instead?"

To her surprise, he actually took a minute to examine both of them. Rose felt her eyelids getting heavier with each step; there was no way she'd make it through this whole place. It was already much bigger than she anticipated. Quite impressive that they'd been able to maintain this pace for so long--how long had it been? It was just more than she felt ready to handle at the moment. Maybe after a nap or something she'd be able to finish their "tour."

He beckoned them forward. "Follow me, we're almost to the dorms."

Thank goodness! She grabbed Aire's hand and continued after him down the hallway. Rose had found a new burst of energy at being granted her request for a nap.

No more than five minutes later, Clayton brought them to a door. She could already tell this part of the Fortress was for people her age.... and possibly from her home. It felt so much friendlier being in this hallway. There were decorations hanging over some of the dreary gray doors, taped to the walls and even fun rugs in front of them. The door they stopped at made her stomach fall. Everything was pink pink pink. Flowers, smiley faces, anything that was over the top girly was taped to the door.

Clayton opened the door and held his arm out to signify for her to walk in. "This is where you'll be sharing your room with two other women. Aire has already been staying here, and she should know how to show you where the bathrooms are."

Rose nodded, biting her lip to keep from asking for a room change. This was not what she'd been hoping for. If they were a badass secret society, weren't they supposed to have some really cool amenities? Like, say, a single room for each person? Or non-pink decorations? Rose was the first to admit she'd had it really good for most of her life; she'd never had to share a room with anyone. It was something she wasn't completely opposed to, yet this room reminded her of a five-year-old girl's bedroom during her girliest phase.

Clayton, sensing her disappointment, leaned close to her ear and whispered, "Sorry that it's not to your satisfaction. We have to make sacrifices in order to have community and safety. You might not understand that yet, but you will."

She shrugged him off. Screw him! He had no idea what she was feeling inside.

Seeing a comfy bed made her want to curl up in a ball and bawl her eyes out for those she'd lost up there; the people she'd seen mauled by those droids. They hadn't even seen it coming.

Thank goodness for Aire, who picked up on Rose getting all emotional. She ran right over to Rose and wrapped her arms around her. "I know you feel bad, Rosie. What happened to those kids wasn't your fault."

Clayton stood awkwardly in front of them. He clearly hadn't dealt with a lot of sad girls before. She wasn't going to cry in front of him, but it was kind of fun to watch him squirm. It brightened her mood enough to shove the emotions deep down inside herself.

She leaned into Aire and sighed. "I know...it's just the guilty feeling of knowing I could have done something to help them. I could have warned them."

Clayton reached out and patted her arm in a strange way. "I've had many of those thoughts myself. It's not worth it to beat yourself up over it...that kind of guilt will only eat away at you until you turn into... into..."

"You?"

He frowned, his eyes sagging along with his mouth. "Yes. Until you turn into me. See? I *was* useful. Now you have a good example of how *not* to treat people."

She laughed so hard a snort came out. Covering up her mouth, Rose walked toward the empty bed and flopped down on the grey covers. The other two beds had different shades of fluffy pink comforters. *Wonderful.*

"You know, I could talk to Bernard about getting you special treatment if you'd like. Nobody has ever been poisoned by the droids and lived to tell about it...you've got something special." Clayton looked away, obviously embarrassed now. "There's got to be something special we can do for you."

Rose did consider that. How nice it would be to have her own room! But then again, she didn't deserve it any more than the next person. She'd stay right here, sharing a room with Aire and some other pink-obsessed girly girl and she'd be just fine.

"I really appreciate that, Clayton. But I need to learn the value of community somehow, right?"

He smirked, this time lighting up his enthralling brown eyes. It brought a peculiar flutter to Rose's stomach. "Good choice. I'll leave you to it then. Aire, please make sure to show her the way to the dining hall in time for the five-thirty dinner. You'll want to get there a little early...I have a feeling people will want to talk to and sit by Rose. It'll be easier for you to have your own section of a table before chaos ensues."

A groan slipped out as Rose fell back onto the pillows. "Why do people keep treating me differently? I'm just me. Nothing special."

"You're something of a celebrity, Rose. People want to know how you did it." He gave her an apologetic smile.

Aire made it apparent that she wanted him out so they could rest. She even shooed Clayton out by giving him a gentle shove toward the door. He left with one final look at Rose. They made eye contact before the door shut; she thanked him with her eyes while he seemed to question her with his. It was a strange balancing act.

She let her heavy eyelids close once they were alone. It was the first time she let herself relax since she'd woken up...and it felt nice.

*** 

Rosabella woke to a loud squealing sound. It startled her awake abruptly. She shot up in her bed, covers tangled with her legs. She wiped sweat off her face and looked around. She didn't remember her dream, but her heart was beating, so it must have been a nightmare—in this case, an "afternoonmare."

Her eyes paused on a pretty girl standing at the foot of her bed; she stared at Rose with an expression of awe twisted into her delicate, porcelain features. She had a slant to her eyes that wrinkled at the corners from the gigantic smile on her face. Didn't it hurt her with her skin pulled back like that? If it did, she showed no signs of losing the smile anytime soon. *Great.*

Aire was still sleeping, so she wasn't going to be any help in identifying this strange girl Rose had never met.

"Umm? Can I help you?" She dropped her legs over the edge of the bed, becoming protective all of a sudden. If this girl tried anything to harm herself or Aire, Rose wouldn't let her get away with it.

The girl nearly burst, she was so excited. "My name is Gianna! I can't believe *Rosabella* is my roommate!"

She fought the urge to roll her eyes. "Oh, um. Yeah, that's me. Am I in your bed or something?"

The girl shook her head with so much energy, Rose's own neck felt sore. A miracle was the only thing keeping Gianna's head attached to her skinny, delicate neck.

Gianna gasped and started bustling around, picking things up that weren't really in the way and putting them in places Rose hadn't even known were there. She shoved things into drawers of the dressers and tossed other things into the little standup closet in the corner. Rose watched, completely frozen with shock. This could not be happening. She did *not* want to wind up with a roommate who was obsessed with her or something. How did she always get to be so unlucky?

Rosabella thought it best to give this girl a chance, so she walked over to a balled up shirt on the ground and held it out. "Is there something I can do to help you clean up?"

Gianna snatched it from her and wagged her finger. "No, no, no. You don't need to clean up after me. You're too important."

What was with the talk of her being important? Were people crazy or something? She literally almost died, that didn't make her special. Maybe if she talked to Logan, he'd be able to do something about that. People would listen to him, she'd seen it.

Gianna couldn't see Rose's blatant annoyance, the poor girl. Rose shouldn't have been so angry with her, but it was difficult when she didn't know where she was, how she'd gotten there, and who was going to treat her like a normal human being.

"Gianna?"

She stopped throwing things into the closet long enough to look at her. "Yes?"

"I'm not special. Please don't treat me any differently." She looked right into Gianna's pretty eyes.

"I'll do my best...but, Rosabella, everyone knows who you are now. Or at the least, they've heard your name." She sighed, trying to look sympathetic. "You might want to start getting used to this now."

She stared at Gianna. Was she saying that every time Rosabella left this dorm she was going to be bombarded by people who wanted to meet her? How frustrating!

"Oh, I almost forgot this too!" Gianna ran over to her desk and handed Rose a big brown envelope. "That guy, Clayton, dropped it off—boy is he cute or what? I mean, I'm happily dating my boyfriend, but I've always thought Clayton was attractive."

Rose didn't have a response for that. She snatched the envelope from her new roommate and brought it to her bed where she tore the top off. Gianna resumed her meaningless cleaning while Aire continued napping.

Rosabella pulled out the small stack of papers and read the top one. Surprisingly, it was a letter from Bernard.

> *Rosabella Porter,*
> *Clayton informed me that you wanted a map of the Fortress drawn out for you so you could keep it with you and use it to find your way around. I've lived here for nearly fifty years and I never thought to do anything like that. Because of your suggestion, we'll be creating a welcome packet much like this for when other new saves like yourself arrive next.*

*Of course, that's only if you approve of the packet. Please take some time to go through it and make sure everything is worth including. Your classmates seem to value your opinion, and that makes me believe that you have things worth sharing.*

*Oh, and one more thing before you open the rest of the packet: Please don't think too harshly of the others here. We aren't used to seeing people survive the droid's poison. You're something of a rarity. They'll all want to meet you and try talking to you. Give them a chance; many of them didn't ask to live down here. Most of the ones your age were born here and others escaped here; but even then, they weren't really given a choice. As you learned from Logan, we are a secret society. It's either join or die. Sometimes we have to let the few go to protect the many. I hope you come to understand that.*

*I would like to set up a meeting with you, one-on-one, as I do with all the new saves, to get to know you and what your ideas for the future are. We want to make you as comfortable as we can. It's important to us that you find your niche here. When all my citizens are happy, I'm happy.*

*Happy first night in your dorm!*

*Bernard*

Wow, that sure was nice of him to write a letter to her. It actually improved Rosabella's mood and put a smile on her face. Even her nerves calmed while reading the letter. Bernard had known exactly what she needed to hear. Maybe the Fortress wouldn't be so bad. Escaping didn't seem like a good option at this point anyway; she had no idea where anything was yet. And Clayton had said something about dinner, so they obviously made sure everyone was fed. Prince's "office" was like a mini clothing store, so they were all dressed properly and comfortably; not to mention, they had a great system to keep everyone's lives a secret, whatever it was. Bernard said he'd been living here for nearly fifty years; that meant they'd managed to stay under the Government's radar for at least that long.

"...He's just so damaged, that poor guy. He needs someone to love him, to pull him out of that rock hard shell."

Rose didn't realize Gianna had been talking to her that whole time. "Sorry, who?"

"Clayton of course. He's got a big chip on his shoulder, worse than I've ever seen."

She set the packet down on her lap. "I'm sorry, who exactly are you? Were you rescued with us?" Rosabella was pretty sure Gianna hadn't come in with them. Rose didn't even recognize her from school or anywhere else.

Gianna laughed and shook her head. "No, no. I was born here."

Intrigued, Rose set the packet aside and crossed her legs on the bed. "Can you tell me about it?"

Her roommate beamed and took a position similar to her on the end of the bed. "My parents were born here too, actually."

"Really? Where do the rest of the people live down here?"

Gianna laughed, but stopped when she saw the serious look on Rose's face. "Oh I thought you were kidding! Didn't someone show you around the Fortress? … Never mind, I'll give you the run down. We all live with our families in the apartments down a few hallways toward the eastern edge of the Fortress. Each apartment has at least one bedroom and can get as big as five, all included with some kind of kitchen and bathroom. Sometimes, if you're lucky, you can get into one of the really nice ones that have living rooms at the front. "

"How many of those apartments are down here?" Rose asked incredulously. This place sounded like your normal neighborhood, except, you know, they were underground.

"Oh I don't know. We've always had enough, that's all I know. Anyway, then, when we turn eight, we start with junior training—that's at the northern end of the Fortress—until we turn twenty-one. That's when we get to have a conversation with Bernard and his Cabinet about what kind of career we'd like to start here at the Fortress."

No way! Rose chewed on the inside of her cheek, absorbed in the world she'd just entered. "Wow! You get to pick your own career?"

Gianna nodded excitedly, brown eyes blinking with each word. "Of course! Well, it also depends on your skill level and knowledge of that profession and how much observation time you have by then...from what I've heard, Bernard and the Cabinet let you speak, and then they give you their opinions. If they think you really wouldn't be a good fit for, let's say a doctor, then you go down the line to the next career preference."

This was all so fascinating! "You said Bernard has a Cabinet? What's that? And what's observation time?"

Gianna giggled. Even her voice was delicate. "I'm glad you're so intrigued by this. I feel the same way about your world too. But to answer your first question, the Cabinet, including Bernard, is comprised of an equal number of men and women: three men and three women. The Head of the Fortress—that would be Bernard right now—elects them into position before he gives his commencement speech."

"Oh, so they're like the Government?"

Gianna gave her a confused smile. "I'm not sure exactly what that is, but I know the Cabinet and Bernard are really understanding of us. Bernard always wants to make sure we have a say in anything he does—unless it requires immediate action...as for observation time, it's what we start in our younger years, when we turn thirteen. When we show an interest in a certain career, they give us special time in our schedules for observation time. You're supposed to get a certain number of hours in the career of your choice and present that to the Cabinet."

"But you haven't done that yet?"

She laughed again. "No of course not! I'm still in training. You choose your career when you've done six months of mission time after your training is over."

"But how do you know all of this then?"

Gianna shrugged and played with her short black hair. "Oh you know, friends who have gone through the process already. Bernard and the Cabinet are very transparent with us and give us the rundown of all the rules. Besides, my parents have told me all this too...it's not like it's a secret."

Rose nodded in agreement. She believed everything Gianna relayed was all part of her belief system; for Gianna, it was all legit. But for Rosabella it was too hard to tell if this was all true. If Bernard and this Cabinet were anything like the Government, they filled everyone's head with lies so they wouldn't get to the heart of their motives. Maybe she would have to do some digging before she officially decided not to escape.

Gianna hopped off her bed and started scrambling around in her dresser drawers for something. She came up with something flat and pink—go figure.

She wrapped it around her wrist and held it up to display it to Rose. "Have you ever used these before?" She presented a thin wrist band, so thin it was almost unnoticeable on her roommate's tiny wrist. It took up about a half an inch of space, width wise, and even had a stylish vibe to it.

"All of us start wearing these once we begin training. It's so they can trace our vitals and food intake." She twirled it around her wrist. "They want to help us stay as healthy as possible. I'm shocked you haven't been informed of that yet."

Rose shrugged and stood up. "Well, I haven't been listening to a lot of what they say."

"You've been through a lot. I'm sure they understand." A quiet pinging sounded from Gianna's wristband. She double-tapped it and headed for the door. "C'mon, we don't want to be late to the second call."

Rose cocked her head. "Second call?"

"For dinner, silly." A last minute thought redirected Gianna to Aire; she began to shake Aire awake. "There are several rounds for dinner. The first call is at four-thirty, when the older population, sixty-five year olds and up, and the families with younger children get to eat before everyone. At five-thirty, the trainee and young adult populations—that would be all eight through twenty-eight year olds—get to eat. That's the majority of the population here, and they have us go last so that we're able to take a little longer. It's the same process for lunch too."

"Oh, that's nice, I guess." Aire still hadn't moved, so Rose thought she'd give waking her a shot. "Here, let me try." She ran to the other end of the bed and jumped onto the mattress. Just as she'd hoped, Aire popped into the air a little, enough to wake her up. Rose knew from experience that she was a really mean person when she woke from a nap. This time was no different.

"What the hell is wrong with you?" Aire shoved Gianna off the bed and sat up, glaring between her and Rose. Gianna backed away a foot or two, seeing the crazed look in Aire's eyes.

Rosabella had learned to never get upset with Aire when she acted like a crazy person; some things were better left alone.

"It's time for dinner, sleepy head." Rose grabbed the packet from Bernard, tucked it under her arm, and headed for the door, hoping her friend would follow. She was used to being mistreated by Aire when she was freshly woken up.

Gianna ambled over, pulling on her shoes. The three of them left the room together, Rose with a strange pit in her stomach. She had lots of people around her who wanted to talk to her and get to know her, yet she didn't want any of that. But why did she still feel so alone?

# Chapter 8

## (ROSABELLA)

T HEY ARRIVED AT THE DINING HALL AND SWIFTLY found a table in the back, per Rose's request. She didn't want to have to deal with people like Gianna anymore. She hoped it was possible that if she just ignored everyone, they'd forget all about how "special" she was.

Aire and Gianna snagged food while Rose held their table. She tried her best to keep her head down, seeing as though people were looking at her with wide eyes. After about five minutes, Rose spotted Aire and Gianna; the two of them hadn't made it very far in the line.

The assembly line process was much different from their high school. Rose was used to seeing students shove one another to get at the last chicken breast or burger. There was a food shortage in schools up above that the country had been battling for almost a decade. Here, people stood in line, calm as can be. Nothing down here was run the same way it was above. Perhaps that's what made this place so interesting to Rosabella. She'd always been a rule follower, but maybe it was time for a change.

Gianna had said something about having a boyfriend earlier, and when Rose saw a skinny man walk up to her, she assumed it was him. Especially when he wrapped his arm around her shoulders and pulled her in close. It was so touching, Rose wished she hadn't seen it. Okay, so that would take a while to get used to. The only people you were allowed to love up there were your family and the person you were paired with. Rose hadn't the slightest idea how to love someone of her own choosing. Her parents were happy considering the circumstances, but they'd also been destined for greatness. Her mom's mom had worked remotely for the Government in her career days, and her dad's mom had been the receptionist for their corporate office here in town for years. Not to mention, her dad's dad had been pretty high up in office too.

From the way Rose understood it, the Cabinet Bernard had was just a smaller version of the Government. Up above it was topped with the twelve most exclusive men and women in the country. Two of each ruled a certain area of the country together. It was broken up into compass directions: the Northeastern Sector, the Southeastern Sector, the Northern Center Sector, the Southern Center Sector, the Northwestern Sector and finally, the Southwestern Sector. After those exclusive leaders came the advisors to the Government, a group made up of handpicked men and women, decided upon by the governmental leaders, as each required two advisers. Rose wasn't even sure what their leaders really needed advising for; they never seemed to share the information on their decisions with the public--if they made any. People usually had to find out from people who'd been affected, like from that last income cut they'd made a few years ago. Those in low-paying jobs really suffered that year. Things had improved since then, but it was still a little shaky for some families. Rose was grateful that their family was in such a high position, with her dad serving as one of the advisors to the female Government Leader of the Northern Center Sector, where they were from.

The rest of the people in the Government were classified, in her opinion, as the people who did their dirty work. She didn't hate the Government per say, but Rose certainly didn't worship them like some of her other classmates and their families. Speaking of, she should check in with them to see how they were transitioning. There should have been six of them besides herself and Aire. In fact, she should check in with Aire. She was one of those people who thought the best of the Government. Aire had an older sister who was one of the people who carried out said dirty work, yet she always managed to be successful no matter what she did. Rose had a theory that Aire's sister did more than carry out their dirty work; she provided a different kind of dirty work herself. Unfortunately, Aire idolized her.

Rose pitied her friend for that. She could never in her wildest dreams forgive someone who constantly disappointed her.

Rose's family had lived pretty comfortably all their lives. She'd never teased or belittled anyone for the lesser positions their families were in like Aire used to do, but somehow, she still felt guilty. Pretty much everyone who lived in her neighborhood had some affiliation to the Government, but they still didn't necessarily have the kind of reach her father did. He could be pretty awesome when he wasn't scolding her for something she most likely didn't even do.

She shook her head to clear it and turned her attention to the papers in front of her. Rose took a look at the map first, studying as much of it as she could. Holy crap! It was a huge place! There were four different "wings" to the Fortress. One wing was at the northernmost end. That's where all the training happened apparently. Someone had scribbled some notes about it, but it was difficult to read. She could make out some of it, enough to put it together herself. It read junior training room, lounge, main training and virtual rooms. A few other labels decorated that hallway, sporadically, it seemed. One was the engineering room, another the meeting headquarters and finally, the mission room. There was a big empty space at the very end of that wing, but nothing was written on it. In between the main training room and the meeting headquarters was the only labeled exit she could find on the poorly hand-drawn map.

She figured the next wing to the right was at the easternmost end of the Fortress, titled the medical wing. That's where the library was too. Rose remembered that place vividly. It had been one of the most beautiful rooms she'd ever seen. The southernmost part was where all the apartments were, including the dining hall, which they were in now, and dressing rooms. The westernmost wing contained all the dorms and overflow...whatever the heck that meant. She had absolutely no clue what any of those labels truly meant--in any of the wings. *Awesome.* So she had a map but it was no closer to getting her around the Fortress than her own exploration would.

After Rosabella finished being annoyed at the map--which she believed Clayton had made specially to piss her off--she took a peek at the other papers. Some of them were more in-depth explanations of each of the rooms. That would be great for her later on when she actually had a desire to visit some of them, but for now, she settled for reading one at the top of the stack. It was a list of all their rules. Her heart sank at seeing a curfew time. She escaped one world's unnecessary curfew, only to stumble upon a secret society that enforced their own. It was nice to see that they extended it for teenagers and young adults--thirteen through seventeen--to midnight. At least that gave them an extra hour. It was more than they'd had up above. The young adults, eighteen and over, were given the curfew of 3 am, same as above. Rose couldn't complain, it was a decent time for them all. Besides, she'd never really stayed up that long anyway, unless she had some big exam the next day, or a project to complete. Wow, her life hadn't been very eventful. Until now, it was always: get up and go to school, work her brain to the breaking point, go back home and do more work for school, and finally go to bed. Then that vicious cycle would restart the next morning.

The only exciting part of Rosabella's life had been her little brother. Nicolai had been born ten years after Rose. If her dad hadn't worked for the Government, more people would have questioned why it took them so long to have a second child. Nobody knew that her mother had struggled to bear even one child, so her brother had taken some time to happen. Rose had been old enough to see all the pain her mom had gone through, and after witnessing all of those awful things, she wasn't too excited to have her own children. But up above she never would have considered not having children; the Government was very strict on its rules that each couple must bear two children if they are able. The only exception was if the woman medically couldn't sustain a child, or if the father couldn't produce enough sperm. They'd banned any artificial kind of pregnancies decades ago. The Government believed it to be "unpatriotic," because they wanted to make natural soldiers out of their citizens. They weren't soldiers who went into battle, since all the wars had ended a long time ago, but they definitely treated their employed citizens as if they went to work to fight in a battle every day. Rose didn't want to live like that. She wanted to be a part of something bigger than herself that actually meant something to people; something that benefited the world in some way.

Aire had never understood Rose's way of thinking. Aire accepted that she was probably going to go into some sort of teaching career like her mom, unless she wanted to do what her sister, Luna, did. Rose shuddered at the thought; she'd hate having to bribe men into letting her get away with things.

Where was Aire? She'd been in line for a while. Rose looked up and saw her sitting at a different table, talking with Clayton. Of all people, why did Aire have to like *him*? Clayton needed to shape up before Rose would ever consider him to be worthy of friend status. If Aire wasn't going to kick him into shape, Rose was going to try herself then. For Aire.

Gianna was now sitting with her boyfriend, Donovan, who was not at all what Rose had been expecting. Unfortunately, what she'd pictured him to look like had been very stereotypical. She just assumed he was some big guy like Clayton or even like Logan, average in height but muscular. This guy was scrawny and thinner than Rose's forearm. He had long greasy blonde hair and dull hazel eyes, nothing like Prince's fierce ones, though she had to cut Donovan some slack. He didn't wear two pounds of makeup on his eyes to enhance the color. That's where Prince had the advantage. Looks weren't the main focus of a relationship, Rose knew, but after meeting Logan and Clayton, among others, she'd just speculated everyone here was fit and built to fight. Prince was an exception of course, but he was also Prince, so it made sense.

So Gianna clearly wasn't going to come back either. Rose was actually a little envious of her roommate's life; she'd lived down here, not having to worry about half as many things as Rose had to up above. Gianna didn't even know what or who the Government was. How refreshing naivety must be. Rose sometimes wondered why she worried about so many things all at once; maybe she inherited that from her dad. He'd always been looking over his shoulder for as long as she could remember.

Without warning, someone sat on the bench across from her.

"Rosabella, I hate to break it to you, but you're never going to make any friends tucked away in the corner by yourself."

"Logan! Am I glad to see you!" She jumped up from her bench and ran around the table to hug him. He wrapped his arms around her and gave her a great big bear hug in return.

Rose pulled away and looked him in the eye. "I never really got a chance to thank you for getting me here safely...so, um, thanks."

They both shared an awkward laugh. Then he leaned back against the wall and smiled at her.

"You're pretty incredible, Rose. You know that?"

She rolled her eyes, fighting the urge to groan. "No, not you too! I'm nothing more than a girl, Logan. Please don't treat me like I'm special. It's...it's so invigorating!"

He let out a light laugh and touched her arm. "Don't worry, I won't call you 'special' anymore, but I can't promise I won't look at you with awe...I don't think you understand just how amazing it was that you survived that."

"Why?"

"Because we've been working on an antitoxin for months, since those things started destroying other neighborhoods like yours."

"Okay? What does that mean?" She wasn't getting any answers here. Logan was such a nice guy, but Rosabella was about to blow a gasket if he didn't give her a straight answer in five seconds.

He must have noticed something in her eyes because he smiled sadly at her. "That means we haven't been successful. We've lost lots of people. Yeah, we've lost people before, but never like this. Not to some kind of uncontrollable poison."

Now she felt bad for demanding so many things from him. All he'd done was help her find her way to safety and now she was ruining his mood by quenching her own curiosity.

"Oh, I'm sorry. I...I didn't know that."

"We're getting through it together, but it'll definitely take some time to figure out what we're up against." He hesitated, searching her face. "That's where you come in."

*What?*

Her jaw dropped. "Excuse me? Did I just hear you right?"

He chuckled again. "Yes, I'm afraid you did. Bernard wants to speak with you as soon as possible. Rose, I'm not sure if you really understand what we do here, but we have countless rounds of training every week for young people. Anyone between the ages of eight and twenty are supposed to start training, no matter if they were born here or if they came in as saves. Do you know why?"

She shook her head. That hadn't been in the papers from Bernard.

"I didn't think so. Why don't I take you to Bernard?" He eyed the empty space in front of her. "Haven't you eaten? If not, he'll be able to order something for you so that you can both talk over dinner."

"I don't know. I'm actually a little scared of him."

Logan, thankfully, didn't think that was silly of her. "I know, quite a few people have said that to me over the years. I think it's because he's the Head of the Fortress. Everyone is always intimidated by authority. I never truly understood that until I grew up."

He stood to go, but Rose pulled on his arm. She sat there, looking up at him, feeling safe here in their little corner. She was afraid that once they left, she'd never feel this way again.

"Will you be there?"

He smiled at her and guided her to her feet. "I don't think Bernard has that in mind for this meeting. If not, I promise to meet you in the hallway right after. Is that okay?"

She bit her lip to keep from showing how scared she was. Then she grabbed her papers and followed him out of the dining hall. Rose begged him silently that he wasn't about to lead her into something that would change her life forever; she'd had enough of those changes to last her for years.

# Chapter 9

## (AIRE)

S HE SPOTTED CLAYTON FROM ACROSS THE DINING HALL, sitting by himself. Aire was honestly surprised to see him sitting all alone. Wasn't he like the coolest guy here? She stole a glance at Rosie, who was sitting all by herself too, but she was busy looking at papers. Aire observed Gianna on the other end of the room sitting with her boyfriend, Donovan.

She knew it would be a while before Rose would emerge from whatever she was reading; she was always letting herself get sucked into new things. Rose had a thirst for knowledge about her that Aire couldn't relate to. She was more of the narrow-minded woman who would do whatever was necessary for those close to her. She didn't mind not having a desire to learn everything like Rosie; in fact, it was kind of nice to not worry about everything all at once. She could focus on one thing at a time and get whatever she could out of that thing.

At this moment in time, it was Clayton.

God, he looked so good, leaning his head on his left hand while he ate with his right. When he thought no one was looking, he seemed a lot happier. Okay, that was a lie; he at least looked less angry. Was he really not much of a people person? Before she could control herself, she walked over to his table, trying to make it seem as if she'd accidentally run into him. She hoped he'd glance up and take her in. She was feeling really good about how her legs looked in these shorts and didn't want that confidence to go to waste.

He didn't look up until she was standing right next to him.

"Oh, hi Clayton! When did you get here?"

His quick glance up at her and then back at the table was very discouraging. He hadn't even looked at her legs.

"Can I sit with you?"

He stopped chewing and blinked at her. "Are you talking to me?"

Aire nodded, trying to smile without her teeth. She always thought she smiled prettier when she didn't use a full mouth of teeth.

Clayton looked around to see if anyone was around. "Umm sure. I'm about to leave though. Gotta grab some food for Clarise."

There it was, the stab in the heart. Why did he have to mention her right now? Couldn't he see how much she wanted him to like *her*? No matter, by the end of this, she'd have what she wanted. She always got what she wanted, one way or another.

He cleared his throat. "So, is there some reason you're sitting with me? Why aren't you with Rose?"

"We're not glued to each other, you know. I can make my own friends." Aire shrugged and started eating the pasta on one section of her plate, ravenous after such a long nap.

He smirked. "Did she send you over here to say that?"

She nearly choked on her noodles. "What? No! Is it really so difficult for you and I to be friends?"

There was an awkward pause before he replied. "It's not *impossible*...I just--look, Aire," he rocked back on the bench, "I think I know what you're trying to do here and I'm sorry, but I'm just not interested, okay?"

She shook her head, trying to play it cool. She knew he didn't really mean that. Right now, he had another woman in his life, and she was clouding his judgement. If this Clarise cared about him, she'd be here with him. But she was nowhere in sight; in fact, he was bringing her food later. What a lazy piece of crap.

"Clayton, I don't mean it like that. I just really think you're awesome and thought we'd make good friends." Saying that was like swallowing acid. Aire didn't want him to think she was desperate; she'd had no other choice but to pull the friends card. They'd get there eventually. She'd be waiting when he came to that realization.

He sighed and continued eating.

Aire spun her fork around on her tray. "So, since we're friends now, can I ask you a question?"

"Okay."

Wow, he actually answered her question! Baby steps. They'd be there in no time. Aire tried to conceal her excitement and shook her head to make her hair fall more naturally around her shoulders.

"What do you do down here? I mean, for your job?" She attempted to seductively suck a noodle into her mouth, but he wasn't even looking at her. He'd resumed looking around the room.

"I'm one of the trainers."

Hmm. So he wanted her to dig deeper by not answering her questions directly? She'd do that without a doubt.

"That's really cool! How did you decide to--?"

She watched the way his eyes landed on something on the other side of the room. Clayton faced her, cutting her off mid sentence, "Listen, Aire. I'm not your typical friend. I don't like people prying into my life, which means I don't like answering questions. I'm sorry, okay, I am, but this is not how I wanted to spend my dinner."

Deflated, she nodded in agreement. Maybe she'd gone too far this time. She really had to pick better times to flirt, not when the man was in the middle of eating.

Aire couldn't meet his eyes anymore, not that he was even looking at her to begin with. "Well, before you go, is there anything you want to know about me?"

"Actually, yes."

She perked up, ready to tell him everything.

"How long have you and Rosabella known each other?" He looked around the room again.

What was he doing? It was like he was looking at someone, or *for* someone. She wanted his eyes on her instead. *Take it easy*, she told herself. He'd get to her level eventually.

"Since we started school together. She's like the only friend I've ever trusted with some of my darkest secrets." She giggled, hoping that sounded mysterious. "She's been my rock through lots of family drama."

"That's nice of her."

"Oh I know! She's always been selfless like that. In fact, even though her parents continued to push her to the breaking point in school, she'd drop anything and give me a call whenever I sounded the least bit upset." She sighed. "Rosie is like the most terrific person I know."

"Hmm. It sure seems like everyone--I mean those who have met her--look up to her." He turned back to Aire, folding his arms on the table. She fought the urge to sigh. That pose made him look intensely more attractive--if that was even possible. It showed off the definition in his arms and chest and set off a ripple effect of pure strength and muscle. Her heart fluttered just *thinking* about looking at him!

"For sure. Did you know she didn't even cry the night we escaped? Sure, she screamed and everything, but not once did she shed a tear! I was so impressed." Aire caught a glimpse of her friend, still sitting at the table in the corner. "There are times when I never truly understand her."

Aire wasn't sure what Clayton was trying to gain by asking her these questions, but she didn't want to lose his attention. Any attention from him was better than no attention at all. He beat her to the punch.

"This is more of a question about you. What made you want to follow Logan to the Fortress? I mean, you didn't know what you were getting yourself into."

She laughed. "No, I certainly didn't. I actually almost didn't follow him, but boy am I glad I did! The only thing that changed my mind was the fact that Rose trusted Logan. I can honestly say that if she hadn't been there, I wouldn't have gone with him."

A small smile formed at the corner of his mouth. "I see."

She wanted to keep him talking. "I mean, of course, I'm strong enough to know what's right for me. I just didn't know if the whole 'join or die' thing was for me, ya know?"

To her amazement, he nodded as if he understood what she meant. "That's sort of how I was."

She gasped. "You're a save too? Where did you come from?"

"Sorry. Like I said before, I don't like people prying into my past."

"Oh, okay. I'm sorry."

"Hey, I have to go. Clarise's already probably wondering where I am." He stood, grabbing his tray from the table.

Well, if he was leaving, then she was going to go back to Rose. She stood up with him and grabbed her own tray. She looked at the table to see if Rose had gotten her own tray, but realized she wasn't there anymore.

"Umm, Clayton? Did you happen to see when Rose got up?"

He turned his head toward the empty table immediately. How had he known where Rose was sitting? "No, I didn't. Was she supposed to meet up with you or something?"

She lowered her eyes, feeling like a terrible friend. "We came in together. She was actually waiting for me to come back to the table."

From the corner of her eye, she saw Clayton tense up and shake his head. "Wow, some friend you are. And I thought *I* was the mean one."

"I--I--I'm sorry."

"I'm not the one you should be apologizing to."

Aire started tearing up. "I've never been a good friend to her...at least one she deserved."

He looked down at her, backing away toward the exit. "Umm. Yeah. So I think that's my cue to leave."

"No wait! Can you help me look for her? I don't know my way around very well yet." Aire rubbed her nose.

He stopped walking away. "Well how the hell did you get here then?"

"Umm, our roommate, Gianna, walked with us."

The loudest scoff she'd ever heard from another person emerged from him. "You mean to say that both of you abandoned her? Wow, two for two on her first day here. Good job you guys."

"I know. I suck as a friend. Are you going to help me find her or what?"

"Sure, I guess. But I'm going to agree with you that you suck as a friend." Clayton laughed in disbelief. "She almost *died* and this is the way you both welcome her to a strange and foreign place?"

Aire sniffled and followed his lead, sliding her tray into the dish room opening. Once she was finished, he pulled back to walk beside her.

"Alright, Aire, oh terrible friend. Where do we start?"

# Chapter 10

## (ROSABELLA)

"WE'RE ALMOST THERE. IS ANYTHING LOOKING FAMILIAR TO you yet?"

Rose's head had been on a swivel the whole time; she wanted to take in as much of her surroundings as possible. So far, all she recognized were the off-white walls and grey tile floors...but that was everywhere she looked.

"Not really. Oh wait! Are we near the entrance? I vaguely remember Clayton running down this hall with me." She shivered at the memory of the pain in her head. "At least everyone made it safely inside, right?"

Logan slowed and wrapped an arm around her shoulders. "Yes, they did. And don't worry, what happened to you wasn't your fault."

How did he know that's what she'd been thinking about? She hated feeling like a burden, which was probably why she'd pushed herself so hard when her parents asked her to. Rosabella swallowed to keep her emotions at bay. Why was she feeling so sad all of a sudden?

She leaned into him, feeling warm and safe. "Logan, can we talk about something else? I just...I can't think about that stuff right now."

"Of course! What are friends for if not to distract from all the bad stuff? Umm, how about we talk about your training. Are you excited to start tomorrow morning?"

Oh, she'd forgotten about that. "I guess I really haven't thought much about it. But, I have to be honest, I've never done any training before. Is it easy to catch on?"

He gave her shoulder a squeeze. "Don't worry, everyone from up above has never been exposed to fighting. They learn at an average pace. Very rarely do they surpass the trainees who are Fortress-born. Clayton was the only exception."

"So, is it more of a competition to your people--the 'Fortress-born'?"

Logan's laugh vibrated against her side. "Yes, *Fortress-born*. And I suppose you could call it that. It just depends on what you want to do with your future. The stronger ones start getting weeded out around fourteen or fifteen, when the boys and girls start retaining muscle mass." He shrugged. "My father was really big into me being the best at everything: training, classes, you name it."

Rose gasped and stopped dead in their tracks. He turned to look at her, and for the first time she really looked at him. They were like two long lost peas in a pod.

She told him so, "My parents have always been so hard on me, I feel so worn down." She rolled her eyes. "I mean, why does it matter if I'm great at everything? Don't I just need to be good at *one* thing to be successful? I still love them, of course, but it's just frustrating. Wait, is it past tense now? *Loved?*"

Logan pulled her in for one of his bear hugs. "If it's love, it's never in the past tense. You will always love them."

They stood there in silence while her tears slowly subsided. She sniffled a few times and then stepped back to rub her drying eyes. Bernard might not understand what she was going through if he saw she was upset. Besides, she didn't want to start their first conversation together by crying like a fool.

"Thank you." She gave Logan a gentle kiss on the cheek.

He grinned and twirled her hair around his finger. "What are friends for, right?"

They both laughed and continued on their trek. Even though they were silent, it wasn't awkward. She didn't despise being silent next to him as she had the first night she met him. Maybe it was because she'd never had the pleasure of having a guy friend. Whatever it was, Rose found it nice to talk to the opposite sex about her feelings for once. Aire always cried along with her, which could get annoying after six or seven times.

Logan hadn't encouraged her not to cry, but he'd comforted her enough for the emotions to stay where they were and not boil over the edge. The more they walked, the more she returned to normal.

Logan stopped her in front of a set of grey doors, the only room in the hallway with two double doors. "Ready? We're here."

She nodded, suddenly nervous again.

He hesitated before opening the doors. "I promise you, he's not scary. He's more like a father-figure to me than anything else, so you can trust me when I say he's really kind and compassionate."

"Okay." Rose nodded firmly this time. "Let's do this."

Logan pushed open the double doors, revealing a large room. It was much longer than it was wide, but still left enough room for large groups of people to occupy it. A lengthy table stretched from the back of the room, almost to the door, surrounded by swivel chairs.

Bernard stood in front of a wall, staring at something on a screen there. He touched the screen and it allowed him to manipulate the angle of the view. He pulled the image down, in search of something specific. He hadn't seen them yet.

"Excuse me, sir? I brought Rosabella here to meet with you." Logan gave her a small encouraging nod. "I'll be right outside if you need anything, I promise."

Then she was left alone with the Head of the Fortress. He stopped what he was working on and smiled at her. It didn't seem fake. In fact, it was really genuine.

"Hello, Miss Porter. What a pleasure it is to finally have a conversation with you, given that the last time, you were a little annoyed with our Clayton, were you not?" He didn't sound angry at all; laughter danced in his eyes. "It's about time someone other than myself had a stern talking to with him. He stopped listening to me a while ago."

"I'm sorry. I really didn't mean to be rude, but he just...I couldn't stand...why is he such a dick?" She gasped in horror and covered her mouth. "Oh, I'm so sorry!"

He laughed a hearty, belly laugh. "Don't worry my dear, I've heard much worse from people who are far less extraordinary. Speaking of, I hear you're a little frustrated that people keep referring to you in that way, am I right?"

Bernard liked to end in questions, she noticed. He pulled out a chair for her and she gratefully took it. He sat down in the one next to her and turned so they were both facing one another.

"Rosabella, I've been here for a long time, and I've never seen anyone fight that poison as you did."

She leaned forward in the chair. "I thought Logan said these droids only started showing up a few months ago?"

"Yes, that is true." He nodded and looked her in the eye. "I only meant that we have been fighting enemies for a long time, and you're one of the few survivors to be attacked by something and live to tell the tale."

"Bernard?"

"Yes, my dear?"

Rose smiled at him. There seemed to be a mutual respect between the two of them. Of all the people here, Bernard could probably understand people's newfound admiration of her the most, since he was in charge and had people looking up to him left and right. The only difference between Bernard and Rosabella was that his respect had been earned and hers had been gained by way of accident.

"I just wanted to let you know that I really enjoyed reading your letter. Thank you for all the information."

He nodded, giving her a little smile. Then he didn't say anything else. Was he waiting for her to say something next?

"So why do you continue to bring people here? What do you call them, saves?"

Bernard smiled again. "What is your take on it?"

"I think you want people to have a better life, so you invite them to live here. But you have conditions. It's not a free ride for anyone. Am I on the right track?"

"Absolutely. We believe that everyone should have the chance to *choose* the way they live."

Rosabella bit back a smile. The two of them sat in silence, both looking at opposite ends of the room.

Eventually, she decided to break the silence and ask something she'd been dying to ask. "Can I ask for a favor?"

He cocked his head, intrigued. "It depends on what you're asking."

She dove right into the deep end. "Is there any way I could go back up to see if my family escaped to somewhere else?"

Bernard stood and headed for the screen on the wall closest to them. He cleared his throat and turned it on, putting the password in at the lock screen. As he did so, he talked to her, "We already sent a search party up there a couple days after you and your friends arrived. We didn't find anyone alive, unfortunately. But we also didn't find many dead other than the ones in the area you escaped from. I can't allow you to go up right now, but there may be a chance in the future-aha!"

The screen allowed him to log in and revealed the screen he'd shut down once she and Logan came in. He'd been looking at a map of their sector. He zoomed out and presented it to her.

"Do you see these purple dots?" He pointed to one for emphasis. There were only a few of them in total.

"Yes, what do they mean?"

"These are the places where we were able to rescue people and bring them in as saves." He shook his head sadly. "Unfortunately, as you may have witnessed, not everyone believes in taking a chance. Or they didn't trust our people--I like to call them ambassadors when they go out like that. Those ambassadors--"

"Is that what Logan does here?" When Rose realized she interrupted him, she apologized again.

Bernard laughed. "No harm done, my dear. And to answer your question, yes and no. He has a much greater role to fulfill down here, but he volunteers to go up every now and again. Now, as I was saying, those ambassadors have been through extensive training on how to best word their little speech in order to retain the most people they can. They are also trained on how to answer their questions without giving too much away. Some people are overly inquisitive, much like yourself. But I don't blame you. I'm not sure if I would have ended up coming to the Fortress if my friend hadn't gone with me."

She was embarrassed thinking back on all the questions she'd asked Logan on the way here. Perhaps she shouldn't tell Bernard that he'd answered most--if not all--of them.

"That's what I wanted to speak to you about. Of course, I have these one-on-one meetings with every new save, but I feel especially inclined to learn what you and your friend, Aire, think of our quaint little society."

"Are you saying you're asking for my opinion, sir?" She had to think for a moment. "Well I definitely think everything is pretty bland down here. It probably takes people twice as long to learn their way around this place because everything looks the same. You should see if anyone with artistic talent would want to paint the walls so they represent the world up above. The moon, the sun, and the--" She stopped when she saw the amused look on his face.

"Oh, don't stop on my account."

Rose shook her head and looked at the floor. "I really shouldn't keep going. I'm overstepping--if that's even possible to do at this point."

That made him laugh one of those deep belly laughs again. "I like you Rosabella. You're not afraid to speak what's on your mind. And thank you for your opinion. I've always wanted to do something to make each wing feel unique, but I haven't come up with a good idea just yet. Please let me know if you have any more. Until then, let's continue." He pointed to a red dot. "Do you see these red dots?"

She nodded. There were nearly ten times as many red dots as there were purple.

"Every one of these dots on the screen represent the locations of the droid attacks. But these red dots in particular show us the places we weren't able to rescue people from."

She gasped. "But that's so many! Are you saying all those people died then?"

He took his seat again. "Not necessarily. That just means we didn't bring anyone new to the Fortress, but it doesn't mean everyone died. It's a high possibility that people were able to escape to another neighborhood or even sector if they had the means to do so."

"Have the other sectors been affected yet?"

"No. And that's what's so interesting. My theory is that the droids had to have been created by someone in this sector." He tapped the desk and the center of it flipped around, revealing a map of their own sector. He pointed to the tallest building in the middle. "It's interesting that they haven't attacked the Government headquarters, don't you think?"

She started catching on to what he was saying.

Bernard continued, "I think there's someone who works in that building who's created these monstrous creatures to weed out the weak. It's as if they're looking for something."

"Or protecting something."

He looked at her. "Why do you say that?"

She pointed to the headquarter's building. "Because my dad worked for the Government--he was pretty high up actually--and recently, I overheard my parents arguing about something when I was supposed to be sleeping. It sounded like his colleagues had started working on a project that my mom didn't approve of or find ethical."

Bernard's mouth nearly dropped open. "Well that changes a lot of things."

She hesitated. "Do you think the Government created the droids to keep their project a secret?"

"Or was their *project* the creation of the droids?" He stroked his chin and rolled his chair over to the door. "Let's continue this conversation. I just need to call some people in here first."

"Bernard, is it possible they had a different plan for the droids, and they lost control of them instead?" She shook her head. "I can't imagine they would allow their spouses and children to be murdered."

He wheeled back over to her. "That's difficult to say...sometimes, you have to sacrifice the few to save the many."

He'd said that in his letter to her, or some other version of that phrase. After staring at him in shock far longer than necessary, Bernard gave Rose's cheek a tender pat.

"I don't mean that's what their intent was, but we have to keep that in mind. I've had to make sacrifices in my time as Head of the Fortress." He leaned back in his chair and rested his hands on his stomach. "But that's a conversation for another time. We have about five minutes. Tell me more about yourself."

Interesting tactic he had, changing the topic like that. "What do you want to know?"

"What makes you who you are?"

"Oh, sure, let's start with the simple questions," She said sarcastically. That brought another laugh out of him. Rosabella took that as encouragement. "I guess you could say I was always pressured to be the best and now that I'm here, I'm wondering if it was even worth it."

He nodded, urging her along.

"Ummm, and now that I'm here, I'm really curious about everything. That includes the layout of the Fortress of course, but I'm really interested to get started with my training. After talking to Logan, I think I'll be able to catch on alright, but I'm curious to see how everyone trains."

Bernard shook his head, smiling at the floor.

"Did I say something again?" asked Rosabella. As the Head of the Fortress, there were probably only a handful of times he was going to put up with her disrespect. She needed to be more careful.

"Oh, no, no, no! I just enjoy listening to you speak. You have this... this confidence in your speech and determination in your eyes. It's quite incredible."

She blushed, not used to receiving compliments. Sure, Aire would say something nice about her every now and again, but it wasn't the same. Aire had known Rose her whole life; they both knew each other's tricks. But when she was complimenting Rose, she usually wanted something from her.

"Don't be so bashful, it's a great quality! I'm sure people above are going to miss that about you."

Her heart flipped upside down. "You mean, I can never see them again?"

He looked her dead in the eye, expression full of compassion. "Unfortunately, it's forbidden to contact anyone up above. I have a contact or two so that I stay in touch with the world up there, but other than that, you may not speak with anyone from your past life..." He patted her hand and smiled sadly. "Anyway, enough about that...now, can you tell me--?"

A knock sounded at the door, startling both of them. Bernard stood and brushed his pants off. He held out his hand to Rose and she accepted. Their time must be up already. That hour had gone by way too fast! She felt like she'd only just sat down.

"Follow me." He winked at her and strode over to the double doors. He pulled them both open and welcomed a group of five people in.

Rose's knees suddenly felt shaky. She wasn't ready to meet anyone else. She couldn't bear to hear any more people talk about how "amazing" she was. When this was all over, she wanted to be able to count on one hand how many times she'd heard that or a similar phrase.

As if they were used to being in this room together, the five of them greeted Bernard and headed for specific chairs around the table. Even with all of them sitting, they didn't take up half of the table. Bernard passed Rosabella on the way to the table and ushered her into a chair beside Logan.

Logan leaned in to whisper in her ear so no one else could hear, "He's letting you stay here? Wow, this never happens. You should feel honored."

She glared directly into his kind green eyes. "Logan--"

He laughed quietly. "I'm not referring to your magical ability to heal from a deadly poison. I'm simply saying that there's a reason you're still here."

Rose looked around at the others then. Bernard had taken his seat at the head of the table. There were two other men and three other women besides herself.

Rosabella turned to Logan and leaned in to his ear to whisper back, "I hope there's a good reason for me to be here. I'm already embarrassed."

He gave her knee a squeeze. "Don't worry, I'm sure there is."

Bernard's voice changed drastically from the informal, fatherly tone he'd used only a few seconds ago with her to a boisterous one. A man capable of commanding the room with one word.

"It's time we meet to go over all we've learned about this threat to our society. But before we get into that, I wanted to introduce one of our newest saves, Rosabella Porter."

She waved at the others, as a chorus of greetings flooded the room. They all laughed at Rose's shy, little wave before turning back to Bernard.

"Rosabella, these are my Cabinet members. They aid me in every single decision I make, big or small. In order to be an active Cabinet member, they must be willing to drop everything without a moment's notice, because, like I said, they help me make every single decision." He was still the kind older man she'd gotten used to speaking with, but now he visually carried more power in his demeanor, even in his eyes. "To my right is Andre Harrison, head of external security. Say something to our new member, please Andre."

Andre shifted in his seat and winked at her. "In case you were wondering, I'm Clayton's best friend. I also--"

Rose held up her hand, utterly baffled by that. "Wait. Clayton has a *friend*? Like by your own free will or is he holding something over you?"

Bernard snorted and some of the others started laughing. She felt bad for saying that, but it had taken her completely by surprise.

"Shoot, I'm so sorry. I have to work on that." She held her breath, waiting for Andre to yell at her for disrespecting his "friend."

Thankfully, he laughed. "Believe me, I've wondered that at times too. But no, I'm pretty much the only one who's seen different sides of him and hasn't shunned him. We all have our flaws." He shrugged and smiled at her. "I was born and raised here in the Fortress. Oh, and I'm twenty-five in case you were wondering."

Rose fought the urge to gag when he winked at her. Again. Now she understood why Andre was friends with Clayton. It was probably because they were both very unlikeable. The two of them would definitely make a great pair, condescension and selfishness included. Andre was attractive just like Clayton, and he definitely knew it too. Andre's eyes were nowhere near as mysterious as Clayton's but he clearly wanted one thing and one thing only. Rose would not fall for his chiseled jaw, beautiful dark brown skin and warm, syrup colored eyes. Men like him could be really dangerous in the feelings department.

Bernard rolled his eyes and continued, "Thank you, Harrison. That's enough. Next is Eden Wells, head of internal security."

Eden, the first woman she'd met other than Gianna, although quite the opposite of Gianna with her buzz-cut style hair, smiled warmly at Rose. "I too am Fortress-born. But that doesn't matter as much as people think. I had to work just as hard as any of the other saves to get to where I am today. Oh, and if we're sharing our ages, I'm twenty-seven. Nice to meet you, Rosabella."

"You can call me Rose."

She replied with a curt nod of her buzzed head. "Rose it is."

Right away, it was settled; she liked Eden.

The woman next to Eden looked like she could be a young teenage girl and had the high pitched voice to match. "I'm Alice Palmer, assistant internal security. I came in from the world up there."

She wondered how a woman of her stature could defend herself, but she knew it was best not to question. Maybe they needed diversity on the Cabinet--it sounded like nearly everyone was Fortress-born--and Alice had been the best trainee from above.

Alice raised her hand and giggled. "Oh and I'm twenty-six."

Rose realized with a start that she was right across from Alice. Was she supposed to say something next? Bernard had already introduced her, so she didn't know what else to say. But she thought it better to fake confidence than to come across as timid and afraid.

"As all of you know by now, I'm Rose. Apparently I'm remarkable or something, so I'll just beat you to it and let you know that I hate being referred to as such." She took a deep breath. "I'm obviously from above, so I'm still figuring things out down here. I'm truly excited to be here though. It's funny, right before the droids attacked us, I was actually trying desperately to find some way to change things up. I realized I was living in an annoyingly small cycle. I needed a change of pace desperately...and now, here I am."

Silence.

"Oh, and I just turned eighteen the night I escaped here."

Some of them smiled, others chuckled. Either way, Rose was pretty pleased with herself for not fearing their judgement. It was time she learned that it was okay to make mistakes. She didn't have to be perfect anymore. There was no more staying up until 3 am doing homework for all those honors classes.

Logan introduced himself next. He looked right at Rose as he spoke. "Well, Rose, I know you already know me by name and that I'm Fortress-born, so I guess all that's left is my title. I'm in the head of mission control. That basically means that I have to make sure everyone who is supposed to leave, makes it in and out without issue."

Bernard chimed in. "Clarke's being modest. It's one of the most important jobs here, Rose. Anyone who passes through the doors, whether they are going in or out, must be confirmed by him. Think of him as our first line of defense...and at only twenty-four."

Logan shook his head. "Don't listen to him, Rose. I don't do nearly as much as the others in this room."

Everyone protested, save for Andre, who looked bored. Rose beamed with pride for her friend. Wow, she didn't know she was sitting next to someone who played such an instrumental role in maintaining the Fortress's safety. It was also refreshing that he was being humble, because she couldn't take another Clayton or Andre in her life.

The woman at the end, to the left of Bernard, leaned in to the table to see her around Logan and smiled. "My name's Naomi Todd. I'm twenty-eight and in charge of engineering, though the process has been kinda slow, what with all this droid stuff happening these last few months and needing all hands on deck."

Bernard nodded along with her. "Well put, Naomi. Thank you. Now, I didn't just invite you here to meet Rose." He caught her eye and nodded. "We have something to discuss."

***

A couple hours later, Rose found herself walking back to her dorm. She ambled on between Andre, who kept bumping into her for some reason, and Logan. They were both talking to one another animatedly over the top of her head.

Andre bounced on the balls of his feet, the muscles in his calves flexing. "Dude that was like, so cool! No one has ever been allowed to sit in on a Cabinet meeting unless they'd been here for a long time and had a major problem--especially not some random chick from up above!"

"She's not some random *chick*, Andre. Watch your mouth," spat Logan, coming to her defense.

Rosabella ignored both of them. How on earth had that just happened? Once Bernard filled them in on what she had brought up about the Government and the droids, he basically let her lead the rest of the meeting to share her thoughts on the droids and perspective on the world above.

Rose had obviously taken her required leadership courses at her high school, but those classes could only prepare a person for so much. The rest was up to the individual. The meeting hadn't felt like a complete bust, and she was confident they didn't think she was dumb. Were there things she could have worded differently? Sure. And was she on point the entire time? No. But that was okay. Collaboration was key if they wanted to come up with some kind of solution. Even though they'd been in that meeting room for two hours, they hadn't been able to come up with an exact solution. Yet. But it was definitely on all of their radars now. Bernard called the meeting when he could see they were no longer getting anywhere. It was nearly 10 pm anyway. She needed to get to sleep if she wanted to be refreshed for her first day of training in the morning.

Andre nudged her in the side. "Damn girl, you got balls talking to some of us the way you did! But don't worry, I don't mind."

She shoved him away. "Andre, please stop. I'm thinking."

Logan burst into laughter. He wrapped an arm around her shoulders and playfully teased Andre, "You hear that, Dre? There's finally one woman who isn't gonna take your crap!"

Rosabella was more gentle with Logan but still shimmied out of his embrace. "Both of you, stop. Please. I need to think."

It was Andre's turn to laugh and point. "Looks like I'm not the only one, Clarke."

Logan, now visibly hurt, didn't say anything more. Rose felt bad for being so rude to him, but they were onto something here. She couldn't just let it slip right through their fingers when they had it in their sights.

Andre pressed a warm hand on Rose's back, already forgetting her command to leave her alone. "Forgive me for being so bold, Rosabella, but has anyone ever told you that you look quite beautiful under these fluorescent lights?"

She halted immediately and placed her hands on her hips. "Andre, let's get something straight. I'm still very new to this whole, 'pick who you want to love' thing, but I'm smart enough to know that you're certainly *not* that person for me. Are we clear?"

His face went slack and he leaned against the wall as if she struck him. "Wow, major loss, man." Then he went right back to smirking and talking about random stuff.

Logan leaned down so Andre couldn't hear. "It's okay. Your thoughts aren't going to slip out of your head while you sleep. I think you can afford to let yourself relax now."

As much as she hated to admit it, he was right. Rose needed to take a deep breath and calm herself. It was just that she was overstimulated, and being in a top secret meeting hadn't helped her to lighten up. She literally hadn't even been awake for twenty-four hours and already she'd met the leaders of the Fortress. Not only that, but she sensed a couple of strong bonds forming between her and those she'd met--aside from Andre and Clayton. She didn't say anything to Logan, but he seemed to understand what was going through her head. Rose had a strong feeling of understanding between her and Logan; he'd probably been through similar thought processes as her at some point or another in his life.

"What did you think of Bernard?" asked Logan, keeping his distance from Rose. She appreciated the effort and smiled.

Andre was still rambling on about something she didn't bother to listen to.

"I actually really enjoyed my time with him." Rose said, smiling at Logan. She rolled her eyes. "Yes, Logan. You were right."

He chuckled. "Wow! After I dropped you off in his office, I wasn't sure if I'd be right."

"I'm not going to say it again, so enjoy it now," she teased.

Andre stopped at one of the doors. The door with pink, frilly decorations. He flicked one of the streamers. "Ya know, Rosie Posie, I didn't take you as a girly-girl."

She turned her nose up at him. "So what if I am?"

The door swung open before Andre could think of a comeback. Aire saw her and lunged at Rose, wrapping her up in a hug. "Damn it, girl! You scared me half to death. Where the hell did you go?"

Andre leaned not so casually against the doorframe, looking Aire up and down. "Now, why haven't I met you yet, hot stuff?" He trailed her long legs a few more times before looking at her face. *Way to be subtle*, Rose thought.

Rose pulled out of Aire's unusually strong hold and glared at Andre. "Don't even try. She's my best friend and I won't have you messing with her."

He sighed and locked eyes on Aire again. "Let's let *Aire* be the judge of that, Rosie Posie."

Rose looked at Logan and scoffed. "Why do I even bother with him? Especially if he's friends with Clayton, he's a lost cause."

Logan cleared his throat and motioned for her to turn around. When she did, her face went from pale to tomato in an instant. There was Clayton, standing in the doorway. Great.

"What about me?" he asked.

"Oh nothing." Rose squinted at him, confused. "Clayton, why are you in my dorm?"

He shrugged, leaning against the doorframe. Then he replied in a sarcastic voice, "Because I wanted to dig through all your personal belongings and steal whatever I could, which happens to be air at this point."

She didn't know if he was joking or not, but she was so tired she didn't even care. "Well, glad I could be of some help in increasing your oxygen supply. Have a good night." She turned back to Logan. "Thanks for walking me home, Logan." Then she pulled Aire into their dorm, shutting the door on Clayton and Andre.

She faintly heard Andre whistle and then shout, "I walked you home too, you know!"

"Oh, give it a rest. Come on," laughed Clayton.

Aire gave her a funny look. "So, ummm. Where were you?"

"I was in a meeting with Bernard." She slipped out of her shoes and flopped onto her bed. Was it possible that it was more comfortable now than it had been earlier this afternoon?

Her friend still didn't move.

Rose sighed. "What is it, Rei?"

She shook her head and went to her own bed. "My meeting with Bernard was only like, half an hour...you were gone for *hours*. Are you sure that's all you want to tell me?"

Rose laughed and pulled the covers over her, nestling into the pillows. "Yes. I wouldn't lie to you. Bernard and I had a great conversation. He and I really hit it off."

Aire crawled under her own covers. "Okay. I just hate when you lie to me, so if there's something else you want to tell me, please do."

Rosabella pretended to be asleep so she wouldn't have to respond.

Gianna was nowhere to be seen, and Rose was totally fine with that. She didn't want to be treated like a celebrity right now--or ever again. She just wanted to sleep. Even with her nap earlier, she didn't feel fully rested. She fell asleep a moment later, easing into a world of dreams.

# Chapter 11

## (ROSABELLA)

THE ALARM WENT OFF MUCH TOO EARLY. ROSE especially didn't like the way the bed shook until she got out of it. Those stupid pressurized sensors didn't offer an easy way to snooze for ten extra minutes. The comfort of the mattress somewhat made up for that.

Rose pushed the covers back and slid onto the floor. She didn't like the absence of windows; that had always been her favorite part of waking up, especially in the summer, having the sun greet her on an early morning.

Aire's alarm blared a little longer than her own. Rose was more of the morning person. She opened the closet door marked with her name in pink frilly paper and was surprised to find clothes hanging in it. A few of them looked really fancy; a sequined dress decorated one corner of the closet, a tight-fitting red dress right next to it. She didn't know why she'd need anything like that. Shaking her head, she pulled open the matching dresser and found a few shirts and shorts, a couple pairs of pants, and other essentials in the top two drawers.

Aire went to her own closet. "I had Prince select a few things for you. I figured you wouldn't want to dress the same as me."

She had that exactly right. Rose was not a scandalous, showy person like Aire could be sometimes. Instead, she preferred her t-shirts and jean shorts. Today, since it was her first day of training, she selected a black shirt--that wouldn't show sweat--and grey athletic shorts. The waistband was nice and stretchy. Sometimes, she had problems finding pants and shorts that fit comfortably over her hips.

She laid her outfit on her bed and began to undress. "Gianna, what are you going to wear?" asked Rose.

Their roommate didn't respond. Rough night last night? Where the heck did she go?

"Aire, have you seen Gianna?"

Her friend shrugged and sat on the edge of her bed to pull her shoes on. "Nope. But don't worry, five nights out of seven, she doesn't spend the night here."

"What? Do you mean she stays out with her boyfriend all night?"

Aire giggled at her stunned expression. "Yes, they are a lot *freer* about relationships down here. Gianna and her boyfriend are happily dating and don't like to be apart for too long."

"Wow, must be nice to have someone love you like that."

"Oh, Rosie. Don't worry. You'll find your someone!"

She didn't respond. She'd never been given the ability to even *think* about loving someone of her own free will. It was a lot to take in.

"You'll want to shower right away after training, so I'll show you how to get there from here." Aire slipped a white tank top over her head and wiggled her eyebrows. "Right this way."

\*\*\*

Rosabella leaned back in her chair, stretching her arms above her head. She'd nearly forgotten what a full belly felt like. Aire leaned her head on her palm and closed her eyes.

Rose tapped her nose and laughed. "Aww, come on Rei! Aren't you excited?"

"You forget that I've been doing this for the past two weeks. Sure, I was excited at first. Now that's pretty much worn off." She sighed and blinked twice to readjust her eyes. "I'm not cut out for this life."

The chair next to Rose squealed across the tile floor. She was completely baffled to see Andre plop down, and even more so when Clayton carefully did the same beside Aire.

Andre leaned in and gave Rose a tight side hug. "Hey ladies! How's it goin'?"

She shoved him off her. No way was this happening. "Is there something you need, Andre?"

He laughed and backed off. "I wouldn't say I *need* something, but if you're offering, I definitely *want* something."

Aire giggled, but then saw the disgusted look on Rose's face. Andre, encouraged by the giggle, beamed and plucked the banana from Rose's tray. Without asking, he peeled it and started chomping on it.

She smacked it out of his hand before he could take another bite. "You'd better have a good reason for coming over here."

Andre just sat there, stunned into silence. Clayton's face brightened and he chuckled at his friend's expense. The deep, authentic sound was almost enough to snap Rose out of her anger. Almost.

"What Andre's not cool enough to say is that he wants to get to know the two of you," Clayton reassured.

Rose glared at him. "And you?"

Aire kicked her under the table. No doubt, she was most certainly enjoying the company of Clayton and Andre. It was clear Aire had a thing for Clayton and didn't want Rose to screw it up. Too bad.

"Eh...I don't know." Clayton's tone was so nonchalant, she wanted to smack him. He smirked at her. "It kinda looks like you want to hurt me."

"Wow, impressive. Now you can read minds too."

Andre leaned away from her, pretending he was scared, eliciting another laugh from Aire. "Wow, you weren't kidding, Clay. This girl is tough. No wonder she survived the poison."

In response, Clayton looked at the digital clock on the wall. "Yep, I told ya. Are you girls ready for training?"

Aire, who'd been pretty much speechless since they arrived, nodded. Rose was appalled to see her look at Clayton from under her lashes. Damn, she was trying way too hard, and Clayton didn't even seem to notice. He just kept looking at Rose.

"Does it mean I get to be away from *him?*" She nudged her head in Andre's direction. He finished off his banana and tossed the peel back onto her tray. No way was she walking with him. It wasn't too far, but she didn't know what he might try to do or say along the way.

"Nope! You're stuck with me, Rosie Posie." He picked something out of his teeth and flicked it away. "I'm doing a special demonstration today."

"Come on." Clayton stood and grabbed Aire's tray. "Andre, grab our friend's tray."

"No," he whined, "Why do *I* have to grab it?"

He glared across the table at Andre. "Because you rudely took her food and put it back on her tray, that's why."

Rose tilted her head up at Clayton. Where had the chivalry come from all of a sudden? He'd even successfully gotten Andre to listen, a skill she assumed had taken years to master.

To cover up her astonishment, Rose asked, "Did you just call us your friends?"

Andre nodded his head, excitement radiating from his toned body. "Yeah, and Clayton Taylor doesn't say that lightly. So you'd better feel lucky."

She rolled her eyes. "I'll feel lucky when my 'friend' is actually kind to me and other people."

The two guys walked away laughing as if she'd just told some insanely funny joke. She was being serious. Clayton and Andre would not be considered her friends until they whipped themselves into shape. Rose followed behind them, Aire to her right.

Aire nudged her in the back of the knee. "Please try to be nice. I really like him!"

"Gross! Why?"

"I don't know. He's hot and talented and hot," she shrugged.

She rolled her eyes and bumped Aire with her hip. "You can do better."

"I don't think it's possible to do better than Clayton Taylor."

*Oh crap.* Clayton was in trouble; Aire wouldn't give up on him until she had her way.

***

Andre chatted their ears off the entire way to the training room. *The entire way.* Rose lost track of how many times he talked about himself, nor could she remember how many times she rolled her eyes. A few times, he'd directed the conversation toward Clayton, who was less than thrilled to speak. As expected, Aire took in every word.

The main training room couldn't appear fast enough.

Andre scurried away, toward a group of older men and women. Rosabella smiled, excitement tickling her bones now that she could finally begin training. Oh, and also because Andre was gone.

Aire gave her arm a squeeze and bounded over to join a different group. Her face turned serious when she reached them. It was obvious she didn't like any of the young men or women, but only Rose could tell, since she knew her friend so well.

She took in the room, eyes trailing along the walls to the high arched ceiling. It gave the massive room a dome-like feel. It reminded her of that one time her parents took her to see a professional football game. They were few and far between these days, and made for a difficult time finding and purchasing tickets.

There were rows of black and silver electric bikes along one wall, all of them facing toward a large screen with training stations and groups. A rack of weights, attached to a row of hooks that held mats stood nearby. Large, thick blue mats--more heavy duty than the ones hanging from the hooks--decorated another corner of the room, where a few teenagers practiced fighting. A grouping of kiosk-like machines squeezed in the third corner of the room, buttons and knobs galore.

Four doors lined the wall between the mats and the bikes, all of them closed but two. Younger kids were on the other side of the first one, practicing the positioning of certain moves Rose had never seen before; then again, she'd never seen any kind of fighting. Unless you counted football, which she really didn't want to. A woman led the younger group, her face serene and her arms and legs firm and fit. Rosabella thought of her own arms and legs, consisting of more obvious squish than anything else.

Her eyes were soon drawn to Andre, who climbed up onto an expansive, raised fighting ring in the middle of the domed room. He nonchalantly leaned on the surrounding elastic, playing with the balance of gravity. Then he glanced around the room, smiling when everyone's eyes focused on him.

"Today, I'll be doing a demonstration for you. Most of you will be able to move forward with your training now that we're a day after the two week mark." He waved someone over. Rose recognized Eden by her short, boyish haircut. "This is my fellow co-head of security, Eden Wells. She's here to assist me with the demonstration. Please, come gather around and make sure you can see!"

Naturally, Rose took his lead, and followed the groups of people. Something clamped around her wrist, pulling her backwards. She stumbled before catching herself.

She turned and faced Clayton, glaring at him. "What the hell is your problem?"

He shook his head and jerked his chin to the left. She followed his gaze to the rows of bikes. They were completely vacant, as if to show how disliked they were.

"No way," she said.

"Yes, *way*. I'm in charge of your training, and I'm telling you to bike for today."

"What do you *mean*, you're in charge of my training?" she seethed. "But what about Andre's demonstration? It's not like this happens every day, right?"

He smirked down at her, his chocolate eyes revealing how much he was enjoying this argument. "Bernard wanted me to be in charge of your training. And I say you need to take it easy today."

"OH NO. I'm not missing this!" Rose turned on her heel and headed for the crowd, now completely surrounding the ring.

Clayton stepped around her, blocking her path. "Rosabella. This is not a suggestion, it's an order." He sighed and looked at the ring. His voice was half apologetic when he whispered, "Besides, you can see the ring from the bikes."

She wanted nothing more than to smack him and storm over to the ring. That didn't seem like the best option, since it was her first day of training and all. It wasn't even a possibility for her to pass him, he was way too fast. And big.

His laugh caught her off guard.

Hands on her hips, she cried, "What's so funny?"

Clayton laughed again, "I feel like you want to hit me."

She rolled her eyes. With that, she strode over to the bikes, leaving him behind. That's where Rose remained for the next hour, sulking in her hatred for Clayton Taylor and his annoyingly gorgeous features she just wanted to smack.

Rosabella observed from afar during Andre and Eden's demonstration. She watched as the two of them masterfully showed the others how to perform hand to hand combat. Her skin itched with anticipation, the need to get in on the action strong. If she could pinpoint their moves, she might be able to try it later...when Clayton stopped sneaking looks at her every few seconds to make sure she was still on the bike.

The bikes were fairly common for a work-out facility. A screen stood out in front of the bike, simulating an outdoor ride. They simulated the gusts of wind on her face as if she were really riding down a hill and released fragrances along with them. The fragrances ranged from sweet flowers to the sharp scent of fresh grass, both of which she'd only smelt a handful of times her whole life. They were hard to come by, and even harder to remember.

Rose sighed and stared longingly at the screen. This was the closest she'd come to the outside world for a while. It wasn't too bad if she closed out the world around her and focused on inhaling the crisp scents of nature. Her legs pulsed along with her breathing, releasing a bundle of tension inside her. Clayton, overbearing as he was, obviously had her best intentions in mind if he wanted her to "take it easy" today. She respected his thoughts, but it didn't mean she wanted to be cooped up in the corner while everyone else learned valuable combat skills.

Someone must have urged Clayton to participate, because the next time Rose saw him, he was up on the ring with Andre. They were both laughing, hands pulled up to protect their faces. When Clayton let his guard down like that, Rose could almost see the man behind the beast. His smile revealed a more lighthearted side of him. Rose paused her peddling, leaning on the handlebars to take a breather. She watched with interest as Clayton drew Andre nearer, who made the first punch. Clayton easily dodged it and took his own swing. For as tall and muscular as Clayton was, he sure moved light on his feet. Every step was graceful, every swing certain. Gradually, their laughing died off, until beads of sweat shone on both foreheads, eyes turning to slits. Andre's teeth ground together, while Clayton's jaw clenched. What a great example of intensity!

While they were occupied, Rose figured it was safe to get off the bike, her legs filled with the tingling sensation she was fond of. It was a strange thing to enjoy, she knew; but it was proof of an exercise well done.

She dared inch toward the ring, glancing at Clayton every so often. She crossed to the center in a matter of minutes, taking in the others' faces; many, scrunched in anticipation, staring on at the two men.

A girl pulled on Rose's arm, snapping her out of her concentration on Clayton's beautiful movements.

"Excuse me?" the girl asked. "Some of us are trying a simpler form of this combat...would you like to join?"

Rose looked once more at Clayton. It was clear their match wasn't going to end any time soon. This would be one of her only chances for a while if Clayton was firm on keeping her on the bikes. She nodded and followed behind the girl, taking the only open space left. She had no idea what she was doing, but she was determined to try out some of Clayton's moves.

The boy in front of her scoffed and stepped away from her. "No way, I'm not fighting with a girl."

Rose drew near him, as she'd seen Clayton do before striking. It took the boy a second to register her fist colliding with his chin. Once he did, fury rose into his eyes. He locked in on Rose, nostrils flaring, and boomed across the mat. He dove straight at her, but she easily stepped to the left and out of the way. She noticed he was too clunky; he didn't do a very good job of carrying his weight on the balls of his feet, something she'd noticed both Clayton and Andre doing.

The boy growled and nearly spit in anger. Then he began circling her, as a hawk would its prey. She gulped in an attempt to swallow her fear, which had grown to a lump just above her clavicle. The boy's energy resurged, seeing her swallow. His anger was unmistakable; she'd recognize a determined glare like that anywhere. It was the way she'd felt every time she had a task to complete or a challenge to beat.

Too bad...for *him*. Rose was not one to give up easily. Even though this was her first go at hand to hand combat fighting, her own rage instilled in her. She feigned going to the right, just enough for him to follow, before leaning to the left instead. She sent a punch square into his stomach. Energy renewed, she fought the urge to whoop with joy. If she did, it might draw Clayton's attention to her. She couldn't have him interrupting her mid-fight.

The boy stumbled, catching his balance by reaching a hand out in front of him. Thoroughly embarrassed, he came at her again. Instead of punching her, as she'd been prepared for, he tackled her to the ground.

Needless to say, she didn't have time to brace herself for the impact. Her neck snapped forward as her body dragged heavily down to the ground. She let out a cry. They both landed in a heap on the mat. She didn't want to think about the pain coursing through her back into her neck. If she pushed it out of her mind, it was bearable.

The boy groaned from his perch on top of her, not making any effort to get off. That was the least of the pain.

"Rosie!"

Aire's face appeared above her. Rose, not wanting to see the worry on her friend's face, looked up at the ceiling. She tried to blink back a slow stream of tears, unsuccessfully. Why on earth was she crying? She was *not* a crier! She squeezed her eyes shut, now embarrassed by her own foolishness. What had she been thinking, jumping into combat when she'd never done it before?

The pressure of the boy's body was lifted off her.

"Rosabella? Talk to me, what hurts?"

She opened her eyes to see Clayton's face close to her own. His chocolate brown eyes only inches from hers, their noses practically touching. He knelt beside her and touched her face, her neck, continuing on to every limb of her body.

"Neck," she whispered, staring up at his face, brows furrowed. There was no telling how many people were around, looking at her laying on her back. This was so embarrassing.

Clayton returned to her face, fingers touching either side of her jaw. "Okay, it's going to be alright. Can I help you sit up? We'll take it slowly."

She muttered a yes, and did her best to help him. He knelt beside her and brought Rose to a sitting position. She gasped at a shot of pain running down from her neck to her toes.

"Sorry, Rose. You doin' okay?"

She bit her lip to keep from gasping again. She attempted a weak smile for him. Something about seeing him so upset didn't sit well with her at all. His eyes so wide, his face so pale, it hurt her more than her neck. And it was all beause of her stupid stubborness.

"I just...I just need to sit for a second. I'll be fine," she managed.

He nodded and wrapped an arm around her, supporting her back. Grateful, she leaned into his hold, letting him take the brunt of her weight.

She noticed the boy then, who was off to the side, his hands red with fresh blood. Was it hers? She thought he merely tackled her, knocking the wind from her chest or something. He glared at Clayton with a ferocity Rose didn't understand. Clayton, who was staring at Rosabella's face with an unnecessary intensity, followed her gaze to the boy.

"As for you, Lucca...we will deal with you later. You'll see what it's like to fight someone of a higher training status. I mean, come on. It wasn't even a fair fight!" Clayton snapped. Veins stood out from his neck as he threatened, "I'll make you hurt, I swear it."

Rose shivered and tugged on the sleeve of his shirt. "No. I'm...okay. I was...holding my...own."

Clayton, with much difficulty, moved his gaze from the boy back to her face. Recognition dawned on his face and he shook his head, trying to shake the anger, no doubt.

"Thank you," he whispered into Rose's hair. "Sometimes, I can go a bit overboard when I'm upset."

She smirked. "No problem....That's what I'm here for...to be your personal anger management coach."

He rolled his eyes, smiling. "Alright coach. Let's get you to the medical wing for a check up."

That would mean missing more of her training time! She wanted to stay here and observe, even if she couldn't participate.

She pushed him away, getting into a kneeling position. "No...I'm already better!"

Clayton's returning grip on her was firm, but gentle. He lifted her to her feet, waiting for her to blink dizzy spots from her eyes.

Andre pushed past Aire, who was staring at them in horror, and ran right up to them. "Clay! We cannot let this stand! There's a strict rule about no tackling during combat training. He broke a rule!"

"So let Eden and her internal training staff take care of it. You're in charge of *external* security, remember." Clayton shrugged and gave his friend a *what are ya gonna do look*. "Besides, Rosabella doesn't want us to...you know, *attack* him as we would."

"Screw what Rose would want. I want justice!"

Rose waved a weak hand in front of Andre's face. "Umm, right here. And anyway, I say no to justice. This was my fault."

Clayton led her away, arm around her waist to keep her upright. Andre huffed and left it alone. Aire, surprisingly, didn't follow after them like she normally would. All the better, she would have tried to drape herself over Clayton anyway. It would have gotten on Rose's nerves, and she would've yelled at her or told her to go away.

It was much better this way.

# Chapter 12

## (AIRE)

WHAT. THE. HELL?! HER HEART PHYSICALLY DEFLATED, IF that was even possible. The sight of Rose with Clayton turned her mind into a spinning wheelhouse of accusations. It dawned on her then, an awareness creeping up from the tips of her toes to the top of her head.

How had she not seen it earlier?

It took everything in her to not run after them, rip Rosie away from him, and take her to the medical wing herself. Yes, Aire was jealous. She was jealous as hell.

Rose always got the looks from the guys; she was always the best at everything. She even managed to get their classmates to respect her without them even knowing her at all. In school, people would move out of the way whenever Rose walked down the hallway. The most aggravating thing about it? Rosie never noticed their silent respect. She commanded an audience as well as the Government enforced their strict rules.

To be honest, Clayton hadn't even looked at Aire since they'd arrived. He'd been too busy stealing glances at Rose. Even Andre had been drawn to her. Why did it always have to be Rose? Perhaps if Aire'd been born with shorter genes the guys would've paid her more attention? Or if she had curvy hips like Rose? Or the orange-red hair that everyone was so captivated by?

Of course, Aire would never tell her best friend she resented her for being who she was. It was just so irritating, the way Rose acted like she was merely an innocent, nothing girl. Compared to Aire, she was nothing but a little girl in stature. When it came to her brains and her heart, Rose surpassed Aire. That much was true. But, where Aire was lacking in smarts, she made up for in flirting.

Aire's older sister, Luna, had taught her how to wrap men around her finger. Aire had many chances to observe her sister attract men like flies to honey. In fact, Aire remembered a time when their parents were too busy with work to pick her up from school.

> *Aire was in high school at the time, only sixteen years old. Luna offered to help their parents out by picking Aire up, promising to have her back before dinner. Aire wasn't thrilled by the thought of sitting in her twenty-year-old sister's office for a couple of hours, but she went with her anyway. She didn't have any other option. It was either that or sit at school and do her homework in a stuffy classroom while she waited for her parents.*
>
> *She and Luna weren't very close leading up to that day, so for Aire, it felt like more of a chore to be with her. That all changed about an hour later, when Aire was just finishing up her math homework.*
>
> *Luna hopped up from her desk, shoved in the corner to make room in the tiny, windowless office. She ran over to Aire, checking her watch.*
>
> *"Aire, I have a meeting coming up in a few minutes. Can you do something for me?"*
>
> *Aire blinked, looking at her sister's death grip on her hands. "Sure," she said, unsure of what this meeting was all about. Did her sister have very confidential things to take care of?*
>
> *"Good," she patted Aire's head. "If this goes well, I'll finally be out of this shithole office. I need you to hide under my desk."*
>
> *What?*
>
> *She crossed her arms. "Luna? Why do I need to hide?"*
>
> *Luna kissed her hand. "Oh, don't get worked up, Rei. You know what happens when you get worked up."*
>
> *Aire nodded, sucking in her cheeks.*

*"That's a good girl. I just can't have you wiggin' out on me today,"* Luna laughed like this was all a simple joke between them.

*She pulled her hands out of Luna's grip. "I'll be fine."*

*Luna snuck a look at her watch again. "Alright, Aire. Time for the show. If you behave yourself and remain unseen, I'll teach you how to get your way in this business."*

*Aire shoved everything into her backpack and swallowed. She'd never seen her sister act so strange. Sure, they had weird conversations, like all kids did, but this was different.*

*Luna gave Aire's head a kiss before she ducked under the desk. Aire immediately felt the cool wood against her back, and smelled the pine scent left over from the manufacturer. Luna scooted the chair up to the desk, completely shutting Aire in.*

*"Comfy?"*

*"No," Aire said with her chin forced to remain on her chest. "How long is this meeting going to be?"*

*Luna laughed. "I have it scheduled for thirty minutes. But I don't anticipate this taking longer than fifteen. He can be...easily swayed."*

*Oh. She was shocked to hear her sister speak with such confidence about convincing this guy of giving her a new office. She really wanted that new office.*

*Aire heard a sharp knock at the door, to which Luna tapped on top of the desk.*

*"Here we go."*

Aire had absolutely no idea going into that "meeting" what exactly her sister was capable of. She remembered hearing some really strange flirtation tactics, and other stuff. From that day forward, Luna had treated Aire with the utmost respect. Now they were friends, true sisters who kept devious secrets.

Luna had been impressed that Aire kept her secret. After that, Aire was invited to visit her at work anytime she wanted, in her new, much bigger office on the third floor of the Government's corporate office. Luna taught Aire everything she needed to know about seducing men into getting what she wanted. It used to make Aire uncomfortable, but then she realized how easy it was to manipulate people. It brought her a kind of satisfaction that made her heart pound with adrenaline. She wasn't sure how to explain it.

Shaking off her anger at Clayton and her jealousy of Rose, Aire turned around and walked in the opposite direction. She'd immerse herself in her training, until she was better than Rose. She was determined to do something better than her. Best friend or not.

# Chapter 13

## (ROSABELLA)

THE MONITORS BEHIND ROSE BEEPED IN THEIR ANNOYING way once the medic was done checking her over. The medic gave Clayton a funny look, before she wrapped up her tools and put them back into their kit case.

"It looks like minor whiplash, and a small cut on her forearm. She should be up and running in a few days or so--*if* you take it slow, Miss Porter." She winked at Rose, who was lying on the white cot. "I'll write up a note so you can stay in here for an hour or so and rest."

Rose felt like such an idiot. Even this medic seemed to know her stubborn nature. Rose couldn't meet her eyes when she thanked her. Her face turned warm, and her eyes hot once the medic walked out, leaving her alone with Clayton. She expected a reprimanding, something that could put any lecture from her parents to shame.

Clayton sat on the edge of her bed and shook his head. He did that a lot, she noticed. "Rosabella..." he trailed off, wincing at whatever he was going to say.

Oh *this* she had to hear.

He took the somewhat expected route. Clayton gave her hand a playful light tap. "Don't you ever follow rules?"

It was her turn to wince. "You know, I actually used to do a lot of that--to a fault even. But now, I'm ready for change."

He smirked, bringing a light to his eyes she hadn't yet seen. "I should've known."

A silence passed between them. She stared at his hand, still on top of hers, unmoving. She considered his outfit: grey sweatpants and a black, tight-fitting breathable shirt.

She giggled, saying the first thing that came to mind, "Hey, we're twinning!"

He tilted his head, a curious expression crossing his face.

She rolled her eyes and laughed. "Well, I just mean we're wearing the same color scheme."

Finally, he smiled at her, flashing his top row of white teeth. "Prince would be absolutely devastated to see our lack of color."

Rose shoved his shoulder. Then that silence passed between them again. It was awkward, the way they both stared at nothing.

After a moment, Clayton patted her hand and stood. "Hey, so I've gotta go finish training this morning. I'll be back to bring you to lunch if you want?"

"Wow," she said, her jaw dropping with fake bewilderment. "Is Clayton Taylor giving me a *choice* instead of an order?"

He picked up a pillow from the bedside chair and threw it at her. She caught it inches from her face, giggling.

"Just be prepared for this afternoon, Miss Porter. I'm not going to let you get away with *anything!*"

Rose was still giggling ridiculously when he exited the room.

Dear god, what was in that water the medic made her drink when she came in earlier? If Rosabella didn't know any better, she'd say he was actually nice to her. More than nice even, he'd been *flirtatious.*

\*\*\*

About forty minutes later, Rose grew tired of counting the grey tiles on the floor. She'd been all alone, staring at nothing for what seemed like forever. If she didn't have something to do, she grew dissatisfied; Rose was the sort of person who constantly had to be doing *something*. It was practically a sin for her to sit here idly like this.

More than anything right now, she wanted to get up and stretch her legs. So that's exactly what she did. In the hallway. On her way out of the medical wing.

Clayton wouldn't be pleased to see she'd left, but he had to understand her desire for movement. Eventually, if he kept listening to her, he'd figure out Rose wasn't going to take no for an answer. If he hadn't already.

This time, she'd been taken to one of the rooms at the end of one of the halls. The nurses and doctor seemed to have gotten wind of her last escape; they weren't going to let it happen again.

As she made her way down the hall, Rose made sure to walk at a steady pace and smile at everyone she passed. If they saw she wasn't hurrying to leave, they would be less likely to assume she was up to something.

Rose heard a familiar voice around the corner and froze. It was Gianna! She had no intention of slowing her pace, nor did she have a desire to talk to her roommate.

A nurse rounded the corner, holding Gianna by the arm. "Dear, you're much overdue for a check up."

"I know, I've just been really busy. I have this new roommate...she's sweet and all, but everybody wants to talk to her, so I've had a hell of a time answering the door..." Gianna trailed off, her head down.

Rose pressed herself against the wall, praying they'd turn in the other direction and go down the other hallway. No such luck. They continued down her hall, heading straight for her.

*Shit!* Before she realized what she was doing, Rose barrelled into the closest room, shutting the door with a snap behind her. Leaning against the wall, she took deep breaths to calm herself. That was way too close!

There was nothing wrong with Gianna...Rosabella simply didn't have the energy to listen to her talk about her boyfriend or anything else. Gianna was just like Aire in that way, save for the fact that Aire didn't actually have a boyfriend. But she certainly acted like she and Clayton were a couple. A bubble of rage formed at the back of Rose's throat at the thought of Clayton and Aire kissing and laughing together.

Rose pressed her ear to the door. When she was positive they were gone, Rose turned around to lean her back on the door. This was some kind of therapy room. She had to squint to see the other end of the room, as it stretched almost as long as the training room. Work-out equipment--the easy kind like dumbbells and movement machines--filled the space, with one long walkway left open in the middle. Rose reached behind her for the doorknob, turned it, and then stopped.

A thin girl stood at the back of the room by herself. She hadn't seen Rose yet. The girl leaned heavily on the walker in front of her, sweat gleaming on her face. Her eyes turned to angry slits while her hands clenched around the walker's handles so hard, her knuckles turned white. Whatever the girl was trying to do, it wasn't going her way. Rose related to that feeling of helplessness.

Rose inched closer, taking care to be quiet. She didn't want to disturb the girl just yet; she wanted to see what she was going to do.

As she neared her, Rose saw the girl's legs. With shorts on, it was easy to see how sickly skinny her legs were. It was like she hadn't used them for walking in years. Curiosity took over her, so much so, that she sat down on the floor, right in the middle of the walkway. A minute or two later, after struggling to stand on her own, the girl let out a frustrated cry and fell backwards. Rose hopped up, her heart jumping into her throat.

The girl landed on her back, staring up at the ceiling. She cried out in frustration again and started to cry.

Rosabella, nervous prickles rising on her arms, knelt beside the girl. "Hey, are you alright?"

The girl shook her head. "No. I'll never be okay."

"Hey now, don't say that," she tucked a stray piece of dark brown hair behind the girl's ear. "You were doing really well!"

The girl pushed herself up onto her elbows, cocking her head at Rose. "If you thought that was good, you should've seen me before this happened. I used to be one of the fastest runners in my school."

They stared at one another. The girl seemed to dare Rose to ask about her injury. Rose knew she didn't really want to talk about it so she shrugged and helped the girl into her wheelchair a few feet away. It wasn't difficult; the girl was tiny, all skin and bones.

"How old are you?" asked Rose.

"Seventeen and a half."

To disguise her shock, Rose giggled, patting her arm rest. "You had to throw the half in there?"

"I'll take anything I can get," the girl said, smiling up at her. "You must be Rosabella."

She smirked. "Do the black bags and confused look in my eyes give it away?"

The girl laughed hard, holding her stomach.

Rose ruffled her hair, feeling protective of this girl. She reminded her of someone, but she couldn't place it. It was probably because she missed her little brother, Nicolai, who had only been eight years old when she left him behind.

The girl grabbed Rose's hand and shook it. "I've heard about you from a lot of people."

Rosabella rolled her eyes. "I just don't get it."

"I understand you, Rosabella," the girl said, staring up at her with determination in her brown eyes.

"You do?"

The girl nodded. "I'm different from the others, like you. I've lived here for years, but people *still* stare at me whenever I enter a room. That's why I stick to my apartment with my brother. He's the one who's told me the most about you."

She thought on that for a moment, realizing she should be grateful for the ability to use her whole body.

"Enough talk about me," Rose said, clapping her hands together. "Why don't we try again?"

The girl's mouth dropped open. "What?"

Rose brought the walker closer to her so she wouldn't have to travel as far. She tapped in on the ground and winked at the girl.

"Rosabella...I'm crippled. I can't do that."

Shaking her head, Rose wrapped her arms around the girl's torso and firmly lifted her off the ground. She didn't argue, letting Rose guide her to the walker.

"Do you want to know a secret?" Rose whispered, leaning into the girl's ear.

She didn't answer, but peeked at Rosabella, eyes curious. The girl smirked, something that really reminded Rose of a person she still couldn't place.

"Well, first I tell myself that I can do anything I want. Then I push myself as hard as I can," Rose whispered. She let the girl go so she could try walking on her own. "If I don't succeed, I brush it off and try some other way to get to my end goal."

"That's great, but I'm not going to be able to do this," the girl huffed, frustrated again. Her brown eyes flashed at Rose.

"You can't learn if you don't try....are you ready? I'll hold onto you to start. Take it one leg at a time. If you try your dominant leg first, that should help you gain your confidence."

"I'll try, but don't expect anything to happen, Rosabella."

"Call me Rose."

"Okay, Rose. Here goes nothing."

She did her best to keep the girl talking. If she thought too hard about moving her legs, she wouldn't get anywhere. "So you said you live in an apartment with your brother?"

The girl, breathing heavy already, nodded. She hadn't made any progress yet.

Rose continued the conversation. "Nice, and how long did you say you've lived here?"

"Years."

"How many?"

The girl huffed and rolled her eyes. "Seven, eight. I don't remember."

Along with the eye-roll came forward movement from the girl's right leg. Rose beamed, shocked the girl had already made progress. It was only half an inch of movement, but it was something. The girl hadn't noticed.

"Were you and your brother rescued together?" Rose released one hand, at this point hardly directing the girl.

"No. He came here before I did. There were...some complications. He wasn't with me at the time because I was at home..." She cleared her throat. "I was born a third child.

Rose gasped. The Government only allowed two children to be born into a family!

"I know, I know. My parents committed a crime, sue them." She sighed, rolling her eyes.

"Anyway, our oldest brother hid me when the droids attacked our home. My second brother--the one I live with now--had been out at the time with his friend, Tess. I didn't see him again until he rescued me days later."

Rose released her, all control in the girl's hands now.

"Wow." Rose stared at the girl's feet, eyebrows raised in surprise. She squeezed the girl's shoulder with encouragement. "Ummm. Did you just see that?"

The girl looked back at her, confused. "See what?"

"You just walked forward with your right leg."

"Wha--?" She looked down at her leg. "Holy shit! I just *walked!*"

Rose hugged her, laughing. They both gave one another a squeeze and pulled away.

A man's voice interrupted them, "Didn't I teach my little sister not to curse?"

The girl and Rose saw him at the same time, leaning against one of the machines. His arms were crossed and he was smirking at them.

The girl leaned forward on her walker and nearly shouted, "Clay! Did you see me?"

"Did I *ever*!" He ran to her and picked her up, swinging her around. In the whirlwind of movement, the two of them tipped the walker over.

The girl squealed and giggled, holding tightly to his arms. Rose couldn't help but blush. *Clayton* was her brother? Everything made sense now, especially the way the girl's smirk had looked so familiar to her. They had the same gorgeous brown eyes too. She was as beautiful as Clayton was handsome.

Allowing them to have this moment alone, Rose slipped away, smiling in triumph. She'd go back to the training room, sit on the bike and obey everyone's orders to take it easy. If this girl could make herself walk again, surely Rose could make herself *not* walk into dangerous situations for a while.

Clayton caught her before she'd made it to the door. He shouted down the walkway, "Rose! Wait!"

Rose turned around to see Clayton smiling. It lit up his whole face, flashing a small dimple on his left cheek. He looked at her with a strong intensity, bringing her to another blush. She rubbed her arm, uncomfortable with the sudden change in the mood of the room. They wound up staring at one another in silence.

The girl nudged him, still in his arms. "Go on. What were you going to say, Clay?"

It was his turn to blush. On him, it didn't look like a tomato exploded on his face; instead, it gave his skin a warm glow. Rose never thought she'd be able to bring Clayton Taylor to a blush. What a day!

He blinked. "Right. Umm, I just wanted to say thank you. For being here--to help Clarise, I mean."

Rose remembered she'd never even asked for the girl's name. Thankfully, Clayton had said it, or she would've been too embarrassed to ask the next time she saw Clarise.

She smiled at him. "I was just in the right place at the right time, that's all. Bye *Clarise*!"

Clarise held out her hand. "Rose?"

"Yes?"

Clarise smiled. "Can we get dinner together tonight?"

Clayton's mouth dropped open, face still red.

Rose beamed, ignoring Clayton's embarrassment. "I was wondering when you'd ask!"

\*\*\*

Once the buzzer overhead sounded, signaling the end of training for the day, Rose hopped off the bike.

She'd gotten right back on the bike after she'd left Clarise and Clayton in the therapy room. Rose had taken a short break to eat lunch, where she was joined by Clayton and Andre. Rose finished early, saying she wanted to get back on the bikes and exercise her legs. She'd remained there ever since.

Her legs tingled all the way up, from her toes to her waist. She nearly laughed at the strange sensation. Rosabella walked around in small circles to induce a regular blood flow.

Aire bounded over, face pink and sweaty. She crossed her arms and glared at Rose. In an attempt to ignore her friend's pettiness, Rose sat on the ground and pretended she was too distracted to notice her presence. Instead, she stretched her legs and rubbed her calves.

Finally Rose couldn't take the angry silence anymore. "Are you just going to stand there, or are you going to talk, Aire?"

Aire huffed. "Where did you go today after lunch? You got up in such a hurry, I couldn't even ask you. And then, Clayton whispered something to Andre and got up to follow you."

Her head shot up. "What? Clayton didn't *follow* me!"

Sure, he'd walked to the training room with her, but he went his own way once they got there. He'd gone into one of the doors on the leftmost wall in the training room. It was an office for the trainers to meet and discuss things.

"Oh really? Are you telling me you didn't spend that time with him until the rest of us went back to training?"

Rose felt her face turning red. She clenched her jaw to keep from saying something that would hurt her friend's feelings. Aire was being so possessive!

She crossed her own arms. "Aire…Clayton and I walked to the training room together. After that, I rode a bike--completely alone. What more do you want in order to believe me?"

"Well, you've just been so distant today. I was really upset when you got hurt earlier today…and then Clayton, helping you like that. It was just so unlike him…I thought maybe--"

"I think maybe I can shed some light on this argument," Clayton said, coming to a stop a few feet away. He locked eyes with Rose before turning to Aire. "You shouldn't worry, Gil. Rose is well taken care of here. I wouldn't argue with her unless for a good reason."

Rose let out a combination of a laugh and a scoff. "Oh, is that right?"

Clayton smirked.

Aire threw her hands up. "Are you two, like, dating?"

All the color drained from Clayton's face. Rose wished that had been an option for her. Instead, a bright red color filled her cheeks as she was rendered speechless.

"Oh, I'm *sorry*, did I hit a sore spot?" Aire's voice dripped with sarcasm. "The truth hurts, doesn't it? Especially when you're such a bitch about hiding it."

Aire's words hit her like a punch to the gut.

"Aire, how could you say that? You know me better than anyone. I wouldn't hide that from you."

Clayton rubbed his arms and glared at Aire. "We are definitely *not* dating. I couldn't feel that way about someone like her."

Rose sucked in her cheeks, eyes stinging with anger. "Aire, you do not have the right to be so…so *possessive* of Clayton just because you think he's attractive! He's so much more than that, you just don't care enough to look past the surface. And you," she shouted, turning on Clayton next. "I have no idea what that's supposed to mean, 'someone like me.' You're so conceited. Maybe you two deserve each *other*."

She turned on her heel and, with an exaggerated pep in her step, Rose stormed off to the kitchen. She had no idea how that had gone so far in such a short span of time. All she wanted to do was talk to Clayton about Clarise, but instead she had the pleasure of receiving two knives in the back. What a day.

# Chapter 14

## (ANDRE)

"DAMN, SHE SAID IT JUST LIKE THAT?" ANDRE whistled. "She sure is somethin', Clay."

He bit off a piece of carrot in his hand and looked over at Rosabella. She and Clarise had come in together earlier, much to everyone's surprise, and sat a few seats down the table from Andre, who'd been waiting for Clayton at the time.

"No doubt," Clayton said, shaking his head. "That girl can drive me crazier than anyone else I've met, and I've only known her for a few days."

Andre and Clayton had been friends for years, ever since he found Clayton at the edge of the Fortress's boundaries. They had nearly killed one another until Bernard broke them up. Since then, he'd been able to tell what Clayton was thinking, a challenge very few people were able to accomplish.

He threw the rest of his carrot back onto his tray, ready to have a heart to heart with his best friend. "Why don't you go talk to her and explain what you meant earlier? I'm sure she's cooled down since then."

Clayton closed his eyes and leaned forward, face in hands. Andre recognized that look. It meant he was trying to talk himself out of doing something he might regret.

He nudged Clayton's arm. "Clay, c'mon. What's the worst that could happen?"

"I'm not sure what you're implying will happen by me explaining myself," Clayton said, his voice low. "I just feel bad for hurting her feelings, that's all."

Andre laughed. "Wow, what a strange turn of events...Clayton Taylor actually feels *bad*? Oh boy. Watch out world, nothing good can come of this."

Clayton looked at him and lightly punched Andre on the shoulder. "Would you shut the hell up, Dre? Is it so rare for me to have feelings?"

"Umm, yes it is," he said, laughing. "Ever since you lost--you know who--you haven't been the same."

"I thought we promised to never speak about that again?"

Andre held his hands up. "Alright, alright. You're the boss I guess."

Thankfully, Logan joined them before their conversation took a turn for the worse. He plopped right down next to Andre, ruffling his hair.

"Hey guys, what's up?" Logan must've sensed the tension between them because he looked warily at Andre. "Something happen today?"

Clayton leaned back on his chair and crossed his arms. "Nope."

"Okay well, I hope things went well with training." Logan shook his protein shake. "How did Rosabella do on her first day?"

Andre watched Clayton bristle at the mention of Rose's name, so he decided to step in. "Oh, you know, she got into a fight and had to be taken to the medical wing. No biggie--how was your day, Logan?"

Logan stopped, mid shake. "She *what*?"

Perturbed, Andre flicked a piece of lettuce off his shirt that had gotten stuck there earlier. "Yeah, she was supposed to sit on the side today, but obviously she got bored."

"Well what did you expect, that Rosabella was just going to sit and *watch* the action?" Logan looked at Clayton, eyes thin lines. "I thought you and I talked about how difficult it was to keep her in line? We had a *plan* for her training for a reason."

Clayton brushed him off. "I decided to change it. She could have gotten into more trouble had she been allowed to actually do the combat training today. So I had her ride the bikes."

"The bikes?" Logan's hand around the shake bottle clenched. Andre wasn't one to turn down a fight, but given the circumstances of the two men, he didn't think it wise to let them hash it out.

"Hey, yo. Why don't we talk about something else?" He scrambled around in his head for something to say. "Oh, I know! Like that friend of Rose's huh? Aire? Isn't she hot? Not as hot as Rosabella, but you know, in her own way."

At the same time, Logan and Clayton grumbled, "Shut up, Dre."

Sometimes he couldn't stop running his mouth. *Oops.*

"Too far? Shit, sorry." Andre chuckled. "But hey, at least you were in agreement on something for a second."

When neither of them responded, Andre exhaled and leaned back in his own chair. Clay and Logan started arguing quietly about how to move forward with Rose's training. Clayton wanted to keep her out of the action and have her stick to the bikes for a week, while Logan wanted her to ease her way into the training process. He thought having her do some independent work at boxing would help start her endurance and keep her safely tucked away in the corner. Andre could be really dumb, but he knew when things were about more than just getting your way. Logan and Clayton had some underlying issues they hadn't yet worked out, and now they were using one little thing to spur into the rabbit hole of arguments.

Andre rested his cheek on his palm and looked over at Rose, blocking their stupid conversation out. The girls had their heads close together. Rose beamed at Clarise affectionately, perhaps even protectively. He wasn't sure where that had come from or how Clarise and Rose had bonded so quickly, but Andre enjoyed seeing Clair happy. He relished in that smile of hers, crooked teeth and all; it'd been a long time since she was truly happy. Not once had he seen Clarise let go and forget all the bad stuff, like being confined to a wheelchair. Until now. Tonight, she was smiling wider than he'd ever seen. It was then Andre wished he'd had his own sibling growing up. Sure, he'd had a couple of cousins down here, but he was never close with any of them, save for one.

Clair and Clayton had a tight bond Andre would never fully understand himself, one only a sibling would ever feel.

Clarise was the one girl here Andre actually respected and behaved around. If he didn't, Clayton would kick his ass. He had strict rules for Clarise, more so than Andre believed necessary, but she never really questioned them. In fact, she never really left their apartment unless necessary. That's what made Rose so amazing; she was able to encourage

Clair to go into public, something she hadn't done since coming to the Fortress.

If Clayton thought he was being smart by trying to push Rose away, he had another thing coming. Something told Andre that Rose wouldn't let him slip away so easily. If they didn't make out at least once, he'd be surprised. But hey, love was weird like that. Andre had never felt a connection for anyone as strongly as he'd seen others--specifically Clayton years ago--but that didn't mean he didn't know what it should feel like.

Andre hadn't always been this dirty minded before. His mom had instilled in him the importance of respecting women; on the other hand, his dad hadn't been a great role model either. Seeing them both together was like watching oil and water mix. Yet they made it work so well. That's probably why he could see something similar brewing between Clay and Rosabella. They had no idea what was up ahead, and Andre was going to enjoy every minute of it.

Man, was she something. How she'd never discovered the Fortress on accident was beyond him. He supposed her family kept it well hidden. The concept of hiding the door in one of the Government official's houses was ingenious. Whoever had the idea was incredibly intelligent. Hiding a secret society right under the Government's nose...that was perfect! Nobody would ever suspect such a place existed, and if they did, they certainly wouldn't think of an official's house as being the entryway.

"Dre, were you listening?" Clayton asked, flicking him on the forehead.

"'Course I wasn't." He stretched his arms above his head. "What do you want?"

Logan laughed and took a drink of his shake. Clearly, the two of them had worked things out enough to stop fighting at the dinner table.

"I said I wanted to go for a walk after dinner. Do you wanna go with me?" Clayton sighed and shook his head. "Logan's already turned me down. Something about wanting to read a chapter in his book before bed."

"*Reading?*" Andre shoved Logan in the side. "Wow, there are days even I can't believe I'm related to you."

"Love you too, cuz," Logan said laughing.

"You two are cousins?"

All three of them turned their heads to Rose, who was standing behind Logan. Clayton straightened his spine and stared dumbly up at her. She gawked down at the three of them.

"Yup, we are," Andre said, ruffling Logan's hair as he'd done when he came to the table.

"But...but, Logan. You're so *nice*...and Andre's so...so..."

Andre finished her sentence for her, "Handsome? Hilarious? Oh I know! Sexy?"

Clarise, who was parked beside Rose, giggled. In response, Andre reached out and tapped her little nose. Gosh, she could be so cute. There were days he wished she wasn't Clayton's sister. Even then, he didn't think he'd have gotten to know her as well had she not been related to his best friend.

Clayton, obviously trying to be cool, said, "I was thinking more along the lines of arrogant and selfish."

Rose placed her hand on her hip. "Oh, you must be confusing him with yourself then."

"Ooooo, burn!" Andre laughed. Logan joined in, almost choking on his salad. Clayton sat silently fuming. That made it even better.

"I don't have time for people who think I'm not worth their time, so we're leaving." She looked right into Clayton's eyes with an intensity Andre hadn't expected. "I just thought it would be courteous of us to let you know where we were going first."

Clay nodded, mouth shut.

Andre kicked him under the table. What was wrong with him?

"Well, it was nice to see you, Logan." She shrugged. "Can't say the same of you two, but you know, any human interaction is good for me, since I was forced to stay in isolation today."

It was Clarise who, with a smirk on her face, spoke next, "Rosie and I are going on a tour of the Fortress. I'll be back before curfew, Clay."

With that, the girls left, leaving the guys awestruck.

Logan looked at Clayton and laughed again. "Wow, I *love* that woman!"

Clayton stood so fast his chair clattered to the floor. "What did you just say?"

Logan stopped. "I just meant that I admire her honesty and spunk. That's all. Why?"

"Nevermind. I'm leaving. See ya." Clayton began cleaning his place at the table. Then he left without another word.

"Be right back, cuz." Andre hopped up and chased after Clayton, catching him at the dish chute.

Aha. So there *was* more to this than Clayton revealed. Andre knew Clay at least had some feelings for her. It was hard not to, seeing her standing there so indignant. The way she'd stuck her hip out in anger, the way her eyes had flashed at Clayton, those were sure signs of someone who had something like love in her heart. Andre prided himself in noticing the signs of someone loving another. He wanted to take Clayton by the shoulders and shake him until he realized how amazing she was.

Instead, he opted for a much more subtle choice of words. "Clay, if you let her walk away without explaining yourself, you're out of your mind."

He shrugged Andre's hand off and scoffed. "I have no idea what you mean by that. She's just a girl."

"You *do* know what I mean. Don't compare her to Tess. They're very different people. You just need to let this happen the way it's going to happen." He looked his best friend in the eye. "You cannot control everything. Sometimes it's good for you to let someone throw you a curveball."

Clayton looked away. "Dre, we promised not to speak about *her*. You know how I feel about that."

"I'm serious, dude. I want you to be happy." He grabbed Clayton's chin and forced his friend to look at him. "Look at me. You're my best friend aren't you?"

He managed a slight nod. "Forever."

"Great. Then please do me the favor of just hearing me out. What happened with Tess was not your fault. You have to move on and get your life back. She wouldn't want you to go through life hating yourself and everyone around you--"

"I don't hate *you*. At least not that much," Clayton teased. Andre knew he really wanted to be alone so he could cry over losing Tess or whatever he did when he was upset. She'd been an incredible woman, clueless when it came to street smarts, but could perform a surgery on a person like no one's business. It didn't matter anymore; she was gone and Clayton needed to forgive himself.

"I know. But for real, you have to trust me. I know what you need in your life. If Rose isn't what you need, then you can punch me later or something. But right now, I can promise you that if you don't give yourself a chance with her, you're going to live with that burden for the rest of your days."

# Chapter 15

## (ROSABELLA)

CLARISE ROLLED OUT OF THE LOUNGE AT NECK breaking speed. "So that's about it. The Fortress is big, but it's not big enough to hide from people. Trust me, I'd know that better than anyone."

The lounge, which consisted of two large, floor to ceiling screens, one for movie watching and the other for playing video games, was a quaint little room. There was also a table with poles sticking out the sides, which connected to little stick figure things. Some were red and others blue. Clair demonstrated the game by releasing a little ball into a hole on the side and spinning the poles to move the little people. An interesting contraption no doubt, that left Rose fumbling around during the short demonstration. She lost to Clarise in a matter of seconds. The room itself had the capacity to hold about fifty people at a time if they all squished together. Rose would much rather sit alone in the library than be surrounded by crazy teenagers. The technology in the Fortress was old anyway; Rose's family had much better gaming systems in her house.

Clarise smiled from the doorway. "Are you ready? There's not much else in here."

Rosabella nodded and continued after her new friend.

"So now that you've seen the whole Fortress, what do you think? What's your favorite place?" asked Clarise.

"Oh, definitely the library," she replied without hesitation.

Clarise grinned like an idiot. "Are you sure? You didn't like the trash room? I thought for sure you'd like it in there."

Rose laughed and poked Clair's shoulder. "I think you're confusing me with your brother."

Clair's face went from jovial to somber in two seconds flat. "He's not that bad, really. You've never seen the side of him I've seen."

Rose hesitated before responding. "I'm sure you're right. I've just never been so angry at another person like this before. It's hard to like someone who continues to insult me."

"It really isn't meant to hurt you, Rose. My brother just doesn't know how to show his emotions." Clarise sighed and stopped wheeling. She turned her chair to face Rosabella. "If there's one thing I know about my brother, it's that he's not the easiest guy to get along with because he's always trying to hide his feelings from people."

Rose pulled her hair back so it was no longer sticking to her sweaty neck. There really was zero air flow down here. It became suffocating if she thought about it too much. If what Clarise was saying was the truth, Rose grew even more confused by the minute. How could someone as rude as Clayton have a good side?

When Rose thought back to today's earlier events, she remembered how carefully Clay had guided her to the medical wing for a checkup. He'd stayed with her the whole time so she wasn't alone with the doctor. And then there was the flirtatious behavior at the end of the check up... what was going through his mind? Could Rose ever be friends with someone like that? The more she thought about it, the more determined she was to coax the good out of him; maybe with a little help, Clayton would change for the better. She didn't want a project, she wanted a friend; but Rose was not one to back down from a challenge.

✳✳✳

When Clarise and Rose arrived at the library, it was completely vacant. Just the way she liked it! They migrated over to the section along the left hand wall, the section Rose had explored yesterday.

Rose beamed at Clarise. "So you're saying I can just come in here whenever I *want*?"

Clarise laughed, swatting her with a book. "Yes, how many times do I have to say it?"

She giggled and put the book back on the shelf. "I'm sorry, I just can't believe it! We have so many rules about checking out books where we come from, remember. Some people refused to even go to the public library because it's easier to read a book on their screen than go through all the logistics."

"Sounds like the lazy way," Clarise smiled. She pulled a book from one of the lower shelves. "I'd much rather hold a physical book in my hands, no matter how outdated it is."

"Me too! And the smell of the pages. You can't get that vivid scent from reading on a screen."

Clarise nodded excitedly. "So true! Here, I have a great series for you to read...if I could just find it. Aha, here it is!"

She held out a book with a blue cover and a beautiful redhead on the front. The title read, *The Selection*.

"No way!" Rose half screamed with glee. "Holy crap, that's one of my favorite series too!"

"It's like we were meant to find each other, Rosie!"

They both giggled. Clarise put the book back and grabbed the second one right next to it.

"Wanna read this with me?"

Rose gasped. "*The Elite*! It's got to be one of the best in the series. Of course."

"What are we waiting for? Let's get reading. We can talk about our favorite parts!"

Rose followed her to the nearest couch in the corner. She let Clarise take the reins and push herself from her wheelchair to the couch in one fluid movement. She didn't make any comments. It was important for her to feel independent.

She settled in beside Clarise and leaned in to see the pages better. "Oh here! Go to page two!"

"Can you read it out loud?"

"Of course!"

Rosabella brushed Clarise's hair back after she rested her head on Rose's shoulder. She missed her brother then, and having the know-how for taking care of someone else. Here, she was uncomfortable in her own skin at the moment, though she told herself it was out of her control. She focused her attention on reading to Clair beside her, a long lost sister she didn't realize she needed. It was different than spending time with Aire, who was always obsessing over the next guy or talking about herself. That was probably the reason Rose couldn't stand Andre; he was the male version of her friend.

"Okay, here I go. Sorry if my reading isn't to your liking." She took a deep breath and began, "'As he moved his head, inhaling just above my hairline, I considered it. What would it be like to simply love Maxon? 'Do you know when the last time was that I really looked at the stars?' He asked."

Clarise clutched her arm. "Wait, skip ahead a little bit."

Rose pointed to a spot in the middle of page three. "Here?"

She sighed happily. "Yes, I love this part."

"'What else are you terrible at?' I asked, running my hand across his starched shirt. Encouraged by the touch, Maxon drew circles on my shoulder with the hand he had wrapped behind my back....'"

They both squealed, Rose louder than Clarise. They laughed about it, agreeing they both wanted a relationship like what America and Maxon had in the book. Rose kept reading, switching off with Clarise every now and then, until they'd read practically the whole book together.

Eventually, Clarise sighed. "I just love him."

"Maxon?"

"Yes. He's so perfect."

Rose leaned her cheek on the top of Clarise's head. "I wouldn't say he's *perfect*. He has a past you know."

"What man doesn't, Rose?" Clarise yawned. "Besides, some of the best men are the damaged ones."

"How so?"

"Well, for starters, they know how to treat their woman. They do their best to make the woman feel loved so they never have to go through the hardships they went through."

Rose, surprised by such strong words for a girl who hadn't seen much of the world yet, gave her a side hug. "I suppose you're right....you don't have feelings for a guy like that do you?"

Clarise's uncontrollable giggles contrasted her small "no." Rose made a mental note to pay attention to any teenage boys who talked to Clarise. Surely she'd give herself away to Rose eventually.

"Can we keep going? He's just about to profess his love for her."

"For the billionth time you mean?"

"Yes, isn't that how it's supposed to be?"

Rose laughed and kissed the top of Clarise's head lightly. "I guess you're right. Gosh, you're so educated in the subject of love for a seventeen-year-old."

"Don't forget the half."

They both laughed again. Rose continued on for a while, the end of the book in sight. She didn't remember where they'd left off. All she knew was that both she and Clarise had fallen asleep at some point.

# Chapter 16

## (ROSABELLA)

ROSABELLA WOKE TO SOMEONE SNORTING WITH LAUGHTER. Her eyes snapped open, revealing Clayton, lounging in the chair next to her. He was gazing at her, covering his mouth to keep from laughing again.

"When did you get here?" She was careful sitting up, making sure not to disturb Clarise. She moved the girl's head from her shoulder to her lap.

"I've been here for a few minutes." He snorted again and pointed at her. "You uh, have something there."

Rose reached up to find drool running down her chin. How embarrassing! She turned red and wiped her face with the back of her sleeve. That would have to do for now, until she could get away from him.

"Don't worry, I won't tell anyone." He got up and ambled over to the couch, kneeling in front of her. He stroked Clarise's cheek, all traces of laughter leaving his face. "She hasn't left her room besides visits to the medical wing since she arrived here. I have no idea how you managed to do this, but I will forever be grateful."

Rose wrapped an arm around Clarise. "All she needed was someone who was willing to listen."

He shook his head and leaned back on his heels, careful to keep his voice low. "All I've done is listen!"

"Well, Clayton, if you listen to her as well as you do me, I could see the problem." Rose smirked at him, waiting to see what he'd say.

Remarkably, he chuckled. "If I had a dime for every time someone said that to me, well, I'd be rich as hell."

They shared a look. At the same time, Rose wanted to smack him and hug him. He acted so misunderstood sometimes, it made her heart hurt; but then again, maybe it wasn't an act. What if she hadn't been giving him the benefit of the doubt?

He broke the silence first. "I wanted to apologize for today. Logan and I had a set training plan for you and I went and changed it at the last second this morning at breakfast."

"Oh."

"Yeah," he rubbed the back of his neck, looking away. "I was being selfish."

"Oh," she said, unable to look away. He was so innocent, being apologetic and open with her. How was it possible to hate someone one second and then sympathize with them the next?

"Yeah."

They sighed at the same time.

"I'm not going to tell you it's okay, because it's not. I really hated you earlier. I hated being cooped up in the corner. I hated being controlled," Rose said, taking a deep breath. "I came to the Fortress looking for a change of pace, and instead I found myself in another cycle of following orders. I don't want to be the girl that does what everyone wants her to do anymore."

He looked back at her, eyes curious. "Why do you think that is?"

She shrugged. "I don't know."

"Do you think it's maybe because you haven't been taking care of yourself?" He smiled at her, noticing her surprised expression. "You just seem like you take care of everyone else around you, but you forget about doing the same for yourself."

"But that would be really selfish of me to not put others first."

Clayton's brown eyes seemed to stare into her soul then. "Rosabella, you need to be able to put making yourself happy at the top of your list." He was back to looking away again, at nothing and everything at the same time. "Trust me. If you don't, you'll end up just like me."

The corners of her mouth turned up in a soft smile. "We wouldn't want that, would we?"

They shared a look again. Clayton and Rose were close enough for her to see the tips of his ears had turned red. She knew her own face matched the blood-red couch across the room at this point. Whatever was going on here was rendering her immobile. Thank goodness she was already sitting or she'd have fallen over. Her legs started shaking. Why were they doing that?

Without warning, Clayton reached out and touched her left knee, staring at his hand there as if he'd never seen something quite like it. The shaking stopped when he touched her. It must have been due to Rose's lack of any ability to think the moment his skin contacted hers.

Rose's breath caught in her throat. She forced herself to breathe slowly, almost forgetting the sensation of filling her lungs with air. Clayton sucked in a breath himself and continued to stare at his hand, as if contemplating whether or not to pull away. His eyes skirted over to the open book beside Rose. He reached his free hand--the other one was still resting on her knee--and pulled it closer.

He smiled knowingly. "*The Elite*? Oh boy, did Clair force you to read this?"

She snatched the book, holding it close to her chest. "No, I happen to love this book!"

"Hmm, I can't say the same, what with America still dating her boyfriend even though she's in love with another man." He tapped her knee, thinking. "Maxon doesn't deserve to be deceived."

"Oh yeah? Well, how about Maxon professing his love for America one minute and then telling her how confused he is about his feelings the next?" She huffed and set the book back down beside her. "If only he'd be honest with himself…"

Clayton chuckled as she trailed off, lost in thought. Rose's eyes darted to his hand on her knee, up his toned arms, finally resting on his eyes. They were cast downward, at his hand. He began to draw circles there.

Rose sucked in a shaky breath. She was unable to control her racing heart.

Clayton's eyes traveled up to meet her wide ones. "Are we still talking about the book?"

"I--I have no idea," she gasped, subtly clutching her chest. Alarm on his face, he took her hands in his. "Are you alright?"

She did her best to nod. Didn't he know what kind of effect his touch had on her? This wasn't natural, the way her heart beat so hard. It was going to explode out of her chest at this rate.

Rose did her best to make light of the strange turn of events. "Do you do this with all the new women?"

He chuckled. "No, just the ones I can't seem to stop thinking about…"

"It hasn't been that long since we've known each other Clayton…"

It was his turn to suck in a breath. "I know, that's why this is so confusing. It's almost as if I like getting yelled at and insulted by you."

She swatted his hands away, laughing. "What the hell?"

"For real. Every time we're done arguing, my heart races uncontrollably," he said. Clayton's voice was so low she had to strain to hear what he said.

"Maybe you just enjoy arguing with people," Rose teased. "I saw you and Logan get into a heated conversation about something tonight at dinner. It seems like you just have a thing for disagreeing with people."

He pretended to be upset. "Well, I disagree with that wholeheartedly, Rosabella."

She giggled before remembering she had a sleeping girl in her lap. Rose reached down and brushed another stray strand of hair from Clarise's face. Clayton hopped up and sat beside them on the couch, taking care to move the book before settling in.

"Rose?"

"Yes?"

He sighed and rested his arm behind her on the couch. "What did you say to Clair to convince her to leave her room?"

"Nothing. We've just talked about everything." She sighed and closed her eyes. "Clarise and I aren't too different. We both came from the world above. We both have lived through tremendous physical challenges. We like a lot of the same things. The list goes on and on."

"Huh."

"She's still just a girl, Clayton. If you don't give her positive encouragement, especially when it comes to her legs, she won't believe in herself.…when I saw her in that therapy room, my heart broke for a second. Then I realized all she needed was someone to tell her she *could* succeed."

"It was that easy?"

"I wouldn't say it was *easy*."

They sat in silence for a few minutes. Rose had begun to doze off when Clayton pulled her back from the brink of sleep, "What I said earlier to Aire about you....I didn't mean for it to come out that way."

She turned her body to look at him. Was he being serious? Rose waited for the "but," except, it never came.

He avoided eye contact with her. "I'm not sure why I said it the way I did, but...I guess I wanted to tell you I'm sorry. "

She waited before speaking, letting the silence eat away at him.

"I accept your apology, Clayton...I'm going to be honest, what you said really made me think." She looked down at her feet. "I've been really difficult to deal with. I haven't given you the benefit of the doubt before ripping you apart with my insults. I'm sorry too....I can be so bold. I really need to learn to fix that part of myself, almost as much as you have to fix your anger problems."

When Clay looked down at her, she smirked. He smiled back, his brown eyes lighting up.

"You shouldn't change anything about yourself. The way you are, that's what intrigues me," he said firmly.

"Clayton--"

"No, just listen....Please," he added as an afterthought. "We don't need to go into my backstory right now, but I just wanted to tell you that you've already helped realign my view of myself, the Fortress, and the people here. Thank you."

"You're welcome. I guess."

He chuckled, wrapping his arms around her to give her a delicate squeeze. Then he gently let go and stood up.

"I hate to do this, but I really do need to get my sister to bed."

Rose's face warmed. She turned her head away to hide it as best she could while Clayton scooped Clarise up. Rose fixed her shorts so they weren't riding up her thighs, and straightened her sweatshirt so it didn't look like she'd fallen asleep on a couch. Clayton leaned down and held out a hand to help Rose up, which she accepted.

"Think you can find your way back to your dorm if I walk with you to the correct wing?"

She nodded, rendered speechless when she looked into his eyes. They were soft and gentle, nothing like the hard and angry ones she'd seen earlier.

Clayton smiled, then set to work, taking care to set Clarise in her wheelchair so as not to wake her. Rose helped him pack pillows from the couches around her. Rose stepped back to watch Clayton drape his sweatshirt over his sister's shoulders.

"You really care about her, don't you?"

He tucked the sweatshirt under Clarise's chin. "I certainly do. She's my sister. She's all I have left from home," he said, his voice breathless.

Rose touched his arm, willing the hurt to leave his mind. There was something more to him that she wasn't going to push to hear about just yet. It was necessary they get to know one another better first, before they both began digging into one another's darkest parts.

"I had a younger brother, so I get it," she said, throat tight. A lump started to form there and she pulled her hand away from Clayton's arm. He caught it between his hands and brought it to his chest. Rosabella had no choice but to look into his eyes.

He searched her face and whispered, "*Had?*"

She bit her lip, the lump growing by the second. "I don't know what became of him when I left." She swallowed. "I just left them all behind. Who just leaves their family behind like that?"

Clayton flinched, crushing her hand. He breathed deeply, not taking his eyes off her. "Someone who is scared and flustered and has no other choice."

They shared a moment of silence, understanding passing between them.

Together, they both whispered, "Join or die."

Rose brought her free hand to his cheek. "Clarise said you came back for her. You didn't leave her behind forever."

He closed his eyes. "I still shouldn't have left her. If I hadn't been with Te--I guess I mean I haven't always been the brother she needs."

She dropped her hand from his face, to join the one on his chest. "From what I can see, you've improved a lot. You should give yourself more credit, Mr. Taylor."

His brown eyes, surrounded by a frightening red, snapped open and landed on her face. He gave her a slight smile and squeezed her hands. Once he let go of her, he began pushing Clarise's wheelchair to the door. Rose let her hands fall back to her sides, wishing he hadn't released her just yet. She wanted his skin to touch hers again, to feel the roughness of his calluses on her own unblemished hands. It was a sign of a true, hard-working person and she was proud of him for it.

"Come on, Rosabella. They're strict with the curfew hours down here. I don't want you to get in trouble after your first day of training."

She stifled a gasp. "Has it really only been *one* day?"

He chuckled quietly, holding the door open for her. The hallway was as dark as night. Clayton carried an old, beaten up flashlight in his hands; he'd come prepared.

"Oh, you just wait until tomorrow."

She shivered inwardly.

"We'll have you actually working with a trainer tomorrow."

Rose perked up at that. "Really?" She swatted his arm. The beam of the flashlight wavered. "Now I won't be able to sleep! Thanks a lot."

Clayton laughed, shaking his head. "I've never met an outsider quite like you, Rosabella Porter."

"Same here, Clayton Taylor," she teased. If only the morning were already here!

Clayton wound up walking Rose to her door, since there was only one flashlight. They had a quick exchange of goodnights before Rose slipped into the equally dark dorm room. She tore off her tennis shoes and fell onto her bed.

She was wrong; she wasn't going to stay up all night. Once her head hit the pillow, she was out like a light.

# Chapter 17

## (ROSABELLA)

IT BECAME ROUTINE FOR CLARISE TO JOIN ROSE for lunch and dinner. Today for lunch, Clarise and Rose sat at a table near the door of the dining hall.

As she was taking a seat, Rose spotted Aire across the dining hall. She sat by herself, tucked into a corner. For a split second, Rose felt bad for avoiding her. She hadn't spoken or even really seen Aire since their argument. But, not long after, that guilt disappeared.

"So, Clair. I need your input," Rose said, tugging on her ponytail.

Clarise set down her fork and linked her hands atop the table. "Alright, lay it on me. What is it? Did my brother say something stupid again?"

She shook her head, already feeling the blush creeping up her neck. If anything, Clayton had been a complete gentleman lately. There'd been no need for her to get angry at him these last weeks. After their conversation in the library, Clay'd been holding his tongue when he got upset with people in training. Rose wasn't necessarily there when it happened, but she observed from afar during her training sessions with Eden. Clayton had kept his word and taken her off the bike weeks ago. He'd assigned Eden to take over Rose's training instead. She spent one on one time with Rose in the mornings, teaching her how to work on her cardio--there were lots of sprints involved unfortunately--and how to tone the muscles in her arms, back and legs in the afternoon.

They started with easy exercises and worked their way to harder workouts, increasing weight when necessary. She'd been surprised with how much Eden knew about this stuff. She was a great trainer! Rose found she actually enjoyed working out, when she wasn't short of breath from running. Honestly, running wasn't her thing. She loved the weights more than anything else. They made her feel powerful; she knew she was making great progress and that internal encouragement kept her going. Not to mention, it kept her busy and away from the others, specifically Aire.

Though, sometimes she missed an instruction from Eden because she was too busy looking across the room at Clayton. What was wrong with her?

"Not yet. But it's only a matter of time, right?" Rose joked, pushing thoughts of Clayton out of her head for now. It didn't make sense for him to cloud her mind when she could hardly stand the guy. "I'm really confused on how this whole observation time stuff works."

Clarise nodded, eyes full of sympathy. "I completely understand. It's very different from what we're taught up above."

"You can say that again," Rose said, releasing a long breath.

"Here, we get to choose our careers. You just have to put in a request to shadow a career you're interested in and 9 times out of 10, they approve it," Clarise informed. "When you get permission to shadow, then you just have to let the trainers know so they're aware. Usually they want you to make up training in some way if you miss more than two hours for shadow time. Basically, if you keep them in the loop, they're fine with it."

"So there's no limitations to what careers I can shadow?" asked Rose.

"Nope."

She scratched her head. "But I don't even know what all the possibilities are!"

"So there's the medical wing. You can shadow our one doctor or nurses, depending on their availability. We definitely need more medical personel...the kitchen is where you can be a full time chef, mission control where you can watch them approve missions...hmmm, let me think. Engineering, internal and external security, training, which you already get to see most of the time...There's a lot of other opportunities. Oh! You could be a teacher if you want! They always need more of them."

"Hold on," gasped Rosabella. "There's a *school* down here?"

Clarise laughed at the baffled expression on Rose's face. "Of course. They do care about people as a whole, not just the physical training aspect of life down here."

"But how come I never see the kids in school? Where do they go for classes?"

"It's all virtual nowadays, at least down here...you seriously didn't know that?"

Rose's head shook back and forth. "Absolutely not! I've been a little preoccupied with dodging people who still insist on calling me a celebrity."

Clair chuckled, her gentle voice lifting like the ringing of bells. "The kids seventeen and under train in the mornings, break for lunch, and then work on their school work for the rest of the day. That's why you never see them after lunch. The majority of them go home or to the lounge together while those eighteen and older train for the rest of the day."

"Wow, I had no idea!"

She patted Rose's hand. "We've really got to educate you on our processes better. Who's in charge of informing you?"

"I'm not sure. Bernard gave me a packet of information, but unfortunately, I haven't had the energy to read through all of it."

Clarise sighed. "You really should, it's important for you to acclimate here as soon as possible. It'll be easier when you know everything. Bernard always says that when someone doesn't understand things, it leaves room for rebellion. That's why he's so transparent with all of us as citizens."

"Alright," Rose said, embarrassed at her own lack of discipline in the reading department. Training took a lot out of her. By the end of the day, she was so drained she could hardly make it through dinner. "I'll go over the packet soon."

"Good." Her eyes caught on something behind Rose's head, causing her to avert her eyes. Clarise shoveled a spoonful of corn in her mouth, all conversation coming to an abrupt end.

Andre, Logan and Clayton appeared to Rose's right. The three guys sat at their table, keeping a few seats between them. They talked with their heads together and voices inaudible. Andre's smirk convinced Rose that she and Clarise were the topic of conversation. Logan snuck a glance at Rose and smiled. Andre pulled on his chin and drew Logan back to their huddle.

Clarise and Rosabella looked at each other and both rolled their eyes.

"Gee, Clarise, it's as if the guys want to sit with us, but are too afraid to," Rose said loudly, winking at Clair.

Immediately, Andre slid down the bench to sit beside Rose. He leaned his head on her shoulder. "Rosie Posie! Hey, what's up? Where were you all day?"

She rolled her eyes and shrugged him off her shoulder. "I was at training, Andre. Where I'm supposed to be every day."

Clayton and Logan joined their trio across from Rose. She involuntarily smiled at them. Clayton caught her eye and sent her the tiniest of smiles before focusing in on his tray. A little discouraging for sure, but Rose knew he had a hard outer shell; she couldn't penalize Clay too much.

Between bites, Logan asked her how training was going.

"Pretty good, I guess," Rose replied. "Eden and I are on the same page most days with my training. Although, I can't wait to actually get started on combat with the other trainees."

Clayton snorted. "Why am I not surprised?"

Rose's eyes shifted from Logan to Clayton, surprised by his jovial tone. She smirked at him. She'd been rendered speechless by his eyes. What on earth?

Thankfully, Clarise saved her from embarrassment, "Rosie and I were just discussing which careers to shadow."

Andre's arm snaked around Rose's waist. "Ooo! Rosie Posie, you can shadow me! I'm the head of external security after all." He shrugged and danced his fingers on her knee. "Basically my word ranks above everyone else. Nobody will question you wanting to shadow the sexiest, smartest--did I mention sexiest--guy in security."

Clayton's foot collided with Andre's shin, enough for him to wince in pain. He released Rose and rubbed the sore spot. "Ow!"

"Leave her alone, Dre. It's her decision, not yours," Clayton growled. Then he swallowed hard and forced a smile onto his face. "If anything, you're only good at running your mouth. I would definitely take sexiest off the table."

Logan laughed and drove a shoulder into Clay's side. "Why? So you can claim the title for yourself, Mr. Conceited?" he teased.

Rose choked on her smoothie. Once she regained her breath she high-fived Logan. "Nice one!"

"Aww come on guys, that's not true," Clarise jumped in. "There's no need to be mean...my brother only goes by the title of arrogant."

"Ha!" Andre cried, smacking his hand on the table. "Holy crap, what is this, a rapid fire session against Clay?"

Clayton crossed his arms and leaned on the table, obviously annoyed. Rose felt a little remorseful for making him the brunt of the joke, but it was the only thing she could think of at the time to cover up her nervous energy that came on when the guys joined them.

"Okay, okay. Let's stop picking on Clayton," Rose urged gently. She couldn't meet his eyes as she spoke. "I'm sure he's not as bad as we all think he is."

Andre slapped her on the back. "Amen to that, sister!"

Clayton rolled his eyes. "Gee, you guys are great. You really know how to boost a guy's confidence."

Rose laughed. "That's what friends are for!"

"Yeah, okay," he replied sarcastically. Then he threw a handful of corn at Rose first, then Andre. Rose made the mistake of opening her mouth to laugh. A few kernels went directly into the back of her throat, causing her to choke and laugh at the same time. This led to Andre throwing a handful of peas back at him, thus spurring a food fight. At least Clayton was in a good mood today. That made her heart soar into the ceiling with delight. Rose was right, he wasn't as bad as he'd been at first. It just took some getting used to him for Rose to understand what Clayton Taylor was all about.

\*\*\*

Andre was set to do another demonstration in the training room today, so he walked with Clayton and Rosabella. Rose just let him run his mouth about how great external security was for a career. If he was going to keep trying to sell her on the position, it would drive her further and further away from it. Rose hated when someone told her what she should do. She was the kind of girl who made her own decisions when it was her own idea in the first place. Telling Rose to do something only turned her off to the possibility, even if it was something she'd be good at.

Andre's hand clamped around Rose's shoulder as they walked into the training room. "Alright Rosie Posie, it's time for me to take up my position in the ring. Try not to miss me," he said puckering his lips to kiss her.

Clayton shoved him in the chest, laughing. "Just go."

Once Andre was gone, Rose went along her way to meet Eden near the thick blue mats. Today, Eden promised Rose she'd show her some more arm workouts. Rose's legs were gaining muscle mass just fine, but her arms could use some more work.

"Rose, wait!" Clayton called to her back.

Rose spun around to see what had him talking to her in front of people. He'd been very closed off any time she started speaking to him in the training room. Rose assumed it was because he was embarrassed to be seen with her or something, considering that she was "famous" and all.

"I almost forgot something. Come with me," he said waving her over. She didn't need to be told twice. Clayton had captured her attention with one look.

He brought her to the grouping of kiosk machines in the corner. The screen lit up when it recognized their movement. Clay placed something across the screen and held it there while the kiosk beeped.

"What are you doing?" Rose asked.

"Hold out your arm."

She squinted at him, annoyed with the command.

He sighed and chuckled. "Please. I promise it's nothing bad." When his fingers brushed against her wrist, she nearly lost her wits.

Why did his touch do that to her? She couldn't speak, couldn't breathe. When he pulled away, a pretty turquoise wristband remained. Rose's teeth clamped together. It matched absolutely nothing she had in her closet or dresser. It fit in with things about as much as she did. That made it perfect for her!

She had to bite the inside of her cheek from shouting her happiness in finally receiving her very own wristband. She'd been wanting one ever since she learned about them from the rest of the trainees. Gianna used hers constantly; everyone was always sending messages to one another with the internal messaging system all the time. It hadn't really bothered Rosabella until recently.

Clayton turned to the kiosk again. "What's your full name? Rosabella Porter?"

She twirled her wristband around and around. "Ummm yes. But add a Mae in the middle. M-A-E."

"Really?"

She smirked to hide her embarrassment. "I'm serious." As if having a four syllable name wasn't enough torture, her parents had to add a middle name.

Clayton laughed, lips curling over his teeth. "It's a beautiful name." He checked over his shoulder. "Can you keep a secret?"

Rose nodded. "Well it depends on the secret, but usually, yes."

He mumbled something she couldn't pick up. Then, he ran his fingers through his hair. "I have a middle name too."

"No way!" Rose leaned in so nobody else heard them. "What is it?"

He shook his head. "It's James. But you can't tell anyone else. Promise me you won't."

She crossed her fingers over her heart. "I promise."

He nodded and looked down at her wrist, his fingers on her skin there. "I'm sorry it took so long for us to get this to you. We've had a shortage. The Fortress is almost at full capacity." He tapped the wristband and showed her how to keep track of her vitals and her eating, sleeping and training routines. It all showed up in a hologram that hovered just above her wrist. She scrolled through a handful of the options, eyes catching on the messaging icon.

Clayton explained what would happen during an emergency, "You'll hear a sharp screeching sound if there's a special announcement that we have to meet for immediately, or an emergency where you have to go back to your dorm for a head count."

"How do I tell the difference?"

He shrugged. "I'm not sure. We've never had an emergency situation, so everyone just assumes it's a special announcement."

"So if I hear a screeching, report to the dining hall?"

He nodded, fingers grazing her palm as he carefully removed his hand from her wrist. She chomped down on a sigh that threatened to spill out.

"Right. Well, have a good afternoon. Bye!" Rose chirped before leaving Clayton alone at the kiosks. Not too casual, but it was the only thing she could think of. Why was she suddenly so aware of him? Clair was right, he was an arrogant guy who didn't care about others' feelings. She should hate him.

But if that was true, then why was her heart beating a mile a minute?

# Chapter 18

## (ROSABELLA)

THE SCENT OF BURNING FLESH BROUGHT ROSE TO her senses. It filled her nostrils, forcing its way down her throat. She gagged, trying to push it back out. It was no use. Her eyes burned, tears narrowly balancing on her bottom lids for a moment before spilling over.

She looked down at her feet. Soon, black tendrils curled around her ankles. Nothing physical held her in place, yet she couldn't move. Her once pale, peach-colored skin slowly turned to a crispy black. The pain was immense, and she couldn't do anything to stop it; fighting to be free of the invisible bounds did nothing.

Rose had never experienced this type of pain before. Every skin cell was alert, burning and melting from the fire. She shook her legs, hoping to stop the flames from crawling up her legs. It didn't take long for the fire to reach her torso.

Screams surrounded her. They weren't her own; other people must be experiencing this too. The inescapable fire. Flames wrapped around her entire body all the way up to her face.

What was happening?

Rosabella joined in the screams of her fellow invisible comrades.

"Rose! Rose! Wake up. It's just a nightmare!"

A pair of strong arms restrained her. Rose opened her eyes and found herself lying on the floor. There was a dull ache in her lower back from sleeping on the hard, grey tiles.

"What?" She rubbed her eyes and looked up. The bright, fluorescent lights hurt her eyes at first, so she had to give them time to adjust. When she did, she immediately found dark brown eyes inches from her face. Below them, a worried frown enhancing deep creases in the tanned skin around a mouth.

Then she remembered where she was.

A red blanket had wound its way around her legs. Pillows and cushions from the couch were strewn all around Rose, one of them wedged between herself and the couch's foot. The ground, icy-cold against her sweaty skin, had a thick smear of blood on it. Without hesitation, she sat up and inspected herself.

Her legs were unharmed, though very exposed in her tiny pajama shorts. They were as pale as ever, the only spot of color a patch of hot, flushed skin just above each of her kneecaps. Her hands moved up to her hips. The space above her jutted out hip bone on the right side was sensitive to the touch. She bit back a scream on contact. When she pulled her hand away, sticky red blood coated her fingertips.

What the hell did she do in her sleep, *attack* herself?

The sensation of being burned alive flashed through her mind. That was only a nightmare, wasn't it?

"Are you alright, Rose? Here." A hand reached out to her.

"Clayton? What are you doing here?" Rose took his hand and allowed him to help her stand. His other hand clasped her elbow on the way up.

She continued to stare at his hand, the one firmly holding her elbow. She was very aware of how fast her heart was beating. The blood from her fingers left a mark on his wrist, where she'd grasped him. If he noticed, he didn't address it.

"I wanted to talk to you about something, but you weren't in your room with the other girls, so I thought I'd look for you in your favorite spot." Clayton gingerly lifted the hem of her long t-shirt up and over her hips. He talked while he inspected her side. "Why are you sleeping here?"

The words caught in her throat. There was no good way to explain the nightmare; he wouldn't understand. The mind was a powerful thing. That had been a terrible, disastrous dream.

His touch was so light against her bare skin, if she closed her eyes again, she could almost imagine tiny butterflies were kissing her. She fought a shiver.

Clayton let out a quiet breath. He didn't sound angry, rather relieved. "Rose, why don't we go get you cleaned up?"

Both his hands moved from her hips to her lower back, encircling her. Was it in her mind, or did *he* just shiver? She followed the muscles from his forearms all the way up to his neck. He swallowed, and she swore his cheeks flushed pink.

He removed one hand from her back and guided her to the door. "Just be quiet, because we aren't supposed to be out in the halls during these hours."

Rosabella let Clayton lead her out of the room and down the dark hall. The only source of light peeked out from under the medical wing's automatic sliding doors, which were shut for the night. There was always one nurse at the desk and another checking on patients. The doctor would be in her own apartment, sleeping, but remained on call at all hours of the night. One phone call and she'd throw on a pair of shoes and race to the wing. If Rose remembered correctly, the doctor and nurses were given apartments at the closest end of the hall so they could easily rush to the medical wing in the case of an emergency.

This was no emergency. Or was it? The singed flesh smell still hadn't left her nose. Rose expected Clayton to take her to the hospital, walk her up to the desk and demand for medical attention as he'd done when she first arrived. Correction, when she was about to die. This was nowhere as severe an injury.

He steered her away from the hospital, directing her toward the southern wing: the apartments. There were signs for each gender's respective bathrooms at the intersecting ends of the wings. The men's room was set between the hospital's doors and the first apartments, the women's room between the dorm hallway and the lounge. Overwhelmed by the weight of his hand on her back, right above where her spine met her tailbone, Rose couldn't find the words to ask him where they were going.

The intersection of the wings was the only place--besides the hospital--that had a dim set of lights on the ceiling. Just enough for a person to see where they were going. It was also perfect for casting shadows over people's faces.

When he steered her in the direction of the men's bathroom, Rosabella finally found her voice.

"Umm?" She nodded her head to the sign on the wall signifying that this bathroom was for men.

"Nobody will bother us, trust me." He put pressure on Rose's back for her to continue, but she kept her feet planted.

She turned herself into the crook of his elbow and smiled up at him, blinking her eyelashes in an attempt to look innocent. "If that's so, Clay, why don't we just go into the women's bathroom? Nobody will bother us there, trust me."

He froze, unmoving. She watched in amazement as every muscle in his face tensed, felt the ones in his arms as they tightened around her.

"Into the frilly, perfume-infested, feminine product-filled, girl's bathroom? I don't know what I might discover in there...there are some things you can't unsee, Rose." The look of horror on his face made her double over laughing.

She leaned on his arm for support. Through her tears of laughter, she peeked up at him. She was both intrigued and frightened to see him looking at her, no, *studying* her. His face began to soften. His deep laugh warmed her right to her core.

Footsteps echoed around them. They were toast! If she was caught, she could get into so much trouble! They'd make her sit out of training for two days at the very least! Rules were important here. Thankfully they didn't enforce their punishments by execution as the Government did.

They both stopped laughing, tense and nervous. Head on a swivel, Rose realized their only choice was to hide out in one of the bathrooms. They were closer to the men's, so that's where she decided to go. Pulling Clayton wasn't easy, but he let her take the lead after picking up on what she was thinking.

"Faster! They're right around the corner," he hissed. A flashlight beam danced around the wall opposite them. Clayton lifted her up and carried her without issue into the men's room.

It was pitch black inside. Clayton carried her deep into the bathroom. If it was the same setup as the women's there were showers at the back of the room, with a dividing wall that separated the sink and toilet area from the showers. A perfect hiding place. He placed her on the ground. Pressing against Rose so her back was flat against the wall, Clayton rested his chin atop her head. The darkness enveloped them, and Rose was grateful he couldn't see how red her face was. Tomato girl was back and brighter than ever. The adrenaline from having him so close to her lips blocked out the pain in her hip.

She felt the warmth from his hands, which were positioned against the wall on either side of her head. His breath tickled her ear and she resisted the urge to laugh. The idea that Clayton's ridiculously strong arms had been around her only minutes ago made her knees feel like jelly.

They listened, sharing air, as someone opened the door to the washroom. Dim light slipped through the cracks between the shower doors. Either the person didn't care enough to investigate, or they assumed someone wouldn't be dumb enough to corner themself there.

The two of them stayed that way for hours, or minutes. Time was lost on her. Even though she had feelings for him that she couldn't quite explain, and she wanted to stay here forever wrapped in his arms, chest to chest against the wall, Rose was the first one to break the silence.

"Clayton," she whispered into his neck. "Do you think you could help me with my hip?"

"Huh? Oh yeah, wait here." She heard his footsteps as he walked away. The absence hit her right away. It was as if a bucket of ice water had been dumped on her head. It filled her all the way down to her ankles and then seeped into her toes.

She grew antsy when she didn't hear him for a while. What if he'd left her? Was this supposed to be some kind of joke? Maybe someone was about to jump out and scare her, teasing her for being in the men's room? She wouldn't put it past Clayton; he'd been rude to her in the beginning. And, if that was the case, she wasn't going to wait around. She'd go back to her dorm before he could tell his friends where to find her. What had she been thinking? She'd only known the guy for a couple weeks.

Rose felt her way along the wall in the dark. She remembered Clayton taking a direct path to the left. The women's showers were on the right; if she was correct, then the setup was flipped. At least she'd caught the left turn, that was lucky. Her heart had caught in her throat and she'd been focusing on not enjoying herself in his arms too much. Clayton confused her emotions, so it was difficult for her to focus when she was around him, especially when he held her in such an intimate way.

A hand clamped over her mouth from behind. She thrashed around and tried to scream, but whoever it was, they were very strong. She was becoming stronger with each day, but it wasn't enough in that moment.

Plus, they had the element of surprise on their side. A hand brushed against the skin on Rose's hip. She winced in pain, but wouldn't let that stop her. She needed to be free! She moved her head to the right, finding her target there. She bit the hand around her mouth and slipped out of their grip when they cried out.

Then she ran.

"Jeeze! Rose, you make this whole 'be quiet' thing very difficult." Clayton cried, from the dark.

She stopped running. Rose reached out a hand, ready to apologize, but thought it better to find the light first. She touched the wall, running her hands up and down, side to side, until a smooth button bumped her hand. She turned the lights on and saw Clayton a few feet away, rubbing his hand...the one she'd bitten.

"I'm sorry, but you scared me Clay! I'm jumpy." She wasn't sure if she should approach him or not, so she stayed in place.

"Yes I'll try to remember that...don't want to lose a finger," he teased. "Or a *hand*." He smiled at her, despite the red marks in the shape of her teeth on his hand. She saw he was holding a dry washcloth and a bandaid. So that's where he'd disappeared to, the other side of the washroom to find a towel and medical supplies. For her.

And all she'd done was bite him.

Guilt spread through Rose's chest just as quickly as the fire in her nightmare had swallowed her up. Then she watched as his eyes drifted down her body to her side. Her first thought was maybe it was because she was half naked with these little pink shorts on. She didn't usually wear things like this, but she hadn't had a say in the choosing of them. Aire and Prince had selected her wardrobe for her without consent. Besides, she wasn't even wearing a bra! This wasn't the type of attention she wanted from Clayton, so she crossed her arms over her stomach to draw his eyes away from her legs.

Clayton, noticing her embarrassment, stepped forward. His brows met in the middle of his head, eyes dark in the dim light. He looked...he looked...handsome. Hungry. Desirable.

Her heart stopped when he paused just in front of her, so close their toes almost touched. He leaned down closer to her face and looked into her eyes. Their noses brushed. There was that shiver in her spine again. Was he about to kiss her? Just as their lips were about to touch, Rose arched her head to get a better position. She'd never kissed someone before, but she and Aire had watched countless kisses in the movies. They always made it look so perfect. That's what Rose wanted.

Unfortunately, that wasn't meant to happen tonight. Clayton dipped his head at the last second and lifted her shirt to get at her hip instead. She gasped when his touch sent a shock of pain through her.

"C'mere. I'll help you get cleaned up." Clayton walked Rose to the sink where he gestured for her to sit up on the counter. She hopped up and watched in complete silence as he ran a washcloth under warm water, her hands folded in her lap. This was the most concentrated she'd ever seen him. If only he spent more time doing kind acts of service for others, like this, rather than belittle them because he wanted to be the tough guy.

He turned the faucet off after the towel was completely soaked. Rose observed his hands. She loved watching the tendons in his hand tighten and release as he wrung the towel out in the sink. He had calluses on almost all of his fingers, but that didn't turn her away. It intrigued her, just like every other part of him. He was a puzzle she was determined to put together at some point. When he was ready. *If* he'd ever be ready.

"Ready?" He asked, eyes cast down on the counter. Was he nervous or just pretending to be for her benefit so she wouldn't be so scared?

She nodded, leaning back against the mirror to get a better angle. She lifted her shirt up over her belly button with shaking hands, silently scolding herself for being so childish. Clayton was just a guy. A guy with crazy nice arms who was about to touch her bare skin near her waistband with a washcloth.

He slowly brought the towel to her skin, taking care to be gentle. She wrapped her fingers around the edge of the counter, preparing herself. That didn't stop it from hurting. She'd given herself a nice deep scratch somehow by scraping off a few layers of skin. The towel soaked up the remaining blood and wiped away any dried, crusted blood left. She closed her eyes and bit down on her back teeth.

Clayton cleared his throat. "Rose, what were you dreaming about?"

She opened her eyes and shuddered, black smoke filling her nose once more. "I don't want to talk about it. The whole thing was horrible."

He brushed a stringy chunk of hair from her forehead, almost as if it was an involuntary action. She shivered, not from the smell of the burning flesh, rather, from his touch. It was as though she'd been zapped by lightning. His eyes widened, and that's when she was sure he felt it too.

Clayton looked away and started washing his hands instead of letting the intimacy evolve into something more.

He dried his hands on a fresh towel, facing away from her. "It's alright, you know that you can talk to me about it if you want. Although, I understand if you don't want to...I like keeping things to myself too."

Rose grabbed the bandage from the counter and peeled the outer packing off. The velvety texture of the bandaid was somewhat comforting. Her father had used many of these on her when she'd fall and scrape her knee after falling on thin air; she was good at that. In fact, if there was a contest to see who could trip on their own feet the best, she'd win the grand prize. Clayton took it from her, tossing the package into a nearby trash chute.

Rose held her shirt up again to give him a wide berth in getting the adhesive to stick on the flat part of her hip. That's when she felt truly embarrassed for the way she looked. Her stomach was too pudgy, nothing like the flat ones all the prettiest women had. Why couldn't she have gotten her mother's willowy figure? Instead, she was stuck with curvy hips and thick thighs. She didn't even want to think of her butt either; that was a whole other story.

Rose held her breath while Clayton pulled the waistband of her shorts and underwear down, just enough to fit the bottom of the bandaid there.

"Thank you," she breathed as his hands pressed the bandaid to her skin.

"Of course, and anyway, it's just a bandaid. Not life or death," he said shrugging. "Oh, and when you take it off, you'll want to rub some antiseptic ointment on it so you don't get an infection. I'll have some sent to you from the hospital—"

"Clayton," she interrupted.

"It should help to heal this, though it may turn into a scar. If it gets any worse, we should bring you to—"

"Clayton!" She grabbed his arm before he could continue blabbering. She'd never heard him talk so quickly before. "I mean it. Thank you,"

Clayton blushed--something he didn't normally do--and still refused to meet her eyes. He cleared his throat again. "Right. Well, let's get you back to your dorm before I get fired from my job."

# Chapter 19

## (ANDRE)

Andre's fist flew through the air, missing Clayton's face by millimeters. He grunted from the effort, stumbling forward, enough for Clayton to swivel around and smack him on the back of the neck.

"Ow!" He cried, cupping his hand there. "This is supposed to be a *workout*, not a full blown match!" Thankfully, they still had another hour before their curfew, which meant they could make all the noise they wanted. Once curfew hit, not even Andre, who'd lived here all his life, would be able to get away with being out of his apartment. Bernard would only punish him mildly, but his disappointment would be worse than anything else.

Clayton shrugged, hands dropping to his sides. "Sorry man. I guess I needed to blow off some steam."

Brushing his hands on his knees, Andre shook his head. "Well, there's no need to take it out on me." After a moment, he added, "What is it this time?"

"Clarise."

Andre did his best to fake disinterest while his chest fluttered. He picked at his cuticle, keeping his eyes away from Clayton's.

"Oh yeah? What about?"

"I dunno, she's just been different around me. It's like she's a whole new person." Clayton hopped down from the fighting ring and walked over to the cluster of machines in the corner.

He followed Clayton's lead, flicking a hangnail into the air. "What am I missing? Is that a bad thing?"

Clayton huffed in his usual, angsty Clayton way and sat down on the floor. He leaned his head back to look at the ceiling. Andre mirrored him, using his elbows to support his weight.

"Clay?"

His friend kept his face toward the ceiling. "Do you ever have a really strange feeling in your chest? You know, even when you *think* about a person?"

Andre laughed, too shocked to prevent it. "I don't think you're referring to Clair."

"Well, she and Rosabella have been hanging out a lot these last couple weeks. I'm not sure what to think of it." He sighed and leaned all the way back, so his head was pressed flat against the concrete.

Andre caught on to how he'd emphasized her name. He'd used an affectionate tone Andre hadn't heard from him in a while.

He tapped the side of Clayton's knee with his foot. "C'mon man. Don't you think this is a good thing? Your sister needs someone to bring her out of her funk."

"I suppose. But why do you think Rose is the one, after all these years, who could do that?" He sighed deeply. "Not even *Tess* accomplished that."

Andre waited before replying. He sat up and peered at Clayton, who was still staring, unblinking, at the ceiling.

"I thought you didn't want to say her name?" Andre crossed his legs, pushing Clayton's arm to get his attention. "That was only like two weeks ago you yelled at me for it. What's changed?"

"Mhh."

Andre jumped up and straddled Clayton, pushing his arms across his chest. "You know I don't understand mumbling. What. Has. Changed?"

He'd expected Clayton to push back, to start a friendly wrestling match, *something*. Andre wanted Clayton to give whatever was on his mind a break. It wasn't like him to lie on the ground in the middle of one of their workouts. In fact, it worried him to see his friend so distraught. There was only one other time he'd seen Clay act that way. And that woman was gone for good.

Clayton blinked, as if he just noticed Andre sitting on his chest. Oh yeah, this was bad.

"I think," he started, blinking up at Andre. "I think she's changing me. I've thought a lot about what happened with Tess...I think I'm accepting it."

"She?" Andre raised an eyebrow. He wanted Clayton to be the one to say it.

"You know who I mean...*Rosabella*."

He watched Clayton relax as he breathed her name. His eyes took on a glassy, far off expression; the muscles in Clayton's waist and torso unclenched. He went into a pure state of bliss.

Andre rolled off and laid next to him. They both stared up, at nothing, thinking about their girls. Clayton clearly had a thing for Rosabella; the way he looked at her during training made even Andre blush--which was difficult to do. But, then the way Clayton acted at meals, as if he didn't care about her at all, confused the hell out of Andre. He bet Rosabella was just as confused as him, furious even. Clayton was not one for admitting his feelings; Andre knew it scared him to think about another woman the same way he used to Tess. She was the center of his world for years as much as he was hers; they would both drop everything for one another and run to their side when needed. And she usually needed Clayton more than he needed her; she was so dependent on him.

Andre on the other hand, thought about the only other girl who was off-limits. She had beautiful, chocolate-brown eyes and long dark brown hair that he wanted to dig his hands into every time he smelled that shampoo she used.

Clarise Taylor.

When Clair first arrived, she'd been way too young for Andre. But the more he hung out with Clay, the more he hung out with Clarise. She was full of as much angst as her brother, but, like Clayton, she still had a big heart. He could understand Rose having feelings for Clay now. That was the only thing they could relate between them.

Andre savored every single one of Clarise's smiles, the ones that would light up her eyes whenever he complimented her. It always made him want more. Once Clarise turned thirteen, he'd done all he could to make her happy; and she even began reciprocating his feelings around the same time--or so he thought.

That was the one thing he couldn't share with his best friend, as you're supposed to be able to with a best friend. If Clayton found out, he'd be toast. Their friendship would go right out the door like it never existed, and Clayton would hate him forever. Clarise would be cooped up in their apartment until she was old enough to move out, and even then, Andre wasn't sure if Clayton would give her the freedom she so desired. He'd vowed to wait until Clarise was at least eighteen before he said anything to her about his feelings. She might not understand now at seventeen, though he had a sneaking suspicion she did.

Girls were so complicated. Did they all expect the guys to make the first move, or did they want to be the ones to ask the guy out? What would it be like for someone to choose Andre's spouse for him as they did above? It would make things easier, that was for sure. He wouldn't know if he'd actually love the woman he was paired with until they got to know each other--*after* they were married. That was too constricting for him; Andre didn't know if he'd be able to handle living up there, whether he'd been raised in the Fortress or not.

Once the silence became uncomfortable, Andre decided to speak. He couldn't have Clayton thinking he liked a girl. Too many questions could lead them to bad things before it was time. He'd tell his best friend some day.

"So have you mended things with Rose?" asked Andre.

Clayton sighed, the breath leaving his nostrils with such forcefulness, Andre didn't know if he was happy or upset.

"I take it you're not satisfied with how things went then?" Andre asked, keeping his voice low. The trainees should all be in bed by now, but the last thing they needed was someone listening to their conversations about Rose. She already had enough to deal with as it was. She wouldn't want the added stress of people teasing her for having a thing with a trainer. Clayton probably had thousands of thoughts running through his mind, that one included.

"To me, it went well. But I know she wants more..." he trailed off, his voice quivering. "I just don't know if I can give her all she deserves because of my past with Tess."

Andre propped his head up on one arm. "Well, have you thought about telling Rosabella about her? I'm sure she'd understand."

He rubbed his eyes with the heels of his hands. "How can I tell Rose this early on about the woman I used to love? Don't you think that's a little inappropriate?"

"Fine, but don't come crawling to me whining when Rose gets upset with you for avoiding her," Andre warned, rolling his eyes. "I may not know a lot about women, but I know they hate being ignored. And knowing Rose...she's going to give you hell for it."

He saw a smile form at the corners of Clayton's mouth. "Boy, do I hope so."

Andre shook his head. "And I thought *women* were confusing! Clay, you're the worst enigma I've ever met!"

"Oh, give it a rest!" Clay shrugged. "I just like the way her eyes focus on me when she's upset. It's like, if she could rip me apart with one look, she would."

He scoffed. "Yeah, and I bet you'd let her beat you up if it came to that, just to see the way her *eyes* blaze. Real romantic."

Clayton laughed and shoved him. "Shut up!"

Andre was serious when he asked, "Have you thought about telling Rose about what you did when she was asleep?"

The smile fell from Clayton's face faster than blood from a broken nose. "What do you mean?"

Andre pushed himself into a sitting position, holding his arms up in surrender. "I come in peace! I just mean when you sat in the hospital room with her day in and day out."

"What about it?" Clayton sat up and crossed his legs, hands balled into fists in his lap.

"Well, you told me that you talked to her while she slept. Don't you think she'd want to know that?"

His friend laughed angrily. "Sure, I'll put that on my list of things under 'creepy.' That'll really work on her."

"Don't shoot the messenger. I just think she'd like to know how protective of her you were," he said. "You were one of the only people who believed she'd make it. I think she ought to know."

Clayton looked away. "I don't know. I think I need to take it slow."

"For her or for you? I mean, when you like someone, you're supposed to put their needs and wants before your own, right?"

Clay sat on that for a second or two. "Andre, when did you become so good at giving relationship advice?"

"I dunno, probably from all those books Clair makes me read." He laughed. "Did she ever have you read--?"

Clayton's stoney expression shut him up right away. "I wasn't aware you and my sister were book club buddies."

He shrugged and picked at his cuticle again. "She's made me read books over the years. You know that I care about her, just like you. If I didn't listen to her and read all those books, she would've run crying to you." He smiled to himself. "I took the lesser of the two evils I guess."

That was as close as Andre dared to get. His heart raced with anticipation. Did Clayton catch on to how he'd drawn out her name? Did he see the way Andre's eyes gleamed, tasting her name on his tongue? Or the way his cheeks and arms burned with blood blush at the thought of her smile? He wished he could share that with Clayton; his intentions were completely honorable of course, but it would be stupid to tell him.

"Hmm, I'll have to see if she made us read the same books then," Clayton finally said.

Andre had to fight to breathe normally, letting the air he'd been holding onto out slowly so as not to raise any flags. Clayton was in a good mood now, but he could switch that around in seconds.

"Well," Clayton said, pushing himself up. He reached out a hand to Andre. "I suppose we should get back to it then."

"Sure, but only if you talk to me about Rose," Andre teased, accepting the hand. "What are you going to say to her? Or better yet, pretend I'm Rose. Practice what you want to say to her the next time you set eyes on her beautiful blue eyes. Imagine her curves under your hands--"

"Careful Harrison, or I'll take you out. It won't just be a workout anymore."

He smiled at his friend, already in his fighting stance. "Was it ever just a workout?"

Clayton smirked. "No." They both raced to get to the ring in the center of the room, shoving one another and laughing.

They "worked out" for a while after that. Andre was shorter than Clayton--at five eleven--but he made up for it in arm strength. Unfortunately, Clayton was light on his feet, always had been. It was infuriating to do combat with him; nine times out of ten, Andre lost. Clayton was just too good at this. He was too good at *everything*. Andre had never been jealous of Clayton; he understood the importance of their training. And he didn't fault Clayton for being one of the top performers.

After a missed blow to Andre's ear, Clayton huffed in anger. He came at Andre again, feet nearly tiptoeing on the floor. How did he manage to be so nimble for such a big guy?

"Okay Taylor, talk to me. What are you going to say to our Rosie Posie?"

"If she was here right now?"

Andre nodded, breathless. Someone pushed the door to the training room open and closed it behind themselves carefully. The motion lights near the entrance were activated, engulfing whoever was there in its fluorescent light. He was busy and didn't want to take a moment of hesitation to see who it was, so he kept his eyes on Clayton.

Clayten faked a punch to Andre's stomach, and as Andre went to protect himself, left his chest wide open. Clayton took the opportunity to hit him right between the clavicles. That sent Andre reeling backward, a sharp feeling spreading up into his throat.

He walked around the edge, letting himself regain composure before grinning at his opponent. "Well shit. I doubt Rose would like *that* as a welcome."

"I would *never* hurt her!" Clayton gasped. When he realized Andre was kidding, he laughed. "Okay, okay. I'd tell her about Tess."

"Oh wow. That's a big step. Do you think she's ready to hear that?"

"I trust her," Clayton shrugged, giving Andre the opening he needed to kick Clayton's legs out from under him. He swooped in then, pinning Clayton to the floor.

Someone gasped a few feet away. Both Andre and Clayton turned their heads in the direction of the sound. It was a medium height, red-haired, curvy girl.

Rosabella.

She took it upon herself to speak, seeing as though the two of them were still on the ground watching her, mouths agape.

It all came out in a rushed sentence. "Sorry, umm I just wanted to get some more weightlifting in since I couldn't sleep because I've been really restless lately, and Aire and I aren't really getting along, so I thought this would be the best place for me." She paused to take in a breath before continuing, "I just didn't think you'd be fighting so rough, being friends and all. It just surprised me. My bad. Carry on."

She turned and headed for the rack of weights beside the bikes, selecting two 25-pound dumbbells. Then she pulled down a mat from the hooks beside it and started stretching. As she was setting her stuff up, Andre locked eyes with Clayton.

"Go get her, man."

\*\*\*

## (ROSABELLA)

Rose tried to block out the guys while she stretched, starting with her arms first. She could hear them shuffling around, doing god only knew what. She sat on the mat and spread her legs out into a "V" shape and reached her hands between her legs. It was really good for her hamstrings, which were extremely sore from working out all week. She bit her tongue to suppress a groan.

"Hey, want some company?"

She shrieked, and jumped to her feet.

"Don't worry, just me," Clayton said, a smile tugging at the corners of his mouth. He stood there, hands in his pockets.

She reddened. *Oh come on Rose*, she scolded herself. There was no reason for her to be so jumpy. Now she was being paranoid.

"I mean, if you want to," she said shrugging. She hoped she sounded relaxed, because she certainly didn't feel that way. "I'm not very good at this, so please don't judge me."

He chuckled in that carefree, lighthearted way of his and reached for her weights. "I'll show you some new drills. I've noticed Eden hasn't been giving you many new exercises."

She cocked her head. "Oh, you've been watching?"

Her mind raced, looking back on her workouts. She'd sweat like a pig during her sprint exercises and knew she'd grimaced many times during weight lifting. If Clayton had been watching her, surely he thought her disgusting at this point.

He shrugged. "Yeah. Now let me show you something different. We're going to the weight room."

"There's a weight room?" she asked, stunned. Why the hell did Eden make her stand in the corner of the room in front of everyone else then?

"Yes." He searched her face. "And before you say anything, I asked Eden to keep you in here so I could watch your progress."

Her heart thumped roughly against her rib cage. What did that mean? Was he worried about her getting hurt again? Or had he simply wanted to watch her? Without waiting for a response, Clayton returned the weights to the rack and began walking toward the wall with all the doors. She followed him, reluctant at first.

They passed Andre, who was on his way out. He winked at Rosabella, and wagged his eyebrows at Clayton. She didn't know what to make of that.

Clayton stopped in front of the second door, the one that was usually closed. She laughed, nervous all of a sudden. The door was the same size and color as the rest of the doors in the Fortress, surprise surprise. There was something very intimate about following Clayton into that room, just the two of them.

He pressed his wristband up to the tiny screen on the door where a handle should have been.

Without looking at her, he asked, "You alright, Rose?"

"It just feels a little like you're leading me into a dark corner of the Fortress to do something bad to me." She elbowed him, a weak attempt to stop the shaking in her hands. "How do I know you're not going to kill me or something?"

He turned back to his serious self again. "Did you hear what I said to Andre earlier? I also said it to you not that long ago."

She nodded, unable to reply. Of course she knew. Clay's brown eyes were striking in that moment of closeness they shared. He walked closer until his face was so close she was breathing the same air as him.

"I said I would *never* hurt you. I mean it, Rose." He brought his hand to her face. He hesitated before cupping her cheek.

She willed herself to say something smart, but the words wouldn't form. Her tongue felt like sandpaper in her mouth and even her toes clenched. Her teeth pressed together against her will, shooting pain up into her gums.

He pulled away, eyes wide as if she struck him. Did he think she was afraid of him? Her heart, which had jumped into her throat when he touched her, stopped beating.

Wasn't she though?

He cleared his throat. "So, umm only trainers have access to this room, that's why it's always locked."

"Clayton?"

"I'll show you some stuff and then you can have free reign of the room for the rest of the night. I'll leave you be."

"Clayton. Stop." Rose tugged on his arm until he looked at her. He looked at her expectantly but of course, she was at a loss for words. She said the first thing that popped into her head, "Umm, I mean. Please *don't* stop."

A strange look crossed his face before smiling. "Don't stop what exactly?"

Well crap. She hadn't thought that far in advance. "Umm, don't stop being kind."

His face fell. "Oh, is that all?"

She threw her hands up. "Well, what did you expect me to say? That I want to feel your hand on my cheek again?"

One step closer to her. "Well, *do* you?"

"Of course I do! Why do you think--?" She sighed loudly, using her diaphragm to push the air out until her chest heaved. "You *confuse* me!"

He looked around the room before taking another step closer, closing the gap between them. If she wanted to, she could put her hands on his chest. For a moment, she considered it. How nice it would be to lean against him, letting him support her weight; to feel his hands in her hair. She pushed that out of her mind; that would be impulsive, even for her.

Not for him apparently. Clayton placed his hands on either side of her waist. "Does *this* confuse you?"

Her eyes probably turned to saucers, gawking up at him.

She nodded.

Encouraged, his hands wrapped around her and met in the space right above her tailbone. She'd always been embarrassed of her curves before, afraid no man would ever want to hold her because her hips jutted out too far. How would they even get their arms around her? But all those fears slipped away when he made it seem so easy, resting his forearms on her hip bones as if they were meant to be there. Rose flinched when he brushed against her bandaid. It had been days since he'd woken her up from her nightmare, but she kept changing out the bandaid to keep it covered during training.

He started to pull back, but she arched her back to keep him close. Her hands reached under his arms, until she linked her fingers behind him. The muscles in his back flexed. He let out a breath into her hair, right above her ear. A shiver of pleasure raced down her spine.

Everything fell into place: the looks they'd shared across the room, the nights he and Clarise walked her home from dinner though she knew her way by then; their intimate moment in the washroom, his nose lightly brushing against her; even that time he met up with her in the library. They'd sat on the same couch--*their* couch--in silence, inches apart at the time. Now she couldn't get close enough to him.

"So this is what it's like to be on Clayton Taylor's good side," she mumbled into his chest. She closed her eyes and breathed in. He was sweaty from his match with Andre, but there was another scent of fresh linen masking it.

His arms around her tightened. He rested his chin atop her head. "I could say the same of you, Rosabella Mae Porter."

"Well, I suppose this means we should stop yelling at one another then." She smiled into the muscles of his chest. She liked the solidness of him, that he didn't feel like he was going to break.

Clayton chuckled, the sound tickling her forehead. She pulled away to see him, bringing her hands to his chest. His eyes were glassy, his curly hair ruffled. But he kept his arms around her, loosening only enough for her to lean back into his hold. The smile on his face reached all the way to his eyes. The dimple in his cheek returned. She stood on her tiptoes and kissed his cheek right there.

Clayton shuddered before briefly touching his lips to her forehead. Then he released her hips and ran his hand along her arm. Once he linked his hand with hers, he turned and opened the door.

She tugged on his arm. It did no good; he was too strong. "Wait. Clayton, can I ask you something?"

The smile he gave her warmed her heart. She was nervous again, worried about what he might say.

"Can you promise not to get mad?"

He tilted his head, eyes squinting. "I'll do my best."

"Who's Tess?"

Silence. His grip on her hand faltered, until Rose was the one holding desperately onto him. She was afraid of what he would do if she let his hand fall. Would everything that had happened between them fall apart just as easily? Was this what a relationship with Clayton was bound to be like? Could she even call it a relationship?

Rose did her best to backtrack, lifting his arm and pressing his hand against her chest. "I just thought I'd ask because I heard you and Andre. You said the next time you saw me you'd tell me about her."

His face was hard, his touch cold. She let his hand go and watched it return to his side, clenched. They stood in silence again, this time neither of them making eye contact. She wished she could take it all back. How stupid could she be? He obviously wasn't ready to talk about something traumatic that happened to him. What right did she think she had, invading his personal private thoughts?

She walked a few steps backward. "I think I should probably just go back to my dorm?" Rose meant for her voice to sound emotionless, but that was far from reality. Her voice trembled on the last word, turning it into a question rather than a statement.

He nodded. "I think that's best."

Rosabella turned away so Clay couldn't see how hurt she was. He would open up when he was ready; she didn't need to push it.

Only when she reached the exit did she turn around. Clayton hadn't moved from his spot at the weight room door. He kept his hands at his sides, feet shoulder length apart, as if preparing for a fight. In a way, he was. It looked like one of the worst fights of all: one against himself. With frustrated tears in her eyes, Rose turned away and left.

She wanted to spend the night on the couch in the library, too upset to go back to her room. Aire would just give her a dirty look and turn over when she heard Rose come in the room anyway. There would be no one to comfort her or help her make sense of what had just happened.

As she made herself comfortable on the couch, Rose closed her eyes and did her best to breathe. The last thing on her mind before she fell asleep was the way Clayton's eyes had looked when she mentioned Tess's name. It had scared her more than she wanted to admit. That was a place he wasn't ready to go yet. After tonight, she wasn't sure if he'd want to go *anywhere* with her ever again.

# Chapter 20

## (AIRE)

AIRE TRUDGED ALONG OBEDIENTLY. THE OTHER TRAINEES FROM her neighborhood were ahead of her, barriers between herself and Logan. He noticed *everything*. It was so stupid how he seemed to know what they were thinking before they did anything!

She'd planned to see her sister, Luna, today. Aire had been in close contact with her sister by leaving her letters at her house. Luna would write back to her and leave it under the front step. Someday, maybe Bernard would allow the communication system to open up so they could use their screens instead of this letter bullshit.

Earlier this week, they agreed to meet up. She was almost certain it wasn't allowed, but it was necessary for her to contact Luna or else she'd go insane. In the long run, it was only helping the Fortress; Bernard couldn't be too upset with her if he found out.

Luna had insisted she had a surprise for Aire and insisted she make her way to the office today. She'd sent an extra five exclamation faces to emphasize the point. When Luna did that, Aire knew she meant business.

They followed Logan through street upon street until Aire became agitated. At some point, she recognized they were near the Hydro Tube station. The buzzing of the underground train was loud in her ears, the all too familiar saltwater smell thick in her nose. She wanted to plug her ears but was afraid of ridicule. The others were way tougher than she was. Or they acted like it.

Aire was not cut out for this life. So far, she'd managed to get countless bruises and cuts on her body in places she never had to think about before. Enough was enough! She wanted to get the hell out of dodge as soon as possible. It was so hard with everyone keeping a close eye on the only entrance and exit in the Fortress.

She'd heard word about there being several ways to get in and out in the past, but once things started getting trickier, they'd closed them all off except for one. The one inside the pantry of Rosabella's house.

The two of them hadn't spoken in nearly a month now. At first, Aire was so angry she could have screamed at Rose for hours about what a terrible friend she was being. Aire had lost people too, it wasn't just Rose who should get all the attention and told she was "strong." Rose didn't know it, but Aire had lectured everyone she passed who said Rose's name. She told them all that Rose was just a normal girl who went through a strange and difficult challenge. She shouldn't be treated like a celebrity because of her strength or whatever the others called it. Her scolding sessions had seemed to do the trick; they hadn't had anyone knock on the door asking to meet Rose for weeks now.

Unfortunately, not even Rose had knocked on the door. She hadn't even spent the night in their dorm since their argument. Where the hell was she sleeping? Aire was growing paranoid that Rose was going to disown her and never speak to her again. Their friendship meant the world to Aire, so she didn't want to give up that easily. Didn't Rose know when enough was enough? Weren't her insides eating away at her too?

If there was one thing Aire knew about her best friend, it was that Rosabella was stubborn. They'd never fought this bad before, so she wasn't sure how to deal with things. Aire hadn't had time to make any other friends, so that left her with their other roommate, Gianna, who was inconveniently away every single night with her boyfriend.

Aire rubbed her arms. The cool afternoon air was crisp today, a sure sign of a change in seasons. She loved this season, fall, the most; being underground for it wasn't going to fly. She silently cursed her clothing decision. She'd opted for a pair of extra short jean shorts the color of the artificial grass and an off the shoulder lime green plain t-shirt. The colors were meant to bring out her brown eyes, and draw guys' eyes to her long legs and thin arms. She'd hoped Clayton would be the one taking them out on a mission, but sadly, she'd gotten Logan.

He was cute and all, but was a few inches shorter than herself. His green eyes were definitely pretty, but the main issue Aire had with the guy was that he was too nice. She liked her men rugged. Clayton was the perfect guy. Unfortunately, for the time being, he obviously had his eye on Rosabella. No matter, Aire would just change his mind.

That's why she wanted to meet Luna today. She only hoped her sister had an idea for how to do that.

"Now, you'll see here that the droids have attacked nearly every building and monument in sight...except for the Hydro Tube Station." Logan turned into a tour guide, walking backward and gesturing to important things she didn't care about. "They haven't attacked here as of now, but that doesn't mean they won't. We've started organizing guards to patrol out here and keep an eye on things, though it's not within our perimeter."

One of the girls in the front raised her hand. Aire recognized her from their days of high school, but she didn't remember her name. "Excuse me?"

Logan pointed to her and smiled showing all his teeth. "Yes, Xyla?"

Aire fought the urge to gag. Did Logan have to be nice to people all the time? She hoped it was all an act, that he was really a normal person underneath all that kindness crap. His skin was a golden caramel color and made him stand out against the mostly white buildings. Girls always blushed when they talked to him, but Aire didn't get it. He was nothing compared to Clayton.

"Well," Xyla started, blushing--surprise surprise! "What will you do when you--if--you find the droids here. We don't have any weapons do we?"

"Excellent point, Xyla. We are still working on that last part. We're hoping to have weapons available to us in the coming year or so. For now, we are going to monitor the droids' movements and actions so we can better combat them when the time comes." He turned away, shaking his head. His voice shifted from an authoritative tone to one much softer and filled with emotion. "Unfortunately, that means people are going to die in the process. We will do the best we can to get as many willing people out of there as possible."

Aire rolled her eyes. He was too emotional for her too. Clayton kept everything to himself, swallowing down the hurt to save face. That was respectable. The way Logan showed his emotions, by wearing everything on his sleeve, made him undesirable to her.

Their group made it to the Tube station then, watching from afar while people--in much smaller groups now that people kept fleeing--ran around as usual. There was something funny about the way their lives continued on in the same cycle and harmony they were used to all their lives. Everyone knew their way in life. The Government provided them security and something to work for every day.

Meanwhile, Aire had been forced to flip her life completely upside down. She didn't even know what she was training to fight for in the Fortress. Everyone was too vague in their answers. Or they didn't know themselves. But Aire pushed on; she trained and she practiced everything they asked for. She'd done it all for Rosabella. The only reason she followed Logan to the Fortress was because her best friend did. Had Rose decided to stay behind in the house that night of the party, Aire would have stayed back with her. They'd both be dead right now, but at least they'd be together.

When Logan finally turned on his heel and faced the other direction, Aire tiptoed away. She hid behind a building until she could no longer hear his voice above the buzzing of the Tube. Heart racing with excitement at her deviousness, Aire made her way along the sidewalks. She knew how to get to the Government Headquarters from here. It had been a while since she'd been near the Tube station, but she'd never forget which track brought her to the city; HQ was a short walk from there. Her parents had insisted she and her sister make something of themselves so they didn't wind up like some of their classmates' families. Apparently, that meant she was forced to learn the ins and outs of the city. Aire would rather die than work at one of the prisons or something atrocious like that. She wasn't going to take anything less than a Government advisor job. Luna would help her, she didn't have to worry about that.

What she *did* need to focus on was explaining her story to anyone who inquired. Aire was probably supposed to be dead; she was sure the Government recorded her death once they found the bodies of her schoolmates after the droid attack during the party.

When she arrived at the Headquarters building, she made sure to introduce herself to the receptionist as Luna's associate.

The woman smiled at her. "She's been expecting you."

"Oh, great. Thanks." Aire walked across the room to the elevator, access granted to her by the receptionist. Once inside, Aire leaned against the back wall and ran her fingers through her hair. It was severely windblown, but that was the least of her worries right now. She wasn't sure how to prepare for her sister's "surprise." The last time Luna had surprised her had been the day she taught Aire how to seduce men to do her bidding.

Her sister met her at the elevator doors on the fifteenth floor, greeting her with an exuberant hug and kiss on the cheek. "You made it! Come on, I can't wait for you to hear what I have planned for today!"

Luna had on a tight black skirt and a hot pink tight fitting blouse tucked into the top of it. Her shoes were shiny pink, skinny five-inch heels that brought her up to Aire's height. Their mom and dad hadn't passed on the genes of height to their eldest daughter. Instead, Aire was the one cursed with the tallness in the family.

"Me either," Aire said. Saying that made her feel more awake. More alive; *excited*, even. She was careful where she placed her feet on the faded red carpet. Many shoes had walked this hallway, and many more would long after Aire.

Her flat tennis shoes were caked with mud on the bottoms, so she did her best to find the darkest patches of red to conceal anything that flaked off as she walked. At least it was soft under her worn soles. She'd need to stop by Prince's on the way back to the dorms tonight to see if she could get a new pair. Although, he may question why she'd been doing so much walking. Aire knew she'd have to come up with a believable lie so he'd authorize her a new pair.

She took in a breath and was disgusted by the smell of cardboard and something else...*metal?* At least Luna's office had an air freshener installed in the vent. It was a relief to smell something other than sweaty kids all day too.

"Alright, Rei," Luna squealed once she shut the door to her office. "I have something for you. It's not here yet."

Aire fell into the couch in the corner. "What did you do this time, Lu?"

Her sister scrambled around in her desk drawers for something. When she didn't find what she was looking for she scoffed. "I swear, if the cleaning crew moves one more thing, I'm going to see them fired. I have the director of maintenance wrapped around my finger now. We're like this," she curled one finger around her middle finger and sighed.

"Luna, it's alright. I don't need a surprise. I want to talk about Rosabella and Clayton--"

She was cut off by the wagging of her sister's finger. "Stop. I don't want to hear about how terrible a friend she is, how hot Clayton is, or how hurt you are that your friend stole your guy." She beamed down at Aire, showing all her teeth, even the ones in the back. "Today is your day to redeem yourself. You are going to gain your confidence back so you can march right up to Clayton and give him a piece of your mind. The Gil's always get what they want."

Aire leaned back on the couch and closed her eyes. "What have you done this time, Lu?"

Her sister giggled. "Just remember that I have your best interests in mind, okay, Rei?"

A loud, sharp knock sounded on the door. Aire's head shot up, eyes wide. Luna fixed her smooth low-hanging bob on the back of her neck and ran to the door.

"Remember what I said, baby sis." She swung the door inward and leaned her head against the door. Aire watched her seductively tilt her head, exposing the skin on her neck to the man in the doorway. He was pretty average-looking, with broad shoulders and a thick, muscular neck. His eyes were gray, a strange contrast to his straight, dark reddish-blonde hair. He didn't even seem to reach past five feet nine inches tall, quite uncommon for a man.

His hands clasped behind his back. He stared down at Luna, unblinking. "You requested a meeting with me, Mrs. Gil?"

She giggled and twirled a loose strand of hair around her finger. "Oh please, Grayson. The formailites are *so* unnecessary. And it's just *Miss*. Haven't found the right match yet."

He cleared his throat and nodded. "Forgive me, but you don't really get a say in your match, do you?"

Her sister shrugged and stepped back to let him in. "Eh, well, perks of being in the Government. I've postponed my pairing for the last three or so years."

Aire stood, her eyes shooting daggers at her sister's head while she closed the door. This wasn't the surprise she wanted. Aire had heard enough from her sister's "meetings" to know this wasn't going to benefit her in any way. Her sister was so conceited sometimes!

"This is Aire," her sister said, winking at her around Grayson. "And Rei, this is Grayson. He's a guard here. Works closely with your friend, Rosabella's dad I believe. Isn't that right?"

Grayson nodded and cleared his throat. He knew something was up. Aire wished her sister could fall through the floor, all the way down to the main level. She hoped a good one hundred story fall would knock some sense into her.

"Well, I'll leave you to it then. Let me know if you need anything," Luna directed at Aire. Then she slipped out of the room, closing--and locking--the door on her way out.

Aire could kill her. She was certain that if her sister was still in the room, Aire would have strangled her by now. That's how murderous she felt.

Grayson's arms fell loosely at his sides. He peered at Aire, his brows knit together. "Umm, is my meeting with you or something?" he questioned. He wasn't quite as kind or awkward as Logan, nor was he rugged or sexy as Clayton. Grayson was a nice in-between. At least her sister had listened to Aire's rants about everyone in the Fortress. It was forbidden to talk to outsiders about it, but this was her sister for crying out loud. Luna had thought her dead for a while before Aire managed to get her a message. She had to leave a letter on Luna's doorstep. The internal messaging system in the Fortress was speedy, but didn't connect to any communication networks other than the ones down here. It was awful, being closed off to the world. Did Bernard just expect them all to drop off the face of the earth up above? Apparently.

If Aire couldn't have Clayton, she could settle for the next best thing. Luna had said Grayson was a guard, that was the equivalent of a trainer in the Fortress, right? Or pretty damn close to it? Aire realized the only way to deal with the situation was to keep going deeper. If she somehow made him fall for her, or at least wrapped him around her finger, she'd regain the confidence she somehow lost in the Fortress. Maybe Luna was onto something.

She moved to the desk and rested her hips on it. *Make him think he's in charge*, she repeated to herself. Luna had given her a step by step guide to seducing men. It was her turn to put that to action now. *He'll think he wants a woman who will listen to what he says, but you need to show him that a woman who knows her own mind is better.* Aire followed the instructions carefully; she crossed her legs, exposing more of her thighs to Grayson. He didn't remove his eyes from her face, not even when she reached down to "tie her shoe."

He squinted and turned for the door. "Miss Gil, is there something you need? If not, I'd like to be dismissed."

"Wait, please!" She ran over to him, pretending to trip and fall. He caught her in his arms at just the right moment, bringing their faces only inches apart. He righted her and let go. She held her hands on his chest and looked down her nose at him. Though she was much taller in height, she could work with this. Now that she was closer, Aire noted how pretty his eyes were, the gray in them standing out from his pale skin.

*Blink slowly a few times and gaze at him from under your lashes.*

Grayson roughly pushed her away. "I'm not sure what kind of operation you're running here, Miss Gil, but I'm leaving now."

She let her bottom lip quiver and her face droop. "Did I do something wrong?"

He stopped with his hand on the door. With his back to her, he spoke in a low voice, "Not you. I'm afraid your sister has been showing you the wrong side of the world. Do yourself a favor and get out while you can. This behavior is atrocious."

Her mouth dropped open, but she couldn't come up with a response fast enough. Just like that he was gone. And so was Aire's energy and confidence. If she couldn't get a man to like her with free will, perhaps Luna had a better idea for how to wrap a man around her finger. One who would do whatever she said.

Speak of the devil, Luna rushed in then, dark hair a mess.

"What happened?" she gasped. "I was only gone for like fifteen minutes!"

Aire scoffed and pointed at her hair. "Yeah, but obviously you found a way to occupy yourself."

"Nevermind me," Luna said, waving her off. "How'd it go with Grayson?"

She shook her head and looked toward the window. "I want to learn from you. What makes you so appealing to men?"

Her sister frowned. "Why?"

"Because. Grayson told me that my behavior was *atrocious*." She sighed. "I guess I'm just not cut out for a life of love. I think I'm doomed."

Luna ran over and took Aire's face in her hands. "Rei, don't you dare say that. We will turn you into the most desirable woman in the whole country. Men like Grayson are just pawns in our game."

Her heart ached. "But why didn't he like me?"

"Nevermind his sorry ass. You're too good for him anyway." Luna ran to the desk, gesturing for Aire to follow. "For now, let's brainstorm some ways we can get you your life back from those stupid bitches in the Sanctuary."

"Fortress," she corrected.

"Whatever. I don't care either way." Luna blinked at her. "Well, come on. Don't just stand there."

# Chapter 21

## (AIRE)

AIRE AND LUNA SPENT A FEW HOURS PLANNING and plotting against Rose and her "bitches" as Luna liked to call them, which included Clayton, Logan, Andre, Clarise and everyone else who idolized Rosabella. After a while, Aire grew tired of hating her best friend and changed the focus of the revenge to the others. One of the plans--Luna's personal favorite--was to bomb the whole place and bring their society to a halt. Aire opted for something a little less *deadly*. She only wanted them to hurt, not get them murdered for crying out loud!

She knew she'd overstayed her welcome when the moon bled through the shaded glass. Luna walked her through the empty cubicles to the elevator and out the front doors. Somehow, she'd gotten a hold of one of the Government's vehicles and was able to drive Aire to the entrance of the Fortress.

Aire didn't speak to her sister the whole ride there. Her sister asked for directions every so often, but that was all the talking she did. She thought back on her days of being best friends with Rosie.

> *"Excuse me," the teacher said. His cold, unseeing eyes trained on Aire.*
>
> *The whole class turned and stared at Aire. Most of their faces wore bored expressions, thankful to have a reason to move in their*

*seats. To have anything else to focus on. Aire had totally called the teacher out on his bullshit. He's been picking on Rosie, and that was unacceptable.*

*Rosabella crossed her arms and bit her lip beside Aire. She was always the good little student every teacher wanted. Aire knew she wouldn't say anything disrespectful to the teacher. She would hear all about it in a rant from Rosie after school later this afternoon. That's how Rose operated. She was not one to disrespect authority.*

*Rose's eyes glared at the top of her desk instead of the teacher, where they very much belonged. He was awful. No matter what anyone said or did, and even if they* agreed *with him, he'd lash out. It was one of the many pleasures of having a robot teacher issued by the Government. They really needed to program these things better. This one must've been dysfunctional or something.*

*Aire caught herself in a staring match with the robo-teacher. Of course, he won, but she wanted him to know how pissed off she was. Rose was only correcting the incorrect formula he'd written on the board. She had every right to raise her hand and speak her mind when called on. She hadn't done anything wrong at all. The dick-bot embarrassed her because he didn't know how else to react. Obviously he hadn't been programmed with the ability to accept responsibility for being wrong.*

*"Sir, you are an extreme asshole. You deserve to rot in a pile of scrap metal," Aire repeated. Take that you piece of shit!*

*Rose grabbed her arm before she could insult him any more. "Aire! Stop it! Do you want to get detention...again?"*

*She didn't really care. If it meant she'd done her civil duty of standing up for her friend, Aire was all in. So what if she had to sit in the empty, lifeless classroom for an extra hour at the end of the day? It never taught her a lesson anyway. If anything, it only made her angrier; more ready to throw down with whoever crossed her path and didn't agree.*

*She brushed Rosie's hand away. "I've got this, don't worry," she whispered, giving her friend a huge grin. "Hey Mr. Suck-bot. Why don't you apologize for embarrassing my friend here?"*

*He whirred over to Aire, eyes scanning the room. "I do not compute embarrassment."*

*Aha! So he didn't* have the ability to feel. *That explained so much now.*

*Aire pointed to Rose. "My friend. You were very rude to her a minute ago. Take it back."*

*The robo-teacher's head swung back and forth. "I can't take it back. It has already been released."*

*She stood to her feet so fast, her chair toppled over.*

*Rose jumped to her side right away. "Aire! Stop it. You're going to get in trouble with the principal and then the Government."*

*"Psh, I'm not afraid of the Government. They're big 'ol softies."*

*"I wouldn't say that," her friend said in a low voice near her ear. "Just please stop."*

*The teacher rolled up to them. "If there is going to be a disturbance, I can send you to the principal. Would you rather that?"*

*Aire played with the fake piercing in her left ear. "Hmm, I guess we could go there... or you could shove your hand in your own ass."*

Aire would always remember that as the first day Rose had gotten so mad at her, she threatened to stop being friends with her. Aire never got why Rose would become so angry right away. She wished she'd be able to read Rosabella's mind sometimes. Her friend was like a puzzle. It had taken their whole lives so far to put *half* of the pieces together.

Before she knew it, Luna dropped her off at the corner of the neighborhood with the entrance to the Fortress. She blew Aire a kiss before driving away. It was comforting to know she had someone who'd be there for her no matter the circumstances. A few weeks ago, she assumed that person was Rose, but things had changed since then.

Nobody crossed her path as she trudged along the sidewalk toward Rose's house. It still boggled her mind that Rose had no idea there had been a secret society underneath her house. All those nights Aire had spent sleeping over and playing games until the early hours of the morning, and not once had they heard anyone underneath them. Did Rosie's dad know about the Fortress? Her mom? Why all the secrets? Aire and Rose would have kept their secrets safe had they known about the Fortress.

In order to get back in, Aire had to scan her thumb and whisper the passphrase into the microphone in the pantry; the updated passphrase was shared with them on the first day of every month. When Logan realized she'd taken a detour from the rest of the group, he was going to be livid...if he didn't already know. Aire had never been destined for rule following, as evidenced by her many detentions and parent-teacher meetings about behavior. Even if she tried her best to be the perfect student, she just couldn't do it. It was way too boring to go with the flow all the time. That's why she idolized her sister, Luna, who could keep a high position in Government and still get away with the things she did every day. What she did in her office… that was completely unacceptable by the Government's standards. She could be fired and banished from Government property for the rest of her life if anyone found out and took it out on her. Luna was a smart woman; she wouldn't get caught unless she wanted to. Aire had no doubt she'd be able to talk herself out of any situation.

When the elevator doors opened at the bottom, Aire's heart dropped. Logan and Bernard stood at the dividing doors, faces tight and postures rigid. She smiled at them. Maybe Logan would be coaxed into liking her if she pretended to play stupid. She reached down to "fix her shoe" when she really wanted to flash as much thigh as possible. No guy could be *that* virtuous. Logan had to have a darker, more easily seducible side to him. Right? Perhaps he could be her new practice target.

"Aire Gil, you need to come with us," Bernard said. He uncrossed his arms and waved her to follow.

"Oh. Sure," she replied, raising her voice to sound more innocent. Suddenly, the off-white walls didn't seem so welcoming. She rubbed her arms as they walked to a meeting room. "Hey guys, what's this about anyway?"

Logan glared at her, stepping back so she could go into the room first. "You know what this is about. It would be better if you worked *with* us, Aire." His face softened. "If not for yourself, then for your friends here."

She scoffed. "Oh yeah? Which friends? It seems nobody thinks I'm important enough to stick around."

Bernard took a seat and leaned back in the chair. "Well perhaps you wouldn't have that problem if you were easier to talk to."

"What's that supposed to mean?" She seethed, standing over him. Her shadow dwarfed him in size. Finally, something good came from being an extremely tall woman.

Logan stepped between her and their leader. "Watch yourself, Gil."

183

He wasn't angry, she noticed. He was sad. His shoulders sagged and his feet shuffled as he took his own seat beside Bernard. Aire settled for a chair across from them. She folded her hands on the table in front of her and stared them both down.

"Can we get this over with quickly please? I'm not in the mood for a lecture tonight."

Bernard shook his head and blinked at her. "We aren't your enemy, Miss Gil. We simply want you to follow the rules."

She scoffed and rolled her eyes. "Yeah, great work. I feel *really* welcomed knowing I have to follow the rules." She crossed her arms. "What makes you any different from the Government you hate so much? To me, they seem to be getting along really well up above."

Logan leaned his forehead in his hand and began massaging his temples. "I'm sorry you aren't finding your place here. Sometimes it takes people a little longer than others."

"But I never had the chance to--"

Bernard held up his hand. "Aire, we know about your sister, Luna. She works for the Government does she not?"

Aire nodded slowly. Where was this going? If they were going to hurt her sister, she'd personally see to it that someone slit Bernard's throat. Family came first for everything. Rose was considered her family no matter what happened between them, so she would be untouched, but Aire couldn't say the same for the rest of the people here who got in the way.

"We only want to talk to you about that. Now, we don't usually give this opportunity to others, but it appears you are having a difficult time adjusting. Our motto is join or die, but in this case, you've already chosen to join. So there's something we can do for you...think of this as a favor that you'll have to pay back at a later point. Bernard sighed and leaned forward. "Because I trust Rosabella and I know you two are good friends, I want to grant you permission to visit with Luna once a week. But I need you to promise me a few things first."

Aire laughed hard, her diaphragm buckling from the pressure. "You're going to 'give me permission?' What the hell?" And what was this talk about Rose?

"Aire please, don't be so difficult," Logan urged, his face tight again.

"What's it to you, Logan?" She was so angry she spit at him.

184

"Because of Rosabella. I know you care about her. I wouldn't want you to have a falling out," he said, eyes heavy with emotion.

Oh no. Not him too? How the hell did Rose manage to make every guy fall for her? Rose probably didn't even know Logan had a thing for her. That was so frustrating! Aire couldn't even get *one* guy to like her and now Rose had like fifty of them! It wasn't fair.

"Mr. Clarke, my best friend and I are no longer on speaking terms. If you want to fix it, why don't you talk to her and tell her I didn't do anything?" She threw her hands up and stared him down again. "She's just so damn stubborn!"

Bernard gave her a sad look, his eyebrows drooping. "Aire, you need to accept responsibility. Just because there was an argument between you and Rosabella doesn't mean you're not at fault. I think you --"

"No. I didn't do anything. She's the one who deceived me. She made it seem like she hated Clayton." She took a deep breath to calm herself. This rant wasn't going to help anything. "But the whole time she was just twisting my view of it. I'm sure Rose and Clayton have done stuff together already."

Logan swallowed and leaned back, stiff as a log. "Stuff?" He was like a wounded puppy.

She wanted Logan to feel the pain she felt too. Her eyes narrowed and she forced a small smile to her face. "Oh come on, Clarke. You're what, like twenty-five? You've got to know by now that when a man and a woman are attracted to one another...things happen."

"Twenty-four," he corrected. "And I don't think they'd do that..."

Aire found it hilarious that he didn't believe himself. She tapped her fingers on the surface of the table and stared at him. Soon, people would begin to realize that Aire was worthy of love. If Logan was already upset, she couldn't wait to see how broken he'd get when he fully realized that Rose and Clayton were together. They weren't yet, but it was only a matter of time. Rosabella had a strange way of letting passion rule her mind and making her decisions based on the feelings of others.

Bernard smacked his hand on the table. "This is not what we're here to discuss! Aire Gil, if you continue to cause rifts between our fellow Fortress members, I'm going to personally remove you from the premises."

"What?" Her mouth fell open against her will. "But I thought the Fortress was all about joining or dying?"

He gave her a knowing look and cleared his throat. "There have been people who've had a difficult time adapting to our life. We make special accommodations, but as you must know, we keep those operations top secret. It would require drastic measures."

"Like what?" Logan asked, brows furrowed. He clearly didn't know what Bernard was talking about either.

He patted Logan on the back. "Clarke, this is for Aire's ears only. I may need to have you step into the hall for a moment, should she decide she wants to learn more."

"Aire?" Logan asked, concern in his face. What did he care? She wanted to slap that worried look from his face. He was only looking out for her now because he wanted Rose to like him. Too bad. Aire'd take over his heart when it broke in a matter of weeks or months. She'd wait around for him. If he didn't develop feelings for her, she'd snap and take Bernard up on his offer. First, she needed to know what it entailed.

"I want to know," she said, keeping her voice low.

"If you wish." Bernard nodded at Logan and motioned for him to leave the room. Once the door shut, he turned to her. "It will require me to...*erase* your life here."

# Chapter 22

## (ROSABELLA)

A COUPLE WEEKS AFTER CLAYTON AND ROSABELLA'S CONFUSING SPAT in the training room, Rosabella was back to her normal, somewhat healthy self. She still had to be careful of her side where the droid poisoned her, but at least it no longer throbbed throughout the day. She wasn't even wearing gauze pads to cover it anymore, now that the wound was closed up. All that remained was a small area of scar tissue around the injection site.

After their...*disagreement* in the training room, Clayton had approached Rose and tried to apologize. At first, she thought it was romantic. They'd almost kissed. They were so close, but then she brought up the Tess thing again because it was killing her inside...and that was the end of that.

She'd stopped wearing bandages over her hip a week ago. It was all healed up for the most part, a little red patch of healing skin the only sign it had ever happened. It was also the only faint sign of Clayton's affection, and she carried it everywhere. Without him, some days she felt alone, even with Clarise's presence. It was all she had; Rose wouldn't turn to Aire to make her feel better this time. That was out of the question.

The two of them hadn't spoken more than a few words to one another in over a month. It was so unlike Rose to let it get this far, but now she was in a new environment; one in which she no longer felt trapped, fearing that she had to keep people happy so they would be nice to her. Far too long had she followed Aire around like a puppy, afraid to lose the one person who gave her the time of day. She couldn't even remember how they'd become friends in the first place, just that their families had been close. It just made sense for Rosabella and Aire to grow up as best friends. Had Rose not known Aire before starting school when they were five, she didn't think they'd have become friends. Aire was too temperamental and selfish.

Thanks to the separation, Rose had questioned how their friendship had even gone on as long as it had.

It didn't help that Gianna was gone every night. There was no one to mediate their conversations--if they'd had any. And thus the cycle of avoidance was born. Rose snuck away every night to sleep on the couches in the library. She'd tested about half the couches in the room at that point, and had already decided on her favorite: the one in the corner she and Clarise had shared while reading together. Rosabella swore to herself it was only because of its comfort, not because she had a fond memory of herself and Clayton there.

Before she ruined it all, she'd felt a sense of safety she hadn't known she was missing. Thanks to her big fat mouth, Rose destroyed any chance they had in no time at all. She didn't accept all responsibility for how things turned out though. It was a two way street.

Rose admitted that it was a little ridiculous to care about a guy so much, so she did her best to focus all her attention on Eden during the day, and Clarise during meals now that the guys sat across the room from them. She was bound and determined to make it work that way for as long as possible.

Tonight would be no different. Rose took up her seat at their usual table, the first one there this time. Clarise typically beat her to the table as she didn't have the same schedule as Rose. It was much more lenient; all Clarise was tasked with during the day was the basic school work the younger trainees were required to do until they turned eighteen, and then her physical therapy later in the day.

Rosabella took a minute to look around, she observed that there weren't many people in the dining hall tonight.

*Odd.*

Rose waited about fifteen minutes for the other trainees to show up, picking at her food and checking her watch. They never came. Only a few people trickled into the dining hall during that time, the majority of them in their late twenties. Nobody from training was here. Nobody from her age bracket was here.

*Where was everyone?*

She ate the rest of her food as fast as she could. Maybe she'd been too quick to leave the training room. What if there was an announcement that she'd missed? Rose ate her banana on the way out of the dining hall, making her way back to the training room. Even the hallways were empty.

When she returned to the training room, she was frustrated to find it empty. Rose tossed her banana peel into the nearest trash chute and resisted the urge to scream. *What the hell?* She crossed the room, peeking into the younger trainees' room to see if people had migrated in there for something.

There was nothing. The motion sensored lights had gone down. The safety lights bathed the room in a spooky, dim orange glow. She slammed the adjoining door, hand tense around the handle. This had to be some kind of trick or something. Was she in a nightmare?

If Clarise hadn't made it to dinner, did that mean something bad was happening? Rose's wristband hadn't alerted her of anything....or maybe it was malfunctioning and she'd missed an announcement or emergency alarm.

She spotted a light under the door near the end of the separating wall. It was the door for the trainers' office.

*Finally*! Someone for her to talk to! Surely they'd help her sort this all out. Rosabella crossed her fingers, thinking, *please be Eden. Please be Eden.* She tucked her hair behind her ears, a nervous habit she hadn't quite shaken. Her mother used to scold her for it; she'd tell Rose she shouldn't be nervous about anything. Great advice mom, tell the nervous girl not to be nervous, *that'll* help for sure!

She lifted a shaking hand to the door, rapping her knuckles three times. She played with the ends of her hair while she stared at the grey door. It reminded her of the bleakness of the roads above. They were perfectly paved and smooth up there, without any imperfections. This door had dents and chips of paint missing; Rose preferred this door to any old road. It had more personality; she could relate to the chips missing too.

The door swung open. A toned-bodied, brown-eyed man filled the doorway. It was Clayton. *Great.*

"Hey. Can I help you with something?" Clayton asked, voice cool.

Her jaw almost fell. She regained her composure and made sure to keep her voice low. "Umm yeah, you can start by telling me why you've been acting so strange these last few weeks."

Clayton looked past her. "Sure, we can talk about your training. Come on in."

She scoffed, the sudden urge to smack him on the chest flooding her thoughts. "If you don't tell me what's going on with you--"

Clayton took her by the arm and pulled her into the room. The door shut with a solid click behind her. He turned the lock on the knob, trapping her inside the room. Had it been anyone else, Rose might have thought it creepy. Since it was Clayton, who was terrible at speaking his mind, she gave him the benefit of the doubt--just as she'd promised she would.

He leaned his back against the door, sighing. "Sorry, I just saw one of the janitors come in to clean the training room. I didn't want them to see you come in here."

Her insides twisted. "Why not?"

His eyes grew wide for a second, and he crossed the room to stand in front of her. "I didn't mean that! I just meant because...well, I'm not exactly sure what I meant." He reached a hand to touch her cheek.

She took a step back. Clayton's hand fell limp at his side.

Crossing her arms, she fumed. "If you're embarrassed to be seen with me, just say it." She turned away. "You know, I'm getting really sick of your mood swings, Clayton. I don't like beating myself up for something I know I didn't do! You're the problem, not me."

"No, no, no! I don't think that about you at all!" He took a step closer, closing the space. "And please believe me, I know. I hate that you've been beating yourself up over this."

"Then, what?" Rose let him take her hands in his, but pretended she didn't feel anything. It was all a lie; she felt every organ inside her turn over, excited to have him touch her again. She hoped he couldn't feel her pulse in her hands, it was everywhere in her body now.

"I'm just--I don't want people to assume things if they see us together." He sighed. "It's difficult enough for people to see you as a normal trainee since you basically survived something impossible. And what would they think if they saw you galavanting around with a hard-ass trainer like me?"

She couldn't help the smile that played on her lips. Her mood was already improving. He wasn't good with words, that's for sure.

"Hard-ass? *Galavanting?*" she asked, smirking up at him.

"You know what I mean! It would ruin your reputation." He wasn't upset, only teasing. Clayton let her hands go and sat down on the table, eye level with her now. He draped an arm over his bent knee, cocked his head and smiled. "What's on your mind?"

"Is this your office? I thought other people shared it with you?" she asked, looking around at the disorganization to distract herself from gazing at Clayton.

The room wasn't huge. It was only big enough to fit a circular table for six and a desk on the back wall. Papers were stacked in piles everywhere, completely covering any of the desk's surface. One wall fit three shelves, which were filled with more books. Rose squinted to get a better look. They were mostly about training and nutrition.

Clay laughed. "It is a little messy isn't it? It's a joint office...I've been trying to get the others to clean up a bit, but they don't have time." He shrugged. "I guess I could do something about it, but I wouldn't want to mess up their piles." He looked around the room, avoiding eye contact. "But that's not why you're here, is it? You came to see me because you wanted to hit me for the way I've been acting lately...am I right?"

Rose shoved his shoulder. It didn't do much. "I came here because I wanted to know where everyone was, it just so happens you were the only one in here. *Unfortunately,*" she added with extra emphasis. Then she tapped her chin, smiling. "But now that you mention it, I would love to take you up on that offer."

He wrapped an arm around her waist, drawing her in. "I'd like to see you try."

Giggling like mad, she pushed against his chest. Clayton was much too strong for her; he'd had years of this extensive training, and she'd had what, a little over a month?

He freed her, but not before brushing a hand against her thigh. She shivered from his touch, speechless again. Rose, unable to move, stood there with her hands on his shoulders for support. She was breathing heavily.

She shook herself out of her daze. "How do you manage that?"

"Manage what?"

"I can get so mad at you one second, and then all of a sudden it's gone like that," she complained, snapping her fingers for emphasis. Not to mention, she enjoyed the goosebumps that rose along her skin from his touch. How was that even possible, to despise and crave someone all at the same time? It was unusual for her to be so calm with someone other than her family and Aire touching her. But she did want a change of pace; and besides, nothing was the same anymore.

"Is it because of my ridiculously good looks? You did tell Aire that I was handsome."

Rose tipped her head back and groaned. "Don't let that get to your head. Besides, you're on very thin ice."

"I know, I know," he laughed, holding his hands up. "I'm sorry. I really am. But I've been really busy with the newest round of saves. Bernard tasked me with being in charge of their training and it's taken a lot out of me, constantly having to monitor them. Besides, you don't want people to see you with me and associate you with my anger and terrible attitude, do you?"

Nowhere in that apology did he mention Tess. Rose was not about to bring it up again. Not yet.

"I thought I was already known as the only girl who survived a droid attack? I'm supposed to be famous or something." She stuck her nose in the air, pretending to be snooty. "Doesn't that give me a pretty good image? Better than you even?"

"You are so cute sometimes, I can't handle it," he said, voice low. Clay placed his hands on her hips.

Too stunned to say anything, she laughed nervously. The lights flickered then. In response, Clayton's face fell, but he didn't let go of her.

Rose looked up at the ceiling. "What is it?"

"Someone just used the elevator. I bet it was those teenagers again."

Oh *right*! She'd nearly forgotten what she came here for in the first place.

"Speaking of teenagers, where is everyone?"

"You mean, you don't know?"

She shook her head. Rose hadn't heard anything from anyone about leaving the Fortress. Surely she'd have remembered.

"Tonight is a full moon. The teenagers like to 'sneak' out and take a trip to the world above to watch the moon." He scoffed, "It's usually where people party the night away and get into trouble. It's basically a tradition for us...among other things."

"Don't we all have training tomorrow?" She didn't realize he'd drawn her even closer to him. Their faces were merely inches apart now.

A gentle squeeze on her hips took the breath from her lungs.

"No, it's Saturday tomorrow, silly."

*Oh.* So she'd been left out of something...again. She hoped things would've been different down here. She'd grown sick of going to school on Mondays up above, specifically after a long weekend of her classmates partying. Rose never enjoyed being left out of anything then, and it sure didn't get easier with time.

She didn't know what expression crossed her face, but Clayton didn't like it, whatever it was. He stood up, snagging his sweatshirt from a nearby chair.

"C'mon. I'll show you."

Rose stood her ground and placed her hands on her hips. "I thought you didn't want to be seen with me."

He let out a sound that was a cross between a laugh and a growl. "Oh would you stop that? I can't stand to look at you when you're being so stubborn."

She fought a smile. "Oh, so now I'm *ugly*? You're not helping your case much."

"You've got to be kidding me. Get over here!" He ran at Rose and lifted her over his shoulder like she weighed nothing more than a flower. "I'm taking you to see the moon whether you like it or not!"

She laughed all the way to the elevator.

# Chapter 23

## (ANDRE)

PEOPLE WERE SPRAWLED OUT EVERYWHERE THERE WAS ROOM. Now that this neighborhood was vacant--thanks to the droid attack that brought Rosabella and her other classmates to the Fortress--they didn't need to be as cautious. They could talk without fear of someone hearing them. They were all supposed to be carrying around fake identification cards with them, just in case they were caught by anyone and were questioned. It would be difficult for anyone to card all the Fortress citizens if they stayed in this big group. Besides, Andre was never one to worry about those details. He didn't need to; he had his brute force to protect himself. He was head of external security for a reason.

Bernard had entrusted him with the perimeter control when he was younger, to see how he handled it, and Andre had taken it very seriously since day one. It was his first choice for a career and he'd been grateful for the opportunity.

He really shouldn't have come tonight. Andre could get into a lot of trouble with Bernard if he were caught. It wasn't technically "illegal," but it was definitely not encouraged for the head of external security. Bernard would scold Andre and probably assign him with an extra mission or two.

It was meant to be a night for the teenagers to be reckless. It was basically a rite of passage for the newbies too. It hadn't originally been in the cards for Andre to go tonight; he'd thought he was too old for these things. But when Clarise batted her big, brown eyes at him, he knew he was done for. She wanted someone "strong" to escort her up the elevator and back, she'd said. He didn't even hesitate in obliging.

Clayton didn't go to these things, so Andre was in the clear. Besides, if Clayton found out Andre had taken his little sister to the moon viewing, he wouldn't think much of it. Or so he hoped. There was no telling with Clayton. Sometimes Andre didn't know if he was going to get carefree, happy Clay or scary, furious Clay.

"Is this a good spot?" he asked, pushing Clarise's wheelchair across the patchy grass. He made sure to stay at the back of the group, in the shadows. She would understand why he couldn't be seen--especially not with her.

Clarise nodded, biting her lip to keep from crying out. He hit a bump and the chair tilted on one wheel. Andre let go of the handles to grab the armrests to right it. In the process, he brushed her wrist. It drove him crazy, not being able to tell her how he really felt.

He released the wheelchair once he straightened it, unsure how she would react. The moonlight on Clarise's skin was making him lose his mind. It cast a dark shadow over her face, making her brown eyes look black. He wanted to kiss her eyelids.

"I'm so sorry, are you alright?" he asked, voice strained. *Wow, way to play it cool, Andre.*

Clarise looked over her shoulder at him, that smirk he loved so much tugging at the corner of her mouth. "Did I make the wrong decision, asking you to bring me, Dre?"

He leaned back casually, letting the tree behind him hold his weight. He wanted to look calm, cool and collected--the complete opposite of how he felt. While he leaned back, he crossed his arms. But where there was supposed to be a tree, wound up being only air. He fell back into a pile of branches and leaves, Clarise laughing at him. He lay on his back and looked up at her curiously. She clutched at her sides, doubled over in her chair.

A smile came to his face, not because he'd looked ridiculous falling over, but because he'd made her laugh.

"Thank you, that was my first trick of the night," he said brushing himself off.

"Umm, oh, Andre the Great, you have a leaf in your hair," she giggled.

He knelt in front of her, face inches away. "Can you get it for me?"

If he didn't know any better, he'd say she sucked in a breath. And she hadn't released it yet. Clarise's eyes grew wide and then she trailed her gaze from his eyes, to his nose, then his mouth.

His own voice sounded breathless when he whispered, "You don't have to do anything you don't want to. In all fairness, I was truly asking for help with the leaf." He angled away to make her less uncomfortable.

She grabbed his face in her hands and pulled him closer. "Don't worry, I'm not scared of you."

Wow. A bold move for a teenager. He grinned from ear to ear and kissed the tip of her nose. They both stopped breathing, Andre with his lips hovering inches from Clarise's.

"We shouldn't do this out in the open," Clarise breathed. "You know, in case anyone tells my brother."

Right. That life threatening detail.

"You're right. Why don't I take you out of your chair? We can rest our backs against this rock."

Clarise smirked, sending his head spinning. "Okay, but don't miss this time," she teased.

He shook his head, laughing. "Let's not talk about that ever again."

"Oh, trust me. I'll be bringing that up any chance I get," she said. Her smile flickered for a second, but stayed on her face while he lifted her out of the chair.

They both knew she wouldn't talk about it with Clayton around. That was a given. Too bad, it was pretty funny. Clayton would have laughed his ass off and teased Andre relentlessly. But he wasn't here and he wasn't supposed to know that it had happened.

Andre folded her chair and hid it behind their big rock. Then he settled in next to Clarise, an arm around her waist. She sighed and leaned into him.

During their workout, Andre hadn't just told *Clayton* to get the girl, he'd also been talking to himself.

\*\*\*

## (ROSABELLA)

Rose and Clay rode the elevator up in the dark. She didn't mind it so much now. It wasn't awful like last time; she wasn't reeling from the pain in her skull. It also helped that Clayton linked their hands.

She didn't want him to hear her little gasps of breath. His touch had a strange effect on her, like every time they made contact, he stole her breath away, even her heartbeat. Couples didn't show much affection up above, perhaps because most of them were paired with people they'd never met. It seemed to take longer for people to "fall in love." That didn't mean Rose was opposed to affection...she just hadn't experienced it in public places before. Her parents were an exception; they'd cuddle on the couch during family movie nights and kiss on the lips in front of Rose and her brother. Those times were rare, and confined to their home.

"I thought we weren't allowed to use the elevator without permission?" Rose asked to distract him from her strange breathing that was now echoing off the walls.

"We aren't. Head of mission control lets us get by on nights like these. It's kind of like an unwritten rite of passage. Sometimes an assistant will take over, but tonight I'm pretty sure it's the head."

"Hmm." She thought about that. Did Bernard know they snuck out? Would the head of mission control get in trouble too? She remembered something from her meeting with Bernard and his Cabinet. "Wait! Isn't *Logan* head of mission control?"

Clayton looped an arm around her waist. He mumbled, "Mhmm."

She pushed him away, as gentle as possible. Who was she kidding? The only time she was able to push Clayton away was when he let her.

"But doesn't that mean he can't enjoy the moon viewing either?"

He sighed and nudged his chin against her forehead. His voice still had that husky edge to it when he replied, "Don't worry about him, Rose. He volunteers for this most of the time."

"Oh." That was awfully kind of him. What would it be like to be that selfless? Logan had done nothing but help Rosabella through some tough situations. She hadn't done much to thank him, she realized. Getting lunch and dinner with him wasn't the same as thanking him. She made a mental note to pull him aside and thank him tomorrow.

The elevator opened to the one way wall. Rose's breath caught in her throat. The last time she'd been in her own home, she'd flirted with death.

Clayton let her lead the way, keeping a few feet between them. She was grateful he respected her space, but she wasn't sure if she wanted him near her or not. They passed from the pantry to the kitchen. The dishes were in the same place she'd seen them that night she escaped.

Her heart fell. She'd half hoped to come up and see her family sitting in the dining room, waiting for her to return.

"It's highly probable they were able to escape somewhere else," Clayton said quietly. It's like he read her thoughts.

To distract herself, Rose turned her face away and looked toward the living room. "How did people come in and out and I never saw them?"

Clay crossed his arms. "We have a camera system set up all around the house, so that helps us to time our exits and entrances. And usually, when you and your family were gone at school and work, we'd take advantage of the empty house."

She froze, thinking of a smirking Andre watching her shower. "Cameras?"

He smiled down at her. "Don't worry, we don't have anything in the bedrooms or bathrooms."

Rosabella wanted to smile, to joke around with him. But it was too difficult. She couldn't stop thinking of what happened to her family. She wished Clayton would touch her, or wrap his arms around her. Rose wanted to feel safe. It's what her mom would've done. That wasn't Clayton's way though; or he just didn't know she wanted that. Clay let her grieve on her own in silence. The last thing she desired was a chance to feel the hurt again.

"Come on," she said, her back to him. He followed obediently until they reached a comfortable place near the back of the crowd. They remained there for a while, long enough for Rose to peek at the rest of her fellow trainees; they were all so happy and peaceful.

She found it fascinating the Fortress-born citizens were so obsessed with coming out to see the moon. It was the simple things in her life she'd taken for granted. At the time, Rose didn't know there *was* anything to be taken for granted--at least not the moon. There'd been no one to tell her about the underground society running around right below her kitchen. All those days she was sick of the same old cycle and yearning for change, she could have just stepped into her pantry downstairs and bam, she'd have a whole new life. Had her parents known? Surely if they had, they would have escaped there, right?

"What's on your mind?" Clayton asked. Leaves clung to the ends of her hair, and he plucked a few out, tossing them away. The grass wasn't real, but the line of trees to their backs certainly were; and this was the time they all started shedding their leaves.

Rose turned on her side to see Clayton better. The artificial grass did nothing to offer her hips any comfort, but she couldn't complain. Not when she was in the arms of Clayton Taylor. He had an arm under her neck, creating a pillow of muscle. She had her arms tucked in close to her body to keep warm, and her legs curled up, pressed against his thighs. She could feel his body heat through his jeans, relishing in the feeling of someone else's body pressed against her own.

"My family," Rose mumbled, pressing her forehead into the space between his shoulder and his neck. It was her favorite place on earth at the moment. She'd only discovered it twenty minutes or so ago, but she knew it was where she was meant to be. It had to be. No other place felt as safe or secure as Clayton's arms. "Where they are. What really happened. You know, the ugly, gritty details."

Clay kissed the tip of her nose and brushed her hair back with his free hand. Then, shifting so he was using the boulder behind him as a backrest, Clayton pulled her up with him.

"Trust me, that's not a place you want to go. Not right now."

Any other previous day, she'd have thought he was kidding. Now Rose knew how to listen for the shift in his tone from teasing to serious. Right now, he was sincere.

She leaned her head back on his chest, staring up at the moon. On a whim, Rose decided to take a chance. "Want to talk about it?"

His arms draped around her, fingers resting near her bellybutton. "No...not yet."

Eyes still on the large moon that seemed to touch the skyline of the buildings, she sighed. "Well, I hope you don't intend to keep this to yourself forever. We should probably get to know one another better."

Clay's fingers danced around on her stomach. "Oh, I thought we knew each other pretty well...my racing heart would say so."

Rose rested her hands on his and giggled, quietly satisfied his heart was beating so fast. "You know what I mean."

He took in a breath. It was a long time before he released the air; when he did, Rosabella sunk further into him.

"I'd like to think I know you by now," he said eventually.

Rose's heart sped up. "Oh yeah?"

"Mhmm," he started. "I know that your neck and cheeks get red when you're embarrassed, your eyes blaze a brighter shade of blue when you're angry, you love to read about love in books, but you've never felt that way before; you give yourself to others before you give to yourself... shall I go on?"

"Oh, is *that* all?" she asked, her voice a whisper. He'd been paying attention to her? Almost as much as she had paid attention to him.

"No." Clay dipped his head to brush his lips against her neck. She happily tilted her head, exposing more skin to him. "I also know that you love the freedom the Fortress offers you. You wanted a change, a new life, and that's exactly what you got here; you have an unquenchable curiosity that even I can't seem to understand...there's more but I'm sure you want to kiss me now, if I'm not mistaken."

A laugh bubbled out of her. Where was the sudden bold attitude coming from? "But--"

"No. No buts. I *insist*. It's the least I can do for you."

"Fine. But on one condition."

He smiled. "I like where this is going."

She pulled away from him and turned, so she was sitting pretzel-legged in the space between his legs, hands resting in her lap. "Now now, I'm not implying what I think you think I'm implying."

He stuck out his bottom lip, teasing, "Well that's disappointing... Okay what is it?"

Rose elbowed his stomach, trying her best not to let him see how flattered--and unbelievably flustered--she was. "How about you get one kiss for every piece of your past you reveal to me?"

He went silent. Clayton turned his head, something in the distance obviously more important than her. Why did she constantly have to rush into things? What was wrong with her? Clayton was right, she did have an unquenchable curiosity. She couldn't stifle it no matter how hard she tried. It wasn't in her nature. Maybe that was the reason she always did well in school. It was really easy to teach someone who wanted to soak up as much knowledge as they could.

He'd been quiet so long, Rose considered getting up and leaving him there. But then he looked down at her, brushed a thumb along her jaw and whispered, "Alright, deal."

That frightened her. Rose knew herself well, and she was conscious enough to admit that learning about Clayton and his past was scary as hell. What if she didn't like what he had to say? Was she more scared of what his past contained, or was she more excited about kissing him? It was both, she admitted.

"Just...just try to have an open mind, alright? I'm not very good at making my life sound glamorous." He leaned back against the rock and casually rested a hand on each of Rose's hips. "I leave that to Prince, who can spin any story and make it sound like a fairytale."

"I promise, cross my heart," she swore solemnly, drawing an invisible X over her heart.

"Don't say I didn't warn you." Clay tried to smile, but it was a failed attempt. His lips curled, similar to a dog ready to attack. "Lay it on me. What's first?" He closed his eyes, forehead scrunching in anticipation.

*Start small*, a voice in her head shouted at her. "Okay, first, how did you discover the Fortress?"

"I'd be happy to tell you about that." He smiled, genuinely this time. "I was about fourteen. My friend and I were outside playing. She had just gotten this new soccer ball from her parents."

Rose's eyebrows rose involuntarily. She'd almost forgotten Clayton was a child at one point. It was so difficult to imagine this big, solemn guy had once been an innocent kid--not *completely* carefree. The Government enforced rules on children's playtime too.

He smiled. "I know. I know. Our parents were really lenient with our household rules. They let us play more than the average child." His hands moved down and started drawing a variety of shapes on her bare knees. Earlier, she wished she'd worn pants tonight instead of her shorts, but now she was glad she hadn't gone back for them. Clayton continued, "My friend, she thought it would be more fun to kick the ball back and forth on the street, because it was smoother. Easier for the ball to roll back and forth.

"As with most kids and their toys, we went slightly too far with the game. The distance between our goals grew wider and wider, until we'd nearly taken up the whole neighborhood's street. That also meant we had to kick the ball further. Harder. I remember how I wound up, taking a few steps back to prep. When the ball came at me, I raced forward and kicked with all my might," Clayton said, laughing at his own memory. "Needless to say, the ball went soaring through the sky way over her head. It hit a rooftop a few houses over, bounced a couple times, and rolled to the other side.

"Naturally, we chased after it, racing to see who'd make it first. I was always faster than her, so I got there, ready to snag the ball. As I rounded the house, I slipped and fell, crashing into someone there. Come to find out, it was seventeen-year-old Andre. I don't remember if he said anything as we fell to the ground, but I definitely remember him punching me in the jaw before pinning my shoulders into the dirt. Even back then, he was skilled in combat." He chuckled at that. Rose liked this side of him: nostalgic.

"That's when my friend showed up. She screamed for him to let me go, too scared to get her hands dirty to pull him off of me. In response, he just punched me again. I still can't say what would've happened if Bernard hadn't stepped in…"

"Why did Andre do that to you?" She asked, hands on his arms now. "I mean, why didn't he just let you take the ball and go away. You didn't know about the Fortress, did you?"

"No we didn't. That's just who he was. Is. That's what makes Dre so valuable to the Fortress and the Cabinet. He'll do what he needs to in order to protect his people."

"Wow."

"Yes, but don't worry…we're friends now," he said, the corners of his mouth twitching.

Rose rolled her eyes. "I guessed as much. Most people don't lie on the floor talking about the deepest parts of themselves with their enemies."

"You're so smart," Clayton replied with sarcasm.

Another smirk, another mischievous glint in his eyes. Oh no. What now?

He cleared his throat, hands coming to a stop on her knees again. "So, I think it's your turn to pay up."

Rose wasn't even sure if she had a human heart, it wasn't beating properly. A memory of a black heart thumping in a droid's chest flashed in her mind. Her hands, sweaty all of a sudden, stuck together.

"Umm, are you sure? I mean, there's got to be more to that story..." she trailed off, seeing the look on his face. It was unmistakable, she was trying to stall.

"You have to hold up your end of the bargain!" Clayton play-whined, leaning closer to her face. It took all she had not to pull away. How terrifying! What had she been thinking? Rose checked their surroundings. Was anyone watching them? No, Clayton and Rose were too far back from the rest of the group. Even still, everyone else was looking up and talking.

"Clay...I'm--I've never...."

He smiled. "What? Kissed someone before?"

She nodded, gazing at her hands.

"I was counting on that."

"What?" she peered at Clay.

"Well you're from up here, so it wouldn't be common for you to go locking lips with just any guy."

Crossing her arms, she glared at him. "Are you saying I'm *unkissable*?!"

"Of course not! In fact, you look more kissable than anyone else I've ever met." His voice was even, calm. Then he looked away and ran his hands down his legs. If Rose didn't know any better, she thought he was wiping sweaty palms. Was he just as nervous as she was? That gave her a nudge of confidence.

"Are you nervous, Clayton?" Rosabella teased, playing into his nerves. It wasn't common for him to show emotion this way; the only emotion he was consistent with was anger. She stopped laughing when he looked back at her. His eyes were full of emotion, his lips clamped together. "Hey, hey I didn't mean anything bad by that," she said, voice quiet. She took his face in her hands and brought their noses together. "Maybe if we--"

Something soft brushed against Rose's lips. With a start, she realized Clayton was kissing her, light at first, lips barely grazing hers. Soon, his hands found their way around her, one landing on her lower back, the other on the back of her head. She wanted more than a butterfly kiss, so she did what any sane woman would do when she was no longer in charge of her own mind, she knelt and tugged at the front of his shirt, forcing him closer. Their teeth knocked against one another and she started to apologize. But then Clay continued kissing her, blocking out the apology she'd already forgotten about. It wasn't a sloppy, wet kiss, but a gentle, *I respect you* kind of kiss.

After seconds, minutes, hours--she'd lost track--Clayton leaned back, breathing heavy. Rose rocked back against her heels and stared up at him. Something like delight and a sense of freedom blossomed in her bones, thawing her freezing legs and aching heart.

"How did I do?" she asked. *What the--who the hell asks that?* Instead of smacking her forehead, like she really considered doing, Rose sighed loudly and leaned all the way back until she was lying flat on the ground, legs resting in front of Clayton. Rosabella stared up at the moon, wondering why the heck she'd just messed a good thing up. Again. Couldn't she learn to keep her fat mouth shut?

She listened to Clayton's breathing slow as it returned to normal, and examined the moon. Sure, it was bright and beautiful, but what about those dark spots on it? Did people ever point those spots out, tell their kids, "Hey, that moon is flawed just like humanity, but we still manage to find the beauty in it"? If Rose ever had children, would she start the new trend? People always seemed to assume that for something to be beautiful, there had to be a complete absence of any flaws. Rose never agreed with that way of thinking. Those flaws were what drew her in; things that people thought were blemishes gave objects and people their true beauty.

Clayton shuffled but she didn't look to see what he was doing. Rose didn't want to watch his back while he left her there alone. Would he treat her the same tomorrow morning? Or would he revert back to his unfeeling gaze, never acknowledging her when they passed one another in the hall or during training?

She felt slight pressure on her stomach and lifted her head to see what it was. Rose's heart stopped. It was Clayton. He was using her as a pillow, head resting carefully on her stomach. She laid her head back down, barely breathing, and bent her legs. A wave of self-consciousness washed over her. What if she breathed out too hard or took in too big a breath and her stomach moved up and down under his head?

Clayton reached a hand behind his head and touched her side, under her sweatshirt. The breath she was trying to regulate caught in her throat when he began drawing circles on her skin.

"Wasn't this something like what Maxon did to America in *The Elite*? He traced her skin like this..." he whispered. His warm fingers sent a ripple effect of chills along her stomach and down her legs. "You can breathe, Rose."

Oh. Right.

"I'm too scared," she said, trembling. In all honesty, Rose *did* try to breathe like usual. The rough, artificial grass underneath them seemed soft and cloud-like then. Her toes curled in her shoes as her hands found their way to his hair. She stared up at the moon.

"Why are you scared? That was fantastic." Clayton sat up and propped himself up on one elbow over her. His eyes turned to slits and a smile played on his lips. "Are you sure you've never kissed anyone before?"

"I'm sure." If she looked at him, she wouldn't be able to control herself. To fix that, she acted as enthralled with the moon as her Fortress-born peers. Clayton saw right through her.

"Hey....*hey*," he said, louder the second time. "Damn it, Rosabella. Would you look at me?"

She squeezed her eyes shut and shook her head.

"Did I do that bad of a job?" he asked. The way his voice faded out at the end led Rose to think he was embarrassed. She needed to set that straight right now.

"No." She cleared her throat and rubbed her eyes. "That was... indescribable."

"Okay, so then why are you acting like I bit you--?" he stopped. "Oh, god. I didn't *bite* you, did I?"

Didn't he know how vulnerable this made her feel? Was he messing with her? She wouldn't be able to handle it if this turned out to be a joke or something that he and Andre came up with. She'd never kissed anyone ever in her life, and this first time was amazing. She feared she was falling in too deeply with Clayton already. The scariest part was that she didn't know what his thoughts were.

Rose pushed herself up on her elbows and glared at him. "No, you didn't bite me."

His eyebrows drew together and his mouth puckered. "Then why are you upset? I thought we were playing a game you wanted."

Why are you doing this?"

"Doing what?"

"Treating me like I matter when I obviously don't?" She dropped her hands to her sides. Her chest heaved, but she didn't feel it. "You ignore me for days and then you say you care about me? And I mean, come on, using *The Elite* to make me like you. To make me trust you. That's low. You should know, I'm not the type of girl you 'play around' with."

"What? It's because I like you! I'm not trying to do anything more than make you happy!" Clayton ran his fingers through his hair. "Women are so confusing. I'll never understand."

Rose had no idea who he was speaking to, and she didn't care anyway. She crossed her arm and glared at his chest.

"Seriously, if you just tell me what's wrong we can get this all straightened out," he said, matching her stance, legs shoulder width apart. "Did you not like our kiss?"

"No, you asshole. It's because I enjoyed our kiss. More than you, it seems." She turned her head. "I don't want to be your toy that you kiss when you feel like it. If it doesn't mean anything to you, I don't want any part of it."

He threw his hands in the air. "I don't know what you think you know, but I absolutely *loved* kissing you. It was exactly how I imagined it."

*What?* The fists she didn't even notice she was making relaxed. "You... you imagined our first kiss?"

He scoffed. "So *now* she listens to me....Yes, Rose. I've been wanting to kiss you for a while now. I thought I made that pretty obvious."

She tried to collect her thoughts before saying anything. The ice was so thin, if she said one word wrong, she'd fall through into the freezing water.

"Clayton, I--I just thought...well because you--"

"Rose," he said, silencing her. "If you are implying that I--"

"No. Let me finish." She held up her hands. "That kiss--*our* kiss--I was just worried it was too good to be true. I shouldn't have jumped to conclusions."

Clay held a hand over his mouth for a second. "You do matter to me, Rose. I don't open myself up to many people...."

She nodded. "Yes, I know."

He stepped a foot closer, eyes on the ground near her feet. "So when I opened myself up, when I *kissed* you, I wasn't messing around. This is real to me."

Rose stepped closer. "I'm glad you said that."

Clayton scoffed. "Are you going to say it too? Or are you just going to leave me out to dry?"

She took one of his hands and guided it to her cheek. She enjoyed watching his eyes trace the lines of her body as he worked his way up to her eyes. Rose covered his hand with hers and leaned into his touch.

"This is real to me too."

His mouth smiled against her nose. "We aren't very good at this whole relationship thing, are we?"

She swallowed. "Relationship?"

"Yes," he said laughing, "if you want, of course."

She lifted her eyes to the sky. "Hmmm, I may need to think about that--" Suddenly, Rose's eyes landed on Andre, partially hidden by a rock. Or rather, Andre and *Clarise.*

# Chapter 24

**(ANDRE)**

"Are you okay? You can have my sweatshirt if you're too cold," Andre said, rubbing Clarise's arms. She was positioned between his legs, her back resting on his chest. She'd been quiet for so long he'd begun to think she was cold or sleeping or something. Andre Harrison was never at a loss for words, so this was a change. It just so happened that, whenever he would say things, they would be inappropriate or demeaning to women. He wasn't going to speak to Clair that way. She meant something different to him. There was no way to explain it.

"I'm alright, thanks."

Was she purposely making her voice sound hollow and uncaring?

"Andre?"

His heart raced at the way she said his name. "What's up?"

"Your heart is beating awfully fast for a moon viewing."

He didn't know whether to laugh or groan, so he made a sound that was a mixture of the two.

"Don't worry, I won't tell anyone," Clarise said. When she turned around to peek at him, he was already looking at her. A strand of hair fell in front of her eyes and he couldn't resist touching her. He tucked it behind her ear, letting his fingers linger a second longer.

"Do you know what I want to do right now?" He asked. *Oops*, probably not the thing to say to a girl you like. Andre really didn't know how to talk to a woman respectfully; he'd spent too many years telling them what they wanted to hear.

She shook her head, rolling her eyes. "Please don't say something you'll regret. Don't ruin this."

Clarise always knew what he was thinking before he did. But this time, he wasn't thinking about anything remotely close to what it sounded like he implied.

Andre tapped her nose--his favorite feature. "No, it's not *that*. I just meant I want to hold you tight and never let you go."

Clair shrugged. "Okay, then. Why don't you?"

He gulped, something hard stuck in his throat. "Clayton would kill me if he heard me say that."

She nodded. "Clayton would kill you if he so much as saw you touch my shoulder. You're as good as dead."

He smiled. "Gee, thanks."

"Just trying to keep you grounded with a big slap of reality."

Andre chuckled. "You're just like him. Both of you have this wit that I can't seem to prepare for no matter how many times I anticipate it."

Clarise's face turned to stone, her chocolate eyes darkened. "No I'm not. Please don't say that."

What did she mean by that? Before he could ask, Andre heard a woman's voice clear as day. It cut through his thoughts, disrupting his moment with Clarise. They both turned toward the voice.

"Well, *Clayton* I think we can actually agree on something."

Clarise gasped when she saw Rose and Clayton standing two or so yards away. Andre covered Clarise's mouth with his hand so she didn't draw their attention. He tucked an arm under her legs and one behind her back and lifted her. Luckily the moon's light hadn't reached their little corner, so they hadn't spotted them yet. Their heads were bent close together and Clay's back was to them, so he hadn't seen his sister with Andre.

"Andre? How do we get out of here without him seeing us?" Clarise hissed in his ear.

"I'm working on that," he said breathless. The pressure was all on Andre now. He couldn't very well just leave Clarise alone. She wouldn't be able to get around all the people lying on the ground in her wheelchair. This reminded him of the first time he'd competed against Clayton in combat after weeks of training. Back then, he'd been confident for about

2.3 seconds before Clayton threw the first punch, nearly knocking Andre off his feet. After that he was a bundle of nerves the whole time. Once Andre let himself get comfortable, life seemed to enjoy slapping him in the face. Clarise wasn't kidding when she said he needed a reality check.

Fully alert, Andre double-checked Clayton's position. He wasn't as worried about Rosabella seeing them. Maybe she wouldn't even register them long enough for them to slip away.

Rose wrapped her arms around Clayton's neck. "I just realized I never held up my end of our deal."

"Oh yeah?" asked Clayton as he leaned down to touch his forehead to hers.

"You told me another secret about yourself and I haven't repaid you yet. You told me you've been wanting to kiss me for a while now," Rosabella's sugary sweet voice sang through the air.

Whatever they were talking about, Andre had no intention of listening. When they started making out, Andre would haul ass back to the Fortress, Clarise in one arm and wheelchair in the other.

"Rose, that doesn't need to count if you don't want it to," Clayton said. "I don't want to make you do something you don't want to do."

Andre hoped they were only talking about kissing. Either that, or Clayton really knew how to move fast! Andre would have to remember to ask his friend for tips--but not to use on Clarise. That was one girl he was going to respect.

"It's okay. I trust you," Rose said, her voice dropping off at the end. They were so bad at flirting! Andre almost had the right mind to march up to them and teach them a thing or two.

He adjusted so Clarise was on his back instead of in his arms, prepping to sprint away the second Clayton and Rose's lips touched.

"When they kiss are you going to make a run for it?" Clair asked. Her arms were tight around Andre's neck, but he didn't dare complain. There was no reason for her to feel bad.

"Yes."

She buried her face in his collar. "Okay, but don't let me look until it's over."

"You got it," he replied, voice husky. He cleared his throat as quiet as possible and bent his knees, ready to pounce.

But then Clayton changed his mind. "How about we slow down a bit? That wasn't really fair of me to throw that at you so soon."

No, no, no! *Screw you, Clayton Taylor, and your stupid chivalry!* It was overrated anyway! Women didn't want a man to do everything they say, they wanted a man with brute force, who could protect them before anything else.

"Okay, thank you," Rose said, smiling without teeth. Andre hated when she did that because it made her look so endearing--especially when she wore blue like the sweatshirt she had on now--and he was supposed to be focused on getting away. Women in general just fascinated him. Especially when he couldn't tell what they were thinking. It was like trying to put a complicated puzzle together and to do so, you had to guess what was on their mind. Andre almost never succeeded in putting the whole puzzle together, but who needed puzzles when you had lips and hands?

Rose wrapped her arms around Clayton's waist and pressed her face to his shoulder. Clayton adapted quickly, wrapping her up in a bear hug. He nuzzled into her neck and stayed there. Was this the moment Andre dared to take?

He detected a flash of blue when Rose adjusted her head on Clayton's shoulder. The two of them made eye contact and Andre's heart stopped. *Please don't tell him, please don't tell him,* he willed to her.

Rose surprised him. She pointed in the direction of the house and mouthed "go." Andre didn't need to hear it twice. He snapped up and ran, not stopping until he and Clarise stood on the Fortress's floor.

# Chapter 25

## (ROSABELLA)

CLAYTON WRAPPED AN ARM AROUND ROSE'S SHOULDERS. "C'MON. Why don't we head back?"

"Sure," she said, keeping a slow pace. She didn't know how long Andre and Clarise would need to get back to the Fortress. Rose couldn't let them get caught. Not tonight. Clay was in too good a mood and that would change at the drop of a hat if he saw his best friend with his little sister.

Rose tugged at her sweatshirt's strings. She kept one arm around Clayton's waist and headed for the Fortress. It had baffled her to see Clarise with Andre--of all people, why did it have to be *him*? Andre was such a dirty, sleazy guy! Not to mention, there were like eight years between the two of them! Rose recalled the conversation she had with Clarise a while ago, the night they first read *The Elite* together. Clarise had seemed so gung-ho on damaged guys with backstories. Little did she know Clair had been referring to Andre. Besides, what was Andre's deal anyway? What had damaged him and turned him into this disrespectful man?

Clayton's pace slowed. "Rose, I just want to say something. Please don't laugh--"

She never got the chance to hear what he had to say. People began shouting and running. Rosabella turned around in time to see a pair of blinding white headlights turn the corner into the neighborhood. The car sped around the corner, tires squealing. She'd recognize a Government car anywhere.

"Oh, shit! You don't have an ID card yet," Clayton shouted. "We have to run!"

Her mind raced. An ID card? What was the point of that? No time to ask about that now. Rose's body said run. She clutched Clayton's hand as he led her away from the car. And away from the Fortress.

"Sorry for...asking," she said, the air catching in her throat. "But shouldn't we...be going *toward* the...Fortress?...You know...for safety?" Her legs burned and her shoulder throbbed from being pulled by Clayton. She didn't even stop to think about the pain in her side. Rose never looked back to see which people the government had decided to pursue.

"We can't lead them there." Clayton thundered forward, putting as much distance between the Government's car and themselves as he could. He was more worried about Rose than she was.

Rosabella wanted to stop but she knew they couldn't. As they wove through houses, houses that had once been familiar to her, she felt her legs begin to shake. If she continued on like this, Rose was going to collapse.

"Clay, how are you...not dying?" she gasped.

The sound of a car's engine covered up whatever he said in response. The bright lights shone on them from behind, Clayton's shadow accentuating his height and build. Rose's on the other hand, looked like a fat potato with stringy hair flying around her head. The epitome of beauty for sure.

"Keep going. Don't stop!" Clayton seethed between closed teeth. His hand on hers squeezed so hard she cried out.

The squealing of tires screeched in her ears. Rose bit her cheeks to keep from screaming. It rang in her head similar to when she'd been immobilized by the whirring pain.

"Damn it," Clayton shouted, coming to an abrupt halt. The car sped ahead of them and whipped around, blocking their way and digging up piles of artificial grass in its wake. Rose smacked into his back and felt rather than heard him growl, "Get behind me."

"No problem, I'm already there." She thought maybe he would smirk at her, but he paid her no mind. His glare was locked on the person jumping out of the car. Rose's heart was in her stomach, dropping lower and lower with each passing second.

"State your names." A woman said in a low gravelly voice. She stopped in front of one of the headlights. Rose put her hand down to shield her eyes. The woman pointed a shiny black object at them. Rose clenched the back of Clayton's shirt in her hands. A *gun*? She'd only read about those in history books. They'd caused too much trouble in the past, especially during the Cataclysmic Civil War. Where had they come by those? Oh, right. They worked for the Government. That about summed it up. If Government guards were using guns this openly, it meant they'd been using them for a while and had been hiding them from the rest of the country. Or maybe everyone knew. She never thought to check in with anything going on up above since she'd woken up in the Fortress.

Rose looked down and felt a surge of anger. Why was she letting Clayton stand in front of her? If he took the bullets from a gun, she'd never forgive herself. He'd been underground far longer than her; Clay wouldn't know how to talk to them. And these people might know her dad. Or better yet, they might know where he was right now.

Rose let go of Clayton's shirt and stepped in front of him. "Do you know Harley Porter?"

Clay's hands wrapped around her and pulled her to the side. "Are you crazy?"

The woman waved the gun in the air. "Shut up! Don't you see what I have in my hands? Stop moving around!"

Rose pushed Clayton away. "Shut up. I got this." She faced the woman and inched her way forward, hands in the air. Rose knew her legs were sickly pale, and in this light they must've looked like a beacon shouting, "hey, come and shoot me."

"Rose?" Clayton asked, holding his hands up.

"State your names and shut the hell up!" The woman screamed, finger poised over the trigger.

She tried again. "Do you know Harley Porter? He's my dad."

The woman squinted. "What's your name?"

A second person jumped out of the car and raced toward them. Clayton groaned and moved next to Rose. She didn't need protection from him; if anything he needed to be protected by *her*. These were people she didn't know, but who might know her father. They'd listen to her before they even looked at Clayton. They kept their hands up, while

Rose waited for the woman to help her get the information she needed. Meanwhile, the man from the car reached them, stepping just out of the way of the headlight, so Rose wasn't able to see his face.

He spoke quickly, "Rosabella Mae Porter? Rose?"

She snuck a look at Clayton. He was staring at her, mouth in a grimace. Only her family--and Clayton--knew her middle name. Then she turned back to the man, using one hand to shield her eyes. The woman with the gun straightened her arm again and pointed it directly at Rose.

The man held out his hand to the woman. "Give me that. This is Rosabella!"

"Sir?" the woman asked as she handed the gun, barrel down, to him.

"Rose," the mystery man said, walking toward her. Rose saw Clayton tense from the corner of her eye. "Your father's been worried sick."

The way he said it, with an edge to his voice, made Rose wary. Her dad? He stepped in the light, shielding her face from it. If eyes could scream with delight, hers would have. She was developing a headache from squinting into the light. He looked like an average man, on the shorter side, with grey eyes and dark reddish hair. Rosabella didn't recognize him. She wondered if Clayton recognized him from before he moved to the Fortress, since they looked similar in age.

"Emily, please go back to the car. I will escort these two there in a moment," his gaze flicked between Clayton and Rose. The woman nodded once and left, leaving them alone with this man she'd never met before. He held out his hand for her to shake, "Now, let's get down to business. We may not have much time before we get you back to Government Headquarters. I'm Grayson. I'm sure your dad told you about me at least once?"

She racked her brain, flipping through every memory around in order to find something about him. She vaguely remembered a man knocking on their door one night while her family was finishing up dinner. Her father excused himself and answered the door. Rose remembered him pulling a man aside, into their living room and having a discussion with him until she went upstairs to bed. A glint of red hair. A flash of grey eyes. She remembered hugging her dad goodnight and nodding to the man before leaving the room.

She shook his hand. "I'm not sure who you are. I just remember you coming to our house one night months ago."

"Good good. So I'm not a *complete* stranger," he chuckled, reaching for Clayton's hand.

Clayton kept his hands to himself, refusing to take Grayson's. His voice was tight and closed. "I'm sure you can understand if I don't want to shake hands with someone I've never met, and don't trust."

"Not a problem. I guess I know more about both of you than you do me, so that's a little awkward, not going to lie," Grayson laughed lightly, rubbing the back of his neck. He looked around to make sure they were alone. "I know all about the Fortress. Bernard and I are acquaintances, and Rose, your parents know all about them too....so I guess that's enough to show you that you can trust me."

Perhaps she was too trusting, or she wanted so badly to believe her family was alive and well that Rose believed Grayson, a man whom she'd never spoken to in her life before now. It was a stretch and a huge risk, but what else did she have to lose?

Before she could get a word in, Clayton stepped forward. "I'm not sure what you're talking about sir. We just wanted to hang out and have fun at the party you just disbanded."

Rose laid her hand on his arm. "It's alright, Clay. Tell me more, Grayson. Where is my family? Are they alright?"

He nodded. "They've been in sanctuary with the Government. They have a bunker not far from HQ--oh wait. Sorry, nevermind. That's classified."

"So is the Fortress," she pointed out.

"Rose!" Clayton seethed, grabbing her arm.

"Touché." Grayson looked over his shoulder again. "I'm the only person your family trusts with this information. You have to believe me," he directed the last part at Clayton. "If you'll let me, I can bring you to them. We can drop off my other guard at the guard's base before taking you to your family in the safe house."

"Wait. Why should we believe you?" Clayton asked.

Grayson smiled sadly. "That's up to you. I can't convince you why you *should* trust me, just that it's important you do. How badly do you want to see your family, Rose?"

Involuntarily, her mother's face flashed in front of Rose's eyes on the last night she'd seen them. She hadn't let herself think about her family until now. Her mother's blue eyes filled with so much hurt when Rose shouted she hated them. Her dad's brown eyes filled with anger after

216

their shouting match, and her brother's scared ones as he watched Rose storm to her room. Her gut twisted until she felt she couldn't breathe anymore.

"Rose?" Clayton's asked, tone gentle. His voice hardly registered in her mind.

She was a terrible sister, and an even worse daughter for abandoning her family when they needed her most. If Rose hadn't gone to that damn party, would she and her parents have slipped safely away into the Fortress together? Or would they have still gone to the bunker? She may never know unless she saw them and spoke to them herself.

She nodded and started for the car. "Let's go. I want to--"

That infamous whirring, squealing sound nearly threw her to the ground. It was strong and piercing again, rendering her speechless. Though it had been weeks since she last felt the pain, Rose would recognize that whirring anywhere. No! Not now! Clayton rushed to her side and Grayson stood there staring at her. She pressed her hands to the sides of her head, but just like last time, it did her no good. Her knees gave out and she fell to the ground, whimpering like a kicked puppy. If there was something she hated more than anything else in her life it was the lack of control and the feeling of weakness. Whatever was going on inside her head did exactly that. Clayton wrapped her arm around his shoulders and hoisted her up, supporting her weight while she screamed.

Grayson, eyes wide, asked, "Is that what happens when--?"

She never got the chance to hear what he said, because the door of the car whipped open and the woman, Emily, ran for them.

"Sir!" she cried. "We have a situation!" Emily never made it to them. A droid swept her feet from underneath her and ripped her head from her shoulders in one motion. Rose screamed for her. No one should go down speechless, without a fight. Emily's head bounced on the grass, rolling toward them. Rose saw Emily's frozen expression, panic stricken. Her eyes were wide and unseeing, her mouth open and dripping with fresh red blood. The ends of her neck were shredded from detachment and drenched in blood. So much blood. So much fear. So much pain.

Rose screamed again, hands twisted in her hair. Grayson turned around and faced the droid that was now barreling toward them. Just like last time, it was faceless and translucent. If she wasn't in so much pain, she may have even admired the beauty of their smooth movements once more. Now was not that time.

"Hang on," Clayton shouted, sweeping Rose into his arms. She continued to scream, both for the pain and for him to stop. They couldn't just leave Grayson alone with that creature! They'd basically just signed his death certificate.

Gunshots rang out, bouncing off the surrounding houses.

"No!" She screamed for herself and for Grayson.

"We just have to be faster than the slowest person," Clayton gasped into her hair, already out of breath from carrying her. They hadn't made it very far, so she tried to swallow the pain. *Please be okay, please be okay,* she willed to Grayson.

When she turned her head on Clayton's shoulder and peeked, she wished she hadn't. Grayson was already on the ground, pinned into the grass under the weight of the droid. He was fighting back with anything he could. The bullets had seemed to slow the droid down, but Grayson still didn't have a chance. Rose gave him points for effort.

"How could you?" She screamed in Clayton's ear, angry tears streaming down her face. She paid them no mind as they ran down her nose, her mouth, her chin. He wasn't much, but he was all she had to tie herself to her parents. She cried for herself and she cried for Grayson. She cried for the family she abandoned. It wasn't fair. None of it was.

# Chapter 26

## (ROSABELLA)

THE PAIN BEGAN TO SUBSIDE THE CLOSER THEY got to the Fortress. The piercing turned into a dull throbbing and eventually only a nagging ache. Rose didn't speak to Clayton until they arrived back at the Fortress.

"Put me down."

He set her on the ground. Once her feet touched the ground, it was unfamiliar. Her feet had gotten used to the artificial grass above again. She felt the cold grey tile through the soles of her shoes and immediately cringed. The off-white walls were too bright, blinding her. She closed her eyes to realign herself.

Clayton kept a hand on her elbow to steady her, but she wanted him to let go. If he did, Rose would fall right to the floor, but she wouldn't tell him that.

"Are you alright?" He asked her in a low voice.

"Don't worry about me, I'll be fine," she seethed. Her eyes were hot and her cheeks burned. "I'm sure the man you just left to die wouldn't say the same."

He sucked in a hard breath and looked down at her. She glared at him, mouth a tight line.

"You don't get it."

She shook her head and shouted, "You're right, I don't. Clayton, how could you let him die like that? He was innocent!"

Clayton released her and turned away. Rose jumped when his fist collided with the wall. She stepped back and let the other wall support her weight. Rose watched his shoulders rise and fall with angry breaths. He leaned his forehead against the wall and sighed.

"I'm sorry," he said, his back to her. "I didn't—I wanted to—If it had been just me, I wouldn't have left him."

All the rage slipped from her head and out through her toes almost as quickly as the color in her face faded. She wrapped her arms around her stomach, clutching at her sides. It was *her* fault they'd left Grayson. Clayton didn't think she'd be able to defend herself and he wasn't sure if he could protect both of them, so he'd opted for running. *She* was the reason Grayson was dying up there all alone—or maybe he was already dead. Rose's heart ached for Clayton then. She pushed off the wall and stumbled forward. If she could only touch him, she could comfort him. She'd take that guilt away from him and put it on her own conscience. He didn't deserve that.

She tripped on her way there and fell into his back. She'd never seen someone move so quickly. Clay turned around and caught her, holding her an arms length away. Rosabella willed him to see the clearness of her mind, so that he knew it was alright for him to share his burdens. Her hands clutched his biceps and she leaned closer. Rose wanted the space between them to disappear. She wanted Clayton to know she was there for him.

"I'm sorry too," she whispered, her lips brushing the skin on his neck. "I didn't think about it that way."

"It's not your fault." His chin rested on her head, his arms snaked around her. Goosebumps rose along his skin. "I didn't mean to get so mad like that in front of you. Are you okay?"

She nodded into his shoulder. "Mhmm."

"Why is it that we always seem to yell at each other no matter what we do?"

Rose heard the smile in his voice. Though her heart hurt from the loss she suffered tonight and her head pulsed with the memory of the pain, Rose found it in herself to laugh.

"Because whenever we're happy for a second, the world turns against us," she mumbled.

He ran his fingers up and down her spine. "So are you saying you were happy tonight? Even despite our argument?"

She rolled her eyes. "Which one?"

"Yikes, you got me." Clay's breath tickled her hair. "Can you please let me take you to the medical wing?"

"Wait." Rose stepped back and brushed at her cheeks, rubbed her eyes, and attempted a smile. "How do I look?"

He looked her up and down. "Hot."

Rose tried to smack him but she was too exhausted. Her arm fell at her side like a limp noodle. "I meant do I look like I've been crying? I can't have anyone see me this way."

Clayton's small smile turned into a frown. He took one of her hands in his. "Nobody is going to fault you for being upset, Rose."

She nodded. "You're right. Because I won't let anyone see me."

"You look beautiful. Strong."

He said nothing more as they walked to the medical wing. When they arrived, the only person left was a single nurse at the desk and another one running regular check-ups to the different rooms with patients. Clayton led Rosabella over to the desk, a hand on her lower back. He told the nurse about what happened and asked for Rose to get some kind of check up right away. Rose was pleased to hear him speak respectfully to the nurse. He'd even said please.

"Right this way," the nurse said, marking something on her screen. She brought Rose to a vacant room and stepped in the doorway to stop Clayton. She looked at Rose, her face calm and serene. "Miss Porter, I'm going to have you undress. If you want him in here that's fine, but I want to confirm with you first."

Rose's face warmed. This was not the way she wanted Clayton to be exposed to her most vulnerable side. She was nowhere near ready for that yet.

Clayton looked at her like she was crazy for even considering sending him away. "Rose, it wouldn't bother me. It's whatever you're comfortable with."

She spoke to his forehead, "Clay, maybe you could go get me a change of clothes?"

"Sure. I'll be back soon."

Then it was just Rose and the nurse. The nurse tossed her a paper gown and pulled a curtain to conceal the room from the door.

"I'll send for the doctor. She should be here within ten minutes. Please let me know if you need anything until then."

Rose smiled at her. "Thank you."

Once the medic left, Rosabella undressed as fast as she could. She didn't want anyone to walk in on her changing. That would add another layer to her infamy here at the Fortress. She folded her blue sweatshirt and grey shorts into a pile on the chair beside the bed.

Rose was guiltily relieved. For a few short minutes, she wouldn't have to be running around or training or arguing with anyone. She could enjoy a few moments of blissful silence. She hopped onto the patient's bed and leaned her head back on the small pillow. Her eyes closed for a short break, but once the doctor came in and Clayton returned with clothes for her, waiting in the hall until the doctor was finished, Rose knew she had to kick back into gear.

Somehow, someway, she was going to find her family. First, she needed to figure out what the heck was going on inside her head, and then she needed to find the safe house. After that, she'd figure out some way for the Fortress to take her family in--Bernard didn't seem like a cruel guy. He'd let them in if she made a deal with him.

Grayson's death would not be in vain.

***

Rose stood in the doorway to Clayton's bedroom. It was the first apartment she'd ever been inside. Clayton and Clarise shared one of the smaller apartments since they were both so young and Clayton was only a trainer, so he hadn't been very high in the order of choosing one. All the walls were the same inside as they were in the halls. The entryway was plain, with only the door and a tray for shoes. When she walked through the arched doorway from the entryway into the kitchen and living room, Roabella looked around for anything that showed her who Clayton was. The walls were bare and open. This was a welcome change from her dorm, which was still covered in pink frilly decorations. Gianna's little section of the room was covered in pictures and memorandums. Rose almost wished she'd been born here so she could have all those things. Everything that belonged to her was up above in her old room. She didn't have the heart to go up and take anything from it.

Their living room separated into a tiny kitchen with an island surrounded by stools, a decent sized bathroom, and two small bedrooms. The doorways were so close together, you had to be careful not to block one doorway with an open door.

When Clayton gave Rose a short tour, she was slightly stunned to find Clayton's room neat and tidy, just like the rest of their apartment. His bed was made and tucked in around the edges, with the edge by the pillows flipped over. It looked so comfortable, Rose had to fight the urge to run and jump onto it. That would be disrespectful to all his hard work, though. She took in the small wooden desk on the wall that separated Clayton and Clarise's rooms. An ancient, half-inch thick desktop computer--an ancient version of their modern screens--sat on top. Clay also had a small closet in the corner to the right of the bed and that was about it. Not a single thing was out of place, nor was there anything representative of Clayton in this room. Rose was a little disappointed he hadn't even put up some sort of knick-knack. That was just like him though: secretive and mysterious.

Clay kissed the top of her head. "It's not much, but it's kept us warm and safe for years...if you need anything, I'll be on the couch, alright?"

She nodded and held her bag closer to her chest. Rosabella silently wished he wouldn't leave her alone in this room for the night. It would be a huge comfort to her if he just laid beside her all night. They didn't have to speak or kiss or anything; she simply wanted someone to protect her from the nightmares she anticipated having tonight.

"Good. And Rose, I can't believe you didn't tell me you were sleeping on the couch in the library this whole time. That night I found you on the floor, I thought you'd just fallen asleep reading." He twirled a piece of her orange-red hair around his forefinger. "You should've told me."

Rose shrugged. "There was no need. I slept just fine."

He stared at her chin. "You know, it might not be my place, but I'm sure if you sat down and had a talk with Aire--"

A hard shake of her head stopped him. "I feel so much freer without her, Clayton. It's difficult to explain...like a weight has been lifted from my shoulders."

"I completely understand that," he said, nodding slowly. Then he kissed the tip of her nose and turned to leave. His voice was strained when he mumbled, "If I don't leave now, I might not ever leave."

On a last-second impulse, she grabbed his arm. "Wait. What if I... what if I don't want you to leave?"

He stopped, one foot in the hallway already. The muscles in his shoulder tensed. Clay kept his face hidden from Rose.

"Why?"

She let go of his arm and continued into the room. "What do you mean why? I don't want to sleep alone right now."

She fought the urge to laugh as he slowly turned on his heel. It was hilarious how serious his face was.

"Are you sure? I don't want you to feel like you have to." Clay tucked his hands into his jean pockets. "The bed isn't huge...I'll be perfectly fine on the couch."

Rose gave him her best, *Yes, I'm sure,* face. "Honestly if you sleep on the couch, I'll probably wind up sleeping on the floor next to you so I'm not alone... Don't you think you'd be doing me a service if you just stayed in the bed?"

Clayton smiled. "Well, when you put it like that..."

She smiled to herself as she dug through her bag of stuff. After they left the medical wing, with the doctor just as confused as them, Rose and Clayton had taken a detour to her dorm to grab anything she needed. He'd insisted on her staying with him, once she accidentally told him she'd be sleeping in the library.

"I'll go brush my teeth then. Be right back," Clayton said, brushing a hand along her arm on his way out.

Rose pulled out a toothbrush, a hairbrush, an extra-large, dark green t-shirt, and some plain grey sweatpants. She closed the door with a silent click and changed into her pajamas. For once in her life, she was grateful she'd grabbed something comfy, yet practical. If she wore shorts to bed, she'd be embarrassed of her legs, more so than she already was. Not that Clayton cared, but she was very self-conscious of her figure.

When he knocked, she opened the door and swapped places with him. Rose did her best to be quiet. She tiptoed past Clarise's room and held the bathroom door knob so it didn't click when the door shut. Her face and arms were warm, so she splashed some cold water on herself. Rose was suddenly very nervous. What had she been thinking, being so bold like that?

She brushed her chattering teeth then, keeping one hand on the sink to steady herself. Nothing was going to happen; Clayton respected her.

He wouldn't do anything she didn't want to do. That didn't mean she was going to be able to stop *herself*. When his lips were on hers, Rose couldn't pay attention to anything going on around her. It was a beautiful thing, to get so lost in Clayton. But it was also going to be the death of her if she wasn't careful.

She gripped the edges of the sink. Her breaths were quick and shallow. *It's just Clayton, nothing to worry about.* It took a minute or two before she could calm herself down. Once she regulated her breathing, she tiptoed back to Clayton's room. She was tempted to stop in and talk to Clarise, but it was already too late. She was probably asleep.

The lights were off when she returned and Clayton was lying on the covers, back against the wall, with his eyes closed. Rosabella left the door open a crack so she could see her way to the bed. The light from the living room was dim enough that it wouldn't disturb her while she slept, and just the right amount for her to see where she was going. Her knees shook as she climbed up onto the mattress.

Clayton blinked lazily when she started pulling the covers back.

"Hey," he said, his voice gravelly. He looked as exhausted as she felt.

"Hi," Rose whispered, her voice shaking.

His arms snaked around her, pulling her close to his chest. She rested her back against him and closed her eyes. His pillows smelled like freshly cleaned linen, and something else she couldn't pinpoint. Was it his shampoo? It's woodsy scent tickled her nose.

His cheek pressed against her cheek. "If it makes you feel any better, I can sleep outside of the sheets," he whispered into her ear.

She bit the insides of her cheek, too scared to tell him thank you. He must've known because he smiled into her neck.

"Clayton?"

"Yes?"

She took in a shaky breath. "Can we finish our game from earlier?"

"Rose, we don't have to."

"I know," she whispered. "I just want to know you better."

His arms encircling her loosened. "What do you want to know?"

"How about, what happened to Clarise?" She rested her hands atop his. When she touched him, Clayton winced and sucked in a breath. Rose wiggled out of his hold and held up his hand into the light. "Get up. Come on."

He groaned. "No, I was just getting comfortable!"

"I won't say it again." She hopped down from the bed, her bare feet chilling to the bone from the grey tiles. Hadn't they ever heard of carpet?

"Yes, *mother*," he said laughing. Clay followed her to the bathroom and sat on the edge of the tub as directed. She hunted around for a rag and ran it under warm water.

"I can't believe you didn't take care of your hand," Rose scolded. "You just punched a wall an hour ago."

He laughed. "You know, you totally ruined the moment."

"I don't care." She went into her motherly mode, bustling around the room and digging around in the cabinet, trying to find a cleaning solution. When she found what she was looking for, Rose knelt on the floor in front of Clayton. She took care in cleaning his hand. The white washcloth turned a light pink as she did.

"Clarise was left up above when my friend and I came here. We didn't know what to think of the world down here right away," Clayton said quietly. "My friend and I did everything we were told, out of fear for our lives. There was no need for fear...I realized that much later. The citizens here were not out to get us. They wanted us to train and find our place. Bernard oversaw our progress."

"Eventually, I got really good at training. Months after I arrived here, Bernard sent me out on a trial mission with some guy much older than me and a bunch of other trainees. When we did a patrol near my old neighborhood, I snuck away to see what was left of my home. I had to be careful, because they couldn't know I was still alive. When you move into the Fortress, it's like you're erased from the world above."

Rosabella rested a hand atop his unscathed one and lifted her eyes to his. Clayton stared at her, without really seeing her. He was somewhere else. She let him keep going.

"I went into my house and found everything disheveled. I couldn't find anyone. My parents were gone. My older brother." Clay shuddered and held her hand tightly. "It looked like there'd been a fight in the living room, and the kitchen was worse. Food was splattered all over the floor and the walls. I continued on throughout the whole house. I needed to know if there was anything upstairs that could help me understand what had happened. I had to be careful because nobody could know I was there. The Fortress is very strict about not visiting your origin home.

"I noticed my brother's door was shut tight. Cautiously, I opened it and made my way to the closet Clarise hid in when we had people over. I held my breath and listened. Suddenly, she made the tiniest, most depressing sound I'd ever heard her make. I yelled and yelled for her to open the door, which was designed to only be opened from the inside once she was old enough to understand the severity of the situation; that having more than two children was illegal. That *she* was illegal. She started screaming my name and yelling for help. She kept saying she couldn't move. I freaked out and made the impulsive decision to break down the door. With my father's ax he kept in the kitchen…" He paused and took a deep breath. "I didn't stop, not even when I heard her screams."

Rose finished wiping his knuckles and moved on to the antiseptic cream. There wasn't much left in the tube. Did he punch things often?

"The door crashed open and I fell. I…I struck a vertebrae in her spine."

Rose's steady fingers faltered. A clump of the goo fell to the floor. She swept it up with the towel; she wanted Clayton to speak at his own pace. She was not going to show emotion on her face until he was done. She needed to hear this almost as much as he needed to say it.

"It's my fault my sister is in a wheelchair. She's been going through therapy and treatment after treatment for nearly eight years and she still can't walk."

She wrapped a thin medical bandage around his hand and tore it with her teeth when she was satisfied it wouldn't fall off in the middle of the night.

"Clayton--" Rose started.

He shook his head and rested his forehead against her shoulder. She stopped cleaning up and knelt there, still and silent. "Please," he started. "Please don't tell me it's not my fault. That I didn't do anything. That she'll be better soon…I've heard it all before. It *is*, yes I *did*, and *no* she won't."

Rose eased to her feet and pulled Clay against her stomach. "I wasn't going to say anything like that. I was going to tell you that it is okay to feel the hurt. It won't go away on its own…telling someone is important to help you." She ran her fingers through his hair, up and down. He turned his face into her and shook. It took Rose a second to connect the shaking with Clayton's sobs. In her less than two months here, she'd never seen him cry. It broke her heart. He wrapped his arms around Rose's waist and clung to her shirt. She continued to sooth him by rubbing his back.

Sometimes there was nothing more that could be done other than to have a good cry.

By the time she and Clayton returned to the bedroom, it was almost one in the morning. They lay there, facing one another for a long time. Rose remembered Clayton kissing her forehead before she fell asleep, feeling safe and calm.

# Chapter 27

## (ROSABELLA)

WHEN SHE WOKE UP THE NEXT MORNING, ROSABELLA was re-energized and ready to get to work. It was Saturday, a day off of training. She yearned for something to do with her hands. If she asked Clayton, she was certain he'd work on some drills with her. Maybe he'd teach her some combat finally.

She stretched and rolled over, only to find the other half of the bed empty. Clayton didn't get scared off that easily did he? Where the heck did he have to go on a *Saturday?* She groaned before forcing herself to get out of bed. Rose knew she must look terrible; she could tell her hair was sticking up everywhere. When you could see your hair standing off your head from the corners of your eyes, there was something wrong. Running her fingers through her hair to straighten what she could, Rose ambled into the short hallway.

A loud sound came from the kitchen. A pan dropping? Rose passed Clarise's room to go there and was abruptly pulled inside.

"Shhh!" Clarise hissed up at her. She closed the door and gestured for Rose to sit on the edge of the bed.

"Clarise, are you okay?"

Clair crossed her arms and glared at Rose. "You didn't tell him you saw Andre and I. Why not?"

Rose sighed in relief. She thought she was going to get the lecture about making sure to treat Clayton right and all that fun, sisterly stuff.

"I'm waiting. Clay isn't going to be in the kitchen forever."

"Clarise!" Rose gasped. "What's gotten into you?"

Her friend's face contorted. Clair lowered her eyes and uncrossed her arms. "I'm sorry, I'm just scared out of my mind! Clayton would kill Andre."

Rose ran a hand along her arm. "I know, that's why I didn't say anything." She paused to listen for Clayton. When the coast was clear she continued, "Clarise, when we were talking about all the cute stuff between Maxon and America months ago, I didn't realize you had *Andre* in mind."

"What's wrong with him?"

She scoffed. "Clarise, have you met the guy? He's so rude and inconsiderate and he always stares at women like they're prizes to be won."

Clarise waved her off. "No, that's all an act. He's so sweet and awkward with me. I love when he stumbles over his words, because it means I surprised him...I love surprising him."

"Oh, are you sure? He's just so...so..."

Clarise finished for Rose, "Rough around the edges? Mysterious? Confusing? Yes I know. That's what's so intriguing. He's not too different from my brother in that regard."

Rose slapped her forehead. "You're totally right!" She laughed, "Clair, what have we gotten ourselves into?"

Clarise's face relaxed. "You mean you're not upset?"

Rosabella hugged her and smiled. "Well, I'm a little grossed out that Andre likes a girl eight years younger than him...but hey, love is love, right?"

Clarise gave her a big squeeze. "Thank you! I was so scared!"

Rose pulled back and looked her in the eye. "I just want you to know that Clayton is going to find out eventually and it's not going to be pretty. If you need someone to talk to about it, I'm here for you. Or if Andre breaks your heart like an idiot. I can kick his ass for you!"

"Thanks, but I'll be fine. And Clayton will listen to you if you talk to him about love and all that stuff. I'm sure he'll understand once you explain it!"

Rose shook her head. "Clayton is stubborn and hot headed. He's not going to change his mind that easily."

"Of course he will. He's already let you spend the night," she said smirking. "He's never done that before."

"Oh, well, I was just--" Rose was at a loss for words.

Clarise giggled. "Don't worry, I don't mind. Only because it's you."

"Gee thanks." She rolled her eyes. Desperate to take the attention away from her, Rose gestured to Clarise's pajamas. "Can I help you get ready?"

"Please!" Clarise wheeled over to her small closet in the corner. She presented all of her favorite outfits to Rose, explaining that Prince updated everyone's closet once every year. On their birthdays to be exact. Clarise also informed Rose how she did her best to spread out which outfits she wore when and mixed and matched as much as possible. Rose wondered why she'd come up with that outfit system if she'd shut herself inside the apartment. How long had she and Andre had a thing? Clarise wasn't even eighteen yet. She had no comprehension of love. Rose could say that, because she didn't even know what it was like to love someone either. If it was anything like what she felt whenever Clayton entered a room, or when he pressed his lips to hers, then she was certain she'd be able to say she loved him soon.

\*\*\*

Rose and Clayton held hands the entire way back to her dorm later that morning. Today was a great day. Her hopes for love were coming true. She'd underestimated the amount of give and take it required to make things work in a relationship, but it was so worth it. She wanted Clayton to thrive in life and experience things that put him in a state of bliss and happiness.

"Clay?" She swung their arms back and forth as they turned the corner into the westernmost wing. Rose's bag in her other hand crashed against her leg.

"Yes, my darling?"

"Yeah, don't ever call me that again," she said as she rolled her eyes. Her dorm was coming up soon and she didn't want to be left alone with Aire if she was there. "Are you sure you can't help me out today? I really want to start combat. Weights are fun, but I'm getting sick of the same old thing every day."

He gave her a sidelong look. "Baby, I wish I could--"

"No. Don't call me 'baby' either," Rose interrupted him. "That's disgusting."

Clayton squeezed her fingers. "Gosh, my woman has quite an independent mindset, doesn't she? Well, I bet if I…"

Her annoyed expression rendered him silent. She waited while he trailed off whatever he was about to say. They arrived at Rose's dorm and stopped in front of the door.

She dropped the bag. Then she wrapped her arms around his neck and looked up. "Can you teach me combat? Pretty please?"

"I don't know, Rose. I'm pretty busy this afternoon. I've been assigned to go on a mission today to patrol the tube station." He sighed and wrapped his arms around her waist. "I would give anything to be able to teach you how to fight today, but I'm not sure when I'll be back. Why don't you talk to Andre? I'm sure he'll teach you some techniques."

Rose pretended to dry heave. "Gross. No, I'm not going to risk getting groped by your best friend." Clayton laughed at that. She took that as a good sign to continue. "I'll reach out to Logan or something. I'm sure he'd be willing to help me out."

Clay's shoulders tensed and his posture turned rigid. "Does it have to be him?"

"Well, he's my friend, isn't he?" She didn't understand the sudden shift in his mood. When Clayton was on, he was on; but when he changed that quickly it was difficult for her to keep up. Rose anticipated being able to figure him out as they spent more time together.

He breathed out and smiled. It didn't reach his eyes, so she knew he didn't mean it. "Of course. Just come find me after if I'm back before you're done. Please?"

"Sure, we'll get dinner together!" She stood on tiptoes to kiss his cheek. "Have a good day. I'll see you tonight."

Clayton's mouth met hers. She melted at the greediness of it. Her lips parted slightly and her neck and hands felt hot. Rose pulled away before he could distract her further. He shouldn't be late for his mission and she needed to get her day started. She'd spent a few wonderful hours this morning in the Taylor apartment, but she wanted to do something more than hang around doing nothing. She could only sit around for so long before getting restless. A kiss on her forehead was the last touch from Clayton she'd be receiving for a while.

"Bye," he said.

She smiled. "Bye." Once he was out of sight, Rose picked up her bag and opened the door. She jumped when she saw Gianna standing at the mirror in her closet, wearing only a sports bra and shorts. "Oh, I'm sorry. I'll be out soon." Rose shut the door quickly and kept her head down as she made her way to her bed.

Gianna sniffled and swiped at her eyes. "Don't worry, you're not bothering me. In fact, I'm open to the company."

Rose perked up at the sound of her roommate's sniffles. She looked up and met Gianna's red and puffy eyes in the mirror. Her back was to Rose, but she could tell something was very different.

"Are you okay, Gianna?"

She sniffled again and wiped her nose on the back of her hand. She dropped something in the process. Rose set her bag down and ran over to pick it up for her. When she handed it to Gianna, she saw it was a pink vinyl strip with measurements on it wrapped all the way around Gianna's stomach. From the side, Rose saw what Gianna was measuring.

Rosabella gasped.

Gianna's eyes widened to the size of saucers. "Please, you can't tell anyone yet. I haven't even told my boyfriend."

Her roommate's stomach protruded from her normally straight, flat figure. Gianna's elastic shorts were pulled up and over the baby bump.

Rose hugged Gianna, careful not to crush her stomach. "I won't tell anyone, I swear! This is a good thing, don't worry! How long have you been pregnant?"

Gianna giggled and swiped at her eyes. "Four months. It's so good to hear someone other than the doctor refer to me being pregnant." She squealed, her grip tight on Rose's shoulders. "I guess I haven't said it out loud yet either."

Rose smiled, feeling like a proud mother, though she didn't know why. "Why haven't you told him yet? What's his name?"

She rested her hand on her stomach, involuntarily Rose noticed. "Donovan. He and I have been dating since we were thirteen."

"Fortress-born?"

"Yes," she said. "I guess we just didn't monitor ourselves as well as we should have."

"What do you think he'll say?" Rose asked. "Will he be happy?"

Gianna's eyes filled with tears while she pulled on a loose fitting long sleeved shirt. "I...I don't know. I'm worried he's going to be upset. We'll have to grow up fast now that we have a baby on the way."

All Rose's thoughts poured into one stream of questions, "How has he not realized yet? Don't you think he'll want to know and go to your appointments with you now? Have you seen what the baby looks like yet?"

"You're kind of overwhelming me, I'm not going to lie. How about we sit down to talk? I'm past the throwing up stage, but I'm still trying to be cautious." Gianna sat down on her bed and patted a spot next to her. "That's why I've been away with Donovan almost every night. I've been telling him that I have some stomach problems and that being away from people helps me relax."

Rose sat gingerly beside her, afraid to move the bed under Gianna. "So you lied to him because you didn't want him to really know what was going on."

"Exactly. And he hasn't questioned it at all. I guess that's the nice thing about guys being oblivious sometimes." Gianna laughed and wrung her hands in her lap. "That's the answer to question number one...number two is that I'm not sure if he'll want to go to appointments with me because he might not care about it."

"There's no good way to know unless you talk to him about it." Rose clapped her hands together and practically bounced up and down on the mattress. "Why don't you ask him over now? Tell him now before you lose your courage! I'll be right here if you need me."

"I'm not sure..."

"Oh, come on. I have faith in you! Donovan might even surprise you and start bawling or something," Rose said, doing her best to sound encouraging. The truth was, she was completely out of her element here. Who was she to say the guy wouldn't go running in the opposite direction? "Besides, doesn't Bernard or Logan need to know that you're pregnant so they give you less dangerous missions?"

Gianna cocked her head to the side, thinking. "Oh, you're right. I guess I didn't think about that...I'll call him over right now."

"Good! Do you want me to stay or go?"

"You can leave--no wait! Can you please stay?" Gianna nodded toward Rose's closet. "If you pretend you're reorganizing or something, he won't see anything weird about us meeting. I don't want him to come here thinking something's wrong."

Rose nodded her agreement. "Good idea! Give him a call. I can't wait!"

Gianna took a deep breath and pulled out her screen. "Alright I can do this." She dialed a number and waited through the ringing until Donovan picked up. "Hey! Can you spare a few minutes right now? I'd love to talk with you about something...no, I'd rather not wait...yes, everything's fine, don't worry!...Okay. Love you."

Rose grinned at Gianna. "Well?"

Gianna bit her lip and smiled. "We're a go!"

Rose pumped a fist in the air and danced around the room. "Hell yes! I'm so excited for you Gianna!"

They spent the next few minutes getting the room ready for Donovan. Rose hadn't yet unpacked her bag from spending the night at Clayton's, so she set to doing that when Donovan knocked.

Rose gave her roommate a double thumbs-up. "Here we go!"

# Chapter 28

## (ROSABELLA)

Gianna's hands shook as she reached for the doorknob. Rose shot her a reassuring smile from across the room. Her roommate, now a friend, forced her lips upward and nodded. She pulled the door open so quickly it slipped from her grip and smashed against the wall. Rose flinched and Gianna jumped back, but Donovan only laughed.

"I'm happy to see you too, baby!" He said drawing her in for a warm hug. Rose tried not to cringe with the last word. He was in love with his girlfriend and so long as Gianna was okay with it Rose wouldn't object. Only if Clayton called her that would she complain.

"I really want to tell you something." Gianna smiled, genuinely this time, and led him to the edge of her bed. They sat there, side by side, Rose's presence already forgotten.

He nodded and took her hand in his. "Oh, right. What is it, babe?"

*Ugh! Gross!* Rose turned away, afraid she'd groan or make a noise that would ruin their moment.

*Get on with it, Gianna,* she wanted to shout. The sooner she told him she was pregnant with his child, the sooner Rosabella could slip out and go to her combat training with Logan. He'd be here soon to walk with her to the training room and she didn't want him to interrupt either.

"Well…I…sorry, you and I…we are going to…ummm, " Gianna stammered, eyes avoiding her boyfriend. Rose did her best to press herself against the wall. She would rather remain unseen if things went south.

Donovan nodded encouragingly. He must be used to this behavior of Gianna's by now. "Yes?"

Gianna looked at him and started crying.

Donovan stood up right away, rubbing the back of his neck. "Are you alright, babe? Did I do something?"

Rose wanted to shake Gianna and tell her to get a grip. Apparently the hormones were getting the best of her. Rosabella debated stepping in to save her but then Gianna grabbed his hands and looked up at him from her perch on the bed.

"Don, I'm pregnant."

His mouth dropped open. "Are you positive?"

She bit her lip and nodded. Rose grew uncomfortable; she shouldn't be here.

He scoffed. "Well why didn't you tell me sooner?"

"I didn't know how. I was worried you'd be mad," Gianna cried, her voice thick with sobs.

Donovan leaned over her. "I'm not mad at all. This is so exciting!"

Gianna shot Rose a look. "Really? That's a relief!"

"Of course I am, baby!" He gently pushed her back into the mattress.

Rose knew that was her cue to get the hell out of there. She averted her eyes while they began sweet talking one another and kissing. She suspected Donovan hadn't known Rosabella was in the room at all. Gianna was the only woman he saw; they loved one another unconditionally. Rose's heart ached for that kind of love. Would she have that with Clayton one day? Sooner rather than later?

As she snuck around the happy couple, her thoughts ran wild. Was she letting herself let Clayton in too soon? Rose was the first to admit that their relationship started on the basis of them shouting at one another and her hating his guts. Not the most romantic way to start out.

When Rose reached the door, she was ready to get as far away from this room as possible. No way was she going to hear them giggling at one another anymore. This was a little too mushy for her taste. What *was* her taste? A guy who was a little rough around the edges, but who would open up for his girl and treat her as the most important person in his life? A gasp caught in her throat as she slipped out of the room and into the hallway. She closed the door behind her and leaned her head against it. Her type was literally Clayton. No wonder she'd taken a liking to him so quickly. He was exactly what she imagined she'd find in her pair. It was almost too good to be true. Or *was* it too good to be true and this was all only temporary?

Before she could contradict herself, someone laid a warm hand on her shoulder. "Rosabella?"

She jumped at the voice. "Logan! Holy crap, you scared me!"

He clutched at his own chest. "Sorry! You scared me, scaring you!"

"No way," Rose laughed and swatted him in the arm. "That's totally something *I* would say!"

Logan backed away and shook his head. He had a big smile on his face. "Are you ready for some new training?"

She nodded and pulled his arm. "Yes, please. Anything to get me out of my dorm for a while."

He frowned. "Aire still giving you trouble?"

Rose was shocked he remembered they were having issues. It was nice to have a friend she didn't have to explain everything to. He was a very observant friend.

"Well yes, but that's not why I want to leave..." she looked back at the door. Her face was hot. "Gianna and her boyfriend are having a good time and I don't want to be in there."

"Oh. Yeah, that's awkward."

When she peeked at him, she thought it was cute that his face was also red. Logan was blushing? *What a modest guy,* she thought. Some woman would be very happy to be loved by him some day. He was proof--and Clayton too--that people didn't have to have sex to have a solid relationship. Apparently that didn't apply to her roommate and Donovan, but not everyone had the same perspective.

"Definitely." Rose decided to change the subject, "So what are we going to start with?"

Logan perked up, returning to his usual happy self. "Oh just wait, you'll get a real workout today!"

She laughed, squeezing his arm she was so excited. "Finally!"

***

Logan held up his gloved hands. "Very good. Now uppercut. Left. Cross. Good!"

Rosabella stepped back and wiped her arm across her forehead. When Logan said she'd be getting a good workout, he wasn't kidding. Rose was disappointed at first when he told her that she was going to have a boxing lesson, but once they'd started, she understood why.

"Awesome job, Rosabella. I mean it." He patted her sweaty back. "Go grab something to drink."

He stepped off to the side to let her through, and she snuck around Logan to grab her water bottle where she'd left it resting against the wall when she came in. While Rose gulped down water like a mad woman, she lifted her shirt up and down to create a breeze on her stomach and back. The rooms down here weren't circulated with air, nor did they have strong air conditioning, so she felt stifled in the small workout room. She'd been practicing in the weight room with Eden for weeks, but never as hard as this, and her sprints had always taken place in the main training room where the large domed ceiling helped to expand the air.

Logan jogged over to her, smiling. "You're good at catching on to this stuff. I'm impressed."

She shrugged him off. "It's easy when you have such a great teacher."

He laughed and knelt down to tie his shoe. Rose wasn't kidding; Logan was really easy to work with. The two of them fell right into sync with one another. They understood what was expected of each other. She watched with interest as the muscles in his caramel shoulders flexed. Logan removed his shirt a while ago, complaining it was too hot. At that moment, Rosabella wished she'd been born a guy. It would've made her less sticky and sweaty to take her shirt off. That was a step she wasn't willing to take, even if Logan was her friend. If Clayton heard she'd gotten half-naked with another guy he was going to shit his pants. And then kill the guy.

She sat on the floor and rested her head on the wall.

Logan matched her position, sitting beside her. "What's going on, Rosabella?"

"Oh, nothing. I guess I'm just a little distracted." What was eating her up inside was the fact that she was holding onto so many things. After her fight with Aire, it's like she started to let all the pain sink in;

Grayson's death was at the top of that list. Then there were all those secrets she was holding inside: Clarise and Andre's relationship and now Gianna's pregnancy.

He bumped her in the hip with his elbow. "Alright, if you say so. But you can talk to me if you want."

"Thanks, I'll keep that in mind," replied Rose. Before she accidentally poured her soul to him, she jumped up and headed back to where she'd thrown her gloves to the side. As she strapped them back on she said, "Can we get back to it? I really need to blow off some steam."

Logan joined her in the center of the room on the mat. "Yeah, sure. Whatever you want."

She adjusted her ponytail and got into her starting stance, arms and fists up to protect her face and upper body. He smiled at her and nodded. She gave a curt nod in response, ready for him to start drilling her.

"Okay, Rosabella. I'm going to have you take charge."

She tipped her head to the side. "You sure?"

He smiled and motioned for her to come closer.

"Alright. But I'm sorry in advance if anything bad happens."

Logan's shoulders lifted. "Well, and if anything does, I'll know it was an accident. Problem solved."

Rose shook her head, mind reeling. "You're too good to me, Mr. Clarke."

"Of anyone else I've met, you're the most deserving, Miss Porter," he called across the mat, a smile reaching up to his cheekbones.

She laughed. "Yeah right. Now, shut up and box."

Rose lost track of time while they worked out together for hours. She barely registered the dinner bell chiming from her sleek wristband. She and Logan ignored the sound and continued boxing until it timed out. Rose ducked as his cross punch sailed through the air. She made a right jab, uppercut, hook combo at him. On her left hook, she connected with his chin. He staggered backward, eyes wide. That was the first time she'd managed to make strong contact with him. All the other times were minor and on his sides or arms. No matter how much she grumbled at him, he refused to hit her. If she didn't know any better, she'd say Logan continued to miss her on purpose. There were quite a few times he should've hit her on the side of the head or the stomach.

"I'm so sorry, Logan!" She cried, running over to him. He leaned back against the wall and started laughing. Her heart clenched when she saw the skin starting to darken in the form of a bruise. She reached out a hand and touched it gently. "You need some ice."

He waved her away. "Don't worry about it, Rose. That's a job well done if you ask me." Logan looked at something over Rose's shoulder. "What did you think, Taylor?"

"I'd say so," Clayton said, his voice husky.

Rosabella whipped around so fast, she nearly tripped on Logan's boxing gloves on the floor.

"Clayton!" she cried, heart fluttering at the sight of him leaning on the doorframe. She ran to him and wrapped her arms around his neck.

He lifted her up and laughed in her hair. "Well, that's one nice hello! I wish everyone greeted me like that."

She let herself slip out of his arms until she felt the ground underfoot. Rose kept her hands on his shoulders and gazed up at him; she wanted him to see just how happy she was to hug him. If Logan hadn't been in the room, she would have kissed Clayton square on the lips. By the mischievous look in Clayton's eyes, she imagined him thinking the same.

"For real, Rose, that was great," Clay said, hands linked and resting in the small of her back.

She blushed and looked away. "How long were you watching?"

He nuzzled her ear. "Long enough to see my girl kick some ass."

*My girl.* Wow. That sent a jittery chill throughout her body. It ran from her head all the way down to her toes. His breath was warm on her neck as he chuckled at her full body shudder. Remembering they weren't alone, Rose gently wriggled out of his arms. She turned so her back rested against Clayton's chest, her head resting perfectly in between his clavicles. His arms circled around her hips and he linked his hands in front of her.

She met the eyes of her friend across the room. "Logan, I'm so so sorry. Can I help you and get an ice pack or something?"

"No, it's totally fine. I've endured worse," he said laughing. "Go on, you two go grab some dinner. I have things to work on, so I'll be late."

Without hesitation, Clayton unwrapped her and headed for the door. Rose gave Logan one last look and followed Clay out of the room. She made sure to snag her sweatshirt and water bottle and toss her gloves into the laundry bin to be washed before exiting.

Part of her was guilty for leaving Logan all by himself. She'd just punched her friend and left him to figure things out on his own. If Rose was in Logan's position, wouldn't she want someone to stay with her?

"Logan's tough. He'll be fine. I think you just surprised him, that's all," Clayton said softly, drawing her in with one arm.

"How did you know what I was thinking?"

He nudged her with his hip. "It's because you're so selfless. I knew right away."

Rose fell into step with Clayton, their arms brushing every so often. She bit her lip to keep from saying anymore. If she said anything it would probably be about Gianna, as that's all she'd been thinking about for hours. Gianna was supposed to have gone in for an appointment right before dinner tonight. A check up, she'd said.

As they walked to the dining hall, Rose pulled out her screen and sent Gianna a message: DO YOU WANT TO GET DINNER TOGETHER?

Her roommate responded within seconds: YES PLZ! CAN WE BRING IT TO THE ROOM AND TALK?

Rose glanced up at Clayton. He looked away quickly. Had he read her message? Did he know about Gianna's pregnancy? She forced herself to breathe. Of course he didn't. Their texts were too vague. But she did want Clayton to know. If someone was going to be in on the secret, she wanted it to be him. Now she was relieved she hadn't told Logan during their workout. If anyone, *Clayton* should be the first to know.

She replied to Gianna: OF COURSE! CAN I BRING CLAY?

It took a while before Gianna responded, but when she did, Rose finally breathed: YES, BUT ONLY HIM.

"You good, Rose?" Clayton asked, stopping beside her. He placed his hand on her arm, turning her to face him. "Is there something going on?"

Rose blinked up at him. How to begin? Did she want to tell him right here that her roommate was pregnant at nineteen? Wait. That was scary. What if it had been Rose instead? Would Clayton drop her like a hot potato if he found out she was pregnant? If that was the case, she never wanted to get pregnant without talking about it first.

"No. And yes," she whispered before looking over her shoulder. "We need to talk. Can we grab dinner and bring it to my room?"

Eyes narrowed, Clayton stared at her. "I will never understand you."

"Please," she pleaded. Rose placed her hand on his chest, hoping her gesture would show him just how important this was.

He looked away, face dark. "Please don't tell me you're sick of me already and that you want to break up."

A sound between a laugh and gasp left her mouth. "What?"

"Rose, trust me. If you want to, I get it. I'm not the easiest guy to get along with." His voice was strained and his jaw clenched. He stepped back and her hand fell to her side.

For a moment, she gaped up at him, mouth dropping to her feet.

Clayton shook his head. Gosh, he looked so good, no matter the lighting. His face was shadowed from the dim lights on the walls, casting a darkness into his eyes that both frightened and excited her. This guarded, caring guy thought she was annoyed with him.

"I didn't realize we were dating," she teased, poking him in the stomach.

Clayton looked at her from the corner of his eyes. "Well, I mean. We slept together last night. Isn't that official enough?"

"Shhh!" She blushed and backed away. "Yeah, but we didn't do *that*. We just slept side by side."

"Did I move too fast? Did I freak you out...is that what this is?" His voice cracked and he looked down at the floor. He shoved his hands in the pockets of his jeans. "I can do better. I'll cherish you better, I'll even--"

"Woah, woah, woah. Clayton, that's not what this is," she cried, grabbing his face in her hands, forcing his eyes to meet hers. "There's a secret I need to tell you. But I can't tell you here."

"That's it?"

She smiled without teeth. "That's it. We're still...*dating*. But I would like to know more about how you're going to 'cherish' me."

A person could not have smiled wider in their lives than the way Clayton smiled then. He looked down at Rose as if she were the only thing in his life that brought him joy. At this point, maybe she was.

"In that case," he half-growled, running his nose along her cheek. "I think we'd better go to my room instead."

A nervous laugh escaped her again. Her fingers dug into the skin on his forearms. "I...I'm not ready for anything just yet."

Clay kissed her forehead. "I know. I just wanted to see what would happen."

Rose laughed and pushed him away. They linked their fingers together, holding hands until they reached Rose's dorm. Rose wondered what Clayton would have to say about Gianna being pregnant. Afterall, it might be illegal here. Just because they didn't force you to marry a certain person didn't mean they were devoid of the same birthing age rules. *Gianna,* she wondered, *What have you gotten yourself into?*

# Chapter 29

**(ROSABELLA)**

Gianna and Rose tidied up the room before Clayton and Donovan came back to their dorm with dinner. Rose tucked her sheets around her bed as tight as they could go and stretched the grey comforter across the top. Everything else in the room was pink. Gianna had chosen her sheets and comforter when she moved to the dorm. A perk of being Fortress-born. Rose was slightly jealous of her roommate. Gianna had lived here her whole life, never worried about making one wrong step and losing her career. Or her life. For as long as Rose could remember, her dad had stressed about his job. He'd always told her they needed to have a backup plan if things went south.

Wait! Did her dad mean the *Fortress*? Rose didn't know what to think of that. He'd warned her that there were people out there who would stop at nothing to have things their way and that there were other people who wanted to live life to the fullest. Which society was which? She assumed the power-hungry people consisted of the Government officials and their supporters, and the ones wanting to live life to the fullest, the Fortress. Before Rosabella could ask Gianna questions about her life in the Fortress, Clayton and Donovan returned.

"Where do you want me to set your tray, Rose?" Clayton asked, balancing a full tray in each hand. Rose rushed over to help him and set hers down on her bed.

"Right here's fine," she said, gesturing to her empty bed. Her heart stopped when she watched Clayton plop down like he was meant to be there. He plumped up the two pillows and leaned them against the wall as a backrest. When he realized Rose wasn't following suit, he waved her over.

"Rose, there's room for you too," he patted the spot next to him. There wasn't a lot of room. They would have to squeeze together.

She swallowed and nodded, crawling onto the bed next to him. They sat side by side, their arms tight against one another. "Okay, but if I fall off, I'm going to be very unhappy."

He smiled, an evil glint in his eyes. "No promises."

Donovan helped Gianna get settled before handing her a tray. He then sat on the edge of the bed to give her space. Rose couldn't help but feel her heart flutter. Would Clayton ever do that for her if *she* was pregnant? There was no time to think about that right now. This was about Gianna, not Rosabella.

Gianna helped break the ice by getting right to the point, "So Clayton...I'm not sure if Rosabella has told you anything, but I'm--I mean, Donovan and I are...we're going to have a baby."

Rose tensed when the muscles in Clayton's thigh against hers flexed. She grabbed his shirt sleeve in case he decided to do or say something stupid. He was too unpredictable, and she didn't know how else to prepare for a catastrophic event.

Clayton surprised her by removing her hand from his side and linking their fingers together. "I thought something like that was going on. Gianna, you haven't been performing as well in your training lately... Now I understand."

Rose squeezed his hand in thanks. She honestly thought he'd freak out. From the looks of it, Clayton was just taken off guard. There was zero hostility in his eyes.

Donovan sighed and grabbed Gianna's hand. "Gee, I'm sure glad you said that. I've been worried sick these last few hours. I thought for sure Gianna and I were going to get in trouble once you found out."

Clayton's eyebrows raised. "Why on earth would I get you in trouble?"

Gianna dropped her spoon onto her tray. "What Donovan means is that we weren't sure how anyone would take the news...but since you're in a position of authority being a trainer and all..."

Clay shook his head. "Don't worry, I wouldn't do anything to jeopardize what you two have. In fact, I think it's somewhat romantic that you've both decided to keep this baby together."

It was Rose's turn to drop her spoon. It clattered to her tray, bringing Clayton's attention back to her.

He kissed her on the side of the head. "Don't worry, Rose. I'm serious. If we were going to have a baby, don't you think we'd want people behind us, supporting us the whole way?"

Rosabella couldn't respond. Her mouth was too busy dropping to her feet. The serious, yet innocent look in his eyes was pretty clear to her. Clayton wanted to help Gianna and Donovan. He sympathized with their struggles and wanted to make sure they felt safe.

Donovan moved his tray over so he could run to Clayton and shake his hand. "Thank you so much, Mr. Taylor. You're the best."

"It's just Clayton." Clayton shook his hand firmly and then nodded for Donovan to return to his seat. Meanwhile, Gianna and Rose made eye contact. Rose's mouth was definitely still open because Gianna motioned for her to calm down.

"So," Clayton said, taking a bite of potatoes, "Have you gotten a 3D visual of the baby yet?

Rose's spoon slipped out of her hand again. Clayton turned to her and laughed. "Rose, I'm not an idiot. I've been alive long enough to hear about pregnancies." He kissed her again. "Remember, Clarise and I have a decent age gap between us. I remember my mom's pregnancy pretty well."

She unlinked her hand from his in order to conceal the shaking. Rose was unable to meet his eyes for the rest of their dinner.

Rose and Clayton listened to Gianna and Donovan talk all about their appointment earlier that night. They described the 3D image of their child so specifically, Rose felt like she'd been right there in the room with them. Donovan couldn't share the story fast enough. Rose loved the way he and Gianna lit up when talking about it. The image they'd seen appeared right at the end of the bed as a hologram. They could touch it and spin it around to see every angle of their little baby inside Gianna's belly.

By the end of their story, Clayton wound up lying on his stomach, head propped up on his hands. Rose, to conserve space, sat between his legs, her back still resting on the pillow backrest. She rested her feet on his lower back.

Clayton waited for them to finish before asking, "Do you think you want to know the gender before the baby's born? Or do you want to be surprised?"

Rose tapped the back of his knees. "Oh don't be ridiculous, there's no such thing as being surprised. The Government makes you know the gender before--"

She stopped the second she remembered they were in the Fortress. She continued to forget that she was in an underground society where the familiar rules no longer applied.

Gianna giggled. "Don't worry, Rose. We don't think it's that important we know the gender. I'm happy knowing we have a healthy baby in there."

Donovan agreed, carrying all four trays to the door. He placed them in front of the door for whoever left first, so they could bring them to the dining hall.

Rose sighed and closed her eyes. "That's amazing. Can you imagine the present you've always wanted, coming as a surprise?"

Donovan dove onto the bed beside Gianna and kissed her neck. "Yes, it's amazing. I only hope people will be accepting of all of this."

"People aren't going to be mad, are they? It's not something you can control." Rose crossed her arms at the thought of some random person yelling at poor little Gianna for accidentally getting pregnant with a man she loved.

"What's not something you can control?" Clayton asked, turning on his side to look back at her.

She shrugged. "Well, you know what I mean...being in love. You can't really control that."

He stared at her. "You're absolutely right."

Gianna's giggles of pleasure made Rose feel embarrassed. She didn't want to infringe on a romantic moment between her and Donovan. She also didn't want to ask Clayton if she could go back with him to his apartment. That would be rude of her to invite herself over.

Thankfully, Clayton read her mind. "Rose? Want to get out of here?"

She nodded and jumped down from the bed. He smiled at her quick response. They slipped on their shoes, said goodbye to Gianna and Donovan, who were already deeply kissing, and grabbed the trays.

They walked in silence all the way to the dining hall's tray chute. When they arrived, their friends were finished eating and hanging out in the dining hall at their usual table along the wall. Clarise and Andre sat on the same side, pushing one another from time to time, and Logan opposite them. She flinched when she saw Logan pressing an ice pack to his jaw. Next, Rose involuntarily scanned the room for Aire before remembering they weren't on speaking terms. Rose headed for the table with their three friends, but Clayton gently grabbed her arm to stop her.

"Can you and I talk?"

She swallowed and nodded. No way in hell did she have the ability to speak right now. He smiled sadly at her and then led her out of the dining hall. Rosabella took a quick peek back at her friends, but they were invested in a story Andre was telling. They probably hadn't even noticed the two of them enter the hall at all.

She didn't recognize that Clayton was leading them toward the medical wing until they were right in front of the sliding doors. She was taken off guard when he continued down the hall and brought Rose to the library doors.

"I thought you wanted to go to your apartment?"

He held the door open for her. "Yeah, well, I'm sure Clair already assumes bad things about us from last night. No need for her to get any more ideas in her head." He placed a hand on her lower back. "Do you want to sit on your favorite couch?"

She nodded. "How'd you know it was my favorite?"

"Because every time I'd come in here, you were on the same couch. Remember that night I woke you up from a nightmare?"

"Of course I do...that's the first night I knew I liked you."

He smiled and ran his hand up and down along Rose's back.

They reached her couch then and sat down together. She and Clayton sat on either end of the couch, facing one another. She bent her knees so they were between his legs and leaned against the armrest. He kept one leg on the couch, between the back and her feet, and the other hanging over the edge. It was incredibly sexy. Rose pried her eyes away before she closed the space between them and started kissing him.

"So, Rosabella. What about our conversation with Gianna and Donovan has you thinking? Your mind has got to be racing right about now."

She shook her head. "I don't know what you mean."

Clay rested one arm casually on the back of the couch and tapped the other on her ankle. "I *mean*, you were making that face of yours that means you were thinking about something."

"What face? I don't have that face."

"Don't worry, Rosabella. You don't have to hide anything from me." His fingers circled her round ankle bone. "The fact that you told me a secret this big shows that you trust me. There's no secrets between us. I now know I can trust you."

She blushed. "I just didn't want to play games with you. I'd rather you know and help us, rather than dance around the truth only to have it shoot back in my face later."

His fingers moved faster. "Oh really? That's the only reason you wanted me in on this particular secret?"

Was he teasing her? What on earth for? She didn't have any intentions in mind if that's what he was implying!

Rose crossed her arms. "Please elaborate a bit more. I'm not sure I understand what you're getting at."

"Gladly," he said, his voice husky. She hated when he did that. No she didn't, she absolutely adored the way his voice turned all gravely when he spoke to her about personal things. "Alright, I'll tell you what I think you're thinking..."

"Go for it," Rose said, shrugging. She had nothing to hide.

"I think you wanted me to be in on this pregnancy secret because you're thinking about the future...you want a family someday and you're wondering how I feel about it. This was a subtle way of diving into my head to discover if I could or could not handle a child."

Her mouth dropped open again. If this kept happening, she was going to unhinge her jaw. He was more than right, he was dead accurate! She wanted to know what his thoughts were on babies. Though, of course, that wouldn't be an option for years and years.

Clayton walked his fingers up her shin to her knee. "It was the first test in a series of tests that you're going to perform on me. It's your way of beating around the bush so that *I'm* the one to bring it up first. Tell me I'm wrong."

"I hate it when you can read my mind. Do you have some telepathic ability to read thoughts? I read a book once where this guy, Edward, could read people's minds."

Clayton smirked. "Yeah, and he was also a vampire. Both of those things are not real."

Rose wasn't sure whether to reel from the fact that he'd read or at least heard of *Twilight*, or the fact that he'd taken Gianna's pregnancy so well.

He patted her knee. "Don't worry, I don't read minds. You're my girl. I'd like to think I'm getting to know you pretty well at this point."

"Well if you know me really well, then what are my own thoughts about pregnancy?" She asked, crawling slowly over the cushions to him. Rose stopped just in front of him and rested on the backs of her heels. Her hands found their way to his chest and stayed there while she waited for an answer.

"Alright," he said, hands moving to her hips. "You want to have a baby someday--hopefully with me--and you want to be surprised. The way you were talking about a baby being the best surprise present ever got me thinking about your thought process. People above always plan--or do their best to plan out when they have children. You like the spontaneity of Gianna and Donovan's pregnancy, because it seems to be bringing them closer together. You want that in your life, whether you're ready for a child or not." He paused and let his hands travel under her sweatshirt to her stomach. "How'd I do?"

"Wow," she breathed, looking into his beautiful brown eyes. "How the hell did you get so good at this?"

He chuckled, his laugh vibrating her hands on his chest. "Well, I think it's easy. You just have to pay attention--"

"If you don't shut up and kiss me right now, Clayton Taylor, you're going to regret it. I'm really in a kissing mood."

He pulled her close until their noses brushed against one another. "Point taken."

She laughed as his lips trailed along her neck and down to her clavicle. His kisses alternated between light, butterfly kisses to rough, needy ones. Rose dug her fingers into his hair.

After they kissed for a while, Clayton slowed down and eventually stopped. He rested his forehead on her bare neck and breathed heavily in and out a few times.

"What do you say we give parenting a try? I'd be pretty good at it!"

Rose smacked the back of his head lightly. "Don't you dare say that!"

He laughed. "What? I thought you were in a baby mood after talking with Gianna and Donovan!"

"Well, yeah. But not for my *own* baby. Besides," she said, shaking her head. "Don't you know the first step you have to take to *get* pregnant?"

He sat up and kissed her nose. "Of course I do, why do you think I brought it up?"

Rose gasped and pushed away. "I'm not ready for that. And especially not on a--a couch!"

Clayton rubbed her arms. "I told you we didn't have to do anything. But if we ever do I'd like to make it romantic for you. I'd plan out this huge night for us."

She rolled her eyes and smiled, loving the attention from him. Rose also loved that he was planning it all out. "How about when? Not if."

The face he made was the look she had when he talked about how romantic a pregnancy could be.

"Alright then, my girl says when. I'll take what I can get."

Rose pushed him back down on the couch and sprawled out on top of him. She rested her head on his chest. "I love when you call me your girl."

His fingers toyed with her hair. "I'm glad. My girl will never be disappointed by me. I'm going to stay true to her and make her feel more loved than anyone else in the whole world."

She giggled and teased, "Promises, promises. Let's hope you can keep them."

"I promise. You're more important to me than anything else, Rose. I will make you happier than any other woman on this planet. If not, you tell me right away and we'll see what we can do to fix that." He wrapped his arms around her back. "You got that? Need me to write it down?"

She laughed and patted his shoulder. "No, no, I've got it. How about you start by kissing me?"

He saluted her. "Absolutely. Wouldn't want to disappoint."

# Chapter 30

## (ROSABELLA)

THE NEXT FEW WEEKS WENT BY IN A blur. Rose and Eden worked closely during that time to transition Rose from one-on-one training to group training with the rest of her age bracket. She made a point of getting to know the other teenagers who escaped with her and Aire from the party. The majority of them had known Rose from school, which made her feel guilty, because she didn't know many of them. She'd been too focused on her own life and family to get to know others besides Aire...but look how that turned out. It was probably better Rose was on her own for a while down here, what with everyone thinking of her as a celebrity or something. Thankfully, that idea of Rose had dwindled down by now.

Rose had been here for months already, though she didn't really believe that. Things were shaping out in every aspect of her life down here. Well, *almost* everything. Aire was still a no-go; she and Rose still hadn't even looked at one another. Gianna and Clarise were Rose's female confidants, Andre a somewhat annoying friend, Logan her best friend, and Clayton her boyfriend. The only thing missing was her family. There was no doubt that she'd found herself a new family down here, but she couldn't help but question her father's subtle references to a different life. Had he always known that the Fortress would take them in if they needed to flee from the Government? How would that even work? Would they have to erase their lives up above? Fake their deaths?

Today, Rose was assigned to duel with Lucca. She assumed Clayton did that on purpose. He wanted her to be able to get back at him for hurting her that first day she'd been in the training room. Rose was way over it; she didn't even care anymore. If anything, it actually helped strengthen things between herself and Clayton. It was also the day she'd met Clarise in the medical wing. Rose knew she'd endure that whiplash all over again if it meant those same events would play out the way they did.

Eden pulled Rose aside and gave her a quick pep talk. "Now, Rosabella, don't worry about what other people are shouting to you. You just get your head in there and you work on those protective maneuvers like we've worked on together."

Rose stretched her arm across her chest to warm up. "Okay, but what about my plan of attack? What do you think I should do?"

Her instructor patted Rose on the arm. "Well, let's try to get you through this fight without a concussion. You can wear him down and then claim the winning title once he's announced defeat."

That pissed Rose off. Did Eden seriously think she couldn't win this by fighting? What good was a trainer if she didn't believe in her pupil? Rose caught Clayton's eye across the room. His smile faltered when he saw the hard set of her mouth.

She turned back to Eden. "Thanks for your advice, but I want to do this my own way. I'm a lot stronger now."

Eden shook her head and crossed her arms. "But so is Lucca. You have to play this smart."

Rose pulled her hair back into a ponytail and stared Eden down. "Would playing it smart apply to a droid fight up above?"

Her face fell. "Rose, this isn't the same thing. This is training."

"But training is for what? I'll tell you...*real life*, Eden. We can't afford to 'play it safe' when we're supposed to be the protectors of the Fortress."

Eden knew she had lost Rose's respect then. Rose didn't even try to argue.

Eden walked away shaking her head. "I didn't mean to offend you Rosabella. Please just think about what I said."

The second Rose stepped onto the mat, she felt guilt tear through her. What right did she have to talk to a person like that? It reminded her of when she'd first heard Clayton speak disrespectfully to that nurse when he carried her here on her first night in the Fortress.

She'd already started to cool down, her face somewhat returning to its normal color. Rosabella took a deep breath and held her arms to protect her face and upper body, just like when she and Logan had trained together. This was different than their friendly sparring. Lucca was out for blood. She'd seen the way he trained with the group, always pushing to be the best, making people feel insecure by commenting on their flaws. He played a mind game more so than physical. She'd have to keep her head on her shoulders and ignore any insults he used.

One of their training peers held up a hand. She relayed the instructions of the fight first, "Alright, you know how this works. We don't fight to knock out, we fight to show our skills and stamina. When you feel you've hit your limit, call for defeat."

Lucca smiled. "Oh, no need for that on my part. Defeat is not in my vocabulary."

The girl rolled her eyes and dropped her hand. Rose transferred her weight on the balls of her feet, making sure to stay light and moveable. The more she could flit around the mat, the better chance she'd have of dodging punches.

Lucca moved right away, throwing a punch to her jaw. Rose ducked and dashed around him. She turned and kicked the back of his knee. He groaned and fell to one knee. She went for an equally hard kick to his other knee, but Lucca fell to the floor and rolled, taking her legs out from under her in the process. Her mind turned on, adrenaline advising her to barrel roll far enough away from him so he couldn't pin her down.

Here, there weren't many rules other than no kicking in the sensitive region of the male body. Hell, there weren't even any specific rules indicating the fight had to stay on the *mat*.

She looked around to make sure there was an open space. When Lucca dove at her, Rose lay there in wait. At the last second, she lifted him up and over herself with her legs. All that weight training had done wonders for the muscles in her thighs and calves. Lucca was at least a foot taller than her and weighed significantly more, yet she'd managed to throw him using only her legs. A few cheers rang in favor of Rose. She didn't have time to think about their encouraging shouts, because she was already jumping to her feet.

Lucca and Rose danced around one another, making their way around the room. People ducked and moved out of the way wherever they went. After another successful kick, Rose jabbed her fist into his spine. He fell to the ground in a heap.

Then Lucca quickly hopped up and rubbed his left elbow. Rose could use that to her advantage if things got messy. She would never intentionally exploit someone's weakness to defeat them, but in this case, she knew Lucca wasn't going to give up easily.

Lucca taunted her, drawing Rose closer to him, "Come on Porter. This is a fight, not a playground."

She ignored him and trained her eyes on the rest of his body, careful not to linger too long. If he noticed her scanning a particular body part, he might anticipate her next move. They walked in a circle, glaring at one another.

Lucca shrugged. "I'd be willing to pretend this was a playground if you wanted to give up now. We can run around, hold hands, sing songs…"

"Shut the hell up," she growled. *Don't let him get to you. Don't let him get in your head.* Rose's advice was stellar, but whether or not she followed it would be a different story.

"In fact," he said smiling. "When I get the first pick of careers here and I choose to be a trainer, maybe you'll be more willing to play around with *me.*"

Rose had no idea what he was talking about; he spoke in riddles. Her eyes trained in on his leg, to trick him into thinking she'd go for his knees again. She feigned a kick, and when Lucca reached down to block it, she threw her elbow into his cheek. He cried out as he lost his balance. Rose jumped on him, straddled him, and pinned him to the floor.

Her forearm pressed into his neck to cut off his air. If she held him this way for long enough, maybe he'd give in. It wouldn't be as short a fight as she'd hoped for, but it would be a win nonetheless.

Lucca wheezed, a disgusting smile still on his face, "Is this…what you do…with your trainer…boytoy? Now I totally…get it…it kinda…turns me on…actually."

"Shut up!"

He laughed, an ugly strained sound. "Now I get…why Clayton…likes you…you have a…very nice…body…all those…curves."

She wound her arm back and drove her fist into his bad elbow.

He let out a howl and started screaming, "Defeat! Defeat!"

At that word, Rosabella released him and crawled off Lucca as if he'd stung her. A nurse ran over to Lucca and started assessing him for injuries. Another nurse, this one male, came to Rose's side and inspected her. She waved him off. The only pain she'd suffered was mental; the nurses couldn't help her with that.

Bernard walked up to Rose, flanked by Andre and Logan. "That was excellent, Miss Porter. Am I to understand that this was your first official combat fight?"

She nodded, rubbing a sore spot on her elbow. Her fingers came away, wet with sticky blood. The force of her elbow hitting Lucca's flesh replayed in her mind. She'd have to get a bandage for it herself, seeing as though the nurse who offered to help her was now helping escort Lucca to the medical wing.

Andre patted Rose on the back. "That was great Rosie Posie! If you keep doing that, you'll have a good future ahead of you in external security."

Logan shook his head. "There are other careers besides security."

Bernard held up his hands before the guys could begin arguing. "No more talking about that. I don't want either of you to recruit for your positions. To *anyone*. Is that clear?" He waited for them to nod. "The career choices our trainees make should be based solely on their interests and skills."

Logan nodded. "Yes, Sir."

Andre gave Bernard a curt nod and stepped away to talk to Eden about something. That left Rose alone with Logan and Bernard.

Their leader looked around. "I'm afraid there are too many prying eyes for me to discuss something important with you, Rosabella. Can we go to my office?"

She immediately searched the room for Clayton. He was staring at her from the other end of the room, where he was overseeing a group of younger trainees' boxing practice. Rose didn't want to go with Bernard. She wanted to stay here and talk to Clayton. Had he watched the whole match with Lucca? Did he think she'd done well or would he have pointers for her?

Logan touched her bare elbow, considering the blood. "Please, Rosabella. We'll get you supplies to wrap this up, too."

She looked back at Clayton and forced a smile. Then she turned her attention to Bernard before Clayton reacted. She didn't want to know what he was thinking. "Okay, sure. Let's go."

Bernard congratulated her on the fight while the three of them walked to his office. It wasn't too far of a walk, just down the hall. She thanked him, instantly embarrassed by his praise. Logan kept a close eye on her while they walked, even placing his hand between her shoulder blades to guide her. Rose wasn't about to pass out or anything. He didn't need to be so worried.

"Why don't you find a seat and I'll go get a bandage for you?" Logan asked, steering her into the huge conference room she'd first met with Bernard.

"Yeah, okay."

Bernard laughed and sat in the chair near the left wall after Logan left. "So I take it you're a little flustered right now?"

She nodded. "I don't know why. I won my first fight. Shouldn't I be excited?"

He patted her hand. "Yes dear, but I heard what Lucca was saying. I want to clear that up for you if I may."

Bernard had heard Lucca talk about her body? Heard him say that the only reason Clayton liked to be around her was because of her curvy figure? Well, not in those exact words, but close enough.

"Clayton Taylor loves you, I can tell. He and I are very close, you know. In all the years he and his sister have been here, I've never seen him love someone the way he loves you. Not even Tess."

Rosabella trained her eyes on the floor. If she looked at Bernard she might reveal something she didn't want him to know. Like the fact that she hadn't officially known Tess was a love interest of Clayton's years ago. No wonder he hadn't told her a lot.

"Don't be upset with Clayton, he's very guarded. I'm impressed he's let you in as much as he has with Clarise and all. I can only give so much advice to that young man."

"He's talked to you about me?" Should Rose be upset? Flattered? How much did Bernard know? Was he aware of Gianna's pregnancy?

"Rosabella?" Bernard snapped his fingers in front of her face. "Mr. Taylor is like my grandson. He trusts me with information and in turn, I keep it to myself. Unless, of course, it can benefit people. In this case, I know hearing that is important to you. Clayton and I share in a weekly breakfast to catch up on things...I started seeing him frequently after Tess--well, I can't tell you *that* just yet--but anyway, I knew he needed some extra help adjusting. He's had a lot of anger built up over the years, which is why you saw him in a different light when you first arrived."

The rushing flow of angry blood in her ears subsided. She shouldn't be upset with Clayton or Bernard. Clayton was simply confiding in a friend, someone who was willing to listen.

"Then you came along and helped him change back into his old self."

Rose shook her head, almost in disbelief. "I don't think that's exactly my doing."

Bernard shrugged. "You're probably right. It's a combination of things. But a very impressive change has been made in Clayton and it started when you arrived. For that, I am very grateful to you. And now--"

A knock at the door cut Bernard off. His voice switched to commanding again as he asked who it was. Logan replied and was welcomed back into the office. He sat in the chair next to Rose, between herself and Bernard.

"Here, can I help you?" Logan took Rose's elbow in his hand and dabbed at the drying blood with a cool, wet antiseptic wipe. He spoke as he got to work, "I'm not sure how they could pair you with that giant."

Rose wrenched her elbow from his hold. "I can do it. And for the record, I'm perfectly capable of winning a fight."

Bernard chuckled to himself and turned to the screen on the wall. He logged in and searched around for a file while Logan gaped at her.

She felt bad for snapping at him and apologized, "I'm sorry, Logan. I'm just frustrated that people think I can't handle myself. What do they think I've been doing for months, sitting and doing *nothing*?" She sighed and handed him the bloody wipe back. He wrapped it in another one and set it on the table, moving quietly. Rose took Logan's hand in hers. "It's just frustrating. I've worked just as hard as the next person here--possibly even harder--and all I get are doubts from people because I'm not...well, let's just say I don't have a very athletic body structure...and probably also because I nearly died the night I was brought here."

Logan shook his head. "That's not why I said that. I just worry about you, Rosabella. The last time you fought with Lucca, you wound up in the medical wing. I'm just trying to look out for you."

"I appreciate it, I really do Logan. But if you're my friend, you'd see how frustrating it is to be put down because of things like that. Lucca told me that the only reason Clayton liked me was because of my...my *body*."

Logan's hands hesitated as he wrapped a bandage around her elbow. "I can't believe that. No way. There's so much more to you than that!"

She blushed and gently took the role of bandaging tape from Logan. Rose finished the bandage herself, wrapping it tighter than necessary, but she didn't mind. It helped to numb the pain.

"Alright you two, it's time we discuss something important." Bernard's deep voice pulled their attention to him. He stood in front of the wall screen, displaying a picture of a strange game board. "Logan already knows the story, so feel free to ask any questions you may have, Rosabella. Oh, and Eden will be joining us shortly."

Rose squinted at the screen. There were countless blank spaces, each in their own color groupings, six colors in total. It looked like a similar version of a board game she used to play...if only she could remember the name of it. While it all looked like fun and games, Bernard wasn't playing around here. That much she knew. So what did it all mean?

"I received word from one of my close contacts from up above that the Government has come across something very instrumental for determining the future of our country," Bernard started, drawing out the last word. "As you can see here," he gestured to the screen and pointed to the first space in the corner, the one titled GO. "This is where we start. Each color represents the different sectors. So there are six different sectors in which the board will take us.

"Additionally, my contact sent me a letter with all of this information. All he knows is that there's a key at the end of each location...a puzzle or a physical object. It's unclear what they'll be exactly. The Government doesn't know they're up against us, they just know that they have an opponent.

"The point of this is that, in order to advance, we must find the correct key at each location. That's where you and Eden come in. We are looking for two skilled Fortress members to go on the first key hunt."

Logan agreed, "Right, and Bernard trusts us with this secret over anyone else. So you can't--"

"Wait. Pause. Why do you trust *me*?" Rose asked, growing even more confused with each passing second.

Bernard smiled at her from his place beside the screen. "Because my dear, you are very trustworthy. I've been keeping tabs on you. If it's for the greater good, you know how to keep a secret, unless of course, you're allowed to share it…"

Was he referring to Gianna's pregnancy? Or something else? If so, what the heck did he mean? How did he even find out about it?

"Can I continue?" He asked gently.

She nodded, her mind spinning. "Oh, wait. Can I ask a question?"

He bobbed his head once.

"So what exactly is at the end of the line? I guess, what I mean is, what are we hoping to discover? Also, does anyone want to explain to me how this came into the picture? How did your contact get a hold of it again, Bernard?"

Bernard and Logan made eye contact. Logan leaned forward in his chair and rested his chin on his palm.

"I honestly can't remember. He said the Government officials came across it at some point about a year ago. I can't say where it originated, or who created it, or even what it leads to. But I do know that if the Government is after whatever's at the end, there's got to be a reason for it," Bernard said, crossing his arms. "What we do know is that the Government will stop at nothing to succeed and get to the end of the journey first, which is why it peaked my contact's interest. The Government is worried about losing their power, as they know they have many flaws that are beginning to upset people again. All of that gives me reason to be nervous they'll play dirty…but never fear, we will win in the end. I can feel it."

"So, we're in a race with the all-powerful Government--the one that could obliterate us in five minutes--for something we don't even exactly know will help us restore humanity to our country?" She tapped the table top. "That doesn't really make much sense to me, I'm sorry Sir."

He smiled at her. "Don't worry my dear, I thought the same thing myself. But my contact works undercover in the Government right now and is very adamant that we go after whatever is at the end of this thing… the letter he sent me was very clear that whatever's at the end of this journey is something that can control the Government. My guess is that it's some kind of old artifact that was hidden away for the day when our country became corrupt again. These things never truly last. There are twists and turns, and sometimes deaths, but in the end, the people leading the system are bound to become corrupt if their morals change."

Wow, this was insanely heavy stuff. Whatever this board led to held the power to change the Government. Rose was definitely up for the challenge, but what would Clayton think if she began keeping all kinds of secrets from him?

Bernard leaned forward and rested his hands on the back of his chair. His posture commanded her attention again. "Well, Porter, what do you think?"

"How many locations will we have to search?"

Logan chimed in, "Well, there's four corners that are already given to us: the GO space, the Jail and Just Visiting space, the Free Space and then the Go to Jail space. There are three Chance options, which means things could get really good for us really fast, or really bad; two utilities and two Community Chest spaces. I believe there's twenty-two other spaces left besides those. The locations with the keys."

"Right," said Bernard. "Then, like the original game, you'll have the option to visit each of the four major Hydro Tube Stations."

"Oh, I see! It's like Monopoly, that really old game with all the money and properties for sale."

Logan nodded. "Precisely. Though, this is much different. Instead of playing for fun, we are fighting for the future of our country."

Rosabella was officially intrigued. This was scary but fascinating at the same time. "So will we have to roll dice like the old game too?"

"Unfortunately, yes," Bernard said, letting out a sigh. He pinched the bridge of his nose, lost in thought.

Someone knocked on the door. Startled, Rose jumped in her seat.

"It's Eden, Sir."

"Good, good." Bernard went to the door to let her in. "Wells, it seems Rosabella has agreed to join us."

Eden beamed at Rose as she took a seat across from her at the table. "I was very impressed with you earlier, Rose. Great work against Lucca."

She blushed at the memory of yelling at Eden. "Thank you, and I'm so sorry for what I said."

Eden waved Rose off. "Not a problem. That was a test of your character, and you did not disappoint."

Rose spun her chair to face Bernard. "That was a *test*?"

Logan and Bernard both chuckled.

"My dear," Bernard said. "It was *my* idea. I needed to see if you were confident in your own skill set. It's important for us to have strong-willed and talented people on our team."

"Oh. Well in any case, Eden, I apologize for being rude to you," Rose said again.

"Not a problem, Miss Porter. Like I said, I was very impressed," Eden said, tipping her hat to Rose.

"Now that that's out of the way," started Bernard, "I need you all to be aware that once we lock in our team, we cannot leave at any time. We are tied to this...this *challenge* until the end--whatever the results may be." He waited a few seconds and made eye contact with each of them. "I have to lock in our team in no more than four months. We have until then to decide if we are going to move forward..."

Rose rubbed her nose, thinking. "But what if we don't join?"

Bernard heaved a sigh and tapped his fingers on the arm of his chair. "Then all will be lost. If the Government wins, they will use the end result to their own advantage. The Government as we know it may change into one that will crush any remaining chance of freedom the citizens above have."

"Right, so basically, we're going to do it no matter what?" Rose rubbed her hands together. "So how does this work now? Do we go out on a mission to find the next key then?" She stared at the screen. "When do we start?"

The three of them laughed. Bernard double-tapped the screen to zoom in on the first space, lined in dark purple. The label remained invisible for the time being. Perhaps it didn't give the names of the locations until the game officially started.

"First, we need to prepare you. You've never been out on a mission before, Rose, and we need to be sure you know what you're doing. As I said earlier, this is a matter of life and death. I need to know you can handle our process before we dive right in."

"But I thought we were on a time crunch! Why can't we--"

Bernard silenced her with the shake of his head. "Absolutely not. Just because you're strong and think you're ready, the second you get out into the world, that might change. I don't want your emotions to get the best of you if you see someone you used to know or realize someone you used to know is dead."

She threw herself into the back of her chair and groaned. "Fine, but I want to go on a mission as soon as possible. I'm ready."

He nodded. "I don't doubt that. We'll have you ready by the end of the week to go on your first mission."

# Chapter 31

## (ROSABELLA)

TRUE TO HIS WORD, BERNARD HAD A MISSION arranged for Rose by Friday afternoon that week. It was supposed to be a minor mission in which she'd be with Andre the whole time. Their job was to do a patrol through the nearby neighborhoods that had been attacked by the droids recently and search for any suspicious activity. Logan showed her how to scan her thumb to operate the elevator and which password to use--they changed once a month--so that she was ready to go the day of.

The only thing left for her to do was to tell Clayton. He wasn't going to like it. But Rose didn't want secrets between them, though she had no choice with the keys and the mysterious board. He'd been sharing stories of Tess with her lately, and it was getting really personal. At least he'd begun to open up more with her. She couldn't bear to have him upset with her and stop their sharing sessions. One of her favorites was one yesterday morning when they both woke up around the same time and he poured his heart into sharing a story about Tess.

Rose was supposed to leave right after lunch this afternoon. That only gave her a couple hours of the morning to tell Clayton about her mission. She didn't need to be so nervous, it's not like it was his decision or anything. Rose knew it would be difficult for him though, seeing as though he lost Tess on a mission. He hadn't gone into detail about it, but she knew he was worried about anyone he cared about going on a mission now. It was no wonder he didn't work in mission control. He wouldn't be able to handle organizing missions and letting people out, knowing they may never return. It was part of the mission process, as Logan had told Rose when he walked her to her dorm after their meeting with Bernard and Eden. Why she didn't tell Clayton right away, she couldn't say. Rose's heart took over at the time, preventing her from causing him any pain at all.

She slipped her gloves over her already bruised knuckles. Today the trainees were working on boxing. Thanks to Eden and Logan, Rose had already received lots of practice. Her boxing skills were nearly perfect at this point.

Rosabella had used her body for training so much lately she had bruises *on* her bruises. She'd started wearing leggings to training instead of shorts due to all the black and blue splotches all over her pale, thick thighs. Her arms were no better, and her elbow was still healing from her fight with Lucca. Clayton had done his best to get her ice packs at night when she stayed with him, but he couldn't help her during the day when she went through training. She didn't want him to anyway, they were her battle scars; proof she was becoming a better, stronger version of herself.

The lessons had consistently increased in difficulty; each day the trainers added more and more physical combat. At this point, the bikes were seldom used and the mats were filled with trainees working on their new instructions.

Finally, Rose took a moment during a quick break to pull Clayton aside.

When they were alone, he handed her his water bottle. "Here, try this. It has electrolytes. It helps your body keep up with all the exercise you've been doing."

Rose tried the drink, letting the blue liquid spill over her tongue. It exploded into a berry flavor. "Yum, this is really good!"

"Right?" He leaned against the wall. "So how's it going today?"

"Good," she shrugged. If she kept her face as neutral as possible, Clayton wouldn't freak out when she dropped the bomb that she was going on a mission.

"Just good?" he asked, brows drawing together.

She passed him the water bottle and diverted his attention to something else. "Are you no longer concerned about what people think of us?"

"Not at all. I want *everyone* to know that you're my girl," he said, pulling her to him. "Now, are you going to tell me what's going on, or do I have to tickle it out of you?" His fingers found the ticklish spot on Rose's side and danced around there.

She backed away, hands up in surrender. "Please don't! I'll--I'll tell you!"

Clayton smiled triumphantly and then gave her a pointed look.

"I'm going above ground this afternoon..." She looked him in the eye so he'd know she was serious. "Bernard and Logan assigned me an easy, harmless mission. I'll be with Andre the whole time, there's nothing to worry about."

He crossed his arms and smiled. "Sweet. So you're going on a practice mission. Why do you seem so nervous then? You'll be great!"

"Well, I know that Tess went on a mission one day and didn't come back...so I just thought you'd be sensitive to me leaving on one too," she said in a quiet voice. It all made her feel a little silly now. She'd overreacted.

Clay kissed her forehead. "You're so sweet. I appreciate you being sympathetic, but if it's just a minor mission, I'm not worried. Tess went on a life-threatening mission. We all knew what she was getting into."

Rose sighed and kissed his cheek. "Oh thank goodness! I'll see you at lunch. Love you!"

"Love you too," Clayton said, giving her a squeeze.

She ran back to her training group, utterly relieved. Clayton was stronger than she gave him credit for. The girl next to Rose nudged her and winked. Rose smiled back to be polite, but she was annoyed that people were so nosey. They shouldn't be so....so...what was the word she was looking for? Whatever the case, Rose was sick of people thinking, now that she was public with Clayton, she was a love expert. It was almost as bad as when they had considered her a celebrity for surviving the droid attack. Seriously, a few girls had come up to her when she was in the food line at dinner a couple days ago. They'd asked her for advice on how to ask their crushes out. Rose just told them to trust their guts and go with a natural approach. Cliche, but effective. If she'd been anything but her authentic self, Clayton wouldn't have liked her--he'd said as much. For once, she was grateful for her outbursts and yelling matches with Clayton. It didn't get any more authentic than that. He'd seen the worst side of her and had still fallen in love with her.

***

Clayton stood at the foot of the elevator with Rose, waiting for Andre to arrive. He was late. Shocker.

"Why are you friends with Andre?" She asked, checking her wrist band. She tapped it and asked for the time. He was ten minutes late.

Clay laughed and patted her on the lower part of her back. "I'm not really sure. I guess he just gets me, you know?"

"Well, I don't get *him*. He's always late to things! How do you even get stuff done with him? How do you make plans to hang out with him if you're on a time crunch? I just don't understand."

"Hold your horses. One question at a time please!" Clayton teased Rose, his lips tickling her ear. "For the record, when I want to plan things with him, I tell him to be there half an hour early so he actually shows up right on time."

She threw her hands up. "That's so rude of him!"

"I know, but what else can I do? I'm not exactly easy to make friends with. Dre's the only one who knows me and sticks around."

While Rose didn't completely understand Andre, she wasn't going to burst Clayton's bubble. Andre would have plenty of time to do that when he told Clayton about him and Clarise. Rose didn't want Clarise to get hurt by Clayton telling her to stay away from Andre, but she still wasn't even entirely convinced that Andre wouldn't hurt Clair. Since she'd met him, Rose was very aware of Andre's lust for practically any woman. Come to think of it, lately she hadn't seen him eyeing other girls. But Rose could also be seeing what she wanted to see. Maybe it was possible for him to change for the girl he liked.

Rose also didn't know why he liked Clarise. She was beautiful, funny, charming and all that, but she was also eight years younger than him! That was a huge age gap, at least where Rosabella was from. People above never married that far apart. They were almost always the same age, since everyone was paired at the age of twenty one. If there was overflow, Rose wasn't sure how the Government handled that. If a man didn't get paired with a woman and vice versa, she had no idea what happened to them. She'd never met anyone who didn't have a pair.

Andre saved Rose from having to respond to Clayton by running down the hall. He stopped at the doors, pressed the up button, and handed Rose an earpiece all within three seconds. "Here Rosie Posie, put this in your ear. Hi, Clay. Bye, Clay," he called back at Clayton.

Rose followed Andre into the elevator, rolling her eyes. Clayton laughed and waved to her. Someone had installed a dim light bulb in the center of the elevator's ceiling. It was actually less scary with the lights completely off. Now Rose could see all the wires and gears that were crudely placed. She leaned against the wall furthest from Andre in the small space. He didn't make any dirty comments to her or even look her way for that matter.

The moment the doors closed, Andre spoke, "Sorry for being late. I was...I was with...umm...Clair."

She reached across the small space and smacked Andre on the arm. "You're so stupid! Do you *want* Clay to kill you?"

He winced and rubbed his arm. "Ouch! Of course I don't want him to kill me, but I can't help myself."

Rose smacked him again in the same place. "You'd better help yourself or else Clayton's going to find out about you two before you're ready. If he isn't eased into it, he's going to snap. And it won't end well for anyone."

"Okay, okay, I got it. Can you just stop hitting me?"

"Only if you promise to respect Clarise. She's impressionable and very, very naive," Rose warned. She tucked her hair back and placed the earpiece into her left ear. "She will be devastated if you do anything that hurts her."

Andre leaned away from her. "I got it. And I'm serious, I really like Clair. I won't hurt her."

She rolled her eyes. "You say that now, but I know you Dre. All you care about is getting one thing from a girl and then you move on."

He glared at her and rose to his full height, shouting down at her, "Clarise is different. I'm not going to hurt her."

The ferocity in his words took her off guard. If she didn't know any better, she'd say Andre really cared for Clair. It could all be an act, but maybe there was truth behind what he said. No matter what happened, Rose would keep her eye on him, for Clarise's sake. When Clayton found out, he was going to be pissed, but he'd understand once Rose told him how she made sure of Andre's intentions.

She watched Andre glare at the floor for the rest of the elevator ride. Once they reached the top, he started filling her in on instructions. She was impressed by his sudden shift to business mode.

"Okay, so it's just you and me today, Rosie Posie. We're going to do a simple perimeter check." He double-tapped his own earpiece and gestured for her to do the same. "These are for Logan and the rest of mission control to keep contact with us. If they see anything on the surveillance cameras that looks suspicious, they'll alert us right away. Just be careful you don't accidentally shut it off."

"Got it, don't touch the earpiece." She felt for the smooth metal in her ear. It was the same color as each of their skin tones, blending in perfectly with their ears. Rose followed Andre to the kitchen. "Can I talk to them too?"

He nodded. "Yes, but you have to hold down the earpiece to talk... Oh, and you'll want to keep the talking to a minimum if you're ever in a pinch. Especially if you're hiding from someone."

Rose was about to ask if he'd ever run into a situation like that, when the front door opened and slammed shut. Andre shoved Rose behind the kitchen island. They both knelt down and waited.

Andre kept his voice quiet and low as he whispered, "Harrison to mission control. What's in the house?"

Rose couldn't hear what the reply was. She wished their earpieces were connected so she could get in on the same information. This was supposed to be a practice for her. She'd be going on extremely dangerous missions soon enough with Eden. That was, if Bernard deemed it okay. He'd told her that this practice was important for her. She was meant to learn the ins and outs of this neighborhood and surrounding areas in case she ran into a situation where she was on her own. At least Rose had an advantage there. She'd lived in this same house her whole life; she knew her way to and from the tube station. If she was ever lost, all she had to do was follow the sounds of the tube and make her way to the east from there to get back to the Fortress.

Andre nodded and thanked mission control. "We're good, Rose. Just someone returning from their own mission."

She nodded and brushed her pants to cover up the excited shaking in her hands. Rose hadn't been nervous at all. In fact, she'd been *excited*. She'd even hoped they'd run into some kind of trouble just to keep things interesting. She could only do the same thing so many times before it became boring. Training was great and all, but she was definitely ready for the action that came with going on a real mission. She'd heard from her other peers about some of their own missions. Only a few of them hated going above, and generally those were the Fortress-born citizens. They didn't appreciate the true beauty of the world above if they disliked their missions. Besides, who could hate a mission, no matter how minor? Their bodies were trained to fight back at all costs. They shouldn't worry about their skill level being inadequate or anything like that. It was all muscle memory.

They'd even spent a day learning about the ways in which to fool the Government. They were given ID cards to show any Government official or guard who inquired about their reasoning for being out and about. Of course, those IDs included their pictures, but not their real names. Each of them was given a fake name and an identity up above. Bernard had a good contact pretty high up in Government who was able to add their fake identities to the country's directory. At the two month mark, they were supposed to have crafted a completely different life for themselves up above. It was their job to pick the sector of their origin and the rest of their lives.

Rose had worked with Clarise to craft a perfect story about her own fake identity. They agreed that Rose's college-aged alter persona had been born in the northernmost part of the Northeastern sector. It was one of the only places they'd believe, based on the paleness of her skin. No way could she have pulled off being from one of the southern sectors. Her family consisted of a mom, a dad, and an older sister, Kaelyx, who was already finished with college. Being the youngest was a better alternative to Rose being the eldest, because it helped to explain her carelessness with being off on her own in a random neighborhood. It was common for college students to wander off campus from time to time. Rose could just play the dumb card and say she'd lost her way from the tube station or something.

She and Clarise had her whole fake life figured out so that it was foolproof. The only problem Rose might have would be if she ran into anyone who knew her dad and even herself. In that case, it was a free for all, and she had permission to terminate the person. Rose hoped like hell she didn't run into anyone like that. She couldn't bear to take anyone's life, especially if they knew her family. She would rather not have another situation like what happened with Grayson.

The other Fortress member stormed into the kitchen then. Rose took in her extra short white shorts and her low-cut pink blouse. Her dark hair was straightened and glistening, her heeled sandals wrapping around her ankles and up her shin.

"Rosie!" The girl cried in surprise, stopping in the doorway. "What are you doing here?"

Rose took a step forward, prepared to brush past her. "Aire, I'm going on a mission. I'm not sure what you were doing, but we actually have serious business to take care of. Come on, Dre."

"Wait, Rosie! I--I miss you. Please talk to me," Aire pleaded, eyes wide.

Rose whisked past her so she wouldn't have to see the tears in her friend's eyes. "I'm a little busy right now. Maybe later."

Andre followed after her. Once they were outside, he leaned down and whispered, "We have important business?"

She brushed him off and laughed angrily. "Well, I wanted to make it sound important. Can you blame me?"

He shook his head and began walking to the street. He gestured for Rose to follow. "I don't understand girls. She was on a mission too, Rose."

"Oh no she wasn't. She was dressed too nicely to be on a mission. Didn't you notice the glitter on her eyes and the blush on her cheeks? She was *definitely* doing something entirely unrelated to the Fortress. Nobody dresses like that."

Andre sighed and continued walking across the street to the first row of houses. "Or maybe she's comfortable that way. Not everyone needs to dress like an ogre, Rose. Just you."

She scowled at him and forced her voice to remain even. "Oh yeah? Then perhaps I should go tell Clayton what you said about my fashion, and while I'm at it, I can bring up a certain relationship between his best friend and his sister."

Andre whirled around, fear in his eyes. He stood there, mouth opening and closing as if trying to say something. Rose tapped her foot in wait, hands on her hips.

Eventually, he looked at the ground. "I know you don't like me, Rose, but I promise my heart is only meant for Clarise. Clay wouldn't understand that...If he found out, he'd take her away from me and I'd be left with nothing."

Against her better judgement, Rose felt her anger for Andre melting away. It only took a second before she sympathized with him. Clayton was pretty difficult when it came to things like this. He wouldn't be quick to understand, and even slower to forgive. Rose thought about the loneliness Andre would feel if Clayton forced him away. It reminded herself of what was currently happening between her and Aire. Everyone deserved to be given a chance, right? In some cases, even a second chance?

"You're right, Andre. He would rip you to pieces. I'm sorry for being so rude about it, I just really don't want Clarise to get hurt." She took a step closer to Andre. "I'm sure you can recall the first few interactions you and I had...you weren't exactly innocent in your comments at the time."

He looked at her, eyes filled with sadness. Her heart cried out to him. "I'm sorry too. I guess I haven't really been a model citizen."

"You can say that again," she laughed sarcastically. Then she reached him and put her arm around him in a gesture of friendly comfort. "I'll do my best to help you and Clarise. I can't make any promises that Clayton isn't going to want to kill you, but I can promise that Clarise reciprocates your feelings."

He leaned gratefully into her arm, wrapping his own around her shoulders. "You know, you're really easy to talk to, Rosie Posie. I think we might actually become great friends, you and I."

She laughed and shoved him off. "We'll see about that. Let's start with this mission first and see how things go."

Andre nodded and headed west. "Sounds like a plan. I bet you'll be following me around like a lost puppy by the end."

"What's that supposed to mean?"

He smirked at her over his shoulder. "I just mean that you're going to find me the funniest friend you've ever had and you'll want to follow me everywhere because you just can't get enough of me...don't worry," he laughed, "I won't tell Clayton."

She shoved him again, rolling her eyes. "Just shut up and lead the way."

# Chapter 32

## (ROSABELLA)

Finally, Rose and Andre arrived at the tube station. It was eerily quiet. Nobody was rushing to catch the tube as she was used to seeing at the end of the day. After school, she and Aire would leave the tube station and head to their respective nearby neighborhoods. Rose's house was closer, so sometimes, Aire would hang out with Rose and her family until her mom picked her up.

Those were the days Rose liked to think back on. The days when she and Aire weren't even in high school yet. Luna started picking Aire up from school once she had her own career and life. As soon as that started happening, Rose felt Aire drawing slowly away from her, whether she knew it or not. Luna always offered a kind of rebellious life. Rose knew all the things Luna did to get her way, which usually involved using men. It was a despicable life and Rose worried about Aire falling into the same thing. But it wasn't her place to tell Aire what she shouldn't be doing, especially since she idolized Luna.

Andre walked up to the side of the building. "Normally we'd do these missions on our own, but ever since the droids showed up, we started going in pairs." He peeked around the corner of the building and walked up to the entrance.

"So what's the plan here?" She asked, tiptoeing behind him. "I thought this was a perimeter check?"

He stopped walking and pressed his earpiece. "Oh, for the love of god, Logan would you please share everything with Rosabella too? She's very nosy and I don't have the patience to answer all her questions."

Rose scoffed and tilted her head, waiting to hear Logan's voice. A squealing sound filled her ears, causing her to cry out.

"Sorry!" Logan cried into her ear. "Hold on a sec...there! Is that better?"

She remembered to press the earpiece to speak, "Much better."

He laughed. "Okay good. Now, follow Andre. I'll fill you in as you go."

"Okay," she replied, already on Andre's heels. She walked into the station behind him, scanning the scene for any people. A woman with a baby sat alone in the first row of chairs, watching the screen mounted on the wall. The random passerby probably wouldn't think their clothes fit in with the environment, but they likely wouldn't be brave enough to talk to Rose or Andre. Apparently, Prince had been living in the Fortress for far too long without a view of the real world above. Or he was just too eccentric to care about blending in.

"So, here's the deal, Rosabella," Logan said. "I had Dre lie about the perimeter check because I knew Clayton wouldn't want you doing anything like this. He'd throw a fit. We've received strange activity on the cameras recently. It appears droids have been surrounding the station at night. Thankfully, nobody's been injured."

Andre walked up to the same screen the woman was looking at. He studied it and held up ten fingers and then five to Rose. She took that as the tube would be arriving in fifteen minutes. He nodded and smiled at the woman before coming back to stand by Rose.

Meanwhile, Logan was still talking, "So, I've asked Andre to take you there. If anything is going to prepare you for...well you know...it would help you to pick up on a droid's trail if possible. Dre's been briefed on what he needs to know, but you and I have more insight into why you're on this particular mission...I could just as easily have sent you with a few of our newer external security guards to walk through the neighborhood and check that the houses were empty, but I figured this would be more beneficial to you."

She nodded along with him. "So I'm supposed to look for traces of the droids...why am I inside if you said they've been surrounding the station?"

"Because," he said, "I also wanted you and Andre to figure out why they've begun to surround the station. There's got to be a reason for that."

"Got it," she said, already searching for something that could be of use to the droids.

"Be safe," Logan said, his voice low. "If you need backup, you call right away, even if it turns out to be a false alarm. I can't have you getting injured."

As he talked, she knelt down behind a chair and looked under every chair in sight. Nothing.

She pressed her earpiece. "Backup. Got it. For real, Logan, we'll be fine."

"Yeah. I know."

Rose rolled her eyes, grateful he couldn't see her. "You're a good friend for worrying, but we've got this. Talk to you later."

Andre walked up to her and kept his voice at a whisper, "I'm going to check over there by the kiosk stand. You can check over there by the luggage return. We'll meet back here in ten minutes."

"Are we riding the tube?" She asked, checking the time on her wristband.

He shook his head, already walking away. "No, but we need to get out of here before people get off. Can't have too much exposure."

"Sounds good. See you soon."

"Don't do anything stupid," he said with a smirk. "I know how clumsy you can be."

She slapped him on the arm. "Shut up! Whatever you think you know is wrong."

He chuckled. "Oh, Clayton's told me a thing or two. It's quite cute how you manage to trip over your own feet sometimes...like when you fell out of the tub in his apartment a few days ago and he had to help you, even though you were dripping wet and naked. Good move on your part."

She glared at Andre. "Shut up. I was only *half* naked. Seriously. I fell and got my leg stuck." Her face warmed as a quick flash of a memory of Clayton wrapping her in a towel surfaced. "And for your information, he kept his eyes closed like a perfect gentleman."

Andre rolled his eyes, an evil smirk on his face. "Sure he did."

Rose stormed away from him so she wouldn't have to hear his evil laughs. It had been pretty pathetic of her, but Clayton had made her feel less idiotic after that. No matter how many dumb things Rose managed to do, he was always there for her, picking her up and giving her the confidence to move on.

Rose went to the luggage chutes as Andre suggested. The first, a return chute, opened up to a swirling metal conveyor belt that carried the luggage down to the people waiting. When there were people, that is. The second chute was for people to drop off their luggage before getting on the tube. It looked the exact same as the first one, but with a conveyor belt that ran in the opposite direction.

She knelt down to check the base of the return chute to see if there was anything important hidden underneath. There was a small gap that she was able to see through, but it was too dark for her to spot anything important. Why would the droids be surrounding this station? What was so important? Was it the tube they were after? The station? Or the people? If that was the case, they wouldn't come at night, they'd attack at the busiest times of the day. Like during rush hour, for instance.

Discouraged, Rose moved on to the drop off belt. She repeated the same useless process of examining the gap between the belt's base and the floor. If there was something under there, she wouldn't know it. A flashlight function on her wristband would've been pretty helpful right about now.

Without warning, the two belts whirred to life. The woman sitting near the tube doors lifted her baby from the seat beside her and hurried over to the drop off belt. Rose smiled at her and waved at the little baby. The little girl, probably only seven or eight months old, clung to her mother's collar and buried her face there. The woman smiled back at her, though she seemed unsure of Rose's intentions. To make the woman more comfortable while she lifted two bags onto the drop off belt, Rose moved away. She proceeded to make herself busy by tying her shoe off to the side.

One of the woman's bags fell from the moving belt. At the same time, her baby dropped the rattle she was playing with. Rose stood and surged forward to assist her.

"Here, let me help you," Rose said, bending over to pick up the rattle. She passed it back to the woman and then moved on to help lift the bag. Rose couldn't help but notice how heavy it was. People didn't normally pack that much for a regular trip.

"Thank you so much." The woman smiled, her weary eyes underlined by black sagging skin. It was clear she was exhausted.

Rose smiled back. "Not a problem. Are you heading out of town for a while?"

The woman squinted at her and took a step back. "Do you know my husband?"

"No. I'm here with my friend," Rose said, pointing to Andre across the room. "We're just waiting for...our other friend."

The woman laughed lightly. "Oh. Yeah, I'm just taking my little girl here on a trip. We need a break."

"A break?"

She shook her head and tucked her hair behind her ear. "Yeah, home life has been a little...rough lately. My husband is struggling at his job."

Rose took the baby's outstretched hand and played with her. "I'm sorry to hear that. What kind of work does he do?"

"He works at the Government Headquarters." The woman's face contorted and her eyes blazed. "They've been working him double time. We hardly see him at home anymore. And when he's home, all he does is yell and--oh sorry. You probably didn't need all that information."

"It's okay. I'm happy to listen," she assured, smiling at the baby.

"Would you like to hold her?" The woman held out her baby to Rose.

Rose glanced at Andre, but he was too busy typing something at the kiosk stand to notice what Rose was doing. She nodded and took the baby in her arms. Automatically, her body began swaying from side to side; she instantly remembered what it was like to hold her brother when he was a baby.

The woman leaned against the belt, an obvious weight on her shoulders. "She likes you."

"What's her name?" Rose asked. She beamed down at the baby, who was playing with Rose's long, red hair.

"Lilianna."

Rose kissed the baby's head. "How sweet. My name has four syllables too."

The woman seemed surprised. "Wow, that's wonderful! I was really worried about the name, but it's a family name, you know. My husband wanted more than anything for her to take his mother's name."

"Well, I love it," Rose said. Lilianna giggled and pulled hard on Rose's hair. Then she spotted Rose's earpiece and reached for it.

Before Rose could stop her, Lilianna pulled it out of her ear and threw it to the floor.

"Oh shoot!" Rose cried as the little metal piece clattered to the floor. It rolled away, past the conveyor belts. The infamous whirring pain started up in Rose's head unannounced. It was more bearable than last time, but slowly increasing. She tried not to move. Maybe it would just go away.

The woman's tired face twisted into a deep frown. "I'm so sorry. I should have warned you. Lilianna loves shiny things. She must have seen your earring." She hurried to pick it up for Rose.

"Oh that's okay," Rose said, attempting to reassure her while managing to not collapse from the sharp-shooting pain in her skull. "I have a little brother, so I'm used to him clawing at my face and throwing things." She shifted so Lilianna was on her left hip, while her right hand pressed into her temple to stop the pain.

"Rose!" Andre cried from across the room.

She turned around just in time to see his panicked expression. Then, the main entrance to the tube station blew open, glass shattering everywhere. Andre jumped back as a droid burst through the collapsed wall. He bumped against the kiosk, eyes wide. The woman screamed and fell to the floor. She covered the back of her head with her hands. Lilianna, alerted to her mother's screams of distress, began screaming and crying herself. Rose slowly took steps backwards to put distance between Lilianna and the droid. It hadn't paid them any mind yet. Her head filled with that awful pinching; she did everything in her power to keep from screaming. The little baby didn't need that anymore than Rose did.

Rosabella looked on in terror as the droid's head snapped in the direction of the woman. It closed the space between them in a matter of seconds and stood over her. It sniffed her air and leaned down, bending unnaturally at the waist. It's faceless head stopped merely inches from the woman's neck. Rose pulled Lilianna's face into her chest to block the view of her mother. As anticipated, the droid ripped at the woman's neck with its teeth, tearing her head clean from her body as easily as if cutting through butter. Rose turned her own face away, tears in her eyes. The pain in her head was still there, but now she had someone else to care for, so she had to push through it.

She spotted Andre. He was speaking into his earpiece. Simultaneously, he was making for the caved-in entrance. He gestured to Rose to start toward him. She made sure to move slowly, so as not to alert the droid of her presence. It wouldn't be long before it caught wind of them, especially with little Lilianna still crying. At least she'd ceased screaming. That might buy them some more time.

When she was close enough to Andre to hear him, Rose turned her back to the droid and ran to him.

He pulled her out into the sunlight, his grip on her arm iron-like. "Where the hell is your earpiece? Logan said he warned you that a droid was coming."

"It fell out back there. That--that woman was helping get it for me," Rose cried, clutching the baby closer. They ran in the direction of the Fortress.

Andre pulled her forward so she could keep up. "And *what* are you doing with a baby?"

"She was the woman's baby. We were just talking...she needed help. I was going to offer her sanctuary in the Fortress..." By now, the tears were running in streams down her face. This poor baby's mother was mauled by a droid. Would her husband be made aware of her death? Rose could tell the woman had been trying to get away from him, but surely he still loved her, right? Was he going to mourn for the loss of his baby too? It was all too much. Rosabella sobbed for Lilianna, now motherless. It sucked not having a mother around anymore, but at least Rose had grown up with one. Lilianna would never have that.

Andre roughly pulled her again. "Damnit Rose, we have to keep going. This wasn't supposed to happen. We're unprepared."

Rose couldn't even see where they were going, blinded by the slowly subsiding pain and tears. She did all she could to make sure to remain upright. She maintained her balance by feeling the artificial ground through the soles of her tennis shoes. Andre's grip on her never faltered, though he did slow down. Only slightly, just enough for her to keep at his quick pace. Her legs were much shorter than his.

The whirring pain grew again. Rose screamed and stumbled. She tripped forward, falling to her knees. She kept a tight grip around Lilianna so she wasn't thrashed around.

Andre said a very bad word before pressing his earpiece. "Backup, Logan. We need backup now! Goddamnit, Rose. Get up! You can't--"

He was cut off by the droid tackling him to the ground. One of its hands gripped Andre's right leg and pulled. Rose struggled to stand. A loud cracking sound filled the air at the same time as Andre's screams. He thrashed under the droid's hold, but it was no use. He wouldn't be getting away. Unless she did something. Rose kissed Lilianna's head. Maybe she'd turn out to be a good luck charm.

Andre caught her eye. "No, Rose! Run!"

Rosabella shook her head no and stealthily walked up to the droid. She rested Lilianna on one hip and used her free hand to tear at the droid's back. To her utter disbelief, she tore right through its skin. Her fingers closed around the cool metal of its organs. On an impulse, she tugged. A small mechanical organ released and came out with her hand, now covered in black goop.

The droid made an inhuman screech then spun around. It smacked Rose on the side of the head. As she flew back, she shielded Lilianna from the ground. Once she stopped rolling, Rose flattened herself over Lilianna, using only her elbows to hold herself up. Lilianna stared up at Rose with red eyes. At least she was quiet. If the droid finished Rose off, maybe it would leave Lilianna alone, long enough for Andre to think of something, or for backup to get here. If anyone was going to make it out alive, Rose was determined to make it be the baby.

The droid pressed against Rose's back, breathing down her neck. She felt a prick on the side of her neck. A thin stream of blood tickled her skin as it dripped down into her shirt. She closed her eyes and waited for the stab of the needle. If the droid poisoned her, did that mean its job was done and that it would leave them? She'd take another few weeks of sleep enduced torture if it helped them escape.

She breathed in and concentrated on Andre's screams. It wasn't the best thing to do, but it was the only thing keeping Rose from screaming herself. The whirring had subsided enough for her to only feel a dull ache, but that was the least of her problems. She shivered beneath the droid and bit her lip. It's face touched the back of her neck, and sniffed. The needle remained positioned at her neck, ready to puncture.

As if by magic, it recoiled it's needle and backed away. Rosabella peeked over her shoulder, holding her breath while the droid straightened and stepped away from her. It reared its head at Andre again and began slinking toward him, it's arm still a needlepoint.

Rose scooped Lilianna up and dove for Andre. She sandwiched the baby between her and Andre's torsos. If her assumption was correct, the droid would leave them alone.

"What are you doing? Clayton is going to kill me for getting us killed," Andre seethed as he squeezed his eyes shut. He couldn't see, but Rose rolled her eyes.

Just in case, she covered his mouth with her hand. "Shut up. Trust me on this."

The droid repeated it's process of sniffing Rose's neck and drawing away. She kept her eyes trained on Lilianna's, holding her breath. The second the droid began pulling away, Rose spun around and reached her hand into its chest. She only had one shot at this. Droids moved with unspeakable speed.

She closed in on her target: the heart. It screeched and flailed, throwing her from side to side. Rose's hold on the heart was too strong, it couldn't rid itself of her. Andre wasn't the only one who had a deathgrip. After one more good yank, she tore its heart from its chest, stumbling backward. She landed on the ground beside Andre, who'd propped himself up on one elbow to watch, Lilianna in his lap. They observed the droid's actions from afar. It writhed on the ground for a few seconds before collapsing.

She and Andre made eye contact. His eyebrows raised. "Is it dead?"

Rose nodded, her chest heaving with big breaths.

His eyes skirted back to the droid. "How are you sure?"

She leaned back until she was flat on the ground. Her eyes closed against her will, completely overcome with exhaustion. "Because the pain in my head is gone."

Rose passed in and out of consciousness until Logan and a rescue team of about fourteen others arrived. She secretly hoped Clayton would be with them, but he wasn't. Instead, Logan knelt at her side and spoke, telling her he'd carry her back to the Fortress.

She sat up and clutched Logan's arm. "Wait, I need to hold Lilianna."

He ordered one of the others to bring the baby to Rose. A couple of them helped Andre to his feet and supported him all the way back to the Fortress. Rose refused to be carried by Logan, though she did let him wrap an arm around her waist.

Rosabella was vaguely aware of Logan and Andre ordering a separate group to carry the droid back with them. The rest of the Fortress's rescue team surrounded Rose and Andre's little groups. They all walked back to the Fortress in a dark silence.

# Chapter 33

## (ROSABELLA)

As they neared the Fortress, Logan spoke to someone in mission control. Rose heard him mention Bernard as they entered her old house, but she was too focused on Lilianna to fully listen to him.

Once they stopped in front of the elevator, Rose tuned back in.

Logan pointed to the woman and man helping Andre. "You two escort Harrison to the medical wing. I'll be right behind you with Rosabella. The rest of you, follow us down and then bring the droid's body to meeting headquarters. We'll talk about what to do in a little while. Wait for my further instruction."

When it was Rose's turn in the elevator with Logan, she thanked him for his help. "You came just in time."

He hesitated before replying, "We didn't do anything. It was all taken care of by the time we got there." Then Logan looked down at the ground and shook his head.

As it was almost dinner time and training was winding down for the day, they passed numerous Fortress citizens on the way to the medical wing. Everyone pressed themselves against the walls to let their group through. Rose tried to hide her face. The last thing she needed was people talking about her again, though, on second thought, they hadn't ever completely stopped. In the process of covering her face by pulling up her hood, she tripped forward. Logan's hands caught her arm before she fell.

"Don't worry, I got you," he whispered close to her ear.

She swallowed and continued her very important duty of keeping her eyes on the floor. Rose tried telling herself that if she couldn't see the people around her, they couldn't see her. It was childish, but it helped her manage some semblance of sanity. She was at the breaking point, nearing tears again.

Whenever she saw Clayton next, she wouldn't be crying. He would already be furious with everyone around them for letting this happen to Rose. Her tears would only make him more upset. Of course, Clay wouldn't take it out on her; he was very good about that. They'd been dealing with things together lately, and she knew that a side of him would always be protective of Rose and her feelings.

Once they entered the medical wing, Rose and Andre were escorted to a double room. Their injuries weren't life threatening enough for either of them to need surgery, and the nurses had told them Bernard requested this room.

The two beds were separated by a thin curtain that reached a few feet in front of the door. They would have some privacy of sight, but not so much sound. The curtain was so thin, Rose could hear Andre's labored breaths as Logan and a nurse helped him into the bed. While Rose situated herself on the bed for a checkup, she set Lilianna on her lap and played with her hands.

"Excuse me, Miss Porter. May I take the baby?"

Rose took in the nurse's kind eyes and decided it was acceptable. "Yes, but please bring her back to me the second she's done with her checkup."

The nurse smiled and picked up Lilianna, who'd begun whining. "Of course."

After Logan was finished helping Andre, he walked around the curtain and sat on the edge of her bed. "How's your head?"

Rosabella shrugged. "I'm fine."

"Can you move everything? Your arms and legs are working like normal?"

She laughed dryly, "Yes. See, everything's intact. I have all my limbs."

Logan crossed his arms and stared at her. "I'm being serious Rose. You took on a droid and survived. You shouldn't be here right now."

Rose didn't know how to respond to that. Thankfully, a nurse knocked on the open door and walked into the room. She headed for Rose and hooked her up to machines on the back wall. Logan moved to stand beside her bed to stay out of the way. Rose jumped when she heard Andre cry out in pain. The other nurse helping him apologized.

The nurse helping Rose felt up and down her arms. "Does it hurt when I do this?"

She laughed without humor again. "Everything hurts. I've been in training, remember. I have bruises everywhere just from that."

"Right, right. Well, let me call in the doctor. She should be finishing up with another patient in a few minutes," the nurse said, her soft voice wavering nervously. Rose immediately regretted talking so harshly to the nurse. She was doing nothing but trying to help.

At the same time as the nurse's departure, Bernard entered. He shouted for the door to be closed upon his arrival. Then he stormed up to Rose's bed, pushing the separating curtain back along the way.

"What on earth happened to you two?" He cried, throwing his arms up. Rose had never seen Bernard so upset before. Then he saw Rose's wide eyes and cooled down enough to turn to the tiny woman behind him. "Palmer, please go tell Mr. Taylor I request his presence in the medical wing. Say nothing more. Just get him here."

"And Clarise Taylor, too!" Rose shouted before Alice was out of the room. Alice stopped and questioned Bernard with her eyes. He nodded and dismissed her with a flick of his hand. That request was for Andre, though nobody else knew but him and Rose. She caught Andre's eye and smiled at him. He mouthed a thank you.

Once Alice was gone and the door was shut, Andre shook his head. "We were ambushed by a droid."

The middle-aged male nurse attending to his leg shook his head and clicked his tongue. "I'm sorry, Andre. It's broken. I'll have an order put in for the doctor to reset it at once."

Bernard waved the nurse away. "Thank you, Michael. Please go now. And don't come back unless you have the doctor with you. These two need assistance at once."

Michael bowed his head. "Yes, sir."

Logan pulled a chair over for Bernard to sit in. "Here, sir. Take a seat."

He did, patting Logan on the back in thanks, and turned back to Andre, "Well, didn't you have enough of a warning from mission control?"

Logan stepped in, "We did alert the two of them, sir, but our cameras didn't even pick it up until it was right outside the tube station. It's not within our perimeter, so those were the only cameras in the area."

Bernard rubbed his temples, sweat glistening on his forehead. "This is deeply troublesome…can you walk me through the events?"

"We were on separate ends of the station," Andre started, "when the droid crashed through the main doors. There was another woman there."

Rose sucked in a breath and looked down at her hands.

Bernard noticed her movement and swung his head in her direction. "Rosabella? Is there more you'd like to add?"

She clenched the muscles in her face, afraid she'd start crying. "I was just talking to her. She needed help with her bags, they fell on the floor. Then she asked if I wanted to hold her baby…" Despite her efforts, Rose's throat clenched. Whatever words she wanted to say were cut off by the bulge deep in her esophagus. She twisted her neck to hide her face from the three men.

Andre continued for her, "The woman screamed and fell to the floor. The droid picked up on her screams and her fear and crossed the room to…to…well she didn't make it very long. Rose and I escaped the station only to get caught a minute or two later out in the open. It tackled us and broke my leg. I'm not sure what all happened after that."

Rose finished, her eyes still on the wall and away from the men. She explained in as much detail as she could, how she was able to tear out an organ from the droid and how it stopped before stabbing her. She shared everything she'd seen and felt, how the droid stopped when she flattened herself over Andre, and how she was able to catch it off guard and tear out its heart. When Rose was done, the room was engulfed in complete silence. Rose glanced at Bernard from the corner of her eyes. His hands were still massaging his temples while he held eye contact with the wall behind Rose's head.

Shouting ensued on the other side of the door. They all turned at the same time as Clayton burst through the door, the doctor hot on his heels. She shouted at him to stop, but nothing could stop Clayton when he was on a mission. His eyes blazed in anger when he spotted Andre. Then his glare travelled to Rose's bed. She felt tears in her eyes at the sight of him. Damn it! She promised she wouldn't cry. They'd only been apart for four or five hours, but after everything that had happened, it seemed like days. She dropped her legs over the edge and practically flew to Clayton. He met her halfway across the room and folded her up in his arms.

"Oh my god, Rose. I was so worried. Alice wouldn't tell me why Bernard wanted to see me in the medical wing. I thought you…" He buried his head in her hair and breathed in and out. Her arms wrapped around his waist and held on tight. Clayton's body shook with deep, heavy breaths. With her face buried in his chest and her own body firmly pressed against him, Rose felt safer than she ever had.

Clayton was here for her and she was here for him. She wasn't dead. She was more awake than ever now that she was back in the Fortress. It was definitely her new home. There was no doubt in her mind that this was where she was meant to be.

Clayton sniffed and scooped her up. "You've got to be in pain and exhausted. Let's get you to the bed."

When he placed her back on the hospital bed, he was gentle and careful. Clay slid his arm out from under her knees and then the one behind her back. Next he took up a protective position at the head of her bed, his hand linked with hers. Bernard ran his fingers through his thinning hair and leaned back in his chair. He tended to do that a lot. The weight of being the Head of the Fortress seemed to take a toll on his body, so much so that he was tired all the time.

Clarise had found her way to Andre's bedside. They were talking in low voices together. Clayton hadn't even glanced in their direction since he'd arrived. Rose was grateful he was so worried about her, enough to keep his mind on her and not the two lovebirds to Rose's right.

"Doctor?" Bernard directed at the frustrated doctor near the door. "Can you take a blood sample? I have a hunch about something."

"From Rosabella?" Logan asked. "Why do you need to take blood?"

Rose gripped Clayton's hand tighter. He'd bristled the moment Logan opened his mouth.

She met Bernard's eyes. "It's alright," said Rose. "I think I know where he's going with this."

A nurse accompanied the doctor to Rose's left side. They disinfected her arm with a spray and then searched for a vein. She watched them, completely awed by their quick, sure hands. She wanted to be good at something like them. At this moment in time, Rose would never be able to narrow in on a career herself. She wasn't sure what her skill set was.

The doctor pushed the needle into a vein near the inside of her elbow. It pinched her a bit, but not enough for it to hurt. Rosabella didn't look away, even as they drew blood into the needle. From the outside, it had the appearance of normal, red blood.

Clayton perched on the edge of her bed. "Am I missing something here? What do you know that I don't?"

"I suspect," Bernard declared, "That Rosabella still has droid poison in her system."

"How do you know?" Clayton asked.

The doctor pulled the needle out of her arm with one swift tug. She tapped the glass container on the end. "We'll be back in a few minutes. Shouldn't take too long. Michael, put my other noncritical patients on hold."

"Because it didn't attack me," she replied. "When the droid held it's poisonous needle to my neck, it sniffed me and then drew back."

"It's true," Andre stated, joining in. "It was about to stab her, I watched it. Then all of a sudden it stopped. It came at me next. When she positioned herself above me, to protect me, it did the same thing."

Clayton whipped his head to her. "Rose, are you kidding me? You put your life in danger not once, but *twice?*"

"It's not like I had much of a choice. I wanted to keep Andre alive, and I already had a sneaking suspicion that there was something about me that made the droid stop." She shrugged, embarrassed by all the eyes on her.

Bernard tapped the arm of the chair in thought. "Droids don't attack their own."

Clayton threw his unoccupied hand in the air. "I thought she was cleared of any poison after she woke up."

Bernard shook his head. "No, it was never actually confirmed that the poison was gone from her system...we all just carried on like normal after she woke up."

"Damn," Andre breathed.

"And you," Clayton yelled at Logan. "How could you let her be cleared for such a dangerous mission?"

Logan backed away. "I didn't know they'd attack in broad daylight. The trend has been consistent with them surrounding the tube station at *night.*"

"The tube station? What the hell kind of perimeter check was this, Harrison?" Clayton shouted at Andre next, rising to his feet. Rose's hand fell from Clayton's grip when he took a step closer to Andre.

"Don't be mad at him, Clayton," Logan said, coaxing Clayton's attention back to him. "We had to lie to get Rose out of the Fortress. You're so controlling, we were worried you wouldn't let her leave... Rosabella can make her own decisions. She's a very intelligent woman."

Clayton pounced on Logan then, throwing him into the wall. He shoved his forearm into Logan's neck, cutting off most of his air. Rose screamed at Clayton to stop, jumping down from the bed. She tugged on Clayton's shirt, but it was no use. She was too weak from recent events to stop him.

His voice was scary calm when he brought his face an inch from Logan's and said, "How could you let this happen? If you cared about Rose like you say you do, you wouldn't have done this to her. She could have *died*."

Logan pulled at his arm. "Don't you think I know that? I feel awful! If she'd have died I wouldn't know what to do with myself!"

Bernard grabbed hold of Clayton's arm. "Let go of him, son. Now is not the time to let your jealousy cloud your judgement. What we have going on is more important than your little love spats."

*Jealousy?* What did that even mean? Clayton was jealous of Logan? Or vice versa? Bernard didn't know what he was talking about. Clayton loved her, and Logan did too, but as a friend. She was certain of that. Wasn't she?

***

## (ANDRE)

Clarise's hands clenched Andre's. He let his arm hang off the bed so she could touch him and hide it from Clayton. Andre hadn't realized how much he wanted to see Clair until she wheeled into the room after Clayton and the doctor. If he'd been alone with her, he would've pulled her in his arms and kissed the hell out of her. But, alas, Clayton was here, so he didn't dare.

His friend was already having a field day with Logan. Anyone could tell that Logan had more than just a friend thing for Rose, but Andre was surprised it'd taken Clay so long to do something about it.

Once Bernard managed to calm Clayton down, he shoved Clayton into the chair. "There. Now, let's talk about the rest of what happened."

Clayton nodded, mouth a tight line, but eyes no longer blazing with fury. "I suppose I was overreacting. You managed to kill the droid, so I should thank you, Logan. While you put her life at risk, you also saved it."

Logan rubbed his neck. "But I didn't. It was dead when we got there."

Andre couldn't help himself. He burst into laughter. This was all so stressful, and his emotions were running rampant. This was the way he released all the pent up pain and confusion. Clarise gave him a concerned look.

"Why are you laughing, Andre?" Clayton asked, eyes cold.

"Because...because Rosie...killed it...all by...herself," Andre wheezed between laughs.

"You left that part out, my dear," Bernard chimed. His eyebrows raised all the way to his hairline.

Rose was standing with her back against the wall. She shrugged. "I just...I don't know, pulled out it's heart. That's it."

Why was she always so modest? This was her moment of glory. She could tell them all about the battle she had with the droid and how she barely survived. It's what Andre would've done if it had been him. Humility had never been one of his strong suits. Clarise didn't seem to mind, so he wasn't going to change. But then he realized how important it was for Bernard to hear the whole story.

Andre explained in detail how Rose had blocked him from the droid and then, bravely killed it. "She's relentless, sir," he finished, speaking to Bernard. "I've never been more impressed by a trainee."

They all stared at Rose. Her face changed from a light pink blush to a tomato-red color. Her embarrassment was cute and all, but Andre never understood how she managed to be so selfless. If he'd have done the same thing in her shoes, it would've been so Clayton didn't kill him later. If he'd gotten Rose killed, Andre would've lost his life at Clayton's hand. It would simply be self-preservation. Not to mention, having droid poison-blood would've been really cool.

The doctor returned, knocking before pushing the door open. "I have the results of the bloodwork. I'm sorry it took so long."

"Not a problem," replied Bernard. "What's the conclusion?"

Andre held his breath.

The doctor nodded. "Miss Porter's blood is a mixture of droid poison and regular, human blood."

"Woah!" Andre cried. Then he winced from the shooting pain in his leg.

Rose's shoulders drooped. She seemed utterly broken and confused. He could relate, especially with the broken part. He was literally broken. His leg, anyway.

"Clarise," Rose said, voice devoid of all emotion. "Can you come with me please?"

Clair surrendered Andre's hand back to him and wheeled after Rose. "Of course."

Clayton and Logan both watched Rose exit the room, each as equally as head over heels for her.

After the two girls were gone, Andre started laughing again. "Man, you two are so ridiculous."

Clayton gave him a dirty look. "Well then maybe Logan should keep his nose out of my girlfriend's life."

Andre stopped laughing. Clayton was usually difficult, but this was a whole new level. At least this time, Clay wasn't wrong in his anger; Logan was definitely stirring the pot. Andre's cousin wasn't doing a very good job of hiding his feelings for Rose.

Logan threw his hands up and stood beside Bernard. "Maybe I wouldn't if you treated your girlfriend better. I'm only trying to make her happy by picking up your slack."

Bernard held a hand up. "That's enough! If you two boys can't control yourselves, I'll place you in isolation. We'll see how you act after you're alone in a white room for days with nothing but a plate of food a day to keep you in shape."

This was no longer funny to Andre. Bernard was a compassionate leader, but when it came to enforcing discipline, he was tougher than a box of nails. That's why Andre liked to stay on the enforcing end of his anger, rather than the receiving end. They both mumbled apologies to Bernard, Logan's by far much more sincere.

The doctor cleared her throat and frowned at Andre's leg. "I'm sorry, I'll need to reset your leg, now."

Andre waved his hand at his leg and bit down. He spoke through clenched teeth. "Have at it."

Bernard and the *drama team* left the room so the doctor could work in peace and reset Andre's bones. Boy did that sucker hurt, a lot. He yowled the whole time, though nobody would hear him admit to it.

# Chapter 34

## (ROSABELLA)

ROSE LAUGHED AT GIANNA, WHO WAS ATTEMPTING TO feed Lilianna mashed green beans. All she'd managed to do was splatter food everywhere. It was all over her clothes, in her hair and on her neck. It looked like a giant had sneezed mucus on her. Clarise made a gagging sound and wheeled backwards, away from the mess.

Since the droid attack at the tube station and the fiasco with Logan and Clayton in the medical wing, the three of them had eaten meals in their dorm room every day. Rose and Clarise agreed that they could use a break from the guys, and Gianna admitted she wanted to stay away from people's prying eyes. They came to the conclusion to create a sort of solidified group consisting of Rose, Clair, Gianna and, at dinner, little Lilianna.

The baby had acclimated quite well, all things considered. She had nothing from home here, so Prince had had a field day when Clayton and Rose had taken Lilianna to get an outfit of her own. What was intended to be a quick trip, one in which they were going to select a couple of outfit changes had turned into a three hour ordeal. Prince wouldn't let them leave until Lilianna had an entire wardrobe selection to her name.

Through everything, Clayton had been an absolute angel. He was there for Rose every step of the way, never questioning her decision to help Lilianna transition.

Rose was the first to recognize her own lack of skills with children, though she had helped out with her brother when he was much younger. Because of that, Rose agreed to leave Lilianna in the childcare center at the medical wing. She'd had absolutely no idea such a place existed until she brought Clarise to see Lilianna for the first time.

The childcare center was open all day and night, so Lilianna had constant care. She was safer there than with Rose anyway. She wasn't equipped to raise Lilianna on her own. The nurses were going to care for her until she was a little older. Then, they'd give her to a family in the Fortress who wanted a child.

Rose visited Lilianna any free chance she had. She'd even received special permission from Bernard to take Lilianna for an hour or two at night. Thus started their trend of feeding Lilianna in Rose's dorm and playing with her in the library until it was time to bring her back to the medical wing.

Clayton hadn't questioned a single thing, though he did get upset when Rosabella declared she wanted to stay in her dorm again. By the end of the day, she was just so exhausted she could hardly make it back to her bed. Babies were so demanding. They required extra care and concentration.

"I've never really been around kids," Gianna admitted, wiping at her face with a towel. "And I'm not very good at this."

Rose patted her on the back. "Don't worry, it just takes some time to get used to. I remember how long it took me to help feed my little brother." She took the spoon and the bowl from Gianna. "Let me try... Lilianna, yummy food."

Clarise laughed at Rose's various coos and other sounds. She didn't even care that Clair thought it was funny, because it worked.

"Gosh, Rosie, you're really good with babies," Gianna said with a twinge of jealousy.

"You'll get the hang of it. Each child is their own person and they respond differently to each person they encounter. Don't take it personally," reassured Rose.

Gianna thanked her and swiped at her eyes. Her pregnancy had been altering her emotions like crazy lately. Sometimes she'd start sobbing uncontrollably around them, and others, she couldn't stop smiling.

"And this is really good practice for you, G," Clarise said encouragingly. They'd told her about Gianna's pregnancy the first night they had dinner together. By now, a lot of other people had started to notice a change in Gianna's mood and appearance. It wasn't easy to glare at everyone, though Rose wanted to every time someone looked disapprovingly at her friend. They were supposed to be living in a free society, but apparently that didn't mean free of judgement.

"Thanks girls. You're so sweet. I'm just going to have to accept the fact that Donovan and I are going to struggle. A lot." Gianna dipped her finger in the green beans on her neck and tried it. She made a face and wiped her finger off. "Now I get why she's so upset. This tastes terrible! My baby will not be eating this shit!"

Rose giggled and shushed Gianna. "Don't swear in front of her! You don't want Lilianna saying that, do you?"

Gianna got up from the bed and went to her closet to find a change of clothes. "Have they found a family for her yet, Rose?"

"No. Not yet." She managed to get Lilianna to eat a spoonful again.

Gianna tore her shirt off and replaced it with another one, loose hanging. "Why don't you and Clayton take care of her together? It's obvious you two are in love. Don't you think this would test your limits as a couple?"

Clarise snorted. "Have you met my brother? Can you imagine him being tied down with a kid?"

Rose considered Gianna's suggestion. Honestly, she'd thought long and hard about it already. She couldn't put that on Clay right now. He had his own life and Rose wasn't about to stifle that. Besides, who was to say they'd be together forever?

When she pictured her future, Rose always saw Clayton with her. But things could easily change. Along with that, Lilianna deserved to grow up in a normal, two-parent home. She'd even considered Prince and his partner as parents for Lilianna, but she didn't want to ask them to take a little baby either. They would probably feel obligated to take her and then it wouldn't be a true family. Whoever was going to take little Lilianna needed to do it of their own free will.

"Clayton didn't ask for this. I don't want him to feel he has to," she replied.

"But *Donovan* and *I* didn't ask for this little baby either. It just happened by accident, but we are adapting," Gianna said. "We're doing it together. I think if you talked to Clayton about it, you might be surprised."

Rose shook her head. "I just don't know. I need more time."

Gianna nodded, smiling sadly at her. "Understandable."

Rose's wristband chimed, signaling a message. She fumbled around on her bed for her screen to read it in full. It was a message from Logan. He asked her to meet him at his apartment. He said it was urgent and that he and Bernard would be waiting.

Clarise wheeled up next to her. "Is everything okay?"

"I have to go to a meeting with Bernard. I don't know how long I'll be gone." Rose eyed Lilianna, now in Gianna's arms. "Can you two bring her back to the medical wing tonight?"

"Of course," Gianna cried, bouncing the giggling baby on her lap. Lilianna normally liked Gianna's belly and would sometimes fall asleep on her. Rose assumed it was because of the baby inside her.

Clair crossed her arms. "Is Logan going to be there?"

Rose shrugged. "Probably. Why?"

"Because I think he's sneaky. He's trying to tear you and Clay apart."

She laughed. "No he's not. He's my friend. And I've made that *very* clear to him."

Clarise regarded her coolly. "If you say so...but just so you know, if you break my brother's heart, I can't promise this friendship will last."

Rose leaned down and hugged Clarise to melt her icy glare. "There's a better chance that Clay will break *my* heart. I care so much about him, I'd never hurt him. I promise."

"Good," Clarise said. Eyes turned to slits, she smirked. "In that case, I'll kick his ass."

Rose kissed her head. "You're the best, Clair. Thank you."

She lifted her shoulders and winked. "I know."

"Like brother, like sister," Rose sang as she left the room.

She replied to Logan on the way to let him know she'd be there in a few minutes. Then she asked for his apartment number before she forgot. She wouldn't be able to find him and Bernard if she didn't know which one he lived in. She'd familiarized herself speedily with the apartment wing of the Fortress after staying with Clayton for so many nights, so it wouldn't take long for Rose to locate it. Just as she expected, she found Logan's in record time and knocked on the door twice, as he'd told her.

The door opened right away. Logan pulled her inside and peeked out to check the halls as Rose took in the entryway. It was similar to

Clayton's, with a closed hallway stretching a yard or two from the door. Unlike Clayton's apartment, pictures lined the walls around her.

She pointed to one picture of Logan with a man and a woman. "Your parents?" Rose asked. The woman had skin a shade darker than Logan's, but she had the same, kind green eyes as him. The man's skin was almost as pale at Rose's and he had a smile just as wide as Logan's in the picture. Logan definitely got his body build from his dad; they were nearly the same height in the picture too.

Logan leaned on the wall next to the photo. "Yeah, my mom and dad. You'd love my mom. She lives at the end of the hall, actually."

"When was this taken?"

He scratched his head. "Oh I don't know, a year or two ago, maybe. Why?"

"Oh no reason, you just look younger," she said, shoving his shoulder. "Or maybe it's just your baby face."

Logan chuckled and rubbed his arm. "Or maybe you just don't recognize me because I'm not covered in bruises."

She winced and looked away. "I'm so sorry."

"Oh, don't worry about it, Rosabella. It was a perfectly calculated shot. And it was a while ago." Logan gave her a one arm hug and led her into the living room just beyond an arched entrance. "Bernard and I came up with an idea that we need your approval on."

Rose took in the room. A cozy little couch faced the wall next to the arched doorway, where a huge screen was set into the wall. The floor was cluttered with papers and writing utensils. There were a few shirts draped over the arm of the couch, wrinkled and dirty. Rose smiled at the clutter; Logan was put together in every aspect but his apartment. She didn't mind the dirty clothes or any of it. It made him human. Two doors stood open on the wall behind the couch. Rose looked into a bathroom with a nice tub and a bedroom, equally as messy as the living room. Unlike the Taylors' apartment, Logan didn't have a kitchen and he only had one bedroom.

"It was entirely Clarke's idea," Bernard said from the couch, startling Rose. "He came up with this all on his own."

"That's great," Rose started, "But what exactly did Logan come up with?"

Logan shoved papers off the couch to create a spot for Rose to sit. "I've created a device with droid poison in it. When I turn it on, it'll simulate the same energy a droid would."

She sat down and crossed one leg over the other. "How does this involve me?"

Bernard patted Rose's knee. "Because, my dear. We need to get your head figured out. I think that, with some consistent exposure, you'll be able to train yourself to handle the pain until it doesn't take over your head anymore."

Rose perked up. "Oooh, I like the sound of that! When do we start?"

"We can start whenever," Bernard responded.

"Then let's start now!" cried Rose.

"Wait, we haven't weighed out all the consequences yet," Logan countered. "I don't want her to just jump right in. For all we know, it causes minor brain damage each time she's exposed to the droids. That could lead to long lasting brain damage."

That didn't sound like the piece of cake she'd been wishing for. Nevertheless, this was merely another challenge that Rose was determined to overcome.

"Logan, don't be so worried. If you invented this thing, I trust you." She gave him her brightest smile. Then she picked up the remote-looking item on the table in front of the couch. "So how does this thing work?"

He shook his head in disbelief. "You're going to be the death of me."

Bernard laughed and stood. He offered his seat to Logan, who accepted and settled in next to Rose. Their knees bumped one another.

"So this top lever swipes up. Each time you pass one of these bars," Logan said, demonstrating it in the air, "It increases in power. So for you to start out, we should begin at the lowest level and work up to the highest. Make sense?"

Rose looked down at the remote. She understood the logic and where he was coming from, but that would take forever. She pretended to need a closer look and snatched the remote away from Logan. Finally, she raised the lever nearly halfway up the energy indicator.

Of course, it was too much and she fell to the ground on her hands and knees, shrieking in pain. Logan knelt beside her and reached for the remote.

"No!" She screamed, maintaining a tight hold on the remote. "I need...to test...my limit."

Bernard watched from afar, eyes wide and mouth open. "You need to be careful Rosabella. Logan's right, too much could cause permanent damage."

She gritted her teeth to keep from screaming. It was rough, but she managed to think about positive memories--mostly ones about Clayton.

After a while, she wasn't really sure how long, Rose turned the lever back to zero. Logan helped her to the couch where she lay down and closed her eyes. She didn't remember what happened after that, all she knew was that sleep beckoned her and she wasn't going to turn down such a generous offer.

# Chapter 35

## (ROSABELLA)

Rose woke to a hand on her shoulder. "Rosabella, time to get up."

She rolled over to get the hand off of her. She was drained of any and all energy. The events of last night replayed in her mind. There wasn't much to remember other than extreme pain in her head. In Rose's heart she believed this was the best technique for her to build up a tolerance to the pain. She would never be able to go on missions again if she couldn't control it. The last one with the droid had simply been luck.

"You have to be at training in five minutes."

At those words, she shot up out of bed. A bed? She'd fallen asleep on Logan's couch last night. Logan! Holy shit! She spun on her heel and faced him beside the bed.

Rose motioned to the bed. "Umm, did you--why am I--?"

He chuckled. "I carried you to my bed last night and I took the couch. Bernard was here to witness, so he can vouch for me."

"Oh good! I mean, not good that you couldn't sleep in your own bed--but umm--thanks." She ran for the door and pulled on her shoes. "I would appreciate it if we kept this to ourselves."

Logan, dressed and ready for the day in a tight-fitting purple t-shirt, grinned at her. "Not to worry, I've been sworn to secrecy by Bernard."

She pulled the door open and stepped into the bright hallway. Shielding her eyes, Rose made her way down the hall to training.

"Rosabella, wait!" Logan called. "Don't you need to change your clothes?"

"Crap, you're right! Oh god, it's going to look so bad if I'm late!" She ran her fingers through her hair.

He tossed her a bag. "I hope you don't mind, but I took a chance this morning to stop in your dorm." He tucked his hands in his pockets. "Your friends were out at breakfast already."

"Thank you so much!" She cried over her shoulder. Rose made it to the bathroom near the center of the Fortress, and changed in a toilet stall. Then she shoved her clothes from last night into the bag and beelined it to the training room. The whistle cueing the start of the training period screeched from the ceiling. Rose covered her ears. The noise was giving her a splitting headache. It may also have been the effects from last night.

She joined her group at the mats. They'd all made it to the same point of difficulty in training. Now, the trainers were less forgiving when they made one wrong move in a boxing sequence or when someone missed an instruction. And they sure didn't appreciate when trainees were late. It was a good thing Rose had made it right on time this morning. She knew the trainers would be watching her for the rest of the week for that. One trainer in particular would be sure to keep an extremely close eye on her both professionally and personally.

The second she entered the room, Rose felt Clayton's questioning eyes on her back. Rose refused to acknowledge him, or anyone for that matter. She hadn't smiled or even looked at Eden or Gianna since arriving. Today was a day to focus on herself. Rose was all for putting her mind to helping people, but lately, she hadn't been helping herself. She was lacking energy so much from sleeping only a handful of hours a night that she wasn't getting the proper nutrition because lack of sleep was causing her to lose her appetite, and the same went with her body; her cuts and bruises were healing at a painfully slow rate.

Rose enjoyed the training; it gave her an escape from everything else in her life. For a few hours, she forgot the world around her and fixated herself on the trainee in front of her. She concentrated every muscle in her body on the task at hand.

By lunch, Rose was sweating and shaking from exertion. But most of all, she was refreshed. Those few hours were necessary for Rose to center herself and be reminded of where and who she was. Not many people could say they escaped to a secret society underground where they were tasked with protecting their livelihood on top of defying the all-powerful Government.

Before anyone could pull Rose off to the side and talk to her, she sprinted to the bag with her clothes from the night before and ran from the training room. Clayton would have a million questions for her later, and she'd take time to talk to him, but right now, she desired peace and quiet.

Rose ran down the hall to the elevator doors and paused. She couldn't afford to ask Logan to grant her access to leave the Fortress without a solid reason. It wouldn't be right either if she went to talk with Logan after she avoided Clayton. Her boyfriend. That would look so bad.

Where was a nice, quiet place where she could sit by herself in the Fortress? *Think*, Rose, *think*. She'd be easily discovered in the Library. A few weeks ago, she'd be safe in her room, as she never spent more than a few minutes in there at a time. Visiting the childcare center in the medical wing would be plain stupid. That's where Gianna would go to find her. The Fortress was only so large and there were only a handful of places Rose hadn't discovered yet.

As the safest choice, Rose opted for a walk. Her friends all had to be at lunch together by now. She only needed a half an hour nap to be able to regenerate. Her feet carried her to Clayton's apartment without her asking them to. It seemed like the best option. Lunch would last for at least forty-five more minutes, so that gave her fifteen minutes of wiggle room, should she wake up late from the nap she planned on taking.

There weren't many reasons for a person to lock their apartment doors down here in the Fortress. Everyone trusted one another, or so she suspected. Even if they wanted to lock their doors, there was only one set of keys to each apartment. If a family lived together in an apartment, they'd have to pass the key around during the day if one of them forgot to grab something and needed to go back. What an inconvenience!

Rose knocked on the door, out of habit, before sneaking into the apartment. The lights were all off, so she turned on the one in the hallway to guide her steps.

She debated whether she should nap on the couch or Clayton's bed. The goal was to take a nap and re-energize for the second half of the day. She concluded a better sleep would come from comfort. Therefore, the verdict was to snuggle into Clayton's bed, where the scent of him remained ensnared in his pillowcase and sheets. She'd missed sleeping beside him, missed the feel of his warm arms around her, of his lips on her hair while he breathed. Tonight, she would get this back. She vowed to return to her old routine, the one in which she told Clayton everything. She owed him that much after all this secrecy.

***

A 30-minute nap did the trick. Rose's wristband alarm went off at just the right time. Rose woke up without grumbling about sleep, as she did most mornings. In fact, she hopped up promptly and scrambled around on the bed. Rose's socks slid off her feet while she slept, and she'd rolled around so much the sheets were half on the floor. Rose straightened the sheets and pulled the comforter over the pillows, just as Clayton had done in the morning.

While she was pulling on her socks, the hair on the back of her neck stood up. She had a feeling someone was watching her. She twisted around to catch whoever was in the doorway off guard.

Clayton rested a shoulder on the doorframe, his face set in a scowl. "Rose? Are you feeling okay?"

Caught red-handed, Rose accepted her fate. He wasn't going to let her leave unless they talked about her, which she hated. Better to get it over with sooner rather than put it off for later.

She sat on the edge of the bed. "I've been really tired lately. I just came here for a nap. I'm sorry."

"Rose," he started, letting out a long sigh. "You don't have to apologize for coming here. In fact, I was hoping to find you here."

"You were?" Rose asked stupidly. She sounded like a child.

"Well, not exactly in my *bed*, but in the apartment," he said chuckling. Then he waved her over. "C'mere. Can we talk?"

Her feet planted a foot or so in front of him, Rose prepared for all kinds of questions about these last few weeks. He knew she was hiding something, but she wasn't supposed to talk about it. Bernard had made it clear she was meant to keep this to herself. If he wanted Clayton to know, Bernard would've told him.

Clay tucked a hand in his pocket and tipped his head to peer at her. "So, Rosabella, what's going on with you?"

Her silence convinced him of an underlying issue. Clayton removed his hand from his pocket and held out both arms to her. At first she thought he was annoyed, but then he smiled at her, the sides of his mouth turning upward just enough to prove to her he wasn't upset. Rose allowed him to hold her. She stood on the tips of her toes and pressed her lips to his for a few seconds.

"I can tell you're tired. But just remember, training is almost over. Once you hit the six month mark, you'll be evaluated for career work." He ran a hand over her hair. "If you pass, like I'm sure you will, your training will be over. Until then, is there anything I can do to help you?"

"No, I'll be okay. I can make it that long. I think it's just because I've been with Lilianna every night." She smiled without showing her teeth. "Babies are a lot of work, Clay."

He chuckled, his throat tickling the top of her head. "They sure are. I think you're amazing for all you've been doing for her."

Rose shrugged to show it was no big deal. "She deserves all the happiness she can get. I'm only helping where I can."

"You'll make an excellent mother someday." Clayton kissed her neck, nibbling at the skin just below her ear. It sent shivers up and down her spine. A warm feeling flooded her bones.

She giggled and swatted him on the arm. "Don't go getting any ideas."

"No promises," he growled.

"Clay, I'm serious!" Rose said, laughing despite clenching her jaw. "And if you don't stop, we're *both* going to be late."

Clayton sighed and draped an arm over her shoulders. "I suppose you're right. I shouldn't show up late to my job."

When they returned to the training room, they were right on time. Rosabella was cutting it a little close again. Tomorrow she'd have to do better. Clayton started walking toward his group across the room, in business mode.

Rose grabbed his arm and pulled him back to her. "Clay, would it be okay if I came over tonight?" She looked over his shoulder at the wall. Why was she so nervous to ask him to sleep at his place? She'd done it before, hadn't she?

"Rose, you don't need to ask me," Clayton laughed. He kissed her on the forehead. "If you want to, of course you can!"

Her heart fluttered. "Okay, I just wasn't sure because it's been a few weeks."

"I've missed you," he whispered, giving her cheek a kiss. "You're welcome anytime. In fact, I *insist* you come over tonight."

Rose pushed away and blew him a kiss. "If you say so."

"I'm looking forward to it," he called after her. She jogged to her group, giving Gianna a smile on the way. Her mood was already far improved from this morning. After dinner tonight, and Logan's apartment for her new droid exercise, Rose was going to spend the night in Clayton's apartment. After a shower of course. That was a must.

With the hopes that everything was on the up and up, Rose finished out the day with a bang.

That night, she and Clayton stayed up late making plans for Clarise's birthday, which was coming up in the next month. Things were already on their way back to being normal. Rose fell asleep in Clayton's arms without hesitation. It was the best night of sleep she'd had in a long time.

# Chapter 36

## (AIRE)

Aire poked her head out of the dining hall in time to spot Rose and Clayton zip down the hall, a baby in Rose's arms. So it *was* true! Rosabella had brought a baby back on one of her missions.

Great, one more person to occupy Rose's time instead of Aire.

No matter how hard she tried to immerse herself in training and the Fortress instead of brooding over good memories of Rosabella, it never worked. Aire's heartbreak resurfaced every time. She'd shared every story with Luna, but venting could only help so much. The only possibility she had was to isolate Rosie. Then the two of them would work on their issues together. Without the distractions of Rose's new friends around her.

For now, Aire would have to deal with the fact that she was on her own. But tonight she was allowed to visit with her sister, Luna. Bernard wanted to see her in a few minutes to discuss the details, but all she cared about was going above ground for a night. When she wasn't training or going on missions, Aire was at a loss for ways to pass her free time. She would sit in the lounge and watch people talking, laughing, and hanging out. And each time, it was like taking a knife to the heart. She would be in their shoes if she still had Rosie.

What had even happened to them? Aire wasn't at fault for this. She was only being protective of herself and Rose's sanity. Rosabella had changed since coming to the Fortress. It was as if the old Rosie was gone for good, replaced by some strong, independent women who looked like the friend Aire remembered, but was nothing like her.

It was disgusting how Rose could prance around the Fortress, everyone's eyes on her. They looked up to Rose, just as people at school had for all those years. They never interrupted her or burst her personal space, yet they idolized her like some famous celebrity. It was annoying. Not to mention, Aire had always been prettier and smarter than Rose. And she'd had a difficult time living in Rose's shadow all her life. If anyone deserved to be treated with the utmost respect, it was Aire. Too bad the only people who recognized that were herself and Luna.

Her sister had never liked Rose. Ever. She'd thought Rose an immature, stuck-up bitch. Aire never understood why Luna hated her so much. Until five or so months ago; then everything went to shit. Was their lifetime of friendship not enough for Rose? Did Aire have to be the one to apologize this time for something she didn't do? To be honest, she'd been surprised when Rose didn't march into their dorm the next day after their fight and apologize. That was *her* job. She was the one who moved on first, the one who was responsible for most of Aire's hardships and felt bad about it.

It sickened her to see people move out of the way when Rose walked down the halls here. Or the way people nodded respectfully at her, the way someone might a queen. Or the way Rose didn't even notice. She acted as if she expected all of the attention and eyes on her. Not once did she correct anyone for their attention, nor did she thank them. It was despicable. Luna would call her the ultimate bitch when she found out about this.

Tonight, they planned to have a sleepover together. Bernard allowed it only because it was at Luna's house and away from the prying eyes of the Government. He made Aire swear up and down that she wouldn't tell her sister where exactly she was living. Luna only needed to know that Aire was safe and living in a different place. That was all. Aire also suspected he was only doing this to make her happy. The way she understood it, the happier she was now, the easier it would be to manipulate her into doing him the favor he briefly mentioned once. It made sense. Why else would he do her any favors? There was nothing that came for free here. Each citizen paid a price whether they knew it or not. So much for a free society.

Aire dumped her tray in the chute and left for Bernard's office, stewing with thoughts of Rosabella.

A few hours later, Aire and Luna settled into the plush couch in her living room. According to her sister, she'd gotten the couch as a present from some guy who thought Luna's work for the Government was "exceptional." Aire knew that meant he'd been one of her "associates." Luna never completed high quality work. She hardly reached the bar for the bare minimum when it came to work ethic. Instead, she had wooed the poor man late last year, resulting in a complete refurbishing of her house. Of course, it had come with the price of "meeting" with him for a few months. But in the end, it paid really well. What a smart idea! And anyway, men were only good for protection. The rest was the woman doing all the work. The female gender was the superior sex by far. By the time she was done with training at the Fortress, Aire was going to have mastered the art of convincing a man the idea she planted in his head was his own, when really *she* was in charge.

"Alright baby sis," Luna said, tucking a blanket around her legs. "Give me all the dirty details. What's happened since we last talked?"

Aire pulled the blanket up to her chin. "I haven't spoken to Rose--"

"Well, that's a given. She's a bitch."

Suddenly upset, Aire jumped to Rose's defense. "No she's not! It's Clayton's fault. He's corrupted her thoughts."

Luna gave her a sympathetic look. "I know why you think that. You don't want to accept the fact that Rose has dumped you for other friends, but, honey, look around you. You're completely alone except for me… and Clayton's a man. Remember what we talked about? He doesn't have the brain capacity to purposely keep Rose away from you. That's her own doing."

Aire held her ground against her sister's accusations. It was too hard to believe what Luna was saying. Sure, Rose had everyone wrapped around her finger, but that didn't mean she'd done it on purpose. In fact, Aire was positive Rose had no idea people treated her in such a way. Luna was wrong in saying Rose was manipulative.

"I don't believe that. I can't imagine Rose ever purposely doing something to spite me," Aire said forcefully.

Her sister laughed and patted her on the knee. "My dear sister, you are so blinded by the old Rosabella. I wish you'd understand how I see her, then you'd know."

Aire swatted at her sister's hand and looked away. "Can we talk about something else?"

"Fine," Luna spat. "But don't come crawling back to me when all of this goes to shit."

"Yeah, whatever," she mumbled into the blanket.

Luna rolled her eyes. "Okay, fine. Tell me about the others...I like your stories about *Dre*."

Aire was always prodded and poked by Luna until she told a story about Andre. At first, it was funny, watching her sister live vicariously through Aire. Now it was bothersome. Luna had some strange obsession with Andre and it was growing more annoying with each passing day.

"Why? I already told you everything I know about him," Aire grumbled.

Luna crossed her arms, a sure sign she was about to get her way. "Fine. then retell me about the time he took you out on a perimeter check."

"We were in a big group. There was nothing special about it," Aire informed her. One look into Luna's large brown eyes and she knew she was going to tell her sister a story or two. She curled up with her knees to her chest and began, "On my first real mission, Andre was in charge of corralling four of us trainees. We were tasked with the middle of the day perimeter check. I was second in line after Gianna--you remember me telling you about how she's one of my roommates?"

Her sister nodded. "Yeah, the pregnant one?"

"Yep. So anyway, Andre stopped behind one of the abandoned houses to give us the rundown of how the mission was supposed to go. I almost--"

Luna squealed, "Ooo! And I bet he was dressed in a tight black shirt, right?"

"Um, it was a white shirt, but yeah, sure. Can I continue?"

"I bet he looked hot with his dark skin against the white! Damn, I'll have to send you with my screen so you can take a picture of him for me," Luna said, already fantasizing about using him to get her way. She spotted Aire's angry expression and came back to reality. "Sorry, continue."

Aire groaned. "Why can't you just shut up and listen to my stories? You're just like--" she stopped herself before she could say Rose's name. Was that why she was so hurt by Rose? Because she was like a sister to Aire? No, it was so much more than that. It was a bond that could not be easily broken. No matter how bad things got, Aire believed she could hold onto the part of Rose who used to sit with Aire on her bed after school and cry about the work and classmates who sucked. That Rosie was still her best friend inside, it just needed a little help coming back to the surface.

As Aire was getting to the part about Andre standing up for her, a loud bang sounded below their feet. It rattled the floor, turning the couch into something like a surfboard on water.

Luna shot up from the couch. "Shit!"

"Lu? What was that?" Aire threw the blanket off and stood her ground on the floor. The rattling stopped. "We've no record of earthquakes here, right? We're in the middle of the country! I thought nothing like that happens here."

"Well, umm...you have to promise not to get mad," Luna said, biting her lip. She twirled a thick strand of her dark brown hair around her forefinger. A small smile blossomed on her face. "Come with me."

Whenever she heard Luna say those words, Aire braced herself for something devious and life-changing. Sweat glistened on her sister's hairline. Aire nodded and followed behind her sister to the basement door. A jolt of fear filled Aire's body when Luna led her into the basement, through another bedroom and into a hallway hidden behind the closet door.

Aire placed her hand on the wall to catch her breath after running down all those steps. Luna paused momentarily and then pushed on again. The hall was so long, Aire couldn't see the end; the darkness was also a factor of that, as she couldn't see her feet or her hands unless they were right in front of her face. Green fluorescent lights decorated the wall. They were spaced out every so often in no particular order, creating a creepy vibe. The smell down here made Aire gag, and Luna to rub her nose in disgust. A cross between urine and blood infiltrated her nostrils. She covered her nose and mouth with the hem of her shirt. The cold air struck Aire's stomach and sent goosebumps all over her exposed skin. She kicked herself for leaving the blanket behind. But who was she to know they'd be visiting a dungeon? She nearly slipped and fell after stepping on a slimy patch of something on the floor. She didn't stop to examine it, afraid she'd vomit or cry.

They trudged on in silence, the sound of Aire's gags and something dripping onto the floor the only noises down here. The walls were completely bare except for streaks stretching from ceiling to floor, the unmistakable evidence of water damage.

Sooner or later, Luna paused at one door on the left wall. A sliver of light shone in the gap between the door and the disgusting floor. Aire was unsure of how much time had passed since they walked through that closet door. Based on the greenish tint to her sister's face, Aire guessed it had been more than just a few minutes. She stepped behind Luna, using her as a shield for whatever was on the other side of the door.

Her sister stopped, hand on the doorknob, and faced Aire. "Okay, Rei, I need you to be calm. What you're about to see is top secret. Something I've been working on for a while now."

"For the Government?" Aire wheezed, doing her best to take in as little breath as possible.

"No," Luna said smiling. "It's a personal project of sorts."

Aire braced herself and wrapped her arms around herself, shirt falling back over her stomach. She shielded her eyes from the bright light in the room and entered behind Luna.

She froze in the doorway. A half-naked mangled human man was strapped onto a rolling bed in the corner. Luna took no time tearing across the room to the man in the bed. Half his body was covered with green and black bruises: an arm, a leg, his chest.

Luna waved a woman with almond shaped hazel eyes away. The woman nodded and proceeded to wash her hands in the sink at the back of the room.

"Luna," the woman said, "I'm sorry, but I had to sedate him again. He woke up and started smashing things again."

"Thank you Andrea," Luna said, her back to the woman.

The woman nodded and gave Aire a sad smile. She patted her shoulder as she passed her to get to the hallway.

Aire ran to the sink and splashed cold water on her face. When she was done, she screamed at her sister, "You'd better explain this to me right now, Lu, or I swear to God I'm running for help."

"Chill, chill. You get upset so easily, sis. This is Grayson." She stepped aside to present the man to Aire. "I thought, surely you'd recognize him."

"What!" Aire ran to the side of the bed and frowned down at the man. His strange gray eyes were closed, but that was definitely him. His blonde-red hair lay in stringy strands, framing his face. It had grown since Aire had last seen him; now, his hair curled up and over the tops of his ears and around the sides of his neck. Aire gasped. "What have you done to him?"

Her sister giggled and prodded at one of his limp arms, the one covered in green and black bruises. "He should be thanking me. I saved his life."

"Explain."

"You have no imagination, sis," Luna said with a disbelieving shake of her head. "Grayson underwent an attack from a droid. I just happened to be driving past--lucky bastard--and found him in a heap on the ground. The droid was dead, he'd killed it with his gun, but not before it had gotten a hold of him...are you still confused? I'm trying to help him."

She shook her head and pushed the heels of her hands into her eyes. "Luna, I'm not sure I believe you. Sometimes you have bad intentions. Are you really trying to help him or are you using him for something else?"

Aire didn't see her sister's face, she couldn't look at her right now; but she pictured Luna biting her lip and smiling.

"This is purely for your benefit. You'll see eventually. If he believes you rescued him, you'll have him doing things for you like that," Luna sneered, snapping her fingers.

It took awhile for Aire to formulate a response without starting an argument with her sister. She moved to the sink, splashed more cool water on her face and waited, leaning over the sink, as it dripped from her face.

Eventually, she wiped the water from her jaw. "Luna, I can honestly say you are the craziest person I've ever met."

Her sister laughed and pulled a thin sheet over a sleeping Grayson. "Why, thank you."

Aire shook her head. "Can we go back upstairs now?"

"Sure thing!" Luna hooked her arm through Aire's. "I'll keep you posted on his improvements."

"Whatever you say," Aire mumbled as they emerged into the hallway.

There were many times Aire couldn't see the end result of something. This was one of those times. Luna was so confusing, yet she always managed to see the bigger picture. She knew the steps to take in order to achieve a final goal. She could paint the picture of them in her mind and work step-by-step toward the end result. Aire would normally do her best to follow her sister's logic, but in this case, there was no sense to this.

The method to her madness was lost on Aire. *I hope you know what you're doing*, she thought.

# Chapter 37

## (ANDRE)

"I T'S ABOUT TIME! WHAT THE HELL WERE YOU two doing?" Andre asked, holding the door open for Clayton and Rose. "You know what, I actually don't want to know. It's probably not appropriate."

Clayton jabbed his elbow in Andre's side. "Absolutely not! And shut up. Rose doesn't like when you talk so dirty."

Andre laughed and jabbed his best friend back. Clayton only ever acted defensive when it came to Rosabella. That led Andre to believe there had been some funny business going on earlier after all.

He closed the heavy double doors behind them, shutting the pouring rain out. Rose unzipped her jacket and revealed a sleeping Lilianna curled against her chest. Not to mention, completely dry.

Andre laughed again and helped Rose out of her jacket. "Looks like you got the worst of it Rosie Posie."

Clayton took his own jacket and the one from Andre. "Absolutely selfless, my girl is."

"Well, don't let me stop you from having fun tonight. Just remember, this is a birthday party for a teenager." Andre winked at Rose. "If you sit in the back seats, I'll know you're not just watching the movie, so don't make me separate the two of you." A feeling of satisfaction came upon Andre at seeing Rose's face darken with an embarrassed blush.

In response, Clayton shoved him. Harder this time. "Knock it off, Andre."

He and Clayton were by far the strongest men in the Fortress, but that didn't mean it hurt any less to get a blow to the stomach. His nose scrunched to cover up the pain. "Alright, alright," Andre coughed. "I get it."

Rose smiled at Andre, her red face slowly returning to normal.

Clayton smirked and wrapped an arm around Rose's waist. "Good, now let's go see the birthday girl…did you have to stop at all, or was it smooth sailing in getting her here?"

Andre's heart flew up into his throat. His feet fumbled and he fell behind Clayton and Rose a step or two. "What? Uhh, yeah. I mean no. We didn't have to stop or anything. I carried her here easily."

Rose peeked at Andre over her shoulder and glared. Would they find out that he and Clarise had stopped a couple times not because of the rain, but because he couldn't stop kissing her? Rose seemed to catch on based on the angry expression on her face. She'd probably hear from Clair about it later and would scold Andre at some point. At least Clayton hadn't picked up on anything.

It had been totally worth it, carrying Clarise from the Fortress to the abandoned movie theater. Who knew that she'd be so good at kissing? Where on earth Clarise had learned such skills he'd never know.

Clayton slapped Andre on the back once he caught up. "Okay, good. And hey, man, thanks for offering to carry her here. I appreciate it."

He shrugged. "Yeah, no big deal. I'd do anything for her."

Clayton gave him a side glance. "You would?"

Rose faced forward again, jaw clenched. Andre had to think fast on his feet if he was going to get out of this with his head still attached. He forced himself to roll his eyes at Clayton. "Yeah, of course man. She's my best friend's sister. I'd do anything for you guys."

"Oh, well thanks dude. I didn't mean for you to get all emotional there," Clayton teased. Andre reached up and realized his face was warm. His eyes had filled with liquid at some point during that interaction. Nervous tears or heartfelt tears? Whatever the case, he'd barely gotten out of that alive. Thank god for Clayton's naivety. And for Andre's smooth charm.

Andre picked a seat one row above Clarise's so he could be close but not so obvious that it alarmed Clayton; this theater wasn't large enough to hide everything.

None of the Fortress-born citizens would be able to tell you when the theater was built, but everyone knew about the fire years ago. At that moment in time, there had only been a dozen theaters left across the country. Everything had been converted directly to home entertainment systems and screens. This theater had been the site for many an illegal party back in Andre's teenage years.

The two massive screening rooms that still stood to this day were all that remained of the once popular theater building. The screens themselves had only suffered minor damage in the fire, if any. The one particular room Clarise decided on for their movie tonight was made up of fifty or so rows; spaced out into single chairs and sets of two-person couches. The top rows, at the back of the theater, had taken on the brunt of the damage. The front twenty rows or so were the only ones without burn holes and ash. The most interesting feature of the theater was it's open concept ceiling. Before the fire, the owner had installed a retractable ceiling that could be opened for certain viewings if desired. During the fire, all of the mechanisms were destroyed, so the ceiling was now permanently left open in this room. And no matter how many scented sprays they'd used in the theater, it could not take the scent of burnt fabric out of the air. Once you were in the room for a while, your nose adjusted to it, so it wasn't a total irritant for the whole night.

In front of Andre, Clarise parked her wheelchair in a handicap spot. A couple girls sat on either side of her. When she'd had time to meet friends, Andre had no idea. Clarise had basically been a recluse in their apartment for years; she'd hardly left for meals for a long time.

Then Rose arrived and everything changed. Whether he'd admit it to Rosabella or not, Andre was grateful to her. She was the catalyst that brought Clarise to life. It was due to Rose's compassion that Clayton hadn't found out about Andre and his feelings for Clair. He understood that eight years was a big difference for many people, but age was just a label. It was not meant to constrict people who loved one another…if their love was true.

Tonight, the hardest part about being here would be keeping his eyes off of Clair. If Clayton suspected anything tonight, he'd come after Andre. It wouldn't matter to him if it was his sister's birthday or not;

there would be a beating and lots of blood. Andre was going to avoid that at all costs. That didn't mean Andre couldn't stick close by Clair. If anything happened, a droid attack or something, his first duty would be to protect her, screw hiding his feelings.

Unfortunately, that meant he couldn't wish Clarise a true happy birthday as he wanted to. In his mind, Andre had planned out a romantic night for her. He would set up some kind of picnic for the two of them and they'd have their own moon viewing party together, wrapped up in a warm blanket under the stars. There was obviously a kissing spree in there somewhere, but nothing more than that. Clarise was special to him and he was going to hold the utmost amount of respect for her.

In all truthfulness, Andre probably could've gotten away with sitting next to Clarise, Clayton was so occupied with Rose that he wouldn't even notice. Better not to try his luck though.

Once everyone was accounted for, Andre leaned back in his chair and activated the movie from a small remote screen. It was a sleek design, with a slim shape that fit the curve of his palm. He had to shuffle through a few genres before he found the one Clarise requested. Andre then prepared for a long night of an aching heart, flicking his gaze toward Clarise in short bursts so as not to raise alarm.

***

## (ROSABELLA)

Gianna and Donovan sat to Rose's left. The two of them leaned close together for most of the movie, their hands linked in Gianna's lap below her bulging stomach.

Donovan peeked around Gianna and smirked at Rosabella. "You know you could've left her back at the Fortress, right? The childcare center is really great."

Rose ran her fingers through Lilianna's short hair, watching her heavy eyelids close. "I don't like being separated from her for too long. Plus, she needs to know she always has me. I won't ever leave her behind."

With that, Donovan chuckled and wrapped his arm around his girlfriend.

The two lovebirds, as well as Rose and Clayton, took up two sets of couches on the side of the group, away from the younger trainees. They had too much energy for Rose and the others. She felt like an old lady thinking that, but it was true. She was just far more mature than them.

Lilianna slept on Rose's chest for the majority of the movie, grounding her. It was comforting to have the rising and falling of someone else's chest on her own. Rose had fallen asleep at some point, Clayton's arm around her.

Not long after, he nudged Rose, jolting her awake. She snapped her eyes open and looked around, searching for some sign of a threat. Not here! Not on such an important night for Clarise!

Clayton tapped the skin on the inside of her elbow. "Rose, calm down. The movie's over and we're leaving now."

She sighed and proceeded to bring her heart rate down. "Did I seriously sleep through all of the movie?" Lilianna started to fuss.

He nodded and smiled. "Yes, but you needed it."

"But that's so lame of me! I'm literally a grandma at heart."

Clayton kissed her forehead. "I don't mind. I think that's kinda sexy actually."

"What does that even mean?" Rose asked, laughing quietly. Lilianna resumed sleeping, thumb safely tucked in her mouth.

He shrugged and helped her to her feet. "I have no idea...but I do know that watching you take care of that baby is making me think of lots of things. For the future, you know?"

Over her shoulder, Rose heard Gianna sigh happily. "Aww, Clayton, that was so cute! Maybe Donovan can give you some fathering tips once we have our little guy or girl...If my guess is correct, it won't be long before the two of you start a family of your own." In response, Donovan squeezed Gianna's butt playfully and smiled at her.

Rose's stomach fluttered. Before Clayton could reply and crush Gianna's hopes, Rose did it for him. "Absolutely not."

To her astonishment, Clayton laughed. "We'll see."

Rose wanted to know what that meant. Did he really see them having a future together? That's all Rose had been thinking about lately, so it would be refreshing to confirm if they had similar hopes and dreams. It would also be a relief to know if he had other plans too. It was the not knowing part that killed her.

Gianna held out her arms to Rose. "Here, I can take Lilianna back to the medical wing tonight. Why don't the two of you take a break?" She followed up with a subtle wink at Rose.

Rose carefully handed Lilianna off to Gianna, sliding one arm out at a time so she didn't disturb the sleeping baby. She was such an easy baby compared to Rose's brother. Nicolai had made feeding a disaster, and bedtime was even worse if that was possible. Rose was silently both guilty and relieved that she could "return" Lilianna at the end of the day. It would make things harder to have to care for a baby overnight rather than for a few hours a day.

"Should we talk to my sister about her gift?" Clayton nodded his chin toward Clarise, who was laughing with a couple girls her age. Rose noted Andre's close proximity to Clair. He would gaze at her and then flick his eyes away for a second before he resumed ogling her. *Crap*!

In order to not call attention to Andre, Rose smiled. She pulled Clayton behind her and said, "Sure! But let's make it quick. I'm super tired."

"Is that code for anything in particular?" he questioned, wagging his eyebrows up and down.

Rose skipped away, down the steps, taunting him. "Definitely not," she jeered. Clayton chased her down the steps while she shrieked with anxious glee. He gave her space to run without being caught, that was, until she reached the ground level. Clay charged up to her and wrapped his arms around her from behind, lifting her off the ground. His lips kissed along the back of her neck, sending her into another round of giggles. Clayton always knew just where she was most ticklish.

"Guys, can you please not do that here?" Clarise scolded as she wheeled up to them.

Rose laughed again and shimmied out of his hold. "I'm sorry Clarise. If it's any consolation, it's all Clay's fault."

"What?" Clayton's eyebrows touched the top of his forehead. "How easily you betray your loved ones."

"Oh my god, I can't listen to this garbage," Clarise mumbled.

Rose stepped in front of her so she couldn't roll away from them. "Hey, wait! How has your birthday been so far?"

She broke into a wide grin. "Amazing! Thanks so much you guys for organizing this. I really needed a reason to get out of the Fortress."

Clayton leaned over and kissed the top of her head. "Not a problem sis. I'd do anything for you. And Andre helped out a lot too...you should thank him."

Clarise squirmed in her seat. Rose tried to cover it up by lunging at her for a hug. Clarise whispered a thank you in her ear.

"Clair...Clayton and I wanted to give you your birthday present. But it's--"

Clayton cut her off and stepped up to cover for Rose, "But it didn't make sense to give it to you here. We'll give it to you in the morning. But just know that it's a really special present that we've been working on getting for you for a looooong time."

Clarise snickered and narrowed her eyes to slits. "Can I at least know what it is?"

Once Clayton and Rose shared a look, he crossed his arms and looked away absentmindedly. "Well, it's just this little thing that could help you walk again...I don't know, you might not even want it..."

Rose had never seen Clarise so excited other than the times they talked about *The Selection*. If she had the ability to, Rose was convinced Clarise would've jumped into Clayton's arms.

Clair looked to Rose for confirmation. "Rose, is this real? Are you being serious?"

"Of course I am!" she cried. She clutched Clarise's hands in hers. "We had to do a lot of searching, but Bernard was able to help us locate someone up above who creates rehabilitation technology. You connect this little device behind your ear and then these probes up and down your legs--like a brace--and you should be able to walk again. It will take some time and lots of patience and concentration, but it'll happen. I believe in you."

"Have I ever told you that you're amazing?" Clarise asked, eyes glistening with tears. She tugged on Rose's arm so that she fell into another hug. Clayton knelt beside them and joined in. Clair swiped at tears as they fell in steady streams down her cheeks. She and Rose laughed, both sniffling to keep a fresh round of tears at bay. Finally, Clarise wiped the back of her hand across her eyes. "Okay, before I become a blubbering puddle, I should probably go. Clay, is it okay if I have a sleepover at Daisy's dorm tonight?"

Clayton rose to his feet and looked at Rose with a sad smile. "Of course. Rose, are you up for a detour before we go back to the apartment?"

"Clay, I can get Clair to her friend's if you two wanna head back," Andre suggested, joining them at the base of the steps.

Clayton turned to his sister. "Only if you're okay with that, Clair. I have no problem bringing you back to the Fortress if that's what you want instead."

"No, that's totally fine. I'm good with that. Andre can take me back. You two go ahead," Clarise said. She spoke so fast, Rose could barely keep up. She made a face she hoped told Clair to chill, but it was difficult to tell if it registered. In a final attempt to keep Clayton's attention on her, Rose hopped on his back and pretended to steer him. He caught her with ease and grasped under her thighs while she wrapped her arms around his neck.

"You heard the girl, let's go Clay!" Rose squealed.

Clayton shot Andre a serious look. "You get my sister back safely or else I'll kill you...my girl's waiting for me, so I gotta go now. Be safe, you two."

Andre saluted them and began prepping Clair for their journey home. "You got it, boss. Have fun, you crazy kids."

Rose buried her red face in Clayton's neck.

Clayton gave her thigh a squeeze. "Ignore him. I've told him we don't do anything that he suggests. You don't have to be embarrassed."

"I know, but I can't help it," she sighed into his neck. The cool night air hit her hot skin. The rain had stopped a while ago; it was refreshing to smell the sweet water mixing with the faraway scent of trees. She wondered what the wet grass would smell like had it been real instead of artificial. She'd never smelled fresh soil before. Would that give the air more of an earthy smell? The rain masked that faint metallic sting in the back of her throat that seemed to hang in the air, the closer she moved toward the tube station.

The theater was only a thirty minute walk or so from the Fortress. When they arrived, Clayton used the password of the month to open the elevator door. Rosabella hadn't bothered to learn the password since she was with a group of people. Not the smartest or safest thing to do, but it was one extra step she hadn't had time to think about when searching for Clarise's birthday present. Speaking of...

"Clay?" She asked when they were in the elevator. He helped her slide down his back and onto the floor. She leaned on him the whole ride down.

"Yes?" he asked, hand linking with hers. "What is it?"

She was thankful for the dim light. "Why didn't you tell Clair about how I lost her present?"

His stubble grazed her temple. Clay's voice was low in her ear, "Because I know we'll find it. No need to upset her."

"Thanks," she replied, leaning into his shoulder.

When the elevator opened at the bottom, they tiptoed down the halls. It was lights-out for most of the citizens here; they didn't want to disrupt anyone sleeping.

Neither of them spoke until they closed the door behind them in the apartment. Rose fell onto the couch in the living room after sluggishly tearing her shoes off. She threw an arm over her eyes and rested there for a few minutes. Something solid poked at her. It must've been another loose spring. The Taylors were in desperate need of a new couch.

Without warning, Clayton lifted her legs into the air and plopped down on the cushion next to her. He draped Rose's legs over his lap and rested his hands on her knees. The scent of fresh linen--Clayton's signature smell--surrounded Rose and clouded her thoughts.

"What are you thinking about, Rose?" he asked.

She removed her arm and squinted at him. "Can I ask another question?"

"You can ask me anything," he said, a small smile on his face. His eyes told her he was serious; that he was listening to her and not playing around with her emotions. He eyed her, anticipating her inquiry.

The mood in the room shifted. Rose felt five years older, more mature than ever before. "Well, I'm just wondering what you meant earlier. When Gianna mentioned kids...do you remember?"

"Of course I remember." Clayton's tone was so matter-of-fact she thought he was done speaking on the topic. Then, he ran his hand up and down her shin. She should've shaved earlier. "What I meant was that I love you and I want to be with you until I die. I've always thought about kids."

Rose shivered under the intensity of his gaze. "Clay, I've only known you for like six months, and we've only been dating for five."

"When you know, you know," he said, shrugging. His eyes followed along the base of the wall, where the grey tiles met the off-white walls. She noticed the rock hard muscles in his back and neck clenching. This was uncomfortable for Rose, but even more so for him. Rose knew Clayton was not one to speak his mind and share his feelings easily. It took a lot for him to trust people. Rosabella was more open than him, but it didn't stop her from sympathizing with Clay. He lost someone dear to him years ago and he hadn't been ready to move on until recently. All she wanted was for him to be comfortable. She herself didn't know if this was going to work out. Rose obviously hoped it would last the rest of their lives, but it was so early in the game. She told him as much.

"But doesn't it feel like it's been years?" he protested, body still taut.

She poked him on the arm to draw his eyes back to her. It didn't work. "What do you mean by that? Are you saying a few months with me has dragged on for you?"

Clay's head snapped in her direction. "Absolutely not! I've loved every second with you. I just meant that...well I...doesn't it feel like we've known each other for a lot longer than five or six months?"

"Yeah, I suppose."

"That's all I meant."

The dejected look on his face upset Rosabella. She didn't want him to feel uncomfortable or worried. She needed to show him that he was important to her without giving up on her own standards and values.

Rose lurched forward. Her lips smashed into Clayton's, slightly parting them. She straddled him on the couch. One hand found its way to his hair, the other to his shirt collar, pulling him closer. It took a second for him to register the kiss, but once he did, he was all in. His hands caressed her back, her hips, her cheek.

They kissed until they had to stop for breaths. They touched foreheads, both of them panting.

Clayton brushed Rose's hair away from her face and smirked. "Hey, do you feel like the couch is stabbing you?"

She nodded, eyes glassy. "Yeah, I think it's one of those stupid springs again."

"Wait, hold on," Clayton said, reaching under the cushion. He pulled out a small silver case and held it up. "I can't believe it," he cried.

Rose's mouth fell open. "Is that...?"

Clayton laughed again and set the case on the cushion next to him. "Holy shit, we found Clair's present! I can't believe it," he said again, breathless.

"Well, I guess kissing on the couch came in handy tonight," she joked while wiping her sweaty palms on her shirt.

"For sure." Clayton nudged Rose's nose with his. "Would you like to continue, to make sure we've found everything?"

"You bring up a good point…It's only right that we're thorough." She yanked on his collar again, bringing his lips to hers.

"For the sake of the couch, you mean," Clayton said against her lips.

She closed her eyes and smiled. "Absolutely."

# Chapter 38

## (ROSABELLA)

ROSE PULLED OUT THE CHAIR AT THE TABLE nearest the door, sitting across from Clarise and Andre. They were sitting close together, almost touching. Andre had his arm on the back of her wheelchair. Rose checked over her shoulder to make sure Clayton was still in line grabbing a tray of food. Rose set her own tray down, acting as casually as she could though her insides were about to burst. She lowered her gaze and started to cut her chicken.

Eyes still on the table, Rose whispered, "You two need to be careful. I don't mind, but if Clayton sees you two…without an explanation…"

They both understood. Andre scooted his chair a few inches away from Clarise. Rose hated to be that person, but she'd rather Andre keep his head; not for her sake, but for Clarise's. Clayton would come around eventually. Hopefully.

"He's coming," Clarise whispered. "Act natural."

Soon Clayton dropped into the chair next to Rose. He handed her an ice pack, which she placed on her forehead, her chicken forgotten. Instant relief flooded her when the cold connected with her bruising skin. She nearly sighed with relief. Clayton gently bumped Rose with his elbow and kissed the side of her head.

When he turned back to his tray, Clay shook his protein shake up and down a few times. Then he moved on to cutting his chicken. Nobody said anything and it was becoming obvious there was something going on. Rose was very uncomfortable with the silence, but she didn't know what to say. She worried she'd give Clair and Andre away if she so much as looked at Clayton. He would be able to see in her eyes that there was something she was hiding, and she wasn't ready to tell him about them. That was a job for Clarise and Andre. It wouldn't be right if she outed them.

Thank goodness Prince showed up. He came up behind Rosabella and gave her a kiss on the cheek, "Mwah! Hey everyone! How are you all doing?"

A chorus of "goods" echoed in return. Rose almost slapped her forehead. This was ridiculous. She gave Prince a kiss on the cheek.

"Careful, Prince. That's my girl you're kissing," Clayton teased giving Prince a wink.

*My girl.* He'd referred to her as his girl again. She was giddy inside. Her heart started going haywire.

"You're lucky you're hot, Taylor," Prince joked. "Mind if we sit here? Rosabella, you remember me telling you about Oaklee," he said motioning to the man beside him.

Rose smiled up at Oaklee, swapping hands with the ice pack before waving up at him. She liked his smile; he had straight white teeth that stood out from his face. He was nowhere near as handsome as Clayton or Andre, or even Logan, but he was cute. He had a mop of curly blonde hair on his head, and a blonde mustache to match--save for the curls. Where Prince was small and bird-like in structure, Oaklee was big and built like a tree. Oaklee was much taller than Prince, by at least a foot. He had to be taller than Clayton, who was about 6'5." A perfect place to keep a little bird safe. Rose was surprised Oaklee didn't have similar crazy colored hair and outfits as Prince did. She appreciated how their opposites complemented one another well.

Rosabella patted the open space on the bench next to her. "Of course! It's nice to finally meet you, Oaklee."

He smiled again and said it was nice to meet her. Man, he was quiet as a mouse, very different from Prince's boisterous personality. Speaking of boisterous, Rose couldn't help but stare at Prince's outfit today. He had on loose-fitting jeans with the cuffs rolled up above his ankles and wore tall, flat tennis shoes. His shirt was bright orange, matching his new shade of hair. Prince's eyeshadow was subtle today: a pale peach shade.

"How was training today, kids?" Prince asked, taking the seat next to Clarise, across from Oaklee. He blinked at Rose. "What's with the ice pack?"

Clayton snorted and Andre choked on his green beans. Rose turned a shade of red that could probably be classified as magenta. Clarise giggled; she hadn't been there, but Andre had obviously told her about it. Rose was surprised Prince hadn't heard about it, since everyone seemed to know everything so quickly down here.

"Oh please, can I tell the story?" Andre cried, laughing.

"Go for it," Rose said, waving her hand at him.

*Rose had just finished up a spontaneous weightlifting drill with Eden. Though they'd taken a break from weight training to work on more combat, hand-to hand stuff with the other trainees, Rosabella couldn't help but focus on the pure bliss that came with working out. That feeling of power filled her veins again, until it pulsed through her whole body. Her favorite part of training was the knowledge that she was doing something with herself that was important; that she was working for a cause bigger than herself. She'd never felt this way before coming to the Fortress. She'd done things the way they were meant to be done and that was that; a perfect rule follower.*

*The part of Rose that gushed pride wanted to run to Clayton, throw herself in his arms, and tell him about her day. It had been a while since she'd been able to add more weight to the bar, but today, Eden increased the weight on the bar and said she was impressed.*

*The adrenaline coursing through Rose cut out all external sound. All she could hear was the blood pumping in her ears. She spotted Clayton across the room, who locked eyes with her when he saw her coming toward him. Focused on him, Rose didn't hear Eden call out to her right away. She kept pushing forward, wishing she was in his strong, steady arms already.*

*The adrenaline started to wear off. The ability to hear returning, Rose spun around to smile at Eden. As she spun, her feet wound up getting tangled with one another. Before she knew what was happening, Rose fell face-first into the ground. Her forehead took most of the blow, and then her chest. Fighting the urge to scream in frustration at her own clumsiness, Rose rolled onto her back.*

*She lied there, staring up at the ceiling, until the light pounding in her head began to subside.* Please god, *she thought,* let that have just been in my imagination.

*Eden was the first to reach her. Then Clayton. Eden lifted her head, turning Rose's face both ways. Her hands smelled of sweat and metal.*

*"I don't think she has a concussion," she said in relief. "That would've set your training back, Rosabella."*

*Clayton knelt, his knees on either side of her head. He leaned down to look into her eyes. Rose gazed up at his upside down figure.*

*"Oh no!" he cried.*

*"What?" Rose asked, her voice weak. Whatever it was couldn't be good.*

*"Do you see that too?" he asked Eden.*

*Now Rose was worried; she hadn't felt much pain other than to her pride, but maybe there was more wrong than she'd originally thought.*

*"Where?" Eden asked. Clayton leaned over Rose and whispered something to Eden. Her confusion melted into something else Rose couldn't quite recognize.*

*"Oh, that! Yeah, I see it now…"*

*If Clayton was upset by something, it was* really *bad.*

*"What is it guys?" Rose asked, squeezing her eyes shut.*

*Clayton brought his face very close to Rose's ear and whispered, "You have…oh, I don't think I can say it." He turned his face away.*

*"You should be the one to tell her, Clay. Go on, it's okay. She'll accept it eventually." Eden patted him on the back. She didn't look at Rose as she spoke.*

*Her heart racing, Rose grew extremely worried; meanwhile, Clayton pressed his lips to her temple. He didn't know that every time he touched Rose, it sent shivers up her spine. The pounding left her head the moment he touched her; Clay had that effect on her.*

*"Guys please just tell me what's wrong...I hate this anticipation."*

*"Okay, only if you're sure." Clayton sighed. "You have...a case of......red hair syndrome."*

*Rose smacked him on the arm and sat straight up, blinking minor dizzy spots from her vision. "Idiot! I thought something was seriously wrong with me!"*

*Clayton doubled over laughing, and the crowd around them began to lighten up when they realized everything was okay. Andre clucked his tongue at them from afar and joined in the laughter.*

*"Oh, but it is serious, Rose. You have one of the rarest hair colors ever known to man. If Bernard is smart, he should lock you up so no one can reach you," joked Clayton, fake seriousness in his voice. Rose groaned and tackled him--well tried to anyway. He was very strong.*

*"Don't do that to me ever again!" She decided to take it out on him by pinning Clay's arms to the floor. He let Rose pin him down; she'd never be able to do so otherwise. That only made him laugh harder.*

"Yeah, not one of my prouder moments," Rose said, staring down at her chicken. Why did Prince have to notice everything? She supposed the ice pack wasn't necessarily blending in with her skin. She didn't fault him for it, he was just making conversation; but she didn't like that her face was turning so red. It matched the welt on her forehead.

Andre hooted and smacked the table with his hand. The silverware rattled, making the others chuckle.

"How was I supposed to know I'd lose my balance? It's not like I plan to be this clumsy!" Rose threw her hands up.

This triggered another round of laughter from her friends. Clayton rubbed her back, smiling at her. She brushed off the embarrassment and laughed to herself. Then Rose set the ice pack down on the table between Prince and herself, proceeding to finish cutting her now-cold chicken.

"Where's Logan today?" asked Clarise, who'd been staring at her own plate of food until then. She looked scared; her face paled and she kept flicking her gaze from Clayton back to her food. Rose willed her to calm down. Clarise's behavior was going to give her and Andre away if she didn't act normal.

Andre shrugged and shoveled in a bite of his own chicken. "I donth know. Heth been buthy all day!" he exclaimed with his mouth full.

"Gross! Don't talk when you're chewing, Dre!" Clarise shoved him in the side. He groaned, pretending she stabbed him. She giggled and tucked her hair behind her ear. Andre smiled, food swallowed, gazing down at her with kind eyes. He rested a hand on her knee. Clarise looked back at him with an equal amount of affection. She didn't remove her hand from his arm and he didn't let go of her leg.

From the corner of her eye, Rose saw Clayton's hand clench around his knife. Oh great, a *knife*. Well, she supposed any object Clayton held in his hand could be used as a weapon, whether it was sharp or not. Could and *would* be used. She wanted to pull his attention to her, but it was too late. He'd already seen. Rose nearly smacked the two of them. They'd worked so hard to hide their feelings in front of Clayton, and now, this one stupid slip-up was going to cost Andre his friendship--and possibly his life based on the way the tips of Clayton's ears darkened in anger. He was impulsive and reckless and was the "act now, apologize later" type of person.

Before Rosabella was able to touch Clayton in an attempt to distract him, someone called out her name. She dropped her fork, startled. Everyone at the table, including her, turned around.

It was Bernard, standing stiff as a board in the doorway. Rose didn't know why he couldn't just come over to their table. Then she noticed the look on his face. His mouth was set in a hard line, a crease between his eyebrows. His arms were crossed over his chest, but not in a menacing way. With the way his shoulders drooped, Rose guessed he was in a dismal mood. But, why?

"Sir?" She asked, fully alert. Her mind raced, immediately going right to Aire. She'd been absent from meals lately but Rose wasn't sure where she spent her free time. All she knew was Aire was bound and determined to keep far away from Rose and vice versa. She rose to her feet and started for Bernard. Clayton, still seated, grabbed her arm to hold her back.

"I don't like the look of Bernard's face, Rose. Something's wrong," said Clayton, his voice low.

Rosabella wanted to find out for herself. If Bernard wanted to talk to her and didn't want to say too much in front of the others, it might be about the board. She wasn't allowed to share that information with anyone who wasn't involved. Was it possible something had happened to

Logan? He'd gone on a mission earlier this morning and Rose hadn't seen him since then.

"Logan...is he--?" She was unable to let herself finish that sentence. Her friend could *not* be dead. Rose felt her knees grow weak, and soon she couldn't feel anything. Blood pounded in her ears, just like when she was pumped up from training; the only evidence that she was still alive.

Clayton stood up to support her. Rose was grateful for it, because another second of standing on her own and she would've fallen over.

"What about Logan?" Clayton asked curtly, staring directly at Bernard. Did his grip just tighten around Rose's arm?

Bernard looked behind him in the hallway. He nodded at someone and stepped out of the way. Logan walked through the doorway and Rose let out a breath. She was too relieved at seeing him alive she didn't think after that. She pulled away from Clayton and ran at Logan. He picked her up and hugged her tightly. She squeezed her arms around his neck.

"From the look on Bernard's face, I thought you were dead," she said, suppressing a relieved sob, into his ear. Rose's body shook with exhaustion, thoroughly worn out. Logan nodded into her shoulder, his arms around her waist.

"What happened?" Andre asked. Rose peeked behind her and saw that, at some point, he'd moved to stand beside Clayton. Prince, Oaklee and Clarise were still sitting at the table, mouths open. Andre squinted at them. "Why are you so upset, Logan?"

Remembering that Clayton was watching from afar, Rose gently wiggled out of Logan's embrace. He didn't put up any resistance, and obliged. She landed on her feet and checked to see what Clayton was thinking. Clay's shoulders were pulled back and his nose flared with angry breaths, but other than that, he hid his emotions well. She hadn't meant anything by hugging Logan. They were friends and that's how you reacted when you found out your friend wasn't dead.

That was Rose's biggest mistake. Now, Clayton was going to ask her questions and that would mean she'd have to lie to him about where and when the two of them hung out. Logan's friendship was too closely linked with the deadly competition they all agreed to join; she couldn't give any details of the truth without telling Clayton everything that happened behind closed doors.

Rose's feet remained planted, standing in front of Logan to protect him if Clayton came at him as he'd done in the medical wing. She wanted to make things right.

She realized that she needed to say something--anything. "Clay, this isn't--"

"Rosabella, maybe we should talk about things another time?" Clayton snapped angrily. "Bernard," he started, facing away from her. "What do you need from Rose? What's going on?"

Bernard's face was solemn as he stepped back once more, guiding a young boy into the dining hall. He kept a hand clamped on one of the boy's shoulders.

Rose cried out in shock and raced forward another time, only to be stopped--yet again--by hands. This time it was Logan. He wrapped his arms around her waist and drew her away from the boy, keeping her back pressed against his chest. Rose fought and kicked as hard as she could, and knew Logan suffered from all the blows, but he refused to let go.

That's when Clayton stepped in.

"Let her go," he growled at Logan, a hand on his shoulder. "Now."

Bernard nodded at Logan. "It's alright. Let her go, son."

Grateful someone actually let her do the thing she wanted to do, Rose dove at the boy. Tears of joy sprung into her eyes, blurring her view of his face. But she didn't need to see his face, it was etched into the back of her mind. It haunted her worst nightmares. He had innocent blue eyes, a cute little nose and a rumpled head of hair that was never tame, no matter what she did about it.

The boy hadn't hit puberty yet, so his voice was still young and quiet when he said her name. Rose wrapped him up in a hug, bringing him to his knees in her lap.

"Rose?" asked Clayton. He hadn't moved from Logan's side, but he'd taken his hand off his arm. That was a start at least.

"This," she began, swallowing. "This is my brother. Nicolai."

All those months ago, Rose thought she'd never see him or their parents again. To have her brother standing here in front of her was the closest to a miracle she'd ever been. His little arms squeezed her in greeting.

Nicolai shivered so Rose wrapped her arms tighter around him to help him take in her body heat. Why was he shivering? More importantly, why did Logan try to stop her from seeing him? Benard hadn't exactly stated his reasons for looking so forlorn either.

"Why is everyone so damn upset?" She looked around at all of them. "This is amazing! My brother is alive!"

Logan pulled Andre and Clayton aside, whispering something to them. Clayton sucked his cheeks in and glanced at her. When their eyes met, he looked away. This was one of the rare times Rose couldn't decipher his expression. Andre whistled and rubbed the back of his head; Prince, clutching Oaklee's hand, leaned across the table to Clarise. Quickly, as if they were playing the telephone game, everyone else was in on the secret and Rose was left to wonder what they were whispering about.

Prince kept his voice low, but the dining hall was so quiet, Rose heard him. "This is better than my soap operas on TV. So much drama in so little time," he said, shaking his head. If he didn't look so sad, she would have laughed.

Rose stood and pulled her brother to his feet. She clutched his hand as if there was nothing else holding her to this earth. In that moment, there wasn't. She led him to the door, but Bernard stepped in her way before they could leave. Nicolai hid behind Rose's leg and clutched the back of her shirt.

She sighed, frustrated and annoyed by everyone around her. "*What is going on?*"

"There's something you need to know, Rosabella," Bernard said, holding up a hand.

Rose shrugged and groaned. "Fine. But it can wait. I want Nico to take a bath. He's probably scared out of his mind…that'll help him. It used to when mom did it."

Logan and Clayton appeared at her sides. What was with all the secrecy? Andre, she saw as she looked past Logan's shoulder, had returned to the table. He was speaking to her friends. His back was to Rose, so she couldn't try reading his lips, but Prince's reaction unsettled her. He covered his mouth with one hand and clutched at Oaklee's chest with the other. Clarise's face had turned a shade whiter than before. She almost blended in with the wall.

Bernard's frown deepened and he stroked the sides of his face. His eyes were red when he finally said, "Rosabella. Your brother has droid poison in his blood."

# Chapter 39

## (ROSABELLA)

Rose could have slapped Bernard across his face. How dare he? How *dare* he! Who said that in front of a vulnerable, innocent little kid?!

Before she went bat-shit crazy and jumped at Bernard's throat, someone wrapped their arms around her. Amidst her struggle, Nico's hand slipped out of her grip and he took a step back. His eyes were red and filled with tears. Rosabella was brought to her senses by the sorrow in his face. She stopped thrashing around.

"Can I trust you if I let go?" Clayton asked near her ear. How had he known she was about to go on a slapping spree?

"Yes, I'm fine," she said, attempting to wrench herself from his grip. Her brother stood in the doorway, pressed against Bernard's leg, who had an arm around Nico protectively. Did he have tears in his eyes too?

Clayton's arms released Rosabella so she could comfort her brother. Her motherly instincts kicked in enough for her to save face for Nicolai. She reached out her hand to him, smiling. "Come with me, Nico."

He took her hand, squeezing it hard. She didn't know why she'd lost her mind for a second, but she wouldn't let it happen again. Not while Nico was around. He'd been through so much--Rose didn't even know all of it--and he needed to feel loved if he was going to survive the poison. If Rose did it, he could do it.

"If you want, Rose," Logan said, placing a hand on her back, "We can take him back to my apartment. If it's a bath he wants, I have a really nice tub."

Rose shot him a weak smile and nodded. Logan stepped into the hallway, waving them to follow him.

Before she could, Clayton took her face in his hands. "I'm coming with you." There was a hard set to his mouth, as if he was biting his cheeks to keep from hurting someone.

"No, I'll be fine. I promise," she said, shaking her head. He kept a firm hold on her eyes.

"I know, but I *want* to be there with you."

"Alright." It wouldn't hurt to have him there. Rose knew she could use the moral support. "Just keep the angst to a minimum, my brother's been through enough," she half-teased, turning her face and kissing his palm.

He didn't smile. "Deal." Turning to Andre, he snapped, "You're coming with too. I want to keep an eye on you. Clair," he called to her at the table. She was watching them with tears in her eyes. "You have Prince and Oaklee walk you home, alright? I'll be back later."

Clarise rolled her eyes. "Clay, I'm fi--"

"No. I mean it. You got that guys?" he directed at the two men on the side, their hands clasped together. It would have been adorable had Rose not been so upset. Then Clayton turned and placed a hand on Rose's lower back, steering her out of the dining hall. Logan did his best attempt at a smile, ruffled Nico's hair, and guided them to his apartment.

Bernard gave Rose's shoulder a gentle squeeze as she passed. "I'm sorry."

A quick shake of her head solidified her belief. "Don't worry about it. He'll be fine. I fought it, so can he."

Rose thought she heard him say, "I hope you're right," but it was too quiet for her to hear accurately. He turned and walked in the direction of his office, head down and hands in his pockets.

Andre followed behind, putting a good distance between himself and Clayton. Rose saw him look back at the dining hall longingly. He probably wanted to go to Clarise, but thought better of it. She prayed Clayton hadn't seen.

They were halfway down the hall, heading toward the center of the Fortress, when Nico looked up at Clayton.

"Who are you?" he asked, his little voice squeaking.

Clayton tried to smile. It looked more like a grimace. "I'm Clayton. And you must be Nico. Your sister has told me so many stories about you."

Her brother sniffed and turned his head away. "It's Nicolai to you, mister."

Rose chided him, "Nico! Don't talk to my friend like that."

Clayton rubbed her lower back. "It's okay, Rose." To Nico he saluted and said, "Yes, sir."

To her surprise, and satisfaction, Nicolai giggled. But then he caught himself. Rose squeezed Clayton's arm encouragingly. It was a start. Clayton tapped her spine and trailed his hand up and down it as they walked.

He smirked down at Nico. "So, Mr. Nicolai, how old are you?"

Nico kept a straight face and looked forward. "How old do you think I am?"

Without hesitation, Clayton said, "Fifteen."

Her brother made a sound between a groan and a laugh. Rose's head snapped to look at her brother, a laugh rising in her own chest. He was trying so hard not to break character. That gave her a warm, happy feeling. If he was walking on his own and joking around with droid poison in him, he'd be okay. She would make sure of it.

"No, I'm eight. Almost nine," Nico replied after collecting himself.

"Oh, my apologies, sir. I thought you were older. You're just so mature." Clayton bowed his head solemnly. Rose's brother beamed, hiding behind her leg. He hated and loved affectionate attention almost as much as she did.

*** 

Rose had been in Logan's apartment many times before to train her mind to combat the whirring of the droids--a product of being stabbed by one all those months ago. Clayton didn't need to know that. She pretended to admire a picture of Logan with his parents near the door she'd already seen before. Logan played along and identified it as his family. The rest of his apartment was the same as it was last time: cluttered.

She slipped her shoes off and directed Nico to do the same. He obeyed and leaned on the wall with one hand. Clayton and Andre made their way inside before them, having slipped out of their shoes faster. They passed through the arched doorway into the living room area.

Logan walked over and ruffled Nicolai's hair. "So champ, do you really like baths?"

"Yep." Nico rolled his eyes.

Rose nudged Logan in the side with her elbow. "Yeah, Logan. Didn't you know that? Gosh," she said, rolling her eyes like her brother.

He bumped her back and laughed. "My bad. Let me take you there." Logan gestured for Nicolai to go ahead of him.

While Rose watched the two of them go into the bathroom to start the water, Clayton came into the doorway, leaning on the wall.

He gazed at her, eyes lazy and half closed. "*Champ*? Who does Logan think he is? He doesn't even know your brother."

Rose walked up to him and ran her fingers along the arm propped on his hip. "And you do?" she asked, standing on tiptoes to whisper in his ear. She laughed and patted his arm before entering the living room, where Andre sat on the couch, head in his hands.

Her heart fell, and Rosabella felt sorry for him. She sat down beside him and wrapped an arm around his back. He flinched, but then realized it was her. Andre glanced up at Clayton, who'd turned and was glaring at him from the doorway.

"Don't worry," she said quietly, giving Andre another side hug. "I'll talk to him."

He shook his head. "It won't be that easy. It's his *sister*. He's fiercely protective of her. Think of your brother and then multiply that ferocity by ten and that's Clayton's reaction to me liking Clarise." Andre didn't bother to keep his voice low; Clayton already knew. The damage was done. Well, the damage had *started*. Andre hadn't been killed yet, so she knew there might still be a chance for him.

Clayton headed for them, fists clenched at his sides. His eyes held a murderous look. Rose understood the meaning of the expression, "if looks could kill" in that moment. If that was true, Andre would've been dead for a while now. Rose felt Andre tense under her touch and tightened her arm around him. Clayton wouldn't hurt him if she was there, would he?

At the last second, Clayton turned abruptly away and walked into the bathroom instead.

They both sighed. Rose patted Andre on the back. "See? He'll be fine...eventually."

"Yeah, but how long is *eventually*? Because from where I'm sitting, it looks like it could take at least a decade of torture first."

A loud thud sounded from the bathroom. Rose sprung on her feet right away. She half-expected to see someone carrying her brother's limp, lifeless body to her. She imagined it would be Clayton. Logan wouldn't be so impulsive as to bring her dead brother's body to her when she was so emotionally unstable.

Just as Rose anticipated, Clayton ran out, holding a soaking wet Nicolai in his arms away from his body. Her brother still had clothes on. Clayton's face was scrunched and his eyes watered. He stopped right in front of Rose. She couldn't bring herself to look at her brother.

Instead, her eyes traveled to Logan leaning on the wall to support himself. He was laughing. Hard. Hysterically, even. Rose connected Clayton's expression as the same thing. Her heart started beating again.

Nicolai--fully alive--reached out to her and giggled. "Want a *big* hug, Rosie?"

"Why the heck not?" she said, laughing. Her shirt was soaked through in an instant, but she didn't care. Rose was grateful her brother was still functioning. She silently scolded herself. *He's going to be fine, don't even think that way.* When she pulled away, she was giggling. "What did I miss?"

Logan was currently gasping for air, so Clayton did the talking, "We were talking about--well, nevermind. We turned our backs for like, two seconds, and then we heard a loud crash and..." he trailed off, biting his lip to keep from laughing. It wasn't working very well.

"He--he slipped on the floor and fell, knocking over everything he possibly could on the way down," Logan said, clutching at his side. He wiped the moisture from his eyes and looked at her. "I now understand how you two are related."

Nico giggled, still in Clayton's arms.

Rose slapped Clayton on the arm for laughing. "It was *one* time!"

***

# (ANDRE)

Rosabella left the room, carrying her wet brother on her back. She claimed she wanted to make sure he actually took a bath this time. Meanwhile, Logan laughed and wiped his eyes. Apparently when there was a lot of tension and anger between people, the thing to do was laugh until you cried. Logan certainly had that down to a science, and Clayton wasn't too far off.

Seeing Clayton relinquish his anger for a moment gave Andre some semblance of hope. If his friend smiled and joked around after finding out Andre and Clarise had a thing going on, was that a sign he wasn't too upset?

Just as Andre caught Clayton's eye and smiled, all faith was lost. Clayton's glare threw daggers at Andre. Good thing Clayton was on the other end of the room. The downside to that meant he had Andre's only escape route blocked. The Fortress was a safe place, until something bad happened between citizens. Andre had a right to fear for his life. He'd known Clayton since he arrived here, but that didn't mean he would hold back if things escalated. This was Clayton's sister they were talking about. Andre had witnessed Clayton's unending ferocity when someone so much as said Clair's name wrong. He was fiercely loyal to his loved ones, and even more protective of them. Andre was truly terrified of what would happen once they were alone.

The three of them didn't speak for a while. Long enough for Andre to see the laughter in Clayton's eyes--put there by Nicolai's fall--fade. Logan tapped his knuckles absentmindedly on the back of the couch, near Andre's shoulder. They all balanced on the fine line between insanity and violence.

"How are you guys?" Logan asked.

Clayton shook his head, gaze cold and unfeeling. "Not now, Clarke."

Logan's attempt at making conversation was appreciated, but it did nothing to unfreeze the layer of ice coating on Clayton right now. Andre was afraid to look at his friend. He could feel Clayton's eyes on him, probably planning out how to kill him slowly and painfully. Andre figured thinking about Clarise would help calm him down and take him elsewhere. But the minute he pictured Clair's smile, her chocolate brown eyes, he worried Clayton knew what was going through his head. He forced himself to imagine one of his combat fights with Clayton. He'd lost every match against his friend, no matter how much he trained. Clayton was always smarter, always one step ahead.

If Andre wanted to save his own skin, all he had to do was point at Logan. He wasn't completely innocent in his "friendship" with Rosabella. It was made extremely obvious today when he and Rosabella had embraced in the dining hall. If Andre hadn't been so fearful of his life, he'd have pulled Logan away from her. Andre didn't doubt that same thought had gone through Clayton's mind. Clayton never wanted to anger Rose or cause her any grief; because of his love for her, he'd kept his composure like a pro in that moment. Even now, with Rose in a different room, Clayton didn't take his chance and beat the shit out of Logan. Probably because Clay knew Andre would bolt when his head was turned in another direction.

Clayton crossed his arms over his chest—a sure sign something serious was about to happen. He glared at Andre. "Can we talk?"

Andre gulped and nodded. He didn't move from the couch. Clayton may feel threatened if he did and would throttle Andre.

Logan straightened behind the couch. "Are you sure now's the best time?"

"If you think talking down to me right now is smart, you must be stupid," Clayton sneered, brown eyes shifting from Andre to Logan. "You're not in the clear either."

Andre cringed when Logan threw his hands up and said, "I don't know what you're talking about."

"Oh really?" Clayton scoffed. He leaned forward, the veins in his neck standing out from his tanned skin.

"Really," Logan spit back, all kindness in his eyes gone.

Andre dropped his head into his hands. "Come on, cuz. Just stop. We all know."

Clayton laughed dryly. "For once, I'm agreeing that you should listen to Andre. He has your best interests in mind. I, however, don't care as much."

An eerie, painful silence enveloped the room. Andre silently begged his cousin to keep his mouth shut. They were all in a pile of shit right now, digging it deeper with every word uttered.

"I just don't understand," Clayton started, hands waving in the air, "when you two decided it was okay to go behind my back and try to steal both of my girls from me. Andre, you and my sister are never going to happen. I'm calling it off right now—"

"They never did anything," Logan interrupted. His testimony might have helped Andre's case slightly, but it didn't help his own.

Clayton's hands slapped against his thighs as they fell. "Are you telling me that I was the only person who didn't know? All of you did?"

"I plead silence," Logan joked, hands up in surrender.

*You idiot*, Andre thought, *you're going to get yourself killed.*

With perfect timing, Rosabella emerged from the bathroom, eyebrows drawn together. Her confusion worried Andre. If she broke down or became upset with either one of them, Clayton was going to unleash all his anger.

The name that fell from her lips threw a bigger ball of tension between Clayton and Logan.

"Logan?" she asked as she rubbed her temples. "Can you explain to me why, if my brother is poisoned, he doesn't have a fresh injection site?"

Uh-oh. Andre stood and backed away from everyone. If Clayton went after Logan, Andre was not going to get in the way. The two of them were going to hash it out eventually. They were men; it was bound to happen.

"Well, umm," Logan stuttered, wringing his hands. "We took a blood sample and discovered that he has droid poison running through his veins too."

She smiled, relief standing out in her bright blue eyes. "That's good, isn't it? I have the same thing and I'm fine."

Logan shook his head and snuck a glance at Clayton. "With you it was different. You recovered and your vitals were all fine...Nicolai has a strange heart condition that we are still working on figuring out."

Clayton raised his hand but didn't wait to be called on before speaking, "Hold on a sec. Are you saying that you've had Rose's brother here for a while?"

Rose's smile faded, the corners of her mouth dropping into a deep frown. "I hadn't even thought of that."

Logan glared at Clayton and cursed him. "Thank you for that, Clayton. It really helped," he said with sarcasm.

Andre thought it was the right moment for him to ease his way toward the exit. He took a few small steps while the three of them started up a shouting match, Rose loudest of all.

"I thought you were my friend, Logan! He must've been so scared! Did you have him tied up like an animal?"

Clayton defended Rose, "I thought you said you cared about Rose. It doesn't seem that way to me."

Logan did his best to defend himself while also deflecting Clayton's jab and reassuring Rose that nothing bad had happened to her brother. It was all so unnecessary. Why did they feel the need to argue? The neighbors all the way down the hall could probably hear their bickering.

Andre could practically smell the desperation in their voices. Didn't they all know this was petty of them? Clayton was really only upset with Logan because he thought he was making a move on his girlfriend. If Andre didn't know his cousin so well, he'd have defended Logan to the death. Now he wasn't so sure. Logan and Rosabella *had* been spending a lot of time together lately; Andre caught Rose letting herself into Logan's apartment one night after dinner without knocking. What was going on in this apartment while Clayton was busy or otherwise unassuming?

Not to mention, when Clayton became upset, he took up as much space as he could to look menacing to the other person. In this case, he blocked the entire doorway to the hall. Andre's only escape; he abandoned his plan to slip out unnoticed and moved closer to the bathroom door. Maybe he'd be able to hang out with the kid for a while until things cooled down.

With each step away from the fighting trio, Andre knew he was already forgotten. Clayton wouldn't yell at him for his relationship with Clarise for a while. Long enough for him to catch his breath and come up with a plan to save his own ass. And Clair's of course.

At the door, a fresh, soapy scent burst into Andre's nose. How much soap did the kid need? He was the size of a twig. Had Rosabella been that small once? She was no longer living in the body of a child; in fact, Rose had a womanlier figure than most Fortress-born girls. That may have been why Andre was so drawn to her at first. She was beautiful, but not in the conventional stick-figure way so many movie actresses were these days. Rose was different. She stood out in a crowd.

So did Clarise.

She was unique because she was wheelchair bound. Even if she wasn't, Andre still would've fallen for her. He was around Clair so much, it was inevitable. He, Clair and Clayton used to stay up late into the night talking about their lives. Andre was one of the only guys Clair was exposed to for as long as he could remember, even though the Taylor's had been living in the Fortress for about eight years.

Andre closed the door behind him, leaving a slight crack so he could listen if anyone were to approach the room. Clayton in particular.

He waved his fingers back and forth at Nicolai, who was covered up to his chin in bubbles. His big blue eyes stared at Andre, out of place among the sudsy floor.

"Hi, kid. My name's Andre," he announced, smiling. He didn't want to scare Nicolai, only to escape the others. They reminded him of his parents. It was about time people grew up and talked their problems out instead of screaming in one another's faces.

Nicolai blinked and waved back. "Hi."

"So, you came from up above, huh?" Andre asked. He hopped on the counter and made himself comfortable.

The kid nodded, eyes still wide. He wasn't unfriendly, just cautious. "Yep. Rosie's my sister."

He smiled slightly. "Yeah, she's a good sister, isn't she?"

"Mhhm."

"Sweet," Andre said, twiddling his thumbs. Gosh, he was terrible with kids. "So what's your favorite—"

"Are they fighting because of me? Because I'm going to die?" Nicolai asked, absolutely matter-of-fact. To this boy, his death didn't seem to frighten him; at least on the outside. Nicolai had clearly accepted this fate a long time ago.

Andre shook his head and attempted to reassure Rose's brother, "No, you're not going to die. Don't be silly."

Nicolai played with a pile of bubbles near the faucet head. "Yes I am. My dad told me so. That's why he sent me here."

"Say what?" Andre exclaimed. White hot embarrassment crawled up his neck to his cheeks. This was not the type of conversation he'd been expecting. If Rose heard them, she was going to throw a fit, and then Clayton really *was* going to kill him! "Let's not say stuff like that. It's going to be fine."

Nicolai shook his head. "No, my dad told me I'm going to die soon. There's nothing we can do about it."

Oh no! Rose's heart was going to break into little tiny pieces everywhere. Andre believed she'd never recover from the death of her little brother…if it was even true. What father told his son that he was about to die?

All Andre could do was shrug and smile. "We'll see, I guess. For now, why don't we talk about something else?"

The boy glared at him. "No. I need to tell them now."

"Okay, okay. I'll be right back." Andre teetered on the edge of the counter, debating who to call in here. Logan was the best option by far, especially because he didn't have any urges to kill Andre.

He went to the door and poked his head out. Rose, Clay and Logan all wore angry, exhausted expressions. If they were all so tired, why continue to argue? Andre never made sense of that.

"Hey, umm Logan? Can you come in here for a sec?"

Rose, wary of the tightness in Andre's voice, followed him. Of course, that meant Clayton trailed after her. Soon, everyone was in the bathroom. The poor kid was naked in the tub; all he wanted was a nice, relaxing bath and, instead, this is what he got.

"What's going on, Nico?" Rose asked. She knelt beside the massive tub and rested her elbows on the ledge. Her tender tone impressed Andre. Even amidst the fear of losing her brother, Rosabella managed to mask it and only display love.

Andre rocked back and forth on his heels, a sticky sweat crawling onto his neck. "You need to hear this, Rose. He said your dad *sent* him here."

Rose's head swiveled while she glanced back and forth between Andre and her brother. Nobody spoke for a while, everyone examining Rose's behavior, waiting for her to blow. Logan remained still off to the side, Clayton in the doorway, readying himself to comfort Rose. Andre watched his eyes transform from anger to sympathy. He lost Tess all those years ago, so he was able to relate to this situation in ways neither Logan nor Andre would ever be able to. While they'd all loved Tess, she was more connected to Clayton than any of them. She'd needed him like he was her source of air.

Rose's brother cupped a handful of bubbles in his palms and spoke, "Dad told me I had to come here because I'm going to die. It's okay,

Rosie. I've known for a while. The treatments never worked when Dad tried."

"Nico?" she asked, hands balling into fists. "What are you talking about? You're not going to die."

He blew the bubbles and watched them float. Only when they landed safely in another pile of bubbles, did Nicolai look over at her. "Rosie, dad told me everything. He knows about the Fortress and he knows about the droid things. That's why he's been injecting me for a while. He wanted me to turn out like you, immune to the droids."

Wow, this eight-year-old knew all of that? And he wasn't screaming and running away? What an extraordinary family. Rose was tough as nails, yet soft as a cloud, and her brother was no different. Both were beyond brave and opinionated—Rosabella slightly more so, but that most likely came with age.

From the pained expression on Rose's face, Andre figured she was not coping well with this new information.

"I'm not sure if you're remembering things right, Nico," Rose whispered. Her face turned red, and her hands started shaking.

Nicolai shook his head. "They both knew about this place. Their job was to protect the entrance at all costs. Don't you remember that night when you and I snuck downstairs for a late-night snack—after mom and dad told us no?"

"Yes," she said, voice weak.

He continued, "And remember how we caught dad doing something in the pantry? He was coating the floor in the same thing he used to dose us with to keep the droids away."

Utter shock hit Andre. Hard. If it was this bad for him, he didn't want to imagine what Rose was going through. She sagged back onto her heels. Clayton was at her side instantly, an arm around her.

Clayton spoke next, "Nicolai, what do you mean, the dose your dad used? Are you saying he *injected* you with droid poison?"

He received a curt nod from Nicolai in return. "Well, he said it was delusional—oh, no, *diluted*. That's what he called it…dad gave it to you for a few weeks before the first attack, Rosie. It was supposed to be a secret. You never even knew."

The magenta of her face gradually faded to a pale white. "But…but why?"

"So we could survive the poison if the droids ever attacked us..." Nico replied.

Goosebumps appeared along Rose's skin so she rubbed her arms. "Why are you saying that you're going to die then if you've had the injections?"

Her brother shrugged and returned to his bubble-playing. "Because it didn't work on me. I'm not strong enough."

Rose grabbed his arms and wrenched him to face her. Andre flinched for the little boy. She nearly screamed in his face, "How are you so calm? How are you okay with this?"

A long pause ensued, while Rose and Nicolai gawked at one another. Andre and Clayton made eye contact, the two of them nodding their understanding. Rose was going to need Clayton around for a while, more so than Clarise. Clayton was silently telling Andre to keep his hands off his sister, or he would kill him, while at the same time showing his concern for his girlfriend. He then tore his eyes off of Andre, putting all his attention on Rosabella. Andre had a sneaking suspicion he wouldn't be seeing much of Clayton for a while. He and Andre had become the new Rose and Aire: old best friends, destined to have problems for months—in this situation, possibly even years.

As a last-ditch effort, Andre tiptoed to the doorway. With Clayton on the floor beside Rose, it left Andre plenty of escape room.

The last piece of conversation he heard was Nicolai's little voice, "Because I can be with mom again. She's dead."

Yep, it was time to get out of there. Andre wanted no part in the sorrow Rose was about to experience. Losing a parent was difficult as hell. He couldn't sit by and watch another person go through what he went through. Time for him to go to his apartment and work through a plan to not let Clayton kill him and a way for Andre to see Clarise every now and then.

Just because someone told him not to be with the girl he liked, did not mean he was going to listen. Andre would just have to be extra careful now.

# Chapter 40

## (ROSABELLA)

"YOU SHOULD REALLY BE MORE CAREFUL, ROSABELLA," LOGAN chided, grabbing onto her elbow to steady her.

"Sorry," she mumbled, righting herself. "It's a little hard to focus on a mission when my brother might be dying. But don't mind me."

Saying it out loud was painful. Like, gut-wrenching, stabbing a knife into her abdomen, painful. Nicolai had been in the Fortress for a few days now. He'd progressively gotten worse, to the point of Rose and Clayton considered moving him into the medical wing; but after much thought, Rose wasn't ready to admit that her brother was on the verge of death. Clay said he'd back up whatever decision Rose made, even if it meant Nicolai took up space in Clayton's bedroom.

A lack of sleep and not eating made for a terrible combination. Rose just couldn't bring herself to eat anything. Yesterday, Clayton had forced Rose to take a tray with food from the dining hall back to his apartment, where he coaxed her until she ate half a grilled cheese sandwich.

Beyond that, she hadn't had any time to see anyone besides Clayton, Logan and Nicolai. Rosabella hadn't spoken to Clarise or Gianna and most of all, missed out on dinners with Lilianna. Her brother required constant attention, but unlike the way it was with Lilianna, he was about to die.

She'd been doing her best to make him as comfortable as possible despite the circumstances.

Logan had offered to give up his room for her brother, but she didn't want to put him in an awkward situation with Nicolai should she not be there and he needed something. Not only that, but she'd have to stay overnight in Logan's apartment and that would be a bit strange for their relationship dynamic. If she'd said yes, Clayton would've probably had a heart attack. He was very sensitive whenever she brought Logan up in conversation, so she was not about to put any doubt in Clayton's mind that she loved him and only him.

The day after Nico arrived, the trainers had awarded the trainees with their official, training completion certificates and badges. Next, Rose and her fellow trainees would go on missions for a few months before eventually deciding on a career in the Fortress. At least Nicolai had the chance to watch Rose walk across the makeshift stage in the dining hall to receive her training certificate before he'd become bedridden. Her brother had made it to the ceremony, where he sat between Clayton and Clarise. The dining hall had been converted into a ceremony room, complete with a stage near the door and a skinny microphone for Bernard to announce each of the trainees' names. Rose had crossed the stage, a smile plastered on her face for the benefit of the other citizens; she'd done it for them, not for herself.

She'd stopped smiling genuinely the minute Nico revealed what had happened back home. Rose refused to think of her mom as being dead. It was much easier for her to pretend their parents were up above, living in a different safe house, riding out the storm. She determined the next steps for her family: once everything with the droids cooled down, they'd move into the Fortress with Rose and Nicolai, who was not going to die if she had anything to say about it.

His decrease in health had happened quickly. Rose didn't see it coming, especially not as fast as it had. Or she didn't want to see it happening so rapidly. One day Nico was in the bathtub, playing with bubbles, the next, he was throwing up and convulsing several times a day. He took naps between convulsions, and he remained in one spot on the bed unless he had to use the bathroom, in which case, Clayton assisted him.

Rose had to hand it to Clayton, he was a trooper. He'd been there for her through each of the Aire and Lilianna situations, only getting upset when she was upset; and now he was right by her side while her brother fought against droid poison.

As she should be right now. Rose hadn't wanted to leave the Fortress, but Bernard and Logan both insisted she take a break and go on a perimeter check mission. This time it was actually what they said the mission was.

"I'm sorry," Logan said, placing a hand on her arm. She looked into his kind green eyes, softening immediately. With the treeline and the setting sun behind him, his eyes stood out from the rest of his features. "I'm not sure what the best thing to say is...but I want you to know that I'm so sorry you have to go through this. If I could reverse the clock and do something about it, I would."

Rose nodded, took his hand from her arm and folded it between hers. After mustering the best non-frown she could, Rose whispered, "I know you would. That's why you're my friend...because you always know what to say even though you think you don't."

For a few moments of silence, Logan's mouth opened and closed over and over. He gaped at her, eyes clouding with something she'd never seen before. It came as a shock when Logan pulled her in for a hug. Their cheeks brushed against one another as he leaned down. Rosabella found herself relaxing in his hold, with her head on his shoulder. That's what Logan was good at: noticing when someone just needed to be held.

As a woman who wanted to be strong and brave, it was sometimes difficult for Rose to relinquish that control. She'd only ever allowed Clayton to hold her before, and now she'd let Logan in. Rose loved both of them, in different ways of course. They'd both supported her when she needed it, and comforted her when she was upset. They were the truest people in her life.

Even her own father couldn't be trusted. He'd known about the Fortress and had never told Rosabella or her brother about it. To keep a secret like that was despicable. If they'd known about it during the first attack, they'd all be together right now. Nico wouldn't have been injected, their mother wouldn't be dead (not dead, just...gone), and their father would be innocent in her eyes.

After Logan couldn't find any words, Rose spun on her heels and continued their route. She'd never been on a mission with Logan before. It came as a shock to her when she wished Andre was here instead. Logan was too emotional sometimes. It wasn't a bad thing...at least not *all* the time. Just now, before she'd tripped, when she needed someone to tell her things would be alright, he'd gotten all choked up and was unable to reply. If Andre was here, he'd make a joke about Rose and Clayton and then they'd move on in silence. The more she learned about Andre, the more Rose didn't hate him. She used to despise Clayton too, and now look at them. People weren't all they seemed on the outside; some people kept things about themselves buried deep in order to give off the image they wanted to instead.

Clayton had been so good to Rose. If this wasn't a test of their love, Rose didn't know what was. Clayton was helping her through this like a champion. He made sure to bring her food every meal, though she didn't want to eat anything, and even stayed up late with her when she sat in a chair beside Nicolai's bed.

The sickly way Nico's skin had begun to wrinkle was disgusting. She'd never tell her brother that; instead, every morning when she woke up and visited him, she told him how great he looked that day. The smell of death had taken root in the bedroom, the smell of rotting organs, like a dead fish lying on the sand out in the burning sun or something. She could only imagine what she herself smelled like when she'd been poisoned by a droid.

She wasn't going to allow herself to accept that Nicolai was dying. He wasn't! So what if he looked worse and worse each passing day? Rose herself had been in a coma of sorts for weeks before regaining consciousness. Nico wasn't going to die. He was too young. His immune system was too strong to allow it to happen.

Rose blinked fresh tears away, thinking about her brother. An innocent little soul like him wouldn't die at this age. He'd outlive her by decades, she vowed. If he died now, then her whole life would be meaningless. That would mean her mom was dead, her dad was a stranger, and Aire truly hated her.

Logan raced after her, arms and legs pumping to keep up. He was a good half a foot taller than her, but was given shorter legs and a longer torso. Not to mention, right now, Logan didn't have the same pain or the anger Rose had stored inside.

He spoke between breaths, "Rosabella, can you...come with...me somewhere...tonight? I want to...introduce you...to someone."

She shook her head and continued on their route. Her old house came into view against the darkening sky. "I can't. I have to stay with my brother. I shouldn't even be here right now--I should be with him."

"You can spare half an hour, Rosabella. Trust me."

Rose hated the way his voice curled up at the end. She didn't like being talked to like a child. Didn't Logan know her at all?

He stopped walking and stood, refusing to move until she herself stopped and turned around. A staring match commenced. The two of them squinted when the wind dried out their eyes. Rose refused to back down. Logan would not have his way if she could help it. This staring match meant everything to her; it meant she'd win more than some silly contest...she'd win the right to speak first.

When she won, she'd convince him that Nico wasn't dying. Logan's listening skills were fantastic. He was always respectful of her and never treated her opinions as if they were less than his own. All in all, Logan Clarke kept the peace in any situation possible.

Logan snapped his head to the side, breaking contact. "This is ridiculous. I can't believe you have me standing here doing this."

Well, so much for speaking first. She tore up patches of artificial grass with the heels of her shoes as they rammed into the ground. When she posed on her tiptoes to get in his face, her mouth was mere inches from his own. She prayed the anger in her words impressed upon him the notion she wasn't giving in to his pity party. Pity was unnecessary. She wasn't going to lose anyone else. Nico would be fine. Why didn't everyone else believe that?

"Logan, you and everyone else need to stop treating me like this."

His feet planted and his knees locked as they made eye contact again. Logan peeked at her lips and then moved his gaze back to her eyes. "What are you talking about?"

"You and everyone else," she yelled, waving her arms, "need to have some faith. *I* went through hell and came back. *I* survived the poison! Why don't you think my brother can?"

He placed hands on each of her shoulders. "You don't understand Rosabella. This is different. You were stabbed by the droid...Nicolai was injected with the poison and it's not compatible with his health... concerns. There's no way for him to survive unless his body decides to fight it, which hasn't happened yet."

Rose rolled her eyes and dropped back down to her flat feet. "I know! That's what I'm saying. He'll be fine. *I* fought it off."

Logan's grip on her arms faltered. "Why don't we talk about this later? I want to take you to meet someone."

"Later," she mumbled. "I'm not in the mood."

He crossed his arms and glared. "I know you're not in the mood. But, as your superior, you're technically supposed to listen to me, and I say I want you to come with me."

She reared her anger at him, "What are you doing? Is this a *power* trip? You're supposed to be my friend!"

Logan tucked his hands in his pockets and shuffled his feet. "You're right, I shouldn't talk like that...but you have to trust me. It's because I'm your friend."

Face still red, and heart still racing, Rose glowered at him. The sunset shining over the houses cast a shadow across his face. With his green eyes darkened and his hands in his pocket, he seemed an entirely different person. Vulnerable yet sure of himself. Rose hated noticing this side of him. Who was Logan to her now? Only minutes ago she'd hated him... not too different from when she first met Clayton...and look how that turned out.

No! This was different. Logan was her closest friend apart from Clarise.

"Fine," she cried, throwing her hands up. "If you insist, then I guess I'd better listen to you."

*\*\*

Many of the Fortress citizens had retired to their rooms and apartments by the time Logan and Rose returned. She'd promised Clayton the moment she came back from her mission, she'd go to his apartment. He and Nicolai would've already eaten dinner together. All she'd have to do was put her brother to bed and promise to see him in the morning.

Each night, when he was fast asleep, she whispered in his ear, telling him that everything would work out, and that he wasn't going to die. If the others weren't going to tell him, then it was up to Rosabella to give her brother hope.

After a detour in which Rose met Logan's mom, a vibrant, vivacious woman, she realized it was time to leave. She'd overstayed her welcome, having been there far after curfew started.

Rose gasped when she saw the time on her wristband and dashed to the door. She waved goodbye to a protesting Tamika, whom Rose decided she adored. and made her departure. When she went to Logan's apartment for a quick brain squeezing session tomorrow, she'd ask him what the heck all this was about. Sure, she had a great time with Logan's mom, but that didn't make it any less random or weird.

After checking her screen for any messages she may have missed, her heart fluttered when she read a text from Clayton. He told her how much he loved her and that he'd stay up with her brother while she grabbed dinner for herself. He had no idea she'd been with Logan and his mother for hours. Hopefully he'd gone to bed after Rosabella didn't return for a while. Surely Nicolai was asleep by now.

Another message sent her heart racing with worry. Her skin became hot, and her legs shook. Rose broke into a run, making a beeline for her dorm, Gianna's text from about an hour ago clouding any other thoughts: WHERE R U? I NEED HELP.

# Chapter 41

## (ROSABELLA)

Rose hesitated before entering their dorm. She knocked and opened the door a crack. "Gianna?"

"Rose? Come in."

She stepped into the dark room, leaving the door open to shed light on the floor. Her eyes adjusted once she reached the foot of Gianna's bed. All Rose could see was Gianna's hump of a stomach under the covers.

Rose perched on the edge of the bed near her friend's feet. "What's wrong, Gianna?"

"I don't know," she groaned, rolling onto one side. "It just hurts so much. One minute I'm fine and then a few minutes later, it hurts so bad I could scream."

"Okay, okay, let's just talk through this together," Rose assured. She rested a hand atop her roommate's. "Did you try messaging Donovan?"

Gianna moaned, tears glistening on her cheeks. "No, I can't. What if he sees me looking disgusting like this?"

With her eyes fully adjusted, Rosabella took in her roommate. Her hair hung in stringy strands around her face, some sticking to her sweaty forehead. Her hands, clammy to the touch, clenched the comforter. Her large stomach, swelled from the growing baby, protruded from the comforter. The cause of Gianna's pain.

A lightbulb idea struck Rose then. She knelt with one knee on the bed and leaned over Gianna. Then Rose touched her stomach. "Alright, Gianna. You tell me when the pain is back and I'll see if we can figure this out."

Her roommate nodded, fresh tears flashing along her cheeks. Rose's heart ached for her friend. As such a fragile woman before pregnancy, she feared for Gianna during the birthing process. If this was really what Rose thought it was, then the baby was coming sooner than expected. With one hand on Gianna's stomach and her screen in the other, Rose prepared to call for reinforcements.

All of a sudden, light flooded the room as a tall, skinny woman entered. She switched on the lights and took in the scene.

Rose blinked the spots away and put a hand over Gianna's eyes to shield her. When she regained her composure, Rose turned around to yell at the woman.

Gianna moaned again and screamed. "It's happening again." Her hands flew out in agony, smacking Rose's screen from her hand.

Aire, Rose's ex-best friend, froze in the doorway. "I--I'm sorry. I didn't know anyone was in here...what's going on?"

Rose felt helpless in this situation. Utter disappointment in herself tingled her limbs all the way from her toes to her head. The tingling died down as she forced herself to keep Gianna calm. Or tried to.

"Aire, can you help me?" Rose cried over Gianna's screams. "I need you to call the doctor!"

Gianna whimpered between screams, "What? Why?"

Rose took Gianna's hand in hers and told her to squeeze when it hurt. It gave both of them something to center themselves. She stroked the side of Gianna's head, brushing away strands of greasy hair.

"Gianna, I think you're going into labor."

Her screams drowned out any response. Gianna's back arched high in the air. Her comforter twisted around her, constricting further movement. Her cries of pain left Rose's head splitting.

"Holy crap!" Aire yelled, hands on the sides of her face. "What are we going to do?"

Rose kept her back to Aire and spoke in her best calm voice, "First of all, we need to be calm, Aire. Second, you need to call the medical wing and request the doctor's presence. Third, you need to call Donovan, Gianna's boyfriend. Any questions?"

Aire's silence gave Rose hope she was following directions. She'd never helped anyone in labor before. It was scary as hell! Like facing the droids but this time she had no control. If this was what all pregnancies were like, Rose wasn't sure if she wanted to partake in it.

When Rose's mom went into labor with Nicolai, Rose was ten years old. They wouldn't allow her in the room at the hospital, so she had to sit in the hallway on an uncomfortable plastic chair, the sounds of her mom's screams in the background for hours. Talk about a traumatic experience. Now she could add this to the list. Childbirth was not looking too hot right about now.

Aire stepped around the bed to perch on the corner near Gianna's feet. She held her screen to her cheek. "Are you sure?...Yes, we're in the dorms....alright, I'll tell them...thank you."

Gianna squeezed Rose's hand again. "What did they say?"

Rose understood the look on Aire's face. After years of friendship, she'd never forget what each expression meant. In this case, it wasn't great news.

Aire's eyes flitted around the room before landing on the tile floor. "The nurse told me they'll send another nurse down to our room right away--so that part's good!"

"But...?" Rose prodded, hoping Aire would just get to the point.

Aire's eyebrows knit together, a sure sign of discomfort. "But the doctor is actually in with another patient who's giving birth right now too."

"So what does that mean?" Gianna cried, wincing from the pain in her abdomen.

Rose gave her hand a gentle squeeze and smiled. "It means you're going to give birth right here, with us by your side. Everything will be okay!"

Gianna shot her an exasperated look. She clenched down on her teeth, drying tears glistening on her flushed cheeks.

"It means they're going to send a medic to help you," Aire replied, taking up a position on the other side of Gianna's bed. Rose and Aire each took a hand and talked while they waited for the medic to arrive.

"Did you message Donovan?" asked Rose. "Did he respond?"

Aire nodded. "Yes and yes. He'll be here as soon as he can. He just came back from a mission."

Gianna's pain subsided enough for her to get comfortable on the mattress. Her chest heaved with big breaths, her forehead dripped with sweat. She smacked her lips together.

Rose noticed how dry her friend's mouth was and reached around her to grab her extra water bottle on the floor beside her own bed. "Do you need something to drink? Some water?"

Gianna nodded weakly. She downed the water in seconds and handed the water bottle back to Rose, chin dripping. Rose fought the urge to wipe her chin.

Then Gianna rested her head on her pillow and sighed. Her eyes closed as she mumbled, "I thought I was prepared for this. Donovan and I went to so many preparation classes in the medical wing...I--I thought I was strong enough to get through this."

Rose patted her hand after tossing the water bottle over her shoulder. "You *are*, Gianna. it's like...well don't you remember going on a mission by yourself for the first time? You spent all those weeks--*months*--training. Even with all that practice, you still had to figure things out on your own, remember? At least I know I did."

Aire, who grew encouraged, added, "Yeah, I remember when I went out for the first time. It was like I was in a totally different world. I had to remember how to walk, I was so confused and nervous. But, with time, it got better."

Gianna swallowed and nodded. "You're right. It just takes some getting used to, that's all."

"There you go!" Rose cried, happy to see her friend looking on the bright side.

"But I don't think I'll ever get used to this pain, no matter how many kids I have--this sucks!"

In response, the three of them laughed, but were interrupted by a new round of screaming a few moments later, courtesy of Gianna's contractions. Rose and Aire said as many soothing things they could think of, all while holding onto Gianna's hands. Rose had to bite her lip to keep from crying out from the bone-crushing pain. For a woman with no visible muscle mass, Gianna's grip was impossible to escape from. Rose was alright with that; so long as Gianna channeled all her pain into the two women holding her hands, it would help take her mind off the contractions, even for a second.

They were all too distracted to hear the knock at the door. Before any of them registered who entered, Donovan appeared at Rose's side. His face was devoid of color and his eyes were bloodshot. His blonde hair matched Gianna's, stringy in texture.

He touched his girlfriend's arm. "Oh my god, Gianna! Are you okay?"

She snarled at him, "Do I look like I'm okay? This is a pain I've never felt before!"

Rose slipped her hand out of Gianna's and passed her off to Donovan. She patted him on the back, her tender touch sympathetic. "Don't take it personally, she's in a lot of pain."

"I've heard that childbirth is one of the most painful things a woman will undergo in her lifetime," Aire chimed. Her own hair had fallen from its bun and damp dark brown curls crawled up her clammy neck. Her brown eyes blinked, revealing a lack of sleep, through black, baggy skin below her drooping lids. If that's how Aire looked, Rose didn't want to see *herself* in a mirror.

"Gianna, baby, I'm right here," Donovan replied, hands shaking as he clutched onto his girlfriend. The sudden moment of anger now gone, Gianna started sobbing and fell into an embrace with him.

Aire and Rose made eye contact across the bed. Aire rolled her eyes and smiled, while Rose giggled silently to herself at the lovesick couple. It was just like old times, when they could read one another's thoughts without hesitation.

To be honest, Rosabella couldn't even remember why they were fighting in the first place.

Aire, sensing the shift in Rose's thoughts, winked. She mouthed "I miss you" over Donovan and Gianna's heads. Rose smiled and began forming the same words on her lips before remembering the main quality in her friend she despised most of all: egocentrism. Whether Aire played at being inconsiderate, or she literally couldn't perceive other people's emotions, Rose didn't care. The fact of the matter was, Aire only cared about herself. If her memory served Rose right, she bet a million dollars that Aire was waiting for her to apologize first. Well, that just wouldn't happen. She'd die before she apologized to Aire. Rose hadn't even done anything wrong...it was all Aire and her stupid bullshit!

Fine! Rose vowed to call for a truce while they helped Gianna, but after that, they were over. For good. Aire was manipulative--not as much as her sister, Luna, but close to it--and she only wanted what was best for herself. Half the memories from their childhood Rose kept in the back of her mind were of times Aire got her way, either by force or sheer manipulation tactics.

"Oh no! It's coming back," Gianna whimpered, burying her face in Donovan's shoulder. He wrapped an arm around her as if to protect her from the pain. It was romantic and all, but didn't help Gianna in any way other than twist her body. She screamed and sobbed into his shirt, tears soaking their way into the fabric.

Aire released Gianna's other hand and pulled her screen from her pocket. She groaned and threw it back onto the bed. "Damn! The nurse said it'll be at least half an hour before they can get here."

"What?" Rose cried in surprise. "I thought they had, like, an abundance of nurses in the medical wing!"

Aire threw her hands up. "Yeah, but I guess not enough are trained in the birthing process."

Gianna's sobs hurt Rose deep in her heart. The poor girl was suffering so much. They were able to give women medication at the time of labor, or at least they did for Rose's mom when she had Nico.

Rose, quick on her feet, ran around the bed and snatched the screen up. "Well, then ask them what we can do to help!"

Aire gaped at her, blinking slowly. "Oh, I guess I hadn't thought of that. Good idea."

She rolled her eyes and punched in the medical wing's main phone number. "Then maybe I should be the one to text them. Or better yet, let's call them."

A woman with a calm, quiet voice picked up the phone and asked what the problem was. Rose explained their situation in detail and asked the nurse for help on how to get through the birth. The nurse was helpful in that she gave Rose a step by step process on how to help her friend, but was way too calm for the circumstance. Rose swallowed her frustration and plowed ahead to help her friend. It would do them no good if Rose's temper got the best of her and she went off on the poor woman. Even if she did sound like she was reading off a script in a robotic tone.

Twenty minutes later, Rose found herself at the foot of the bed staring at Gianna's...well, private area, gloves on her hands. The nurse stayed on the line with her the whole time, informing her she had to speak calmly in order for Gianna to feel taken care of and safe. Aire couldn't bear to see what was happening at the foot of the bed, so she opted to run around and grab things at Rose's request.

Suddenly, Rose spotted the baby's head peaking. "Aha! You're doing great Gianna! Keep pushing. The baby's almost out. This is almost over."

Gianna's body sank into the mattress, screams of pain on her lips. "I--I can't do anymore!"

Rose continued following the nurse's instructions, placing her hands on Gianna's legs to keep them spread. The end was so close Rose could cry happy tears.

"No way, Gianna. You can do this. One big push is all I need, then I can help you."

Donovan encouraged her too, "Come on, babe. You can do it."

An ear splitting scream and a big push later, Rose was holding Gianna's little baby in her hands. It was a beautiful thing, to have helped someone bring their child into the world. What a fascinating process! Rose was speechless. Then came the afterbirth, which was disgusting and totally awful, but Rose held her tongue. If not for her own sake, then for Gianna's. Her friend had been through enough already, she didn't need Rose's commentary on the functions of a female body during birth. Gianna felt enough of it as it was. She'd been through hell and back.

Rose had never had a child herself, but the scariest part must've been not knowing if you were safe giving birth earlier than expected. She was no expert, but from what Rose could see, the baby was just a smaller, wrinklier version of Nicolai on the day of his birth.

And man, was that baby loud!

Gianna flopped back on her pillow, sweat pooling on her exposed neck and shoulders. She laughed with relief, complete and utter satisfaction dusting her pink cheeks.

Donovan laughed along with her and ran to the foot of the bed where Rose was still staring at the baby in awe. "Is the baby okay? Can we hold it?"

"Is it a boy or a girl?" Gianna whispered, afraid of raising her voice and frightening the baby. Rose soothed the baby by cradling it in the crook of her arm. It was still goopy from the birthing process, but she didn't care. She nodded at Donovan and brought the baby to Gianna, beaming at her friend.

"You did it, G. Here's your baby," Rose said, placing the baby on its mother's chest.

Gianna sighed and closed her eyes. "It's a boy! Donovan, we have a son!" The baby stopped screaming shortly after touching Gianna's chest and hearing her voice. The bond between a baby and its mother was unmistakably strong.

Donovan clapped his hands together. When his eyes travelled from the baby to Gianna's face, he cheered. "We have a son!" He jumped onto the bed and joined Gianna and the baby, wrapping his arms around his girlfriend.

Rose's heart tickled against her rib cage. The sight of the happy family gave her certain desires she hadn't felt before.

Aire fell backwards onto her own bed and threw an arm over her eyes. "I'm so glad that's over!"

"You and me both," Gianna chuckled in a light tone. Her long, willowy fingers traced the baby's spine. He was small enough to reside in the crevice of Gianna's neck.

Rose patted her friend's knee, "It's alright Gianna. At least there was some reward in it!"

Aire gasped and rubbed her eyes. "Speak for yourself! That was torture. I'm never having kids."

"Okay, okay. Let's not diminish the happy couple's moment, Rei." Just like that, at the drop of a hat, Rose had used her old nickname. If Aire noticed it, she didn't say anything.

Gianna and Donovan, attention on their naked, little baby boy, paid no mind to the girls. Rose went to the closet to search for new sheets; they should move Gianna to a more comfortable environment. Nobody should have to sit in the same sheets they gave birth in only minutes before.

There was a solid knock at the door. A woman's voice shouted through the metal, "Hi in there. How's our new baby doing? Can we come in?"

Donovan tucked the sheets and the comforter around Gianna. "Absolutely!"

The woman who'd helped walk Rosabella through Gianna's birth opened the door so fast it hit the wall. "Oopsies! I didn't mean to do that. I'm just so excited!"

"We are too," Gianna said, breathless. "I can't believe I just gave birth."

"Believe it honey, because now you have someone to depend on you for the rest of your life." The nurse rushed to the bed in a flurry of waving arms and glints of metal. The male nurse, Michael, entered next, pushing a wheelchair in front of him. He and Donovan shared a curt nod. The female nurse took the baby from Gianna and looked him over, to which he began screaming again.

*Oh, please just give him back to his mother*, Rose screamed in her head. What more could the nurse need to see? Gianna and the baby were supposed to bond now.

The nurse continued to examine the baby. "From what I can see right now, your baby boy is healthy as can be. Just a tad earlier than expected!"

Donovan laughed again. "That's an understatement."

"You're lucky you have such good friends around you, Gianna dear," she tittered. "Had they not been here, you probably would still be in labor."

Rose blushed and carried the sheets over to them. "Don't mention it. I can't believe I just witnessed that. How magnificent it must feel to be a mother now, G."

"And to have your baby delivered by Rosabella Porter, nonetheless!" the nurse squealed. "My my, you are lucky indeed!"

Gianna beamed at Rose, face tired yet emanating pride and joy. "She's more than her name. She's a wonderful friend."

Rose mouthed a thank you.

Gianna winked back and reached out her arms. "Can I have him back please?"

"Of course, of course," the nurse said. "Let's get you two to the medical wing to take a couple tests to determine both of your vitals first." She handed the baby off to Donovan and, together with Rose, helped ease Gianna into the wheelchair. "Michael, please get these soiled sheets to the wash station."

"You got it," he chipped, the smile on his face never wavering. He set to work once Gianna was cleared of the bed. He began wrapping up everything into a neat pile of sheets and comforter, still strewn with blood and fluids.

Once the four of them left, plus the baby, Rose started the process of tucking the new fitted bottom sheet around the corners of the mattress. Rose and Aire stayed behind to clean up a bit more. Besides, getting in the way of the new family seemed sinful.

Aire lended a hand with the next sheet, making small talk as they worked, "So I've been seeing my sister."

"Really? Does Bernard know, or have you been sneaking out?"

She laughed and waved Rose's question away. "Of course he knows. He's the one who lets me out once a week."

Rose processed her claims. "Oh…what's it like at the HQ? I haven't been there in such a long time… before we discovered the Fortress."

"Nothing's changed. It's all the same. You should come with me next time! We can visit Luna in her new office," Aire suggested, a smile on her face.

Now uncomfortable, Rose looked away and ran her hand along the sheet to get all the bumps out. "Oh, I don't know….I've never been a fan of your sister."

The hope in Aire's eyes slowly diminished. She dropped her corner of the sheet. "What's that supposed to mean?"

How to continue without offending Aire? Would it be rude to tell her what exactly Rose thought of Luna? That she was a slutty woman with no morals or self respect? That she had a reputation like that of a power-hungry conceited bitch? No. Treading lightly was her only option.

"Umm, I just don't feel comfortable around her."

*Wow, way to go.* Now Aire wouldn't be curious about the meaning behind that at all.

"Excuse me? What are you saying? That my sister is a bad person? That you're *afraid* of her?" Aire said, voice raising to a shrill cry.

Rose decided it was best to just move on from the conversation. Honesty would not aid her here. "No, no! Of course not!"

"No, please…tell me what you really think, Rosabella. You've always been good at that," Aire seethed.

She kept her head bent to tuck in the top sheet. "Luna doesn't have the best methods for doing things, you know? She's just…okay…Rei, she's manipulative. Haven't you noticed she only does things that benefit herself?"

"My sister isn't manipulative! In fact, it's kinda funny…she says the same thing about you!"

Rose's voice raised to an inappropriate level. "Oh really? Well I think Luna's filling your head with a bunch of crap! Your sister doesn't live an honest, moral life."

Aire's foot stomped on the floor. "No one in the Government ever does! Besides…you're just jealous."

Rose scoffed, so angry, her shaking hands dropped the comforter in a pile of fluffy pink. "You're joking! I could never be jealous of someone who uses her body to get what she wants. That's...that's disgusting! I don't want the same for you either, Aire! But from the looks of it, you're turning out just like your sister."

Aire's mouth opened as if to spit a comeback, but Rose beat her to it.

"And don't you dare tell me that I'm wrong! Don't think I've missed the clothes you choose to wear every day, showing more and more skin with each wardrobe change." Rose slammed her fist into the bright pink pile and angrily began flattening it across the mattress. "Gosh, Aire, there's more to you than your body. The right guy is going to love you for who you are, not how much skin you reveal. Luna is alone for a reason."

"So you're saying I'm unloveable?" Aire screamed, kicking the bed frame. "Luna was right about you...you only care about yourself. It's no wonder you're upset with my sister. You want everyone to bow at your feet, and she won't."

"Where is this coming from, Rei?" Rose asked. Her face was hot with blood blush.

Aire shook her head and backed away. "No. Don't call me that. You don't have the right to my nickname. I hate that you've become someone I can't recognize."

"Why? Because I'm finally happy not being your puppy dog?" she screamed, ripping the comforter over the corner. "Well, newsflash, Aire, the Fortress is the perfect place for me. I'm finally free. You should be happy for me."

She could practically smell the rage pouring off of Aire. Her glare could kill if she wanted it to. Rose's nose scrunched. It was all she could do to keep her insults inside.

Aire's face contorted and her palm connected with her forehead. She took in a long, deep breath. "I think," she started, "that you and I are not meant to be friends right now. I can't handle this world, and it's obvious you don't care."

Rose was in disbelief. "You can't handle being free?"

"This is not freedom, Rose," Aire complained. "Up above, at least the Government cares about the people. Bernard doesn't put much effort into getting to know us."

"What?" Rose asked. "He and I have been talking a lot. He's been very gracious with me, especially since I woke up after two weeks of being in a dead sleep."

Aire scoffed and rolled her eyes. "Of course he's been. You're the 'queen' and anyone would lay down their lives to protect you. That's how it's always been."

"You don't know me very well if you think that," Rose said, her heart dropping into her toes. "I've lived in your shadow for years."

Aire headed for the door. "You're more conceited than I thought. Have a good life, Rosie."

What did that mean? Aire was insane if she expected Rose to fall at her feet and beg for forgiveness. Whatever she meant by leaving in angry haste, Rose may never know. Aire was such a child. Not everything was about her! The fact that she thought Rose was the selfish one...it was simply crazy! Aire had been the controlling one in their friendship.

Perhaps she was right in that it was time for the two women to separate for a while. With Gianna moving in with Donovan soon, Rose and Aire wouldn't be able to handle living alone. Not that they saw much of one another anyway. She'd have to ask Bernard to make an exception for her and allow her to move into an apartment soon. He was a compassionate man, right? He'd seemed to like her thus far and that hopefully gave her an advantage.

Soon, she'd have to pick a career down here anyway, and once that happened, she'd move into an apartment of her own, with Nico. He could use his own space as much as her. So it wasn't like she was being totally unreasonable.

# Chapter 42

## (AIRE)

No way. No way was Rose allowed to speak to her like that! Didn't she know people worshiped her? What person was so naive they didn't see that everyone around her was dedicated to every breath she took?

Aire walked into the Government Headquarters building. After scanning her eye for access--granted illegally by her sister--she glided across the floor, right up to the elevator without a second thought. The receptionist knew her by now. She'd been visiting frequently since she escaped the droid attack. She was sick of living underground; sick of the life she was forced to live now.

The Fortress was not her safe house. It would never bring her the life she wanted. She wanted to live the life of her sister, Luna. Her sister was so good at manipulating people; they did things for her because they thought *they* wanted to. It was masterful, and so unfair. Luna always came up with the most devious plans for getting her way. In fact, Aire was convinced her sister was made of pure devilish genius. Their parents had never been great with people, but they'd been great at writing laws and creating plans for the Government. Where Luna lacked in writing, she excelled in speaking and controlling. Aire wanted to be just like her someday.

The faded red carpeted halls were familiar to her now. She could find her way to her sister's office with a blindfold on.

When the elevator door opened, Aire stepped out, breathing in the scent of the office complex. It was the smell only an office could pull off: a mixture of cardboard and metal. Strange, yet comforting to her.

As Aire headed for her sister's office, she nodded at anyone who looked at her. She held her head high, to show them she was important and that they better pay attention to how powerful she was. If things kept progressing this way, Aire was convinced she'd have a similar career to her sister--maybe even higher up. She was going to shoot for the role of advisor. Rosabella's dad could do it and so would Aire. But, unlike Mr. Porter, Aire wouldn't back down when something was against her morals. What a weak man, abstaining from a vote when he didn't agree with it.

Luna's door was shut when she arrived. Leaning her ear against the door didn't help much. All Aire could hear were muffled voices. She rapped her knuckles on the solid wood and the voices stopped. Aire heard something heavy dragging along the floor inside and looked over her shoulder. Everyone was busy at their desks, paying no mind to the strange noise. It vibrated the ground under her feet. She clenched her teeth, anticipating what she usually heard her sister doing when she was working on getting her way. Aire was *not* in the mood to deal with that today. She wanted her sister to listen to her.

Another few seconds of the dragging endured while Aire twiddled her thumbs. She'd never stood outside the office this long before. Would people notice?

The door opened finally, but before Aire could say anything, Luna pulled her inside. Then she shut and locked the door. Aire walked away from her sister, heading for the comfy chair in the corner.

"Wait. Before you see anything, I need to explain myself," Luna said, breathing heavy. Her face was flushed and her eyes were bright. She looked at Aire, and an expression of recognition registered on her face. "But it seems you have something to tell me about. I can see you're upset."

Aire ran her fingers through her hair. Turning her face away so her sister couldn't see how red and puffy her eyes were, she headed for the window.

Luna pulled on her arm. "Stop! Don't go over there. Talk to me. What did Rosabella do this time? Or was it Clayton?"

A strange request, but Aire obliged. She clutched the hem of her t-shirt. Today, it was low cut enough to show the top of her chest--a trick she'd learned from Luna. It even worked for women like them, with the flattest chests on the planet. It wasn't practical for a mission, but it was comfortable enough that she wasn't constantly tugging on it to stay in place. Sometimes, she had difficulty getting the necklines of her shirts to stay low.

"She--she's replaced me…" Aire sobbed. Saying it out loud made it so much worse. It solidified her thoughts, turning them into reality. "I don't know what to do anymore. I try so hard--"

Luna drew her against her chest, rubbing her back. "Oh honey, she's delusional right now. The Fortress has her all screwed up….don't worry, I have a plan to help you."

Aire let herself be held for a minute. That's all she got today. Bernard and Logan weren't going to believe she was doing her rounds for longer than an hour. She'd already taken too much time sneaking away to visit her sister. They gave her permission to leave every so often, but she wasn't sure they'd be merciful if she started sneaking out on her own again. When she pulled away, Luna brushed away the tears from her cheeks. It was an affectionate gesture she hadn't expected.

She rubbed her eyes. "What do you mean you have a plan, Lu?"

Her sister released her and rubbed her hands together. "Are you ready for this?" Luna looked over her shoulder at the door, but nobody was there. They wouldn't get in with the door bolted anyway. "You can't scream. You can't yell. No sounds Rei, got it?"

"Umm sure, Lu. Whatever you say." The hair on her arms stood up; there was something awry going on. Luna hadn't killed anyone, had she?

That's when Aire saw her sister's desk had been moved. It was normally much closer to the window, but today it was pushed toward the door. That was the source of the loud dragging sound. Oh god, was there a body behind the desk?

"Okay here I go. Stay behind me." Luna crept over to the desk. Once there, she leaned over the edge to see whatever was on the ground.

Aire wasn't as eager to peek. She wanted to keep the perfect image of her sister in the back of her mind. She wouldn't let it be soiled by something tragic.

"Are you sure?" She asked suspiciously, arms crossed over her flat chest.

Her sister laughed and pulled her closer. "Yes. Trust me, this is going to solve all your problems."

Aire squeezed her eyes shut. Her sister's hand around her arm tightened, convincing her that everything was alright. She peered at the ground, one eye open, one shut. She gasped and was about to scream when Luna's hand clamped around her mouth. It was warm and sweaty; Luna only ever sweat when she was overly excited.

"Shhhh! I know...isn't it wild?!" Luna's voice was full of pride. For herself. "I can't believe I actually *did* it!"

Aire wrenched herself away from her sister. "What the actual *hell*, Lu? What are you thinking? That's a man...it's Grayson for crying out loud! He's supposed to be in your basement! What are you--"

Luna held up a finger, silencing her. "It looks worse than it is. Remember when you practiced on Grayson and it didn't work? Well I realized there was something I could do about it. Call it an experiment of sorts. I realized, with all the droid replacements Andrea and I gave him, just how strong he was. You know how ruthless they are..."

Aire sighed. "Get to the point."

Her sister giggled. "Well, with those limbs come artificial neurons. I was able to create a program. I installed a chip into the bone marrow above his right ear. Watch--" she whispered, grabbing a screen from her desk. It was tiny and compact, even smaller than the ones they used for calls and video chats. She watched Luna type something into it.

At once, Grayson's eyes snapped open. He sat up and looked around. His eyes locked on Aire's, almost begging for help. Luna brought the screen to her lips and whispered something so quietly it was inaudible to Aire. Grayson scrambled to his feet and stormed over to Aire. She wanted to scream, but remembered her sister's instructions. He grabbed her by the shoulders roughly and smashed his lips against hers, so hard she flinched.

A sigh of pleasure sounded. It took her a second to realize it was her own sigh.

Luna squealed, giggling when Aire didn't pull away. "Isn't this great! He does whatever I say!"

"Oh. I thought..." Aire pulled away. Grayson kept trying to kiss her, and she kept shoving him until Luna typed something else into the screen. When it registered, he stopped and stood still as a statue. The only part of him moving were his eyes, snapping between her and Luna.

"You thought he kissed you because he changed his mind? Honey, he's a stubborn man, he's not gonna have a change of heart that fast," Luna spoke to her like she was a child who needed reprimanding. "It was really difficult to get the program right with him fighting everything I did, but here we are. The mind is a powerful tool that can be used for destruction if done right."

"Why did you make me do that?" He growled, "*How* did you make me do that?"

Luna's eyes grew wide and she looked from Grayson to her screen. "What the--? How are you able to talk?"

His eyes squinted and he spit as he quoted, "The mind is a powerful tool."

Aire took a step away and turned her back, heading for the window. She pulled up the shades Luna had drawn earlier. She didn't want to see this. If her sister thought gifting her a man who would do exactly what she told him was the way to her heart, she was mistaken. This was wrong. This was disgusting. She couldn't take the free will away from a person. What she needed was a plan that could take away the bad parts of a person, while still allowing them the free will to make their own decisions.

"It doesn't matter. You belong to me. This is your brain now," her sister said, voice rising. Aire imagined her waving the screen in the air, right in front of Grayson's nose. She peered over her shoulder at them.

"When they find out that I'm gone--" Grayson started, jaw clenched.

"They won't. I'm putting out a report to HR this afternoon to let them know you were killed in a brutal attack with those pesky droids," Luna said sweetly, batting her eyelashes. "It was a pathetic death. You didn't see it coming and they decapitated you from behind." She tapped the screen against Grayson's temple. "Maybe this will teach you a lesson not to disobey your Government when they ask you to do something."

Aire had had enough; she started toward her sister, "Luna--"

"All of this," she gestured to Grayson. "Is for *you*! I've stood by and watched while Rosabella got all the glory and praise because she was good at *every damn thing*. Now it's your turn, Rei. It's *our* turn."

She shook her head, stopping dead in her tracks. "Lu, can't you see how terrible this is? You've taken away his ability to be *human*. He's no more than the car you drive around. You're in control, you decide what happens to him. That--that's so...wrong."

"Rei, you don't get it. He is yours now. Besides, apparently he can still process what I'm saying--which is kind of a problem right now, but I'll get it figured out. Oh, and I bet you'll never guess what else I found out," she said, her lips curling with a sick smile. Luna put Grayson back to sleep. He slowly lowered himself to the ground, first to his knees, then to his stomach. "I couldn't do this on my own, you know. I'm not a surgeon or a doctor. I didn't know the first thing about cutting off infected body parts and replacing them....I had help. Can you guess who it was?"

Arms crossed and eyes glaring at her sister, Aire said, "No. Tell me."

"Well," Luna started, leaning on the edge of the desk as she'd done countless times. "It's the woman you saw helping me that one time. Her name is Andrea Ward. Maiden name: Andrea Thomas...."

Aire waited for dramatic effect, but she wasn't catching on. She'd never heard that name in her life. She said so, making sure to keep one eye on the hand that held the screen. The last thing she needed was for her sister to send Grayson against her.

"Oh come on girlie, you can do this. It's not that difficult. Who have we talked about numerous times?" Luna paused again, but dissatisfied, kept going. "I wouldn't have recognized her had I not known her earlier in life. She's changed her hair, dyed it brown, and wears contacts--hazel to be exact." She was taunting Aire now.

"I swear to you Luna, I will run out of this room and scream for help if you don't get to your point quickly. Sister or not."

Her sister straightened her spine at that. She jumped up and stood nose to nose in front of Aire. "Her name is a fake. It's all a cover. Her real identity is Tess Aabrams."

Something turned in Aire's stomach. All of a sudden, she felt lightheaded, sick. She ran back to the window again, wanting to stare at the sunset for relief, on the verge of vomiting. It had been the only consistent thing in her life and they'd stripped her of that too. She hated the Fortress and she hated everything and every*one* inside it. Except for Rose; no matter how angry she got, she could never hate her best friend.

The sunset would fade soon, and she'd be left with nothing again. What could she do to make sure that didn't happen? Rose used to be the equivalent of the sunset for her. She'd been there for Aire through everything. That was before Lilianna; before Clarise; before Logan; before *Clayton*. How could she guarantee Rose's unfailing dedication again? She realized two things quickly; it only took about two seconds to piece them together.

She whipped around. "Where is she?"

Luna's knowing smile disgusted and excited her at the same time. Aire was not going to back down and that scared her. The results would bring pain to a lot of people.

"At my house. She's...*coping* with everything there. I promised her an escape for a short while."

Aire ripped the screen from her sister's clutches and typed in commands. Grayson got up, eyes locked on Aire's. He looked so hopeful she wanted to puke again.

Instead, she took in a breath and headed for the door. "Come on you two, we have some work to do."

# Chapter 43

## (ROSABELLA)

Clayton eyed Rose across the kitchen counter. He leaned forward and took a sip out of a ceramic mug that screamed, "World's Best Dad" in bright blue letters. It was probably from up above, before he moved to the Fortress. His own father's maybe? He trailed his fingers across the countertop, thinking.

"I just don't understand why you want to move into an apartment, Rose."

She rested one knee atop a stool and placed her palms on the cool surface of the counter. "What don't you understand? It's pretty obvious. I want to move out of my dorm. It's going to happen sooner or later, and I opt for sooner."

He didn't support this, and she couldn't pinpoint why. Ever since they'd met, Clayton knew how independent Rose was. She assumed he'd been prepared for this conversation. And, if anything, she was actually moving *closer* to him by getting an apartment. The apartment wing was large, but compact. She came here to his apartment first to tell him because she wanted Clayton to help her choose the right one. The apartments varied in size and she didn't need a large one. A one-bedroom would suit her just fine; maybe with a kitchen or a living room. It would depend on the options.

"Rosabella, I love you, you know that. So can I be honest with you?" He held a hand up. "Without you getting mad at me?"

Rose rolled her eyes. "No promises."

He chuckled and set his mug down. "Figures." He rested his forearms on the counter and bent at the waist. "So, a few of the trainers have been getting together with Bernard and a handful of engineers lately. We are at maximum capacity right now."

She gasped. "But, how are you going to--?"

"Please let me finish..." Clayton cut her off, his voice gentle. It still pissed her off, but she held her tongue. "Our goal has always been to better humanity and create a society of freedom for all who reside down here. But now, we've been letting in more people than we have room for. Just last week, a new group of saves came down here. Our dorms are crammed full of people. Instead of three, like you and your roommates, we've started shoving five or even six people in a dorm.

"It's become an issue, because now we won't have enough apartments for people. The singles are going to become doubles and triples at the least. Clarise and I are lucky that we have such a close connection with Bernard, or we'd be among the first families to combine with another... do you see what I'm getting at?"

If he was trying to convince her to keep living with Aire, he was sorely mistaken. Rose wouldn't do that; she refused. If she had to sleep on the couches in the library again to stay away from her, she would.

"What I'm trying to tell you is that you wouldn't be living on your own. They might place you with a random person down here you haven't yet met. Do you want that?" he asked, eyes intense.

"Of course I don't, but I'll find the teeny tiniest one so I won't take up too much space," she pleaded, desperate now. Rose was surprised by her selfishness. There were people here who needed an apartment more than she did. Who did she think she was, asking for her own? She shook her head and apologized to Clayton, "I'm sorry, you're right. I'd be conceited if I asked Bernard to make an exception for me. Even if he did--which I'm sure he won't--I would feel so guilty."

Clay rounded the counter and wrapped a strong arm around her. She leaned on him, feeling his sturdy chest against her back. He rubbed his hand up and down her arm. "You're not conceited, Rose. You're just excited to move on, to have even more independence. I get that, I'm just worried about you. I know how you can let your emotions get the best of you, and I don't want you to feel that."

Rose smiled, turning her head into his arm. Her lips kissed the skin on his bicep. "Are you sure it's not because you want me sharing your room with you again?" She didn't add, *once my brother is better.*

Clayton kissed the top of her head. Then the tip of her ear. "Well, there's that too. Move in with a buddy, and you can save so much space."

She laughed and shoved him in the chest. "You're really too much."

He chuckled and hooked his fingers around her chin to kiss her.

"If you're trying to distract me, you're doing a good job," she said against his lips. He groaned when she pulled away. Rose danced away toward the living room. "I should really go check on my brother. He's been asleep for awhile this morning."

Clayton watched her go. "I love you, Rosabella Mae Porter."

She rolled her eyes on her way out the door, "And I love you, Clayton James Taylor."

Well, that conversation hadn't gone as she'd expected. But at least Clayton helped Rose to open her eyes. It really would be selfish of her to move into an apartment by herself. While that sounded like a wonderful, independent step for her, she knew it would only be a matter of time before she surrendered her space anyway.

Logan had suggested Nicolai take up a permanent room in the medical wing, but Rose and Clayton thought otherwise. When Rose went to his apartment late last night for her droid "treatment," they'd talked about her apartment wish as well as the status of her brother's health. He'd brought up his mother, and how she loved Rosabella that day they met. Rose had seen Mrs. Clarke around the Fortress quite a bit after that, and they'd always stopped and engaged in friendly conversation. It helped to take away the pain of losing her own mother, which Rose refused to think about. She set her mind to going on missions, visiting Lilianna, helping Gianna move into Donovan's apartment and caring for Nicolai. Beyond all that, there remained very little time for her to meet up with Logan at night. When she did, all he wanted to do was discuss her feelings and her pain. It was as if he wanted her to suffer through losing her mom, hating her dad, and worrying about her brother. Nicolai would be fine, but right now, worrying was not in her best interest.

Rose tapped her knuckles on the bedroom door. When there was no response, she readied herself to wake him up with a funny song and dance. Nico had always loved when their mom did that for him.

Oh *crap*. Their mom. She'd had the brightest smile and the kindest eyes of anyone she'd ever met, even more so than Logan.

Nope. *Don't feel. Don't let in the hurt.* If Rose closed her eyes, she was able to push all thoughts of her mom out of her head. She forced in other thoughts, like Clayton. She sucked in a deep breath, held it until it made her dizzy, and released it in a loud burst. She turned the knob on the door and pushed it open. Her brother's little shape on the bed encouraged her to put on her silly face, all thoughts of their mom gone.

Nicolai had always been a late sleeper, but this was beyond ridiculous. They'd already eaten lunch today. Granted, Rose and Clayton ate a little earlier today, seeing as though they'd skipped breakfast. Saturdays were her favorite days. They provided a whole day of relaxation and the ability to do almost anything she wanted. Like today, she planned to meet up with Eden and work on combat. They were going to make an afternoon of it together. Working on combat and weight lifting blocked out any bad thoughts and forced Rose to put all her energy into the moment. In other words, training was the best mind block she'd ever experienced.

Ever since she'd reached the six month mark, Rose hadn't been consistently training anymore. After those six months, trainees were officially "graduated" from training. For the next six months, they were supposed to go on assigned missions--which were at least five times a week in Rose's case, mostly to practice for the mission Bernard would have her go on soon. Once those six months were up, they would choose their career.

Would she be happy with a career down here, such as training other saves, like Clayton? Or would she want to work in mission control, like Logan? At least, that way, she'd be able to monitor the outside. Or even work external security, as Andre did. Those citizens underwent extra training in order to work up above on a consistent basis. It was different from simply going on missions, Andre explained. Sure, they did their time every few days a week or so, but it was mostly hanging out around the perimeter, making sure things were spick and span. They were meant to blend in with their surroundings. It was no wonder Rose had never seen them on her own missions before.

Rose's screen buzzed in her pocket. She silenced it by tapping her wristband four times, a new version of messaging that hadn't been loaded into Rose's wristband until recently. The message popped up in front of her. Eden's face appeared in thin air.

"Hey Rose, just checking in. Are we still meeting?"

Rose stepped into the hallway so as not to disturb her brother. She didn't want him to wake up all crabby because he heard her talking to Eden. A crabby Nico would be dissatisfied for the majority of the day. She wished that upon nobody, not even Aire. He could be a real handful.

Once the door closed with a soft click, Rose leaned against the wall. "Hey Eden! I'm so sorry! I must've lost track of time."

She laughed and shook her head. "Clayton occupy most of your morning?"

Rose blushed and turned her head away. "I'll be there in five."

Eden chuckled again. "I'm sorry, I couldn't help myself! And don't meet me in the training room. Bernard wants to see us in his office. ASAP."

That could only mean one thing. They were talking about the game.

"Got it. Do I need to bring anything?"

Eden shrugged. "He didn't say, so probably not. Just bring your wits and your charmingly bright smile," Eden winked. The two of them had been joking a lot lately, which mostly consisted of them picking on one another for their features and personalities.

"On my way!" Rose said, laughing. She poked her head into the kitchen on her way out to let Clayton know where she was headed. "Hey, I'm late to meet Eden. Can you wake my brother up, please? Be gentle, a crabby Nico is never good for anyone."

He nodded, smiling from ear to ear. "Believe me, I get it...it must run in the family!"

"Shut up!" She cried, picking up a pillow from the couch. He dodged it with ease, laughing so hard he choked on his coffee.

"Love you, Rose!" he called to her.

Over her shoulder, she echoed him, "Love you too, Clay!" Rose passed Clarise on her way out. She reached down and hugged her friend. "And I love *you*, Clair!"

"Someone's in a good mood," Clarise said, her voice cheerful.

Rose winked at her. "I'm not going to ask what's got *you* in such a good mood because I probably don't want to know. But I know you're

378

smart. Just be careful you don't get caught again. Clayton isn't going to let Dre walk free and easy for a while."

"You got it," Clarise said, beaming. Oh boy, Clair had that lovesick expression on her face she got whenever she'd been around Andre.

Clayton had yet to beat Andre up, and Rose wanted to keep it that way. Clayton was going overboard with this anger at Andre. She wished he'd calm down, but any time she brought it up, they always wound up arguing about it. It was one of those things she only brought up if Clayton was in a good mood. There was no need to encourage an angry person to beat on someone they were already upset with. Violence was never the answer, unless it was in self-defense, or protecting loved ones.

***

"Come in, Porter," Bernard called through the door. When she entered, Logan, Eden and Bernard were already crowded at the table. None of them sat in the comfy chairs, rather, they were all standing, leaning over something in the center.

"Is this about the board, sir?" she asked, joining them. Her eyes widened in surprise. A large hologram of the board stood before her eyes. In a beautiful array of colors made of energy and light, Rose was mesmerized by the detail and the complexity of it. She reached her hand out to touch it, but Bernard pulled her arm back. His hold was firm, all tenderness lost.

His eyes clouded as he shook his head. "No, don't touch it. We don't know what'll happen."

Rose did a 180 turn to find Logan's eyes. If she could connect with him, she'd be able to understand what was going on. The intensity in the room choked her. It thrust itself down her throat, blocking her airway. She couldn't handle it if another person died. She couldn't bear to hear from Bernard that they'd lost someone else to the droids. As promised, Logan's eyes found hers.

He held out a hand for her. "Here, Rose, come stand by me." She moved next to him and leaned forward to get a good look at the hologram. She was no longer tempted by its beauty; Bernard had scared the curiosity right out of her.

"Rosabella, I'm sorry to be so abrupt with you, but I'm not sure what this means for us." Bernard wiped at his glistening forehead. "My contact up above sent me this earlier today. It came with a pair of virtual dice that I rolled to see what would happen…."

She sucked in a breath. The second purple colored space on the board was highlighted. It read: GOVERNMENT HQ -- GREEN BAY, WISCONSIN.

"Green Bay?" she asked, playing with a loose string on her shirt. "Where's that? I thought the Government Headquarters was right here in the Northern Center Sector?"

Eden chuckled lightly. A laugh that didn't reach her eyes, nor comfort Rose. "The country used to be divided into states, and within those, cities. Now we've separated them into regions, or sectors."

Bernard tapped his chin. "We're actually right under part of what used to be known as Green Bay decades ago." He stared at the hologram a while longer before clearing his throat. "Anyway, we must get started. Don't you see the count-down clock?" He pointed to a space on the furthest corner of the board where a digital clock was counting down from 14.

"Is that in months?" Logan asked, puzzled by the number. "It's too difficult to tell."

"Days," replied Bernard, lost in thought. His focus was clearly elsewhere, what with his eyes staring off into the distance and all.

Rose and Eden shared a worried look. Rose took it upon herself to propel forward. She needed answers now. "Bernard? What happened when you rolled the dice?"

He physically shook himself out of whatever daze he'd been in. "The board did *that*," he said, pointing to the highlighted space. "I rolled a three using the holographic dice and that's what happened. I--I'm afraid to touch it."

"Okay, so that's where we have to go then, right?" she asked, mind racing. "What happens when--?"

Bernard shrugged, his eyes flashing. "I honestly can't say. We never should've gotten involved with this, it's too dangerous."

"What? No way!" Rose cried. She raced up to Bernard and placed a hand on his arm. He flinched but didn't shove her away. "Bernard, we've been working so hard to prepare ourselves mentally for this…you know what I've had to do," she added in a whisper, shivering. "We cannot just give up now. If this is for the greater good of society, then count me in."

Eden straightened. "I'm with Rosabella. We cannot let the Government win. If freedom comes at a price, I'm willing to pay it."

"That may be so, my dear," Bernard said, turning to Eden. "But freedom is not always what is most desired by others. Eventually, a flower without sunlight and oxygen is bound to perish."

Logan huffed and leaned on the table. "I'm not sure what you're getting at, sir."

Bernard smiled without teeth, the corners of his mouth turning up grimly. "Not everyone has the same source of sunlight and oxygen."

It was then that Rose and Logan made eye contact again. Was Bernard losing his mind? Had he'd lived in the Fortress long enough for insanity to set in?

"Perhaps when you're all my age, you'll understand what I mean," he said in response to the silence. "For now, all of you need to be in defensive mode. We cannot afford to lose any one of you...I've been planning this out all morning. When I rolled the dice this hologram did all the work for me. It began counting down right away, which means we have two weeks to find the first key. It also spit this out at me," Bernard added, holding out a solid piece of paper.

Logan took it first and passed it on to Rose next, who stared at it.

"How the heck did you get a physical piece of paper out of a hologram?" She asked.

Bernard lifted his shoulders. "I have no idea. I guess technology has advanced far beyond my comprehension. Anyway, read it. It's a riddle of sorts. A message."

*Welcome.*

*You've just begun a game you can't back out of at any stage. A word of caution: this journey is not for the faint of heart. No matter if you are here for all the wrong reasons or the right ones, the journey is no different. Each one who embarks on the journey falls victim to perilous situations at least once.*

*As you know by now, the dice controls the board, which controls your journey. Do not attempt to cheat, or your death will be instantaneous. The board is programmed to self-destruct at any moment it detects such actions.*

*Know that these are all the instructions you'll receive from me, the creator. I applaud your efforts, as this is no easy feat. Simply getting here is a start, and if you're reading this, you've already accomplished your first task of rolling the dice. Congratulations to you.*

*Stay safe my friends. And I hope to see you at the end. Should you have the right intentions for what I deem an appropriate use of the end result, you'll be rewarded. If not…you'd better say your goodbyes now.*

*Additional instructions are included on the back of this page.*

*Yours in freedom.*

Eden rubbed her arms. "Did anyone else get the chills?"

Rose nodded, biting her lip to keep from shivering herself. She flipped the page over and read the instructions, stomach flipping and flopping with nervous energy.

### Rules
1. *To start off, one "team" rolls the dice to determine where they move to*
   a. *If you land on a space/location (22 colored, 4 Tube Stations, 2 Utilities), you have two options…*
      i. *If unowned: You can have free reign of the space to search for the key on your own by purchasing the space for a set price*
      ii. *If owned: You have to pay the owner/make a deal if unable to pay*
         1. *Payment can include literal $ or other deals. For instance, you can take one roll away from your own team in order to use the space to look for the designated "key."*
2. *Community Chest (2) vs. Chance (3)*
   a. *The Community Chest cards can either give you a set amount of $ or take away a set amount of $ depending on the card…no deals are allowed. You are unable to get out of this unless you claim bankruptcy, in which case, you'd be sent straight to Jail.*
   b. *The Chance cards move you to another random location, and can either help or hinder you.*

c. *Note: There is one get out of jail free card in each deck*

3. *In order to get out of Jail, you must pay a certain amount for each player in Jail ($50,000) or you have to roll the dice three times once it gets to your turn--if you're unable to roll a double at the end of the three tries, you must either claim bankruptcy or you must pay for everyone to get out.*

4. *You must wait your turn to roll the dice*

   a. *All participants must be locked in before anyone can begin*

   b. *Once you find the "key" in your location, you can move on by rolling the dice → but you have to wait until the other teams roll their dice.*

      i. *Just because someone rolls the dice before you doesn't mean you can't roll the dice right after.*

         1. *When you roll, you have 2 weeks to find the key, and if you don't, then the next team may roll the dice.*

5. *The "Key" rules*

   a. *The "Key" can sometimes be a clue or puzzle that leads you to a particular passphrase you must type into the system, or a physical object you must scan into the holograph machine.*

6. *You must reach the "Go" space after doing one full loop around the board in order to figure out the final key.*

   a. *The hologram will calculate out your key results from the rest of the board, and will give you one final key to decipher.*

Rosabella felt bile rising in her throat. It was too late to back out now. Maybe if they'd known all of this before they locked in their team?... *No*, she silently scolded herself. This was their future and their fate. If she showed fear or doubt, the others around her would feed off of her own feelings. She had to keep things locked up tight and exude as much optimism as possible if they were going to succeed. If they didn't succeed...the results would be the end of them.

"Who's ready for their next mission?" Bernard asked pointedly to Eden and Rose.

Logan shook his head at the hologram. "How on earth am I supposed to just stand by and watch people get hurt? What if one of you doesn't come back?"

Rose wrapped an arm across his shoulders. "Don't worry, Logan. Eden and I are pretty badass."

"Yeah, we know how to defend ourselves. It's *you* we're worried about, Clarke," Eden joked, punching him in the stomach. Then she faced their leader. "Do we have any more information on where to start looking once we get to HQ, sir?"

"No. What you know is what I know." He rubbed his tired eyes. "This is all so vague. I have no doubt you two will accomplish your task, but I fear what stands in the way first."

Rose crossed her arms and turned her mouth into a set, stiff line. "Well, whatever it is, we can do this. I'm ready….When do we start?"

Bernard smiled at her. "I'm glad you're so strong-willed, Porter. It will hopefully serve you well. I'll send for Prince so he can get you two proper fighting gear before we start this afternoon. He'll be sworn to secrecy, so don't worry about him blabbing to anyone."

"But--" she started.

"No," he said firmly, holding a hand up. "A t-shirt and shorts is not the proper gear. You need something more suitable for what you may face."

She rolled her eyes. "Okay, fine."

Their leader laughed and patted her on the back. "Sacrifices must be made for the greater good, my dear. I hope you can understand that."

"I do. I just wish it didn't involve me getting a whole new outfit that's probably going to be skin-tight."

Bernard chuckled. "It won't be that bad, will it?"

She blinked slowly at him. "Of course it will be, it's *Prince*!"

# Chapter 44

## (ROSABELLA)

Eden and Rose took in the warm summer air, both adjusting their thin navy jackets, which were just as form fitting as Rose had feared. Prince claimed it was so they could move more fluidly and not have to worry about getting caught on anything. While their black pants were skin-tight, at least they were breathable; they moved when Rose moved, fitting like a second skin. When she'd seen herself in the mirror, Rosabella almost didn't believe the bright eyed, curvy girl was her. She didn't hate the way she looked aymore. She attributed it to the unending freedom she'd experienced by living in the Fortress. After spending years despising her hips, her bright red hair, and her pale skin, she now had a new confidence about her. A confidence which allowed her to see a different side of life, one that she was in no hurry to change.

Rose stopped to adjust her earpiece. All that jogging had jostled the little metal piece around. Before she lost it amidst a sea of artificial grass and smooth black pavement that smelled of rubber in the setting sunlight, Rose tucked it safely back into her ear.

Just as she was running to catch up with her mission partner, Logan's voice filled her ear, "Remember, you two....you sense any funny business, you get out of there. Got it?"

Rose knew their ear pieces were synched when Eden caught her eye and silently mocked Logan.

"Just because I can't see you doesn't mean I can't pick up on the signals that you're making fun of me," he said, startling Rosabella.

Eden let out a surprised cry, covering her mouth with a sharp slap.

Rose exploded into a fit of laughter. "Nice catch, Clarke."

He chuckled along with her. "Thank you. But I am serious...now, get back to your mission you two."

"Yes, sir," Rose saluted to her earpiece. He couldn't see her of course. They weren't dumb enough to risk a holographic meeting on missions like these. She'd left her wristband back home anyway.

They trekked alongside the road in silence longer than Rose expected. This was supposed to be her time to catch up with Eden and get all the details on her life. How to start the conversation? *So Eden, got any new news about internal security?* No, that would be dumb. Rose didn't have clearance to receive any specific information about security. It would only put Eden in an awkward position. How about, *Hey Eden, isn't the weather beautiful today?* No way! The *weather*? What was she, eighty?

As she continued a wrestling match of thoughts in her head, Eden tilted her head back to take in the remaining rays of sun.

When she spoke, her voice held reverence and awe, "This is my favorite part about being alive."

"What is?"

Eden slowed to a walk. Rose matched her pace. "Seeing this. The beauty of the world. The earth continues its cycle no matter what we do. I love being able to pave my own path, but I'm grateful for at least some consistency. If the earth ever stops spinning, I think I might die inside."

Rose patted her friend on the back. "You're so good at living in the moment, Eden. I wish I was more like you."

She laughed. "No you don't."

A hand on Eden's shoulder brought her to a halt. Rose groaned, spotting the tube station in the distance. She needed to settle this before they went any further. "What do you mean?"

"It's nothing. Come on, before we miss the tube," sighed Eden, the usual strength in her voice fading.

Rose put her foot down, crossing her arms to show she meant business. "No way. You need to talk to me."

"Ugh, fine! If you insist," Eden said, a hand cupping the back of her neck. "I just don't think I'm good enough for the Fortress. I mean, everyone there's always so talented and--"

"Eden," Rose interjected, "*You're* talented. Look at you. You're one of three people the leader of a secret society trusts with life-changing information. Oh and, you're head of internal security...not to mention you're on the Cabinet...Shall I continue?"

Eden's face colored, bringing out beautiful speckles of green in her hazel eyes. "Please don't...I--I don't do well with compliments."

"Me neither, but you know what? If it makes the other person feel good to give me a compliment, who am I to stop them?" Rose spoke as though she were speaking to her brother, scolding him for messing with her room at home. Oh, how she suddenly missed their house. She definitely didn't miss her old life, just some of the people she'd met and the memories she'd made over the years. "Anyway, I just hope you know how valuable you are to the Fortress. Who else would teach me to kick other people's butts better than you?"

Eden was not an affectionate person. Rose had never seen her make physical contact with another human being. It wasn't her way. What was characteristic of Eden was a small smile, combined with a dazed look into the distance. Rose imagined Eden's thoughts filtering through her mind, bouncing off the sides of her brain with each new compliment. This time was no different, though Eden's lips curled into a bigger smile than her usual smirk. Maybe Rose had gotten through to her. Her jaw clenched and released. Then her eyes met Rose's and her mouth opened to respond.

"Umm, hi ladies," Logan said, interrupting them. "I don't know what's going on up there, but your trackers are showing that you're not moving. Is everything alright?"

Rose made sure to press her earpiece so Logan could listen to her loud, obnoxious groan. "Come on, Logan! Eden and I are having a heart to heart here."

He apologized, "Sorry, but we have a mission to complete. I'm all for friendships and relationships, but not when your lives are in danger. I want you two back here as soon as humanly possible...preferably with the first key in hand."

"We're almost to the tube." She rolled her eyes. Eden didn't laugh, but she did send Rose a small smirk. It was a start.

"Good. Please report back with any updates as they occur." He paused before adding, "I'm done now. Carry on."

Rose shook her head. "That man is a gem," she complained sarcastically.

"Yeah, I guess." Eden's smile was only half-hearted. A distracted expression crossed her face.

She elbowed Eden as they picked back up into their jog. "What's got you thinking?"

"Nothing," Eden shook her off.

"Come on, Eden, it's not nothing. I can see you're concerned about something."

Finally, they reached the tube station. The damages from the droid attack on Andre and Rose months ago were all patched up. In fact, Rose couldn't even remember what the shattered door looked like. Shortly after she and Andre were attacked, Rose had nightmares about being stabbed to death by droids. Only Clayton knew about them, and would keep it to himself until the day he died.

A group of less than ten people crowded under the large screen mounted on the wall when they entered. Eden tapped Rose on the shoulder and nodded her head in the direction of the crowd. They joined behind a clump of teenage girls laughing about something. Rose was still technically a teenager herself. Just because she was almost nineteen didn't mean she wasn't a full-fledged adult mentally. Sometimes her age was lost on her when she was underground, or maybe it was time.

Rose spotted the luggage return stand. A lump formed in her throat, rendering her speechless. A flash of Lilianna's mother lying on the ground, hands covering the back of her head, danced in front of her eyes; the droid swiping the woman's head clean from her body as if it were merely playing a game. Lilianna's confused eyes while she layed on the ground, shielded by Rose. She shuddered at the ghost of a droid's needle pricking the skin on the side of her neck.

How easily memories came back to a person, especially ones that had scarred them. The only thing that had gotten Rose through all of the pain and hurt of witnessing Grayson's death, the woman's death, and hearing of her mother's death was the community around her. Clayton comforted her whenever she needed to feel his arms around her; Logan distracted her so she wouldn't feel the hurt; Andre joked around and made her so angry she was too busy plotting a punch to his face to even think about their deaths; Lilianna was so innocent and adorable, Rose got lost in playing with her; Clarise and Gianna talked about their own lives to keep Rose from remembering all the bad memories she had, and the list continued on. The moral of the story was that nobody could get through their lives without the comfort of their family and friends around them.

The fresh scent of water brought her back to the present. She wrenched her gaze away from the luggage stands and faced forward. She and Eden stood out in the crowd. Prince probably hadn't thought that through so much as the practicality of the material.

As the tube pulled into the station with an air-sucking pop, the girls in front of them caught a glimpse of their outfits. The girl in the middle, the leader, snickered and pulled her friends in close. They leaned in without question, eating up every word their ring leader had to say. As if on cue, all three girls glared at Rose at the same time. She was probably only a year or two older than them, but in that moment, she felt decades older. After the things she'd been through, the world she'd seen, Rose diagnosed herself with a case of accelerated maturity. Especially compared to those girls. Despite her stomach clenching in anger and her eyes blazing, Rose smiled with all her teeth. The girls spun right around and ignored them after that. Good. Serves them right. If they really wanted to mess with her, she'd win by a landslide. She'd been training in hand-to-hand combat for months now. It was in their best interest to ignore her and move on.

Since it was rush hour traffic, lines upon lines of people emerged from the tube, each of them heading to their homes nearby. The majority of them would have to walk at least four miles. The closest houses were the ones owned by the Government officials and their families, which didn't make sense to Rose at all. If the Government officials were the ones with the cars, why not have them move farther away from the tube to allow other people a closer walking distance from their transportation? She wanted to take each person involved in writing the laws and shake them until their brains registered how unfair they were. Their hierarchy was incredibly disappointing. If you weren't among the top two or three levels of the government you were underprivileged from the moment of your birth.

Rose and Eden filed onto the tube after the arrivals exited. The two of them sat near the back, where the fewest number of people sat. The majority of their little group moved up to the front after entering the cabin. Rose rested her head on the window to her left. As the tube went underground, the scenery wasn't pleasant. The windows offered pictures taken from the world above. They played the same ones over and over again until people grew numb from looking at them. Now that she lived underground, Rose had a new appreciation for the pictures.

The tube started up again, the smell of water stronger than ever. The tube was built like a submarine, with all the features of underwater travel and the design of a sleek, shiny bullet casing. It reminded her of the structure of bullets she'd once read about in the history books in the school's library. There was always some kind of explanation of bullets in the most recent literature. People, she concluded, enjoyed writing and speaking about the things they didn't have. When something was taken away, it was the very thing people fought to have returned to them.

For instance, the American government had become more of a dictatorship, causing the citizens at the time to live in fear of stepping out of line. Thus, their "new and improved" Government came into being. Because, once their freedom was taken, it was the thing the people missed the most. But, as with most leaders, the people grew tired of abiding by the same old rules all the time. And so the new democracy was formed, with two leaders from each sector representing the people in each geographical region. Why didn't they try dividing the country into different Kingdoms instead? It wasn't a terrible thought. A King and Queen would be assigned to their own Kingdom and sectors instead of the whole country. At this rate, they couldn't do anything worse.

Eden bumped elbows with her. "Hey, I'm sorry about before. I've just been sensitive lately, I guess." She looked at her feet. "You'll never hear those words come out of my mouth ever again."

Rose laughed, beyond elated with Eden opening up. She patted Eden's hand to show her affection for her friend without making things uncomfortable. "It's not a bad thing to show your feelings, Eden."

"You're one to talk," she teased. "What's the difference between what I just said and you not wanting to cry in front of people?"

Rosabella tossed around a variety of responses that didn't seem true or good enough. "I don't know."

"That's what I thought," Eden said laughing. Then she spotted something at the front of the cabin. "Are you ever afraid of the future? That something's going to alter your world drastically?"

Where was she going with this? Rose needed to play the quiet card here. Eden always talked more when she was received with silence; it pushed her to fill the space.

"Because, lately I've been afraid of the future. Like what if I start to regret my career decision? Or the fact that I've enjoyed being without a man or woman in my life?"

The use of the word "woman" romantically in her sentence took Rose by surprise. She wasn't completely used to hearing the same gendered relationships, but that didn't mean she wasn't in support of it. From what she'd seen between Prince and Oaklee, love was the most important part of a relationship. Nothing else mattered so long as you and the other person loved and respected each other.

Eden continued. "I don't know why I'm so worried about that. I'm only twenty-seven. I have my whole life ahead of me yet."

Rose nodded to show her support. "Yes you do. Don't let yourself feel that what you've done with your life thus far is something to feel regret over. If anything, I think you're a huge inspiration. A woman shouldn't need a relationship to get through life. It's her friends and the community around her that are the key."

She ducked her head and laughed. "Sure. But if that's true, what about you and Clayton?"

"Since when did this become a conversation about me?" Rose cried, sinking back into her padded seat.

"Since I wanted to bring up your birthday." Eden laughed at Rose's open-mouthed expression. "I had to find some way to redirect the topic to you without being obvious--But I really *have* been thinking about all that stuff, it's not made up."

Rose glared at Eden, blood rushing to her face. "No. Absolutely not. We don't need to talk about my birthday. Did Clay put you up to this? Tell him I don't want a celebration."

"Aww, come on," she whined. "Why not? Clayton and Clarise have been working really hard!"

Rose turned her head away, facing the windows again. "Tell them to stop. I'm not in the mood to celebrate this year. Not after my last birthday was soiled by the deaths of my classmates, some droid poisoning, and an entire shift in my world."

"Ah, right. The droid attack was on your birthday," Eden agreed, nodding. "But that's why Clayton wants you to have a special day this year."

She crossed her arms and slit her eyes. "Well, then I won't go. They can celebrate without me. I'm serious."

"Alright. Fine. I'll tell him to call it off."

They rode in silence after that. When the tube arrived in the city, near Government Headquarters, they both got off. Fewer people took their places on the tube, the setting sun an indicator of the end to a non-work day. On Saturdays, everyone took time to go out and about with their friends or families. Thus, rush hour didn't alter much.

"I haven't been to HQ in a while," Eden breathed as she took in the massive building. All one hundred floors of the building loomed over them, blocking out the sun from their view. It gave the streets a sense of an eerie emptiness. The heart of the sector, what some people referred to as the City Center, was nowhere near as large as cities on the eastern or western coasts. A handful of shops resided here, with a sprinkling of health-food restaurants. No more fast food joints; those restaurants had been banned nearly half a century ago. A small mall complex rested somewhere near the center of the city, with the Government Headquarters standing strong and solid next door. A grade school was housed just down the road from HQ, the only one the Government approved within a sixty-mile radius. There had been an overflow of students there for as long as Rosabella could remember; the highschool she used to attend was no different.

The memories of her past life were hard to imagine now. Were they even real or had they been figments of her imagination? If Rose didn't think back on her earlier life, she was able to pretend it had never happened at all, that she'd been born in the Fortress and grown up there. Of course, it wasn't the truth, but why settle for the truth when a fake reality was so much sweeter?

Rosabella pulled Eden in the direction of the back doors. They slipped behind the trash chute and huddled together. "Logan, we're at HQ. Have you worked out a way for us to get in?"

They both waited for a response. But all they got was static.

"What? The signal's never been blocked before!" Rose snapped. She repeated herself, but was met with silence again.

Eden peeked around the corner to make sure they were alone. "I don't know why the signal isn't working. The only people that have access to the country's broadcast channels are the Government--oh wait." She walked around the corner and out of sight.

"Eden?" Rose asked, following her around the corner to the front of the building. "What are you doing? We're supposed to stay out of sight."

"Hold on. I think I know what's going on." She tapped the glass, testing the invisible security lasers that consistently guarded the doors during the HQ's off-hours. Rose waited for the screeching of the alarm, but it never came. Eden beamed over her shoulder at the partially-hidden Rose. "See? I bet whoever's working on the board managed to get the communications shut down at the building. They must've gotten the same number on their dice as we did…" She pushed the smooth glass door open with a cheer. "That means the cameras must be down too. We can get in without being detected."

Rose looked around. "Eden…I'm not sure. What if there are guards inside? Just because we can get in, doesn't mean we'll be able to get out."

"Oh, don't be such a worrywart. That's Logan's job." She pushed her way into the building, leaving Rose alone in the alley.

What if it was a trap? They didn't even have the ability to contact the Fortress for backup. Or what if the droids made an appearance? Sure, Rose was technically "immune" to the droids, but that didn't mean Eden was. She needed Rose's protection if she was going to make it through this.

Completely against her own judgement, Rose raced in after Eden.

# Chapter 45

## (LOGAN)

Logan was a good guy. He'd never interrupt another person during their presentation. He had mean thoughts before; he wasn't perfect. But, in order to not offend anyone, he gave everyone his full attention whenever they requested a meeting with him. He enjoyed helping people. Loved seeing the smiles on their faces when he told them he'd take care of their problem; watching the stress visibly melt from their shoulders.

He prided himself in his patience and his ability to block out any other thoughts. He was always able to focus on the present moment, a skill he'd learned from Eden back when she used to train the Fortress-born teenagers and new saves. She'd been promoted shortly after Logan finished the first half of training, and after that, there was a period of time when Bernard would take charge and lead them in the next stages of training.

When Bernard hand selected Logan to sit on the Cabinet, he'd been surprised but mostly honored. To this day, he still didn't know why he'd been chosen. Bernard said he was drawn to Logan's "goodness" and kind heart. Bashfully, he'd taken up Bernard's offer. He now sat directly to Bernard's left, where he'd been for almost six years. He worked hard to keep a level head and to not take sides in an argument by keeping his attention trained on the conversation at hand.

So why couldn't he pay attention to Andre's presentation now? What was distracting him so much that his attention was skewed for the first time in six years? He was human and bound to make mistakes...but he never made them like this before. Not in a Cabinet meeting.

Alice Palmer raised her hand and Andre nodded to her, a signal for her to speak. "I'm just curious, Andre, on how you expect us to rebuild the run-down part of the Fortress, when we're busy running trainings for the younger members? The adults all have their careers to focus on."

Bernard leaned forward. "Alice, I think you bring up a great point... Andre, have we considered adjusting a requirement of training to have the younger ones help rebuild?"

Andre tapped the stylus on his chin. "Of course! They'll be taught lessons on collaboration. Genius, sir."

Bernard nodded, concealing his smile. "It's what I'm here for, son." He tapped Logan's forearm. "What do you think, Clarke?"

Logan shook himself from his thoughts about not paying attention and considered Andre's proposal. "I think it's highly possible, but we should have the air quality team check it out first. Do a sweep to determine how much damage is still left over from the flood and what needs to be done to repair it."

Andre groaned. "But that could take additional time to get all the tests done! We can't--"

Bernard silenced him with a singular raised eyebrow. "If it means providing the utmost safety of our citizens, a little extra time is worth it."

Logan cocked his head, squinting to see Andre's poorly drawn chart on the wall. He held up a hand, requesting permission to speak. "If all goes well with the inspection, we still have to think about the possibility of only half the space being open for renovations. From what I've seen, there's so much damage over there it'll be difficult to say how much of it will be useable."

"But--but I'm certain it'll work out," Andre stuttered.

Bernard tapped his cheek. "Or the possibility that *none* of it will be safe to use."

Logan nodded at Bernard. "Precisely. I didn't want to be the downer here, but we have to keep in mind that it's been nearly two decades since the flood."

Andre, growing more impatient with each second, glared at Logan. "Thank you, cuz. I think I can come up with a backup plan worthy of your standards."

Something hard dropped in the bottom of his stomach. Was Andre upset with him? He hadn't meant to offend his cousin. He simply had the lives of their citizens in mind; it was up to him and the rest of the Cabinet to preserve the free human race down here. Until better conditions were developed above, they were stuck down here.

"Sorry, Dre," he said, casting his eyes to the tabletop and away from his cousin. Logan's mom was going to be so mad at him if she caught wind that he embarrassed her deceased brother's son at a meeting.

Bernard pounded his fist on the table three times to gather their attention. Not hard enough to startle anyone, though. "First off, don't apologize, Clarke. There's no need. Second of all, Logan did you notice something in Andre's diagram? I saw you squinting."

Andre's eyes blazed, so Logan knew he was annoyed. But Logan had never been one to disobey an order. Ever. He knew the lesser of the two evils was to go against his cousin and point out the flaw in his plan. He'd get over it; they were family after all. "I just noticed, in your new plan, that you marked the renovated location as a site for more apartments. But then you'd be separating the living quarters. I'm not sure people would be jumping on the chance to move across the Fortress from their friends and even families."

Logan's cousin came back to life, eyes no longer staring daggers at him. "Well, see that's what I thought originally. But then I remembered the special treatment for the Head of the Fortress. Bernard, wouldn't you want to have a separate apartment away from the rest of the citizens? It would be more private."

There was an earsplitting silence for a moment or two while Bernard tapped his finger on the top of the table. Instantly, he'd clenched his jaw, a dangerous sign.

Eventually, he pointed his forefinger at Andre, wagging it from side to side. "Shame on you, Andre."

Logan's head whipped in the direction of his cousin, whose face had gone slack. His hand fell to his side, the stylus dropping to the ground with a clack. It rolled under the table, landing near Logan's shoe. Logan bent down to pick it up for Andre, nervous for what Bernard would say.

The look in Bernard's eyes told him there was about to be a lecture.

"Andre Harrison, how dare you suggest that the Head of the Fortress should receive special privileges!" He stared Andre down. "I thought I taught you better than that. I am not going to turn into that type of leader. Why do you think we didn't carry on the title of government or president down here?… If anything, I should live in the worst apartment we have down here so I can connect with each of the citizens."

"I'm sorry, sir, I didn't mean anything by it," Andre said, voice practically a whisper.

With his mind, Logan begged Bernard to stop lecturing Andre. If he wanted to pull him aside *after* the meeting, then fine. But don't yell at the poor guy in front of the whole Cabinet.

Bernard grunted. "Good, you should be. Now, anyone else have a question before we move on?

Logan turned his chair to catch Bernard's eye. "Excuse me, sir, but I thought Andre had more to say about the plans?" He sent Andre a small smile, but it was received with the coldest expression his cousin had ever given him.

"No. It's fine, *cuz*. I guess I'll just let everyone ignore all my ideas so we can move on to 'better things.'" Andre's emphasis on the word "cuz" shot like a bullet straight into Logan's heart. Maybe it was going to take a little longer for the two of them to mend this.

He did feel bad about somewhat discrediting Andre's ideas. He didn't mean to hurt his pride by pointing out the apartment situation. And Bernard could be a hard-ass sometimes, but his anger wasn't usually pointed directly at someone as it was now. Were there some underlying issues that Logan wasn't aware of? Had Andre recently gotten in trouble for something stupid? He usually did dumb stuff, but Bernard, being gracious, always gave Andre a somewhat free pass. He customarily received a punishment like dish duty for a week or something.

On the other hand, Bernard was dealing with a lot of stress regarding the mission Rosabella and Eden were on right now. They hadn't heard any updates from them in a while, which wasn't always a bad sign. After their joking around earlier, Logan assumed Rosabella had turned off her earpiece. If she knew how. It wasn't easy. Would Eden though? She was pretty strict about following the rules, like himself.

Logan's pocket screeched at the same time as Andre's. He shoved his hand in his jeans to pull out his screen. An image popped up into a hologram, showing him a fuzzy image of two women entering the pantry.

Andre, being external security, received the same poor quality video alert. Were Eden and Rosabella back already? They'd only just left two hours ago. They'd anticipated the mission would take at least three.

Bernard drew close to Logan and whispered, "Rosabella and Eden?"

"Too difficult to tell," said Logan. The screen set off the sound of tinkling bells. "Well, it looks like they knew the password of the month, so it's not a security breach...I should meet them at the elevator doors--with your permission to leave the meeting early, of course."

He waved Logan away. "Do what you must. But if it's the two of them, you know that we have to do a rundown before they can be released for dinner, right?"

"Of course."

"Good. Now go," Bernard stood to see Logan off.

Andre requested permission to leave with him. Bernard grumbled something about slacking on his duties, but proceeded to allow him leave.

Andre caught up with Logan, but, before he could apologize, Andre jabbed his elbow into Logan's stomach. "I'm not going to even begin to tell you how pissed I am."

He rubbed the sore spot, wincing from the sharp pain slowly expanding up into his chest. "I really am sorry, Andre. I didn't mean anything by it."

Rubbing his temples, Andre sighed. "I know you didn't. You're too nice. That's what's so frustrating! Why do you have to be so good at everything? Can't you see the rest of us are suffering?"

"The rest of *who*?" He didn't mean Rosabella, right? He'd be heartbroken if he ever hurt her.

"The Cabinet, that's who. You're always the star of the meetings. God, can't you just shut up for once in your life? Bernard loves you and you take all his attention away from us....Wait, what did you think I meant?" His head snapped sideways. "Oh no. Don't you dare do that. Don't take away the only good thing in his life."

Logan continued on, ignoring his cousin. The elevator was just around the corner now. If he could only see Rosabella was alright, that she was safe, he'd be able to breathe again.

"Logan, man. Listen to me," Andre pulled Logan's arm so he was forced to look up at Andre. "You cannot--I repeat, you can*not* take Rose away from Clay. If you're the good person everyone believes you are, you'll hold back. I mean it--shit! Why did you have to choose her? I know she's hot and all, but even *I* didn't make a move on her for the sake of my best friend."

They stopped at the closed metal doors. Logan bounced on the balls of his feet. A few more seconds. Just a few more. Then he'd get to hug Rosabella and welcome her back to the Fortress. Shoot, was he too sweaty for a hug? He tugged on the armpit of his t-shirt, testing it for dampness. Nope. All good. But what if he didn't smell good? Dang it! He should've sprayed more cologne on before leaving his apartment this morning.

"Cuz? Are you even listening to me?" Andre slapped his cheek, hard enough for Logan to jump, but not so much that it stung. "Were you listening to me at all?"

"Yes I was...but, Dre. She's so special to me." He rubbed his eyes, exhaustion setting in. When he got all worked up about seeing her, he crashed not long after. "Why can't you tell Clayton to leave her alone? He's only going to hurt her in the end. He can be so awful to people."

Andre threw his hands up and let out a sarcastic laugh. "Yeah, sure. Lemme just go tell my best friend that my cousin wants his girlfriend, so he should back off. I'm sure that'll sit well with him."

"You're not on the best of terms with him right now, as evidenced by his threat to beat you up if you ever speak to Clarise again, so why are you defending him?"

He considered Logan's words. "No, you know what? Clay has every right to be upset with me...And you're more in the wrong here than he is. You're sneaking behind his back with *his girl*, man. That's low. Did your momma teach you nothin'?"

"Don't talk to me about my mom. She is no more in control of my emotions than you are," Logan spat back. Andre knew when Logan was angry it was serious. He was rarely ever angry; disappointed at times, sure, but never angry. "Rosabella and I get along better than she and Clayton do. I mean, come on, he's so wrong for her!" Logan's heart raced simply thinking about her beautiful blue eyes. Clayton didn't deserve her. Not when he had a knack for ruining people's moods with his negativity.

Andre backed up a couple feet and let out a noise between a growl and a snicker. "I don't know who you are right now, cuz. You've always been the best of us. The only good man...and did you ever think about how-- look at it this way. Maybe Clay isn't right for her, but did you ever consider that she's right for *him*?"

*Oh.* No, in fact, Logan had never considered that. Clayton was always the strong one, the guy who everyone wanted to be as far as strength went. He kept his emotions in check (if by keeping your emotions in check, you mean never smiling or laughing) which people seemed to think was an example of bravery or something. In all fairness, Logan just assumed Clayton was angry with life because that's how he wanted to be, not that he needed someone to pull him from the dark and into the light.

But why did it have to be Rosabella? He'd met her first, not Clayton. Logan thought about her all the time. He did anything he could to make sure she was happy. Was it too much to ask that she reciprocate his feelings? He'd taken Rosabella to meet his mom for crying out loud!

Admittedly, Logan was not one to diminish someone's happiness. If he somehow managed to get Rosabella, what would that make him? A destroyer of relationships. It would hurt her more than it would help himself. That little flicker inside Logan's chest whenever he saw her in the dining hall, sitting at their usual table, waiting for him, it would never go away. But, for the sake of the woman he had feelings for, Logan knew he needed to back off.

He was ready to do it too. Once those doors opened, he didn't dare look up. Seeing her blue eyes and the way her orange hair shone in the light...it would all be too much for him. If he did, he'd instantly retract his promise to himself. He couldn't hurt her like that. So he kept his eyes trained on his cousin, as if he was telling the most amazing story.

"What the hell?" Andre cried, face contorting. He stood stiff as a board, staring into the elevator.

Was something wrong? Was it Rosabella? Was she alright? Logan snuck a glance into the open elevator, expecting to see a blood-soaked Rosabella and a few missing limbs.

He spotted the first woman and glared at her. "Aire? Who gave you clearance to leave?" He stepped in her way, blocking her path to the Fortress.

She spoke with so much hatred for him, she spit. "Bernard did, like two days ago. I was allowed to spend the weekend with my sister. Why do you care?"

Logan racked his brain for a response, unsure if he should trust Aire's claims. "We'll have to double check on that before you can return to your dorm. Come on in for now." Logan stepped to the side to let her pass. He locked eyes on the next woman to ask her where she'd been all day too. His mouth puckered in response.

"Logey?" The woman cried, rushing to him. She embraced him as an old friend would. Her slender build fit against him as it used to. Her brown hair tickled his nose. She still smelled like fresh fruit. Just like old times. Without hesitation, she was on Andre for a hug next. "I thought you guys had forgotten me!"

Logan had to steady himself against the wall. Shock and fear had knocked the wind out of him. The tightening of his diaphragm straining for more air gave him an acid feeling just below his throat.

Andre kept an arm around the woman's shoulders, nervously smiling sideways at her. "Never," he said. "We never forgot about you. Right, *Logey?*"

Logan blinked to cover up his brain's slow processing. "How? Where did you come from? Where the hell *were* you?"

Andre laughed a dry, rude laugh. "Well cuz, I guess you won't have to worry about hurting Clay. Looks like he's got his own issues to settle now."

Aire snickered off to the side. Logan shot his eyes in her direction, but when he caught sight of her, she'd already stopped. Her hand rested under her chin, supported by her other arm, as if watching a movie on a screen. Did she know what she'd just done? Logan wanted to believe there was good in Aire, that she didn't bring home the one person who could wreck everything between Rosabella and Clayton. He didn't feel good about this. Not one bit. Even if it meant Rosabella would be single in the end, he wouldn't have asked for it to happen this way.

"Well," Logan started, doing all he could to not send her back up the elevator. "I guess we'll have to call a meeting with Bernard. This has never happened before."

"Didn't you guys *miss* me?" The woman asked, blinking at him. "I can go back if you want. I just thought you'd all be happy to see me, that's all."

Logan gestured for her to lead the way. She knew this place as well as he did. As well as anyone who'd trained, ate, and slept here for years did.

"After you, Tess."

# Chapter 46

## (LOGAN)

"Hmmm," Bernard mumbled, his eyes scanning Tess up and down. "I'm not sure I can allow you back into the Fortress Miss Aabrams. This is all too convenient. Let's go over your story again." Something Logan couldn't pinpoint passed between Tess and their leader; Bernard's voice was too flat, too devoid of emotion. There was more to this, but what was it?

Tess crossed her legs and leaned forward. She touched Bernard's hand. "I'm sorry, sir. I know this may come as a shock to you. All of you," she directed to Andre and Logan, who stood behind Bernard's chair.

Logan took it all in. The return of Tess Aabrams, their old friend. She'd been a sweetheart, but so blind sometimes. As nurturing as she was, the poor girl couldn't read a room at all to save her life. Logan couldn't imagine what Clayton was going to say; what Rosabella would do when she saw the woman Clayton used to love above all else right in front of her. The world would have to open and swallow him up before he allowed Clayton and Tess to reunite before Rosabella was warned.

"And don't think I've forgotten your medical talents," Logan heard Bernard say; he was only half-listening to them. The other part of him was busy playing out the scenario of Rosabella discovering Tess had returned to the Fortress.

Strange as the situation was, the story of how Aire and Tess had first met was still a little fuzzy to him. Too many holes. Too many uncertainties. He still couldn't get over the initial shock either.

Tess smiled at their leader. "I'm happy to help! Maybe I can teach some of the younger trainees a few tricks and tips I've learned over the years above."

Andre stepped around Bernard, towering over Tess. "You were up above living your life like normal while we were all down here mourning your loss? What about Clayton? You just left him that easily?"

"I don't expect you to understand, Andre. It's not as simple as it sounds. There were so many factors I can't discuss." Tess wrung her hands together. She ducked her head down, waiting for Andre to say more. When it didn't happen, she peeked up at the three men. "Is...is Clay okay?"

Logan sighed and Bernard let out a strangled laugh.

Andre scoffed. "Seriously, Tess? Do you know how badly Clay took your 'death?' He hardly ate for days, didn't sleep for weeks, still hasn't let himself smile or laugh much because of it. You ruined his life. You shouldn't be allowed back in."

Aire stepped forward out of the corner she'd been cowering in. "Now wait a minute. Tess is one of us, right? Don't you think she deserves a fair chance at receiving sanctuary?"

Andre whipped around, a snarl curled in his upper lip. "Keep out of this. You've ruined my day enough already."

Tess sniffled and swiped at her cheeks. "It ruined your day for me to come back?"

"No, no. It's not that...are you crying? I'm sorry. Gosh, please don't tell Clayton I made you cry." Andre laughed awkwardly and patted Tess on the head, arm extended so he stayed as far from her as possible. "We aren't exactly on speaking terms right now."

She wiped her nose on the sleeve of her thin, pink sweater. "What? You and Clay are inseparable!"

"Yeah, well," Andre patted her head again, messing up her frizzy brown hair that used to be short and blonde. "Lots of things have changed since you left." He and Logan made eye contact. Andre's eyes widened, questioning and confused. Logan was at just as much a loss as his cousin was.

At the last second, he was saved by the bell, literally. His screen alerted him to someone's entrance into the Fortress. They were already in the elevator. If it was Rosabella, he had to intercept her before she got word of Tess being here.

He stepped toward the door. "Bernard, sir. I'm going to umm, welcome Rosabella and Eden back."

Bernard turned his chair, the wheel screeching against the grey tile. "Oh. Right. I forgot about *that* tiny detail."

Andre scoffed. "That's an understatement."

Logan closed the door from the outside, shutting the drama in the meeting room. He'd keep it there as long as possible. Would everything go back to normal if he ignored it was there in the first place? Ignored the fact that Tess was back?

"Hey, Logan. Is Bernard in a meeting right now?"

Logan yelped, frightened by the voice. He was even more freaked out and flustered when he realized it was Clayton. "Clayton! What are you doing here?"

Clayton fell against the wall to their left. His shoulders sagged. "I need to give Bernard some news."

Logan ran his fingers through his hair. "I'm sorry, but Bernard is going to be in there a while. Is there anything I can help with?"

Too drained to argue or insult Logan, Clayton shook his head. He scratched his chin, nails running across the newly grown stubble there. It made the sound of two bricks rubbing together.

Logan cringed and attempted a smile. "I'll do my best to get you in to see Bernard, but there's some pretty big stuff going on right now. I'm actually on my way to meet Rosabella and Eden, so I'll catch you later."

Clayton gripped his arm, nails digging into the skin of his forearm. "Why are you meeting Rose and Eden? I thought they were just working out together."

"They did. And then they went out on a small mission together. Bernard's request." Crap crap *crap*! Logan was blowing Rosabella's cover already and it hadn't even been a full minute. Clayton was going to be mad at her for deceiving him. But seeing Tess may change all that, so it was really hard to tell how he'd react to Rosabella lying to him.

"A small mission you said?" Clayton asked, slowing his scratching.

"Yup. So, I'll see you later then."

"Wait," Clayton shouted. "If it's not too much trouble, I'd like to go with you. To welcome Rose back and all."

Logan gulped. "Oh, thanks. But that's okay. I got this."

Clayton swallowed and pushed himself from the wall. The light reflected a blackness in his eyes, fiercer than ever. "No. I insist. If you're going to sneak my girlfriend out of the Fortress without my knowing I think you owe me this much, don't you?"

With Tess on the other side of the door, Rosabella on her way down in the elevator, and Clayton about to start a fight, Logan's head started pounding. Nobody was cut out for this. He'd never be successful as the Head of the Fortress. Too many things happened all at once, especially at moments you least expected them.

His skin itched then. Logan scratched at his shoulder first. Whenever stress began to consume him, he did this. An image of bugs crawling up and down his back made him shudder.

"You good, Clarke?" Clayton asked, eyeing him curiously.

"Yeah, all good. Just itchy."

Clayton patted Logan on the back. His hand could've shoved its way through his ribs and pulled out his heart if it had been possible. Logan knew his friend enough to point out an anger spree when it was about to happen. This was a terrible way to welcome Rosabella back! She didn't deserve anger and jealousy to be the first emotions she encountered. Especially not from the man she had feelings for.

Footsteps bounced off the walls, preventing Logan from ordering Clayton to keep his mouth shut. Thank goodness too, because he would've laid Logan out flat if he'd said anything more about Rosabella. Clayton wasn't an idiot. He could tell Logan had feelings for Rosabella too. It was written on his face. In the way his eyes turned to slits whenever her name left Logan's lips.

Rosabella turned the corner, black tennis shoes slapping the floor in pounding bursts. She spotted Logan and Clayton and stormed right up to them. The left side of her face was covered in splattered blood all over her skin. Her jacket was wet and dark, a match for the mysterious blood on her face.

Clayton's hard expression melted when he saw her. He held his arms out. "Hey, Rose."

She shoved his arms back down to his sides. "Don't. Logan," she faced him. "Where's Bernard? I need to talk to him."

Logan rolled his eyes playfully. "You and everyone else apparently."

She slapped him on the arm. It was not a gentle, *I'm-only-joking-around* slap. "Stop it. I need to talk to him right now."

"Sure. Let's go in together."

Clayton nudged him. "What the hell, man? I told you *I* needed to speak to him and you told me no."

"This is different, Clayton," said Logan. "You don't have the clearance for it."

Clayton threw Logan against the wall, hand clamped around his throat. "You mean I don't have clearance to watch you snuggle up to my girlfriend and take her from me?"

Rosabella pulled on the back of Clayton's collar. "Knock it off, both of you. Logan, get me in to see Bernard. *Now*. Or I'll walk in myself."

Logan looked over Clayton's shoulder at her. Rosabella's pupils were dilated, her blue irises dark. Her nose scrunched whenever she was upset, as it did now. Her mouth, unsmiling. She meant business.

"Rosabella, you know I would, but I seriously suggest that you wait. He's in an extremely important--and confidential--meeting right now."

She screamed in anger, fingers tangling in her hair.

Clayton released Logan, suddenly alert. "Hey, what's wrong?"

Then Logan realized there was one person missing from their group. "Rosabella?" he asked. "Where's Eden?"

She shook her head and pulled her jacket up and over her face. Rose screamed into it, the thin fabric barely muffling the sound. Logan and Clayton waited for her to calm down.

That could only mean one thing.

Eden was gone.

\*\*\*

# (ROSABELLA)

A heavy sob clawed at Rose's chest. Her arms were covered with raised goosebumps. Her head felt dizzy and her heart raced faster than the tube at max speed. So this is what it was like to grieve. For Grayson, her mom, all those classmates she lost almost a year ago, and now Eden. A friend. An inspirational woman.

If Rosabella was going to put on a brave face for her remaining loved ones, she'd have to pull herself together. She wasn't ready to talk about what had happened to her up there, and she sure as hell wasn't going to let herself think about it. Rose took in a long, deep breath until her head was light and airy. Then she released it in a slow stream.

She dropped her jacket so it fell away from her splotchy red face. Rose was embarrassed for screaming in front of the two men, especially since they'd waited patiently for her to calm down. In her attempt to shut off the bad emotions, she also shut out the good. It only took an instant for her to forget what it was to love someone. Or so she told herself. It was better than letting in all the anger, the hurt, the pain.

"Alright, I'm going in whether you want me to or not, Logan." She knocked twice on the door, announced herself and barreled into the room.

Logan ran in after her, stumbling around her to block her from the people in the room. All she could see were Andre, Bernard and Aire. Was Aire in trouble or something? So this was what Logan was protecting her from? Seeing Aire, her ex-best friend? Under any other circumstances, Rosabella would've thanked him with her eyes; but right now, he wasn't being sweet, he was posing as an inconvenience.

Clayton shoved in after them. His hand gripped Logan's wrist. "Logan, leave her alone. What are you doi--?" His husky voice dropped off before he could finish the question.

Rose watched Clayton as he spotted something beside Bernard at the table. His eyes softened, his eyebrows relaxed. She watched him experience shock and then sadness and then eventually joy. His hand fell from Logan's arm without another thought. Logan stepped in front of Clayton then, revealing a woman Rose had never seen before. A beautiful woman with brown hair and hazel eyes sat to Bernard's left, where Rose usually liked to sit when she had meetings with him. Bernard held one of the woman's hands between his own. His eyes softened when he glanced over at Rose. The woman scrambled to her feet so quickly the chair rolled back into the wall with a thump.

Each person in front of Rose slowly turned to see her reaction. Why were they all looking at Rose? And who was Bernard talking to, a new save? Bernard pushed off the table and stood beside the woman.

He looked Rose up and down. His mouth made an "o" and his eyebrows reached his hairline. "Rosabella, what on earth happened to you?"

Rose crossed her arms, refusing to go into the story. Eden was gone and Rosabella had the key...that's all they needed to know. "I'm not talking about it."

Aire reached out a hand. "Rosie, can I help? You look awful."

She stepped back out of Aire's reach. Logan moved toward her next, but Rose smacked his hands away. Clayton hadn't looked at her since he'd spotted the woman.

"Would everyone just leave me alone?" cried Rosabella, fumbling to take off her jacket. The left sleeve stuck to her skin, sticky with drying blood. A deep cut ran the length of her bicep, ending just before her elbow. Where had that come from? She bit her lip to keep from wincing.

Bernard shook his head, disappointed with her. "I don't know what happened to you, Rosabella, but that's no way to speak to people who care for you." Then his eyes flitted past her into the hall. "Where's Eden?"

Logan motioned for Bernard to stop right there. He caught on and frowned, the corners of his lips curling downward. "Nevermind, we can discuss this later. Now, how do we go about this, since all of you know?"

All of them knew *what*? Was this girl special to him somehow? A granddaughter? Her brown hair rested atop her shoulders, her almond shaped hazel eyes wide and probing. The woman's eyes had not left one particular person: Clayton. He stared back at her with equal amounts of awe and confusion.

Clay's voice shook, "You...you're dead."

On a normal day, Rose would've comforted Clayton when he sounded so anguished as he did now. Even this morning she would've kissed him or pulled him in for a hug to make all his pain go away. Now, she felt like running from the room. Rose wanted to get as far away from him as possible.

Andre sprinted to Clayton and clutched at his arm. "Hey Clay, why don't we all talk about this another time? Bernard really needs to finish gathering Tess' story."

With one word, Andre confirmed Rose's greatest fears, crushing her from the inside out.

The floor shook. The walls collapsed. But worst of all, Rose's heart dropped right through the floor, a gaping hole left in her chest. So

Clayton couldn't take his eyes off the woman because it was the woman he'd known since childhood. The same woman he joined the Fortress with. The same one he'd fallen in love with for the first time, shared intimate moments with for years. The same woman he'd mourned for so long, the effects of which had changed him into an angry, rude person.

Whose gentle hands touched Rose's elbow? Who spoke in a low voice in her ear? More importantly, why couldn't she move? Why wouldn't Clayton just *look* at her?

Because he was too busy running to Tess. Too occupied with wrapping her up in his arms. With burying his face in her neck and sobbing.

Rose's throat ached to scream. Her chest heaved. The air in the room was no longer enough for her. She felt claustrophobic; the walls started squeezing in around her. Before she could start sobbing in front of everyone, Rose backed out of the room. Disbelief clouded her eyes, making it hard to see where she was going. Or maybe it was the tears. So this was what heartbreak felt like. It squeezed your lungs until you wanted to throw up from lack of air; shoved its way into your head, making the world spin and tilt around you. Filled your bones so they were heavy as lead and just as difficult to move. Caught you off guard, sending your world into a spiral when you were least expecting it.

She found her way to the elevator by feeling along the walls. Rules be damned, she had to get out of here. Rose forgot one tiny detail...only mission control could open the doors from the inside to allow her out.

Someone touched her shoulder, gently encouraging her to face them. "Rosabella, I'm so sorry."

She smacked her palms into Logan's chest. "Leave me alone. And get me the hell out of here!"

He tilted his chin up, indignant. "Why? What good would that do for you?"

"It would do a world of good for *you*," she seethed. Spots of red danced before her eyes. Her only emotion: anger. "Because I have the sudden urge to beat the shit out of anyone who gets in my way."

He let out a long sigh, pulling out his screen. Logan then typed in a number of commands. Once he was done, the doors slid open.

"Alright, then let's go. Together." He placed a hand on her lower back and steered her into the open elevator.

# Chapter 47

## (LOGAN)

CLAYTON WAS DESPICABLE! LOGAN EXPECTED THAT BEHAVIOR FROM his cousin, but not Clayton. How could he throw away all those months with Rosabella? She was the perfect woman. Plus, she had feelings and a brain. It had only taken her a few seconds to put things together. Tess was a kind hearted woman too, but she was nowhere near as important to Logan as Rosabella was. Apparently the same couldn't be said of Clayton. He just left Rosabella standing here, blood all over her, a gash in her arm, and a freshly broken heart.

Logan sat at Rosabella's old kitchen table stewing. He'd been waiting there for a while. Rosabella had gone immediately upstairs to her old room. He wasn't even sure how long they'd been in her old house. Logan didn't care either. He had plenty of angry thoughts about Clayton to keep him occupied.

Andre had sent him five messages, called him at least three times and requested access to leave the Fortress a handful of those as well. Logan ignored any messages or calls and denied all requests. It was funny though, Clayton hadn't reached out at all. He should've followed Rosabella out of that meeting room the second she left. Logan shouldn't be the one comforting her when Clayton was the one who was at fault here. He'd taken Rosabella's giving heart and stomped on it.

Tess didn't even know what she was getting herself into, but it was her fault for leaving them and deciding to appear out of the blue years later. Though, Aire seemed to know exactly the effect this would have on Clayton and Rosabella's relationship, so she wasn't cleared of the blame either.

Pounding feet sounded above him. Rosabella barreled down the stairs shortly after. She shot off the bottom step, passing Logan in a flurry of frustrated tears and bloody clothes. She'd promised him she'd change when they went back to the Fortress, but he'd hoped there were clothes up here she'd want to put on instead. You know, to have some memories of her old home. To have some semblance of normalcy.

"Rosabella, wait!" Logan jumped from the chair and raced after her.

Being so selfless could really take a toll on a person. She was strong-willed and wouldn't admit it out loud to anyone else, but Logan understood her well, whether she knew or not. Pouring her heart and soul into so many other people, investing her own happiness into them so they felt the same joy, could drain someone dry. Rosabella had taken Clayton's blow hard, he could see it in the way her cheeks flushed and her usually smooth movements had turned choppy.

When he caught up with her, she was sitting on the front porch. Her shoulders shook with defeated sobs. Logan hated to see her so upset. In that moment, Logan silently promised he'd never let her cry so long as he could help it. Rosabella was not one to cry easily. Clayton had broken that part of her. He deserved nothing more than to rot.

Logan wished he could stop thinking such mean thoughts, but it was difficult when the one woman he'd ever loved was in so much pain.

"Rosabella?" He asked, kneeling next to her. "Do you want to talk about it? Or is this one of those moments where you and I sit in silence and stare at the wall?"

To his relief, she smiled and even let out a little, strained chuckle. Rose turned to him, face streaked with tears. It was a surprising sight, and it made her eyes startlingly blue.

Rosabella's eyes held his. Neither of them looked away for a long time. Long enough for him to make a decision.

"Those are the most beautiful eyes I've ever seen," Logan said softly, reaching up to brush her hair back.

She blushed and turned away. "Yeah sure, tell the sobbing girl that she looks beautiful. That'll solve everything," teased Rosabella.

He took her hand, careful to be gentle. She didn't like anyone forcefully touching her, which was interesting seeing as though she was training to fight people. Logan had to fight himself internally. He wanted to bury his hands in her hair and make her forget about her sorrow.

"I find you beautiful at all hours of the day." He sucked in a breath and held it. That was the first time he'd said anything to her about his feelings. He'd kept them to himself for her sake. Clayton's threats to harm him should he touch Rosabella were no matter now. Logan had only backed off for her, because he didn't want Rosabella to have to make a difficult decision--that was, if she even had feelings for Logan. He could sacrifice his own pained heart if it meant she was happy. He could be the one on the side, supporting and caring for her without disturbing her own love story. He just wished it would have started with him.

After a while of Logan's hand in Rosabella's lap, stroking her bloodied hand, he decided to give her some space. She wasn't ready to share her feelings with him. At this point, he was certain she didn't have *any* feelings for him, at least not the way he'd hoped. He gave her hand one final squeeze and moved to his feet to give her some peace and quiet as he'd been doing for months.

Once his hand touched the door handle, Rosabella hopped up and grabbed his arm, not too kindly if he might add. It wasn't difficult to turn and look at her, he was always looking at her. This time, she just happened to be looking back. There, on the porch, lit only by the small light in the ceiling, they stared at one another for a while, neither moving nor speaking. Her eyes were just as bright under these lights as they were any other time of day.

Rosabella finally blinked at him, the corners of her mouth lifting into a small smile. "Logan--"

He held up his hand, abruptly pulling his arm out of her grip, which she hadn't let go of since standing. "Rosabella, I get it. You're in love with Clayton. I wouldn't want to confuse you." He sighed, turning to go. In the process of closing the door behind him, Rosabella's voice broke through the dejected film surrounding him.

"Logan, wait!" she called, voice breaking at the end.

He stopped, rather against his own will. He always did when he heard that voice say his name. When she said it, things were right in the world; Logan's life made sense.

Rosabella thrust the door open until she stood in the doorway, eyes on him. She eased one foot in front of the other until she stopped in front of him. He didn't speak, didn't move, didn't breathe. When Rosabella took his face in her hands Logan fought a shiver. Her touch was so gentle, her skin so soft. It all sent his heart waltzing in a mad panic, pounding into his ribcage so hard, he feared it would burst out. Was this what love really felt like?

"You know you're special to me right?" began Rosabella, sympathy coating her words. So there it was, the friends card. He let out a breath and prepared himself for what she'd say next. "The more time I spend with you, the more I begin to realize just how much you mean to me. I want to be honest with you....no matter what he's done, I still have strong feelings for Clayton."

Logan nodded like the good, obedient friend he was. He remembered to keep his chest moving up and down without her noticing that he'd lost his breath the moment she'd touched him. Scratch that. The moment she *looked* at him.

She pulled her hands from his face and leaned against him, pressed chest to chest, her back arched so she could look him in the eye. "Logan, I'm starting to recognize that I may have been wrong about some things--stop staring at me like I'm about to stab you through the heart."

"Well, then don't stab me through the heart." Logan wheezed under his breath, looking away. *Keep your eyes trained on the living room couch.* If he stared into those eyes for much longer, he was going to do something he'd really regret, like kiss her.

Rosabella gave him a punch on the arm. Her hips accidentally shifted, fitting herself perfectly against him. "Stop that! I want to finish," Rosabella said, blinking away fresh tears. She took a deep breath. "I already feel like you're one of my best friends. Hell, I tell you things I vow to keep to myself! But somehow, you convince me to trust you."

Logan's heart soared up into the ceiling. The back of his hand ran along her cheek. She leaned into his touch and closed her eyes.

One thing was for certain. His voice was quiet but firm, "I will wait for as long as it takes. I will."

Rosabella's eyes snapped open. She pulled back and glared at him. "Logan! I'm trying to tell you to go live your life! You don't need to wait for me. I couldn't live with myself if I continue to torture you by loving

Clayton. Even if he doesn't love me back anymore. It's just not fair to you."

"But he's an *awful* person! I bet he doesn't even treat you well at all, Rosabella!" Logan lost his cool. It had to be said. He wanted to protect her from Clayton. When they went back to the Fortress, he wasn't going to come running to her. He was going to stay by Tess' side until the day he died. Logan wouldn't put it past Clayton to forget all about his and Rosabella's relationship. "Clayton is nothing but trouble for you."

Rosabella backed away from him, head shaking right to left in a flurry of orange-red hair. "I thought you'd understand. You should really go find yourself a kind, sweet woman. If what you say is true, then in *this* relationship," she waved her hands back and forth between his chest and hers, "should there ever be a relationship--I would be the Clayton to *you*! Logan, you're so generous and good-hearted that I'd ruin that part of you. I'd taint you by drawing you toward the dark side."

Logan scoffed so hard it made his throat feel like he'd swallowed a hot iron. "See? This is Clayton getting to your head. He shouldn't make you feel like you're any less pure than you are...and now he's gone and changed the view you have of yourself! How can you stand to be with someone like that?"

Her face got all red, and her eyes blazed. Damn Rosabella and her incredibly distracting blue eyes!

Rosabella's voice escalated and her arms shook with rage. "I can't help who I fall in love with, Logan!"

His voice low and his gaze serious, he whispered, "Neither can I."

Her face immediately drained all of it's anger, and along with it, its color. She'd turned more pale than a white bedsheet. Caught in a staring match, Logan's heart pulsed in every limb. His toes pulsed with blood, his arms, his neck. She had a hypnotic effect on him. He bet Clayton never felt this way about Rosabella before.

Unexpectedly, she stormed over to him and stood on her tip-toes. It was adorable to watch her attempt to reach his height. A handful of realizations flashed through his brain. The first: Clayton loved being the one in control; he was a full foot taller than Rosabella...not a coincidence. He probably liked being bigger than her, intimidating her as if she were an animal. How despicable! Clayton had a disastrous way of thinking; didn't he ever think about other people?

Rosabella smacked him on the chest. "Logan......damn it!" She tugged on the collar of his shirt and kissed him hard. His arms slid around her waist, drawing her close. Soon they were pressed up against one another, as close as they could possibly get. Their kisses passionate and tear streaked. Was he crying or her? Or were both of them? What did this mean?

His knees weakened and wobbled, so he decided to try his luck and pick her up by the waist. She didn't fight him, and easily followed his lead, wrapping her legs around his waist. They soon found themselves on the dusty couch in the living room.

Minutes, maybe even hours, went by. Logan lost himself in Rosabella. His hands ran up and down her arms, her back, her neck. Of course, he was careful of the cut on her bicep. He couldn't get enough of her. Apparently she felt the same way, because, as they took a breath to look at one another, she pushed his shoulders so he lay on his back on the couch. He wanted her to keep kissing him. This was his happy place. Better than anything he imagined. He knew, from this moment on, he'd always love her, no matter what she said. No matter if she broke his heart in a second.

# Chapter 48

## (ANDRE)

ANDRE WAS NOT A SENTIMENTAL GUY. HE DIDN'T care about many people, nor did he pay attention to their feelings. The more he'd hung around Rosabella, the more he started picking up on signals. Like the hurt that crossed Rose's face a few minutes ago. He'd watched her strut out of the room, head high and chin wobbling. If Clayton couldn't see her pain and Andre could, there was something wrong. The whole universe was misaligned.

Tess' return was shocking, and incredibly inconvenient. Thanks to Aire, their world was rocked yet again. How did Aire know exactly which buttons to press before someone exploded? Andre hated her with all his heart. She was a disaster waiting to happen.

Clayton and Tess stood side by side. Bernard smiled at the two of them, though it never reached his eyes. It was certainly a blast from the past. Just like old times. This was all so extraordinarily wrong.

Aire ambled up to Andre and linked her arm with his. "Wow, didn't see that coming."

He wiggled his arm free of her hold. "Yes you did. This was all done on purpose."

Her mock expression of surprise disgusted him. He should hit Aire, punch her in the gut. A similar match for the pain he'd seen on Rose's face.

"I don't know what you're implying."

"Of course you do," said Andre, voice escalating. He poked a sturdy finger into her gaunt shoulder. "You planned all of this so Clayton and Rose would break up. You wanted to see her unhappy because you two haven't been getting along. What a horrible friend you are, because, guess what? It worked."

Clayton jumped to attention. "Hold on a minute. *What* worked?"

Andre blinked at him while Aire huffed off to the side. Did he really not see it? "Aire just ruined your relationship, Clay."

"I don't know what you're talking about. Rose and I are not breaking up. Why would we?" Clayton's brows furrowed, wrinkling the skin between his eyebrows just above his nose; mouth turning to a stern, flat line.

Bernard patted the table, considering the best way to reply. "Well, son, you didn't make a motion to explain things to Rosabella. Didn't you see her rush out?"

He whipped his head around, looking for her. "Shit! I should've been more aware of that. All I could think about was that Tess was back." He rubbed the back of his neck, thinking, "I should apologize to her."

"Exactly!" cried Andre. "She's hurt man. And trust me, if *I* can pick that up, you're off your game. You're normally so good at noticing this stuff."

At least all of this confusion meant Clayton would be so busy sorting out things with Tess and Rose that he wouldn't be paying much attention to Clarise. Andre would be able to see her more frequently!

Tess leaned into Clayton. "Was that pretty girl your girlfriend, Clay?"

He nodded and leaned the opposite direction, as if remembering he was spoken for. "Yes. And I love her more than anything." He looked at Bernard then. "Bernard, sir, before I forget, there's something I need to talk to you about."

"Alright, son. After we get things sorted out."

Andre held his breath, worried Tess was about to get upset by Clay's comment about loving Rosabella more than anything. Tess had always been easy to offend. If she did, there was no telling what Clayton would do. Way back when the two of them were dating, he'd set everything down and make her happy. Clay couldn't do that anymore if he was with Rose. Unless he made the decision to break up with Rosabella, whom he just claimed to love.

Aire sighed. "Man, you guys are so dramatic."

Clayton and Andre spoke together, "Shut up."

Tess broke into a grin and pulled on Clayton's arm. "That's fantastic! I'm so happy for you Clay! Can I meet her? If she's worthy enough for you, she must be pretty special."

Andre wanted to smack her. Didn't Tess see the way her return had hurt Rosabella? She'd run out of the room, obviously crushed!

Instead of saying something rude about Tess' ignorance, Andre snorted and crossed his arms. "I think you have it the other way around, Tess. Since you've been gone, Clay's been a real pain in the ass. Rosabella changed him for the better. She's way out of his league."

"Watch it, Andre, you're already on thin ice with me," growled Clayton. He took a step toward Andre, fists clenched at his sides. Andre flinched toward the door in case he'd need to make a beeline out of there.

Tess stepped between them, placing a hand on Clayton's chest. "What on earth is going on? You two are best friends. What's gotten into you?"

Clayton lowered his voice and his eyes so they locked on Tess'. "Dre here decided it was alright to hit on my sister. You know, the one who's eight years younger than him. He's lucky I've let him go this long without kicking his ass."

She shook her head, eyes sad. "I can't believe you, Clay. Love is love. I thought we both discussed this a long time ago. You should be ashamed of yourself. That girl you call your girlfriend looked much younger than you too."

"She's only like four years younger than me," replied Clayton, voice unsure. He frowned at the floor.

"What if someone had gotten between the two of you?" asked Tess, hand still on his chest. "What if she had an older brother who told you to stay away from her or they'd kick your...well you get the point."

Clayton groaned, his head tilting toward the ceiling. He rubbed his stubbled chin and sighed. "Would it discourage you?" she continued.

His hands clenched around his elbows. "Not if I really loved her, which I do."

Bernard cleared his throat and interjected, "I don't mean to interrupt this epiphany moment, but I think you need to go find Miss Porter and tell her that nothing is going to change because Tess is back. I'm sure she just wants to hear that from you."

Clayton nodded slowly, pieces of the puzzle clicking into place in his mind. "You're right." He paused in the doorway. Over his shoulder, he caught Andre's eye. "Wanna come with me?"

"Me? Are you sure?" Andre asked, wary of the small smile on his friend's face. "You're not going to beat me up once we're alone, are you?" He wiped his sweaty hands on his shorts.

He laughed and held out his hand. "No. Truce?"

"No, you're not sure? Or no, you're not going to beat me up?"

Clayton rolled his eyes, hand still out for him to take. "Yes, I'm sure. And no, I'm not going to beat you up. Happy now?"

Andre eyed him with suspicion. With all these witnesses around, what was the harm in shaking Clayton's hand? They shook on it, one firm grip shared between them.

Aire whined from the corner. "Can I come with?" She stepped closer to them. "Rosie is my best friend."

"Tess, feel free to go to my apartment once you're done talking to Bernard. I'm sure he can find someone to walk you there....I'll bring Rose back with me. I want you to meet her. You'll love her." Clayton said, ignoring Aire. It was no small feat, as her voice pierced Andre's concentration and attempted to block her out.

"Wait!" Aire cried, tugging on Andre's arm. "Why won't you talk to me? I want to come with!"

Clayton got in her face. "I don't want you to come with because you tried ruining what Rose and I have. You don't get a second chance with me, Aire. I'm writing you off here and now."

Her jaw dropped, face completely devoid of color. "You're going to regret saying that, Clayton. I can make your life a living hell."

"That's too bad, Aire, because you can't make my life miserable when I've got Rose."

Andre urged him to stop poking the bear. Aire was a scary woman, probably filled with secret skills none of them had been exposed to yet. Watch her be a prodigy in kicking a guy in his most sensitive place. That would put the icing on the cake.

Instead of bending down and covering himself for protection, as was his first instinct, Andre pulled on his friend's arm. "Ready, Clay?"

Clayton finished whispering something to Bernard that made him pale, then nodded and left the room. "Yeah, I am."

"I hate you, Clayton Taylor!" Aire screeched. When she finally accepted that he wasn't going to turn around and apologize any time soon, she ran up to Bernard. "You've got to help me, Bernard. I'm ready to take you up on your offer."

Andre left the two of them to talk about whatever deal Aire thought they'd made. He and Clayton walked down the dimming hall together, the first time in a long time Clayton wasn't shooting death glares at him.

***

"Where could she have gone? The Fortress is only so big," Clayton complained, annoyed they kept coming up empty in their search for Rosabella. They'd started in the library, checked every possible place Rose found comfort in, and eventually doubled back to the library.

Andre had a feeling Rose wasn't even in the Fortress. Logan was nowhere to be seen either. After Logan followed her out of the meeting room, the two of them had been difficult to find. After Logan denied each of his requests to leave the Fortress to look for Rose, he grew suspicious of his cousin. Now was not the time to bring that up.

Andre knelt on the floor and peeked under one of the small tables beside the couch. "Nope, not under here."

Clayton glared at him. "This isn't the time for jokes, Andre. Rose has never disappeared like this before. I shouldn't have gone to Tess. I should've run right to Rose. She looked terrible too and I just ignored it..."

"Can I offer a suggestion?" asked Andre. "Maybe don't say it that way when you find her."

He rolled his eyes and headed for the door. "I'm not an idiot, Andre. I know when to sugar coat things to a woman."

Andre raised an eyebrow.

"Ok. I'll admit, that didn't sound great either," Clayton said. "But let's face it, I've never been great with words."

He pulled them back to the task at hand, "So what's the plan? You wanna keep looking?"

"No," replied Clayton. "I think I'll head back to my apartment. If she wants to be found, she'll come to me. If not, then I'll make another round in an hour or two. I need to shower." He rubbed his forehead and sighed. "There's something I need to talk to her about. It's not going to be a good conversation to have and I need to prepare myself."

He respected that. If Clayton and Rose were going to talk about things, chances were good that Rose would initiate it. "Fair enough. Do you want me to join you again?"

Clayton shrugged and passed through the doorway. "I'm not sure. I'll let you know." He poked his head back in the room briefly. "And just so you know, I don't fully approve of you and my sister, but if you want to see her from time to time...I guess I'm fine with that."

"Wow, man," Andre whispered, eyes stinging. "Thanks so much. You don't don't know how much I've missed her."

He held up a hand. "But don't think I'll allow you to talk about her like you do your other lady friends. My sister is not one of your toys. You're going to treat her with respect."

"The utmost," confirmed Andre. "You can count on it."

"I'd better, otherwise I'm really going to beat you up."

Andre nodded quickly. "Yes, I get it...but trust me, Clair's special to me."

Clayton groaned again. "Why did it have to be *her*? Did you really have to fall for my sister? What does she see in you anyway?"

"Hey," cried Andre, slightly offended his best friend couldn't point out any good qualities in him. "There's plenty of good things about me!"

"Oh yeah?" Clayton laughed. "Like what? Belching? Hitting on any girl you see?"

"I mean it, Clay, those days are behind me."

"You'd better be right."

Andre nodded. "I am."

"Good." Clay left for his apartment, leaving Andre behind to sift around his thoughts. First thing was first, he needed to tell Clarise about their conversation.

# Chapter 49

## (LOGAN)

Without warning Rosabella lifted her head hastily from Logan's chest. "I think we should head back to the Fortress. People might notice we're gone. Both of us."

Logan knew she wasn't just making a statement. There was more to it than her wanting to go back. She wouldn't look him in the eye, even after they both stood up. He reached for her hand to draw her in and kiss her on the cheek, but she pulled away as if he'd stung her. The way she'd turned cold toward him really pained Logan. It cut him deep. He'd just shared a very vulnerable part of himself with her.

"Rosabella?" His voice didn't come out as firm as he wanted it to. So long as he didn't cry, it would be okay.

Her back to him, she mumbled, "What?"

"Why do we need to go back so soon? We still have time." He should have ended it there. He should have just kept his mouth shut and moved on. That's clearly what Rosabella wanted. Instead, he said, "Or is that not what Clayton would want you to do? You know, since you're so set on letting him crush your heart and all."

He'd never seen her turn around so fast before. Rosabella came at him, until he wasn't sure if she'd stop. It seemed she might run right into him and tackle him to the ground.

Her face was inches from his own when she came to a halt and glared at him. "Logan. I already told you, I can't help my feelings."

Logan took a step around her to leave the room and kept his eyes far from hers. "I just wish you'd see how happy I could make you! I'd never ever do anything that would upset you, I swear."

Rosabella's voice was quiet and gentle as she replied, "Hey--Logan, please look at me."

Against his better judgement, he turned back to her and looked her dead in the eye.

"You are so good and that's why I can't be with you. This never should have happened. It's my fault. I'm sorry."

The anger building up inside him was about ready to burst. He felt it deep in his stomach, where a pit was forming. All of Logan's limbs turned heavy. For a short while, he thought he had the world in his hands. He thought the woman he had feelings for reciprocated them.

"Then why did you kiss me?" He tried keeping his voice even and calm. It didn't come out that way, but he didn't care as much at that point. Logan wanted answers.

Rosabella ran her fingers through her hair and looked at the ceiling. "Logan, I really don't know. Something inside me seemed to pull me toward you. I couldn't help myself...You understand why I have to put an end to this though, right?"

"No, I don't. I *never* will. When the day comes Clayton breaks your heart--because it will come--I know I'll just let myself slip right back into these feelings. I don't want you to hurt me, but it'll happen because I'm so stuck on you." Logan's voice shook.

He got lost in her eyes, which were so blue right now, it was as if he was looking at the pure blue sky during the daytime.

Logan needed to focus on being angry, not on how much he loved her right now. She took a step forward and touched his arm. He didn't flinch as he'd expected to. Instead, Logan felt himself sinking back into the love he had for her. He knew this would happen. It was basically a given, since he'd had such a long time to work on his feelings. Not many men would usually take that long in figuring out their own feelings for a woman, but he wanted to be sure he truly loved her. He'd only ever had little relationships when he was a teenager, but they didn't mean anything. He'd never been in love. Not this way before.

"I'm sorry I kissed you. I shouldn't have encouraged this. That was completely my fault, and I--"

He stopped Rosabella. "Do you regret it?"

"What?"

"Did. You. Regret it? I want your honest answer. That's all I need and then I'll leave you alone to be with Clayton or whoever you choose next to break your heart and treat you badly."

Rosabella shook her head. "Come on, that's just not fair. I don't rip on girls that you talk to and have feelings for."

"That's because..." he had to take a breath or else he'd start crying. "There isn't a single girl I've met here who compares to you." He turned away and walked to the kitchen. He just needed to get out of here.

"No."

Logan stopped in the doorway between the two rooms. "No what?"

Rosabella looked him dead in the eye. "No, I don't regret passionately kissing you."

Logan had to fight to keep the huge smile off his face. Instead, he nodded solemnly. "Thank you for your honesty. Oh, and Rosabella? Happy early birthday. I suppose I won't see you for a while so I'll give it to you now." He pulled a folded envelope out of his pocket and tossed it across the room to her.

She caught it with ease, staring at him with her mouth open.

He forced himself to smile over his shoulder at her. These past few weeks, every time he was alone with Rosabella, he'd felt that they would have an amazing future together. They'd get married here in the Fortress, move into an apartment down here together and start a family when they were both ready. He had a steady career and there was no reason she wouldn't find one, since she had so many skills and successful training. They would be perfectly happy together. Why Rosabella couldn't see that, he'd never understand. They fit so well together. Unlike Clayton, Logan wasn't arguing with her all the time. Sure, she and Logan had their disputes too, like the one they just had. But it wasn't anything that would make him leave the room hating her.

"Just open it. I'm going to head back now. Feel free to come back whenever you're ready."

"Thank you." She whispered to him as he left.

Rosabella would love her present. It was easy to figure out what to get for her; Logan was always listening to her. She'd been dying for her own apartment recently, and he'd talked to Bernard about it for days. It certainly hadn't been easy, but Logan was able to convince Bernard to let Rosabella have a small apartment of her own. It had two bedrooms, a small kitchen and a nice bathroom with a fancy tub. She loved bathtubs. She said they were so relaxing. Nicolai would love it too; that little guy was all about the tubs. Logan had personally taken a tour of the apartment to make sure everything was just the way she'd want. Bernard had been a little suspicious when he found out that Logan wanted to give Rosabella such a huge gift for her birthday, but he hadn't pressed further. Bernard may never understand.

When Logan climbed back into the elevator, he shivered. That hadn't gone the way he'd hoped, but at least she loved her gift. He could tell by how breathless she was. *Better luck next time, buddy*, he told himself. What if there wasn't a next time? What if Clayton changed his ways and didn't screw their relationship up? Clay would be an idiot to let a woman like Rosabella go, but Logan wouldn't put it past him. He just hoped he wouldn't be too late to pick up her broken pieces.

# Chapter 50

## (ROSABELLA)

Rose's head had been stuffed full of fluff, or at least that's what it felt like. Her insides were completely twisted and tangled together. Why? She and Logan hadn't meant anything by their kiss, right? In fact, Rose had pretended she was kissing Clayton, not Logan. They were friends, nothing more. No need to keep stressing over what had happened.

So why was she still pacing in front of Clayton's apartment door?

Rose really ought to have gone straight to her dorm and showered and changed before coming over here. Her arm still had an unclean cut from her mission, her clothes drenched in blood. Not her own.

But when she'd set foot back in the Fortress after being in her old house for a while, the grey tiled floors and off-white walls a familiar sight, her body went numb. She'd worked herself up so much on the ride down, her blood neglected to pump at a steady rate. The only thing on her mind was to see Clayton and explain herself to him. Maybe he'd understand why she'd done it, why she'd kissed a man who wasn't her boyfriend. In all fairness, it was his fault; he'd hurt Rose deeper than ever before. How easy it had been for him to dismiss her and go running back to the first love of his life, and possibly the *only* based on that reaction.

Rose's body lurched forward, hand knocking on the door in a light pattering of knuckles. Better to get this over with. Anticipating an argument was almost worse than having one. She held her breath until someone opened the door.

When nobody called for her to enter, and the door wasn't opened to welcome her inside, Rose drew herself up to her full five feet, five inches height and turned the knob. The dimmed entryway threw her off guard. Clayton never turned the entry light off. Sometimes she'd come back really late at night, while he slept; he always left it on for her to find her way. She didn't even need the light, she was so familiar with the Taylors' apartment. It was a sign of Clayton's affection for her by leaving the light on. One Rosabella never ceased to smile at.

With it being off this time, did that mean he didn't want her here? Well, if that was the case, then too bad for him! She was here and ready to talk, even if it meant this was the last time she stepped foot in the apartment. There was also the possibility Clarise had turned the light off, too. Rose shouldn't be so quick to incriminate Clayton. Especially since she still loved him...who was she kidding? Rose knew she would always love him, no matter what happened. Which was why she had to tell him about her and Logan. The one-time occurrence wouldn't happen again, she could promise that, despite the potential for him to break up with her.

She swept past the welcome mat, keeping her shoes on in case a swift exit was necessary. Rose wished she could scream, but that would only freak people out. She was such an awful person. How could she go behind Clay's back like this? What gave her the right to kiss someone else out of anger? It was shameful. Was she destined to hurt everyone around her? She had a horrible way of ruining things. It was because of Rose that Grayson and Eden were dead; her fault that Lilianna was an orphan. She'd already driven Aire away, a friend she'd had since Kindergarten... was Clayton next?

As Rose approached the living room, the bright lights blinded her. Once she blinked away black spots, she called out for Clayton, "Clay? Are you here?"

There was no response, so she perched on the edge of the couch to wait. She'd wait as long as it took. Rose's hand ran along the sheet over the couch. Clayton had turned it into a bed for himself so Nicolai could take his bedroom. The two of them had a difficult time fitting on the couch to sleep together at first. Now they had it down to a science; they fit together like two perfect puzzle pieces.

A crash came from a kitchen a second later, startling the socks off Rosabella. She leapt to her feet and spun in the direction of the kitchen. The bathroom door was immediately wrenched open. Steam spilled into the living room, thickening the air. A dripping wet Tess ran out, wrapped in only a towel. Her hair hung damp around her face, giving her an alluring look that no man would be able to turn down.

*Seriously, Clayton?* That didn't take very long.

Tess froze when she spotted Rose. Her perfectly shaped mouth twisted into a sheepish smile. Her plump pink lips smacked together to dampen them as if they'd been busy doing something else...like kissing Clayton. Tess *should* be nervous; Rose was about to murder someone. Perhaps she should forget about Clayton and pretend she was really going to see her brother. Her eyes scanned the room and landed on the bedroom door.

"Don't go in there," Tess said, her voice soft and sympathetic.

Rose scoffed. "Are you telling me that you two...? You've been here for what, two *hours*?"

Tess shook her head, golden blonde hair swinging back and forth with her head motions. Wait, hadn't she been a brunette in the meeting room?

Her disdain for Clayton really hit home when he ran into the living room, pan in hand, completely shirtless. "That was a mess, but everything's okay now," he called to Tess, who was still staring at Rose, shock preventing her from speaking. Clayton hadn't seen Rose yet. He lowered his voice, using that gentle tone Rose adored, "Tess? Are you okay?"

Tess nodded her head in Rose's direction and bit her lip, green eyes wide. Rose could've sworn her eyes were hazel only a few hours ago. Tess wasted no time backing into the bathroom and closing the door on them. A sure sign of guilt. Suddenly, Rose didn't feel too bad for kissing Logan.

Clayton peeked over his shoulder. Once he saw Rose, he ran to her. His arms slid around her, hands locking at her lower back. He looked down at her with sad eyes. "There you are! I was so worried you did something reckless like left the Fortress. Listen, we need to talk. Something happened--"

She pounded her fist on his chest. "Well, lucky for you, I was gone long enough for you to hook up with your old girlfriend. I guess I'm pretty easy to forget about, huh?"

His mouth fell open, arms releasing her. "What the hell?"

"You sure didn't waste any time, did you? And to think I came here to *apologize* to you!" She shook her head and laughed dryly. "Why don't you just go back to making out with Tess?" Bile rose at the back of her throat, an acid taste burning Rose's mouth.

Clayton's face darkened. "Are you implying that Tess and I--? Never! *You're* my girlfriend!"

"Too bad you didn't remember that when--"

"When what?" Clay shouted, furious. "When I hugged an old friend I thought was dead? When I told her all about how much I loved *you*? How *you're* the one?"

Even though she was angry enough to smack Clayton, Rose's heart fluttered. To conceal her pain, she shoved against his chest. He rocked back on his heels from the force.

"Clayton, don't pretend like you don't know what I'm talking about! I watched you rush to Tess and welcome her back as if she were the only one you've ever loved."

He threw his hands up. "Because she was the first friend I ever had! My *best* friend before she disappeared. Cut me some slack! Wouldn't you do the same for Aire? Or Clarise? Or even Logan if you hadn't seen him for years?"

Rose's cheeks flushed. A hot wave of embarrassment spread throughout her body, starting in her toes, all the way up to the top of her head. She fiddled with the hem on her jacket, unzipped by Logan's soft hands. Oh no.

Clayton caught on to her silence, taking that as a sign to continue. "Rose, you should know that a part of me will always love Tess...but I've had a long time to realize the love I felt for her is nothing compared to what you and I have."

Rose blinked back angry tears, more at herself than Clayton. "But--"

"No buts." Clayton rubbed his arm and looked away. "How could you even think that?"

Rose poked his bare chest with a gentle finger this time. "Umm, why don't we start with your bare upper body? What was I supposed to think?"

His head snapped down. Clayton looked at his chest and huffed. "I made a mess in the kitchen cooking a late-night meal--for *you* by the way because I figured you'd be hungry, and also because I thought you could use some cheering up. Then I spilled sauce all over my shirt. I literally just ripped it off before I came out here to tell Tess what happened."

The hot flash of anger drained out through her toes and fingertips. He was telling the truth. Rosabella always knew when Clayton lied, and now was not one of those times.

Clayton noticed an opening and stepped closer. "Hey, I promise you, I'd never hurt you like that...Andre and I looked all around the Fortress for you and I just came back here like ten minutes ago."

A tear slipped out and rolled down her cheek. Then another. "I'm so sorry, Clayton," said Rose, gripping at her elbows.

He closed the space between them and took Rose's face in his callused hands. "Don't apologize. I now see how all this looks. It's my fault. I shouldn't have let Tess come back to the apartment. I just thought some familiarity would be good for her."

Her heart twisted, achieving the maximum amount of guilt she'd ever felt before. She couldn't tell Clayton about Logan. At least, not right now. If he really loved her as he said he did, Clayton would be heartbroken by hearing that. Rose couldn't bear for him to feel the same pain she felt when she thought Clayton had left her.

Rose's hand traced Clayton's jaw, over his stubbled chin and down to his chest. His brown eyes, inches away, searched her face. He started by kissing the tip of her nose and then her cheek. Meanwhile, his hand on her back explored the vertebrae on her spine, coming to rest at her tailbone. The other hand cupped her chin, drawing her mouth to his. Rose closed her eyes and breathed in the scent of fresh linen. Her eyes squeezed out another few tear droplets, the salty taste mixing with the warmth of Clayton's lips.

"I have one more question," Rose mumbled on his lips, a hand on his chest. This time not to smack, but to rest comfortably on his smooth skin.

"Anything," he sighed into her hair. "I'll tell you anything you want to know."

"Why did Tess tell me not to go into the bedroom? Did you move Nicolai to the medical wing after all? That's why I thought there was something going on between you and Tess."

The hand tangled in her hair stopped moving. "Ummm..."

She snickered and pulled away to look into Clayton's face. "Umm, what? I didn't realize that was a difficult question? I thought you said I could ask you anything."

"Anything...except that." He brought her to his chest and rested his chin atop her head. "I'm so sorry Rose. It happened so suddenly, I couldn't do anything to help him."

Her heart flew into her throat. "To help *who?*"

Clayton's shoulders shook with sad sighs, rocking against Rose's cheek.

The Fortress no longer existed. Clayton's arms weren't around her. She was falling. Falling into a deep, dark pit into the core of the earth. That darkness swallowed her up. It reached tendrils through her nose into her chest cavity where it wrapped around her lungs.

It wasn't true. It was impossible.

Nicolai couldn't be dead.

\*\*\*

"Just keep this clean, you got that, Rosabella?"

Rose blinked up at the doctor. "Mhm."

She shook her head, a glint of tears in her eyes. "I'm so sorry about your brother. We did everything we could, but the poison was too much..."

Rose blinked again. She'd lost feeling in her hands. Was that why she was in the medical wing? Because she was completely numb? Was her heart even beating?

Clayton had helped her here late last night. That she recalled. She'd spent the night here so the doctor was able to check in on her this morning without having to hunt her down. Oh, now she remembered... Clayton had slept with his head on the bed, right beside her hip. She'd woken up with their hands intertwined.

Rose swallowed, blankly staring up at the doctor. "My brother?" She glanced around the room. Where was Clayton? Oh, yeah. He left when the doctor came in to replace the bloodied bandage on her arm. She swallowed again. Her tongue stuck to the roof of her dry mouth. "Did Clayton say if he'll be back?"

"You're free to go." The doctor mumbled something else about what a pity something was, and patted Rose's hand. "Remember, you're meeting Mr. Taylor in the dining hall?"

"Right. Thanks."

The doctor started to leave and then pointed to a stack of clothes on the chair beside the bed. "Clayton brought those for you to change into this morning....you take care now, dear."

Did the doctor leave because she saw the room spinning too? Rose dropped her legs over the side of the bed and slid to the floor. Her bare feet landed on the tile with a sticky slap. The silly sound made her giggle. Her toes cracked, a sharp crackling that brought her to tears of laughter. Rose wiggled her feet a couple more times so she could hear the cracking again. Once she finished, she swiped at the tears pouring over her numb cheeks. Why didn't other people do this more often?

Changing clothes turned out to be a slow process. The walls tilted one way, so she compensated for it, and then they tilted the other way, sending her into a spinning circle of laughter every time.

Rose emerged from the hospital room wearing her favorite jean shorts and a black t-shirt with the picture of the country on it. Each of the sectors was highlighted in a different color. Her favorite was the Northern Center Sector, where they all lived; its chunk of the nation was a funny dark purple hue. On her way out of the medical wing, Rose hatched a plan.

She'd leave the Fortress and start a new life elsewhere, pretending she was someone else entirely. And she'd do it now so as not to remember any of the bad memories...whatever they were. She forced everything out of her mind and told herself they were all just nightmares. She was a completely different person from the one who'd endured all those deaths and all that pain. It couldn't be her, not when she had such a happy life down here.

That boy, Nicolai, he would forever be some distant dream of hers. Rose didn't have a brother, or a mother, or a father. There was just Rosabella. Gone were the days of crying from loss. Gone were the days of feelings. Those were so overrated anyway; especially when she had such a life to live. Maybe she'd try college. The Government would find her a home and a person to marry; force her to have two children and a specific career. All she'd ever been good at was yelling at people apparently, so maybe they'd give her a job as a manager somewhere. She'd go on as if life down in the Fortress had been only a dream.

Goodbye freedom. It acted as the devil disguised by an angel facade. Nobody was ever really free. So why not let someone else decide her fate? Her livelihood? It would be so much easier that way. No more choosing her own path. No more questioning if she'd made the right decision. No more hurting those around her with her rash behavior. No more getting hurt by loving people with all her heart.

The pitter patter of her dancing feet along the tile became the sole focus of her walk. *Oooh look!* There was the library from her dreams, the one she'd spent many a night in. The place that guy Clayton had found her with a scratch in her side. And there was the bathroom they nearly shared a first kiss in; the first place she realized how electrifying it felt to touch Clayton's skin; to have him touch her side.

What a great dream that had been!

There was the meeting room she'd first been introduced to Bernard, a strong, sturdy man who'd been nothing but kind and gracious to her dream character.

Aha! Last but not least the metal elevator doors she'd first ridden down in that other guy Logan's arms. He was a nice friend to her in those dreams. His lips were kind and soft too, just like his eyes. It was too bad her dream character self had stolen his screen from his pocket during their kisses. The one piece of equipment that could allow her to leave so she could join reality again. She didn't know why she did it at the time, just that she needed to. It would take him a long time to realize it was missing; he wasn't on duty today. Rose would be long gone by then.

She placed the screen at the foot of the elevator and entered the small space.

*Adios dream self. Sayonara. See ya on the flip side.*

The doors closed on Rose, Rosie, Rosie Posie, Rosabella Mae Porter.

From here on out, she was someone else entirely. The dreams she once adored, behind her forever.

# Epilogue

## (ROSABELLA)

A HAND CLAMPED DOWN ON HER SHOULDER. "ARE YOU ready?"
"No. Get your hands off of me!" screamed Rosabella. "How dare
you do this to me!"

A woman she'd never seen tapped Rose's cheek with her palm. "You
have no idea what this means for you, do you?"

Rose bit at the hand on her face, but the woman pulled away too
fast. She then spit on the woman's shoes. "If I did, I'm pretty sure I'd
remember!"

The woman laughed and yanked on the cuffs restraining Rose's
wrists. "Come on. That's enough anger for today. Wouldn't want you to
feel empowered to fight back again."

Rose scrambled to her feet, prepared to take this woman down.
"What do you mean, *again?*"

"Ahh, yes. It's quite the nuisance." She revealed something from her
shirt pocket. A mask. She pulled it over Rose's head, blinding her. "You
should really cut back on your anger problems. It's not good for the
heart."

Rose swung her fists but contacted only air. All she managed to
accomplish was driving the cuffs deeper into her skin. She bit down hard
on her tongue to keep a cry of pain inside. She wouldn't let this woman

have the satisfaction of knowing she was in pain. The tangy, metallic taste of blood in her mouth restored her strength.

The woman dragged her forward. In order to display her strength, Rosabella forced herself to stay on her feet. She fumbled along, stepping on the woman's heels a handful of times. They descended a set of steps, making it nearly impossible for Rose to remain upright. But she gritted her teeth and pushed onward. The prize? An icy cold tunnel. *Oh, joy.*

Someone joined them at the end of the tunnel: a man. He replaced the woman as Rose's handler. "Again? Are you absolutely certain?"

"Don't you dare question me!" A sound of the woman striking him stopped Rose from saying something evil. She fought the urge to jump. In this brisk temperature, if the woman hit him hard enough, she could split his skin. He might be bleeding right now.

His voice shook, but he held his ground. "I only mean because you just--"

"If you don't get her in there and hook her up to the machine, I'll kill you and then kill her."

Rose was tugged forward again and swiftly shoved onto a soft, plush surface. Once her wrists and ankles were strapped to the surface, the mask was ripped from her face. Rose stared up into the eyes of a man she'd never seen before either. He touched the inside of her arm, right above her elbow. His head faced away and his eyes squeezed shut as he attached something to her skin there. The shadows concealed his face too much; she couldn't identify him.

To say what happened next was complete torture would be sugar coating it. Her limbs burned. Had they shoved the sun itself into her veins? This time, holding back screams wasn't an option. She let it all out. Every burden, every heartache. Every tear and every injury.

Once the pain stopped, and she lied on the comfy surface, a warm hand touched her cheek. She squeezed her eyes shut.

A woman's voice spoke in her ear, soft and certain, "Tell me, do you remember?"

"Remember what?" she whimpered. Who was this woman? What did she want?

"I'm going to list off some names. When you recognize one of them I want you to nod." The woman's hand brushed back loose strands of hair away from her forehead. "Do you understand? Nod if you do."

She nodded her understanding.

"Gianna."
Nothing.
"Lilianna."
No idea.
"Clarise."
Didn't ring a bell at all.

She lay there stiff as a board, waiting for a name she'd recognize. What was this, a game? Would she win if she recognized a name? Or was the purpose of the game to *not* have a clue who this woman was talking about?

"Logan."
No, ma'am.
"Aire."
*What a pretty name*, she thought.
"Rosabella."

Such a long name. What parents would do that to their child? Still nothing.

"Good good." She heard a smile in the woman's voice. "Last one and then we're done. Are you ready?"

She nodded again.

"Clayton."

Her heart raced; her pulse picked up. She should know that name. She willed herself to think back. Waaaaay back in her reservoir of memories. But each time she dove in, she came up empty.

The woman clicked her tongue. "I'll say it one more time...*Clayton*."

She shook her head and opened her eyes. "No. None of those names are familiar to me...should they be?"

The woman's laugh, like tinkling bells, rang in her ear. "Not at all, darling...you're ready."

\*\*\*

**End of Book 1**